[Indigo Romeo Lima]

Veronica Tracey Spy/PI
Book Six

I0561770

[Cat Connor]

For information regarding permission email the publisher at 9mmPressNZ@gmail.com, subject line: Permission.

First beta reader: Rebekah Shelley & Robyn Myers
Editor: Nicky Hurle
Formatting: 9mm Press
Publisher: 9mm Press, New Zealand
Publication date: April 2025
Country of first publication: New Zealand.

ISBN Print: 978-1-0670083-3-8
ISBN ePub: 978-1-0670083-4-5
ISBN D2D Print: 978-1-0670560-2-5

Note from the Author:

As an author I am delighted that you chose to read my work.

Rest assured I wrote each and every word with my own fingers and with my brain ~~mostly~~ engaged.

I did not use AI to create any part of this work.

The characters, plots, concept, theme (if you think there is one) were created by me.

Cheers,
Cat x

"Private Investigator Veronica Tracey must navigate a web of forgotten memories and international intrigue to rescue her abducted colleague, Emily Jones, and uncover why foreign agents are desperate to find her." - [Indigo Romeo Lima]

Dedicated to the memory of a bloody good man,
Duigald Myers,
for whom there will always be Old Time Rock & Roll,
tiramisu, ratchet screwdrivers, and red wine.
We miss you.

Thomas Duigald Hodgson Myers
15th of October 1951 - 16th of July 2024

Chapter One:
[Ronnie: So, you say.]

Wednesday took a turn before lunch. Welcome to my life.

"Look sharp," Enzo said as he threw a notebook at me.

I caught it and flicked through it. Then flipped it over and fanned the pages. A small, folded piece of paper fell to the ground.

I bent down, picked it up, then tucked the notebook into my back pocket. It was a dark green pocket-sized soft-covered Moleskine, not some cheap $2 shop notebook. I'd take my time with the notebook, later.

"Let's have a look." Enzo held out his hand for the note.

The woman we detained sat quietly on a dining room chair in the middle of Emily's lounge. New Zealand's fierce summer sun streamed in through the windows heating the room to an uncomfortable degree.

Enzo opened the note, looked at it, then handed it back to me.

I read it.

"Code," I said. "How fun."

Enzo addressed the woman. "Coded messages make us suspicious."

She tipped her head back and stared at him. Nothing registered in her eyes. It was hard to know what was going on in her mind.

"Is there a reason you were snooping around in Emily's yard?" Enzo asked.

She dropped her gaze and stared straight ahead.

My turn. "Do you know Emily?" She blinked her brown eyes at me. "Do you know her?"

Nothing. "Let's move this party to the office."

"Copy that," Enzo replied. He encouraged the woman to stand. She didn't struggle.

I checked the street. Nothing but heat rising from the melting tar on the road. It was too hot for dog walkers. "Clear."

"Unlock your car," Enzo said. "I'll leave the Harley here."

Keys jangled in my hand. The car chirped when I pressed the unlock button.

"You settle her. I'll lock up."

I flipped through the keys on my keyring and found Emily's front door key, then locked the door. Emily was at work. She didn't know about the snooping woman, yet.

Our guest was safely ensconced in the backseat handcuffed to the armrest in the door. Enzo was in the driver's seat. Okay. Fine. I smiled and slid into the front passenger seat.

"C's or yours?" Enzo asked, starting the engine.

"C's out on a job. His office is empty." I lifted a key from the keyring in my hand. "I've got his spare key."

"Okay. I'm game if you are." He grinned at me. "How come you have a key? I don't have a key?"

"He likes me."

Enzo laughed. "We all like you."

My name is Veronica Tracey, Ronnie to most people. I own a private investigation company with my two best friends Steph and Jenn. Mostly it's commonplace arseholes and thefts by really silly people but every now and then my former profession comes knocking. I'm a reformed espionage officer who used to work for New Zealand. Now I do jobs that intrigue me and pay well. I also work for a top-secret global organisation, *Genesis*. And I'm engaged to a well-known American actor who is also in the espionage game.

I turned on the AC. The heat was stifling in the car.

From the backseat a voice piped up, "Who are you people?"

"Emily's friends," Enzo shot back. "Settle in."

Eight minutes later we were cruising down Camp Street. Enzo parked behind the office, and we escorted the woman in the back door. Enzo pushed her into a chair in Crockett's office. Together we secured her with restraints. Her wrists and ankles were attached to the chair arms and front chair legs with hefty cable ties. They weren't tight enough to cause her too much discomfort, but enough so she wasn't going anywhere fast.

We began asking questions all over again.

"Tell us why you were casing our friend's home," I asked.

"I wouldn't know how to do that."

Butter wouldn't melt. I shook my head slowly from side to side.

4

"We think you do know," Enzo said. "It's in your interest to tell us what you know and why you were there."

"I don't know anything."

I nodded. "We'll just let you go then. You can go back to whatever you were doing outside our friend's home."

She started to stand but realised she couldn't. Bugger. She was still restrained. Enzo smiled. She jerked her wrists against the chair arms and glared at me. Fair response.

"Changed my mind," I said. "Looks like you'll have to talk after all."

Enzo crouched down in front of the woman, not close enough that she could kick out if she got free, but close. "See from our point of view … we snapped you casing our friend's place."

"I told you. I wouldn't know how to do that."

"At least she's consistent," I said. "I appreciate consistency." I was trying to get a handle on her accent. Whatever it was it was subtle. Europe somewhere perhaps.

"Don't talk about me like I'm not here."

"What's your name?" Enzo asked.

"I don't have to tell you. You're not police."

Enzo shrugged and smiled at me. He stood, no longer on her level but once again towering over her.

"You can't do anything to me," she said. "You'll be arrested."

"Aw. That's sweet," I said. "And I think you really

believe that too." She frowned. "We should move this along." I checked my watch. The day was galloping away. Sooner or later this needed to end, or had to end, or I could walk away and let Enzo finish off. That was pretty tempting. She wasn't helping herself.

I motioned to Enzo, and he followed me out of the room closing the door behind us.

"What are you thinking?" he asked, his voice hushed.

"Call in two teams and set up surveillance before we turn her loose. If she won't tell us what she's up to, then we'll get that information via surveillance."

"Yeah. Let's do it." Enzo pulled his phone from his pocket. "One of mine and one of yours?"

"Yeah, we'll run them together."

Enzo and I made phone calls.

"Hey, Steph, who've we got free for a surveillance gig?"

"One sec." I could hear her typing. "Okay, we've got Adam and Sonya."

"Right. I want them in play. Sending you a photo of the target. Female, late thirties early forties. Run the photo. She doesn't want to give us a name."

"Why are we interested?"

"Found her creeping around Emily's home. Wasn't the first time. Got her on camera yesterday too but didn't get there in time."

"Emily know?"

"Not as far as I know."

"I'll flash the photo and see if Emily knows her."

"Good. Let me know when you get something on Ms

6

Jane Doe."

"Do you want to brief the team?"

"Not necessary. It's a run of the mill surveillance job but they will be coordinating with one of Enzo's teams."

"Okay."

"I'll get Enzo to have his team meet up with ours prior to setting up." I don't know when Enzo gathered his own team, but I was pleased he did. I also didn't know who was in his team. Were they skilled in Enzo's special interrogation tactics?

"I'll let them know that's happening. Photos?"

"Yes. Everywhere she goes and everything she does and everyone she meets with."

"I'll check back later. We'll set Jane free as soon as the teams are in place."

"Give us an hour," Steph said.

"Done." I hung up to find Enzo waiting for me with a grin on his face.

"All good?" he asked.

"Yep."

"How long do we hold her?"

"Until Steph rings back and they're all in place."

"Coffee?" Enzo asked.

"Yep."

We were in Crockett's office a few doors down from a bakery. It was a perfect place to have a coffee. Enzo and Crockett made excellent coffee. I knew Enzo would make our coffee and then go get the sweet treats from the bakery.

Enzo smiled. "Custard square?"

"Of course."

"Copy that."

I walked back into the main office while Enzo went into Crockett's kitchen to start the coffee. Our guest glared at me.

"Hi, how are you feeling? Can I get you anything?"

She rolled her eyes.

"I don't know what you people want."

"The truth," I said. "It's not a mystery. Why were you wandering around on private property?"

She said nothing.

Enzo bowled in the door.

"He's on his way," he announced.

"We should clear out and let him deal with this then," I replied. "He's messy. It's not nice to watch."

"Who?" the woman asked, while tugging against the restraints.

"A friend. This is his office," I said, knowing full well there was nothing in the office to suggest who worked here. "We're off then. Take care."

I opened the door. Enzo and I left the room. The woman shouted after us, "Let me go! I haven't done anything."

"Sucks to suck then I guess," I replied and shut the door behind me.

Enzo and I sat in the outer office while Jane Doe rocked the chair back and forth, banging it against the floor when she dropped forward. Enzo went into the kitchen and returned with coffee. It's never too hot for a decent coffee.

"She's agitated," I said stirring the coffee Enzo handed me. "Did you notice how she didn't mention calling police? Or going to police with her tale of woe about how we held her against her will."

He shrugged and sat beside me with his coffee. "Give her a minute."

"You think she'll start with the threats then?"

"People who don't want to draw attention to whatever they are up to rarely threaten going to authorities. If they do, they're empty threats."

Yeah. He had a good point. Would she want to explain herself? I doubted it. Subject change. "Good coffee."

Before Enzo could reply, Crockett's six feet two-inch muscular frame swung through the outer door with a sparkle in his blue eyes and a smile on his face. "Heard we have a guest."

"Jane Doe in your office," Enzo said. "Coffee? Just made a pot."

"Sure."

The thumping continued in Crockett's office. We drank coffee. There was almost a coffee morning vibe. If a coffee morning took place with captives throwing themselves around in the next room.

"She's the one who triggered the alerts when she wandered around Emily's?" Crockett tipped his head toward his closed office door. "Same person, yes?"

"Yes," Enzo said. "It was a good idea to enable Ronnie

and me to get those alerts too."

"How long are we holding her?" Crockett asked with a head tilt toward his closed office door.

"She can go when she explains why she was casing Emily's place," I said. "Or when Enzo and I have surveillance teams ready to roll on her."

My phone rang. A glance at the screen told me it was Steph. I answered. "Whatcha got for me?"

"Jane Doe is Kerrin Costa. Argentinian National."

"And she's here because?"

"No idea."

"She got any flags?"

"Not that I can see."

"Okay, thanks. I'll see what Crockett can find."

Enzo and Crockett waited patiently as I finished the conversation and hung up. The joy of being us is that we have ways of finding things out. I'm not the only espionage officer in my tight circle. Crockett is an Australian spy. Enzo is also an Australian spy although he does less espionage work now that he's my cousin's devoted husband. Both Enzo and Crockett would look right at home in a bikie gang. They were both tall, muscular, take-no-shit kind of guys. Not to mention how much black they wear and their leather jackets. The biggest difference was Crockett's speckles of grey in his brown hair. Enzo's hair was almost black with no obvious grey strands. And they were waiting for me to speak. I shook my head a little and zoomed back in on the problem at hand.

"According to our Steph ... that woman is an Argentinian. Her name is Kerrin Costa."

"Interesting," Enzo said. "I would've picked her as a European."

"She's got bugger-all accent, but yeah, I would've picked her for a European."

"An Argentinian snooping around Emily," Crockett muttered. "What's Kerrin Costa doing in New Zealand?"

"Steph couldn't find out. Sounds like a job for you or me, but your office is closest," I said, with a grin. "Maybe we should all go have a chat?"

"That's a great idea," Crockett said, putting his mug on the coffee table. "After you."

I put my mug down and stood up.

Crockett reached around me and opened the door. I ducked under his arm and entered.

"We're back," I said tapping the woman on the head. "Miss us?"

She didn't respond. Crockett moved around the woman and sat behind his desk. I perched on the left edge of the desk, Enzo on the right.

"Let me make the introductions." I smiled. "Kerrin Costa, meet all of us."

Her eyes widened momentarily. "You don't have names?"

I definitely did not hear an accent that indicated South America.

"Not today," I replied. "But you do, so that's nice."

Crockett spoke, his voice edged with sharp barbs, "You

and I need to have a chat."

That was our cue to vacate. Guess Crockett wanted to dig in and get real answers.

"We'll catch you later," Enzo said, pushing off the desk at the same moment I did.

"I'll call you if there's anything to clean up," Crockett replied.

"Awesome," I said following Enzo out the door. He waited for me and shut the door behind us, then closed the outside door securely. We weren't taking the car. It was a nice day for a bit of a walk. We sauntered down the street and around the corner.

"The Tote?" Enzo suggested.

It was just along the road.

"We're so close it would be rude not to have one drink."

Also, Enzo didn't come through with a custard square, so a drink was now required by Ronnie Law. We shall call it a custard tax. We entered the dim bar. It wasn't dark but the lighting was low. No sun reached the interior of the main bar which made it the perfect mid-summer watering hole.

The bartender addressed us; Enzo ordered a pint of Panhead then looked at me. "Pinot Gris," I said. "House is fine."

It's a hard wine to screw up.

We took our drinks and found a booth.

"Hey, about Costa. Everything about her is off, right?"

"Yes, Enzo, that is my finding."

"She must've known we'd swoop on her and that we had her on video," Enzo said.

"The external cameras aren't hidden and there is a sign in the window saying surveillance cameras are operating." It's not like we hid anything.

"She knew. Why come back again?" he asked.

"So, someone would grab her up ...," I suggested.

"Why did she want to be snatched?"

"Either she has information, or she wants information."

"And yet she said nothing," Enzo said and sipped his beer. "Unless it wasn't *us* she wanted to talk to."

"Pretty extreme way to get close to Crockett." I paused. "She had nothing but the notebook and the piece of paper, right?"

"Correct. No weapon. No ID. No wallet. No keys."

I tugged the notebook from my back pocket. "Maybe there are answers in this."

Enzo passed the note to me from his pocket. "They were together so perhaps they go together in some way?"

I looked at him. "You are one hundred percent sure we didn't leave Crockett with an armed nut, right?"

He rocked his open left hand back and forth. "You don't need a weapon to kill."

"That's comforting." I drank some wine.

"He can take care of himself. She couldn't get out of the restraints."

True. It's not that hard to get out of cable ties or duct tape. If you know how. People like us know how.

"Could've been an act."

"Crockett can handle it, no matter what."

I nodded and sipped more wine. "It's weird though. That chick lurking around Emily's."

"Not disputing the weird factor. Could she be someone Emily used to know?"

"Maybe. I don't know. She was a cop before she came to work for me as a PI, maybe they'd crossed paths."

"You've got a photo. We could swing by the bookshop and see if Emily recognises her."

I nodded. "Steph was going to show her the photo. Let's hold off until we hear from Crockett."

He nodded and took a swig of beer. "Have you and Ben set a date yet?"

"Not you as well?"

Enzo grinned and shrugged. "Just set a date and make Nana and Donald happy."

"Ah, so you were asked to prompt me. Sneaky."

The bartender appeared at our table.

"You're Ronnie Tracey, the private investigator, right?"

"I am. Can I help you?" I smiled.

"I think I have a problem."

Interesting.

"I'm not too bad at solving problems."

"Do you mind?" She gestured to the bench seat opposite us.

"Not at all. Sit. Share. This is Enzo, he's pretty good at solving problems too." I scooped the notebook, and note, up and put them in my top pocket.

"I'm Roxy. I think I have a stalker."

I lifted my glass. "Intriguing."

"What makes you think that?" Enzo asked, magically pulling a different notebook and a pen from a pocket inside his leather motorbike jacket. Or an invisible pocket which is what I preferred to think.

"For the last few weeks, I keep seeing this one guy. He's everywhere."

"It's Upper Hutt," I said. "If that was stalker criteria then the mayor, and half the town, would be in trouble."

"What else?" Enzo asked with a smile. "Ronnie's right though."

"I know," Roxy said. "He's here now at the far end of the bar. Near the toilets."

"Yep. Got him," I said. I had an unobstructed line of vision. "He got a name?"

"If he does, I don't know it. He calls himself something stupid; Rockstar."

I laughed and caught him looking our way. Refocusing on Roxy I pulled a business card from my bag and slid it to her.

"You've got cameras in here?"

"Yes."

"Okay. If we have a look at the footage maybe we can get a bit of an idea and start to build a profile on the Rockstar."

"I have cameras at home too."

"Cool. Let's start with the bar footage first then see if your home cameras have anything."

Enzo said, "Is there a digital trail or even a paper trail? Has he sent you emails, notes, gifts?"

"He's been emailing the bar."

"Okay. Can we have copies, please?" Enzo asked.

"Social media?" I asked her.

"I'll get you the emails and my social media is private so it's the bar social media that he pops up on trying to message me or leaving creepy comments on posts."

"Do you go out much?" Enzo asked.

"No. This is a pretty social job, and the hours aren't great for going out with friends. I'm always at work when they want to go out."

"Fair enough."

"Supermarket?"

"I shop online."

Enzo nodded. "That's probably a good thing."

Roxy's eyes widened. "Really?"

"If he's stalking you then limiting the ways for him to see you or get to you is smart." Enzo looked around the bar. "What happens when you leave?"

A slight frown flittered across her face. I watched her for a beat. "Where's your car parked?"

"At home. I actually live around the corner."

"Totara Street?"

"Yes."

"Does he follow?"

"I don't think so. He's not usually around at closing and there is always someone who walks me home."

"A security guard?"

She nodded. "They come in before closing to secure the cash. One of them walks me home after lockup."

That was good to know.

"When is the best time for us to view the CCTV?"

"I can give you the sign-in and you can check it whenever you have time," Roxy said, standing. Someone was approaching the bar. "I'll get back to work. Come see me at the bar and I'll write it all down for you."

"Great. Thanks," I said and watched Roxy hurry to the bar and resume work.

Enzo finished his beer. I followed suit with my wine.

"What do you think?" Enzo asked.

"I think I have to look into it."

"I'm not averse to that idea. Count me in."

"Things quiet for you at the moment?"

"There's a lull. We work well together so it would be fun."

I nodded. That is true.

"Okay then, you're in. I'll get Steph to send you the documentation so I can pay you."

Enzo grinned. "Nah. I'll do it for fun."

"You sure?"

"Absolutely."

"I think that just made you Steph's favourite person."

We stopped at the bar on our way out. Roxy wrote the information we needed on the back of a business card.

"Brilliant. We'll get onto it as soon as," I said. "You've got my number; anything off happens and you call me, okay?"

She nodded. "Thanks for this Ronnie."

"My office manager will be in touch with fees and whatnot." I smiled at her. "If you need help paying our fees then tell her. We have options for some people. You are now one of those people."

"Thanks, Ronnie," Roxy said.

I was pretty sure I saw relief flick through her eyes.

"We're off. You'll hear from one of us soonish."

She waved and turned to a new customer who was waiting down the bar. "What can I get you?"

Enzo and I left the dim interior. The heat of the day hit me square in the face and caused me to blink a few times. We made it back to Crockett's office without picking up any more jobs, without me setting a wedding date, and with no one expiring under the burning sun.

Chapter Two:
[Ronnie: Here we go.]

We let ourselves in the back door and quietly listened in the vicinity of Crockett's closed office door. His voice. Her voice. Conversational tones. Nothing that required us to burst through the door.

We sat on the couch under the net-curtained front window of the outer office. The room felt cool and fresh. I took Costa's notebook from my pocket and flicked through the pages.

"I think it's a travel journal," I said, turning a page and seeing place names.

"Written in?"

"Spanish, by the look of it."

"Know anyone who could translate for us?" Enzo asked.

"Not that I can think of immediately." I used my phone and photographed every page. In the end, I had twenty photographs of journal pages and one of the coded note.

"Are we sure this is a code?" I asked, passing him the note.

"Could be a bank account," Enzo said handing it back to me.

"I guess it could." I slipped the note back into the book.

Enzo pulled out his phone and used the login

information supplied by Roxy. He spent the next little while looking at bar footage. Every time our mate Mr Rockstar appeared he made a note in his notebook. I watched him working. It wouldn't be bad to have him on staff. Maybe that's something I should explore. No time like the present.

"Hey Enzo?"

He looked up from his screen. "Ronnie?"

"How attached are you to your role with ASIO?"

He smiled. "How do you know I have a role with ASIO?"

"Well, you don't freelance, and you were deep undercover like Crockett at the same time, I believe."

"He was working for the Yanks then ..."

"Yeah, but he was on secondment from ASIO, right?"

He nodded. "Funny thing about that job, neither of us knew the other one was undercover."

"Yeah, I got that impression when we thought you'd come to shorten Crockett's life; you know, before I found out you were here on a completely not-that-reason, reason. And had a serious crush on my cousin Donald."

Enzo laughed. "Pretty sure there was an easier way to say that sentence."

Probably.

"And?"

"I'm not exactly ASIO and I'm not exactly the other well-known alphabet company that you like to refer to as Charlie Indigo Alpha."

"What does that mean, not exactly?" I watched his

eyes. "Are you freelancing?"

His eyebrows rose. "What if I was?"

I had no problem with anyone freelancing, if I did it'd be a tad hypocritical. "Nothing. Just curious and maybe I want to offer you a regular gig with *Wherefore Art Thou.*"

"As?"

"Special investigator."

"You want me to be Jack Reacher?"

Laugher grew from deep within my belly and erupted from my mouth. It took me by surprise. I reckoned he could pull it off.

"Would you consider joining the firm?"

Enzo smiled. "Yeah. I'm sure I could fit *Wherefore Art Thou* into my schedule."

"Great." I offered him my hand. We shook. "Welcome aboard the crazy train."

And just like that, we were a family business.

"It'll be fun," he said.

He's got a weird idea of fun. Couldn't be better suited to join the staff at *Wherefore Art Thou.*

"What do you suppose is happening in there?" I tipped my head toward the closed door.

"We could go in and find out."

"Tell me what you found on the CCTV first."

"Mr Rockstar is only in the bar on Roxy's shifts. He's not hanging around when the male bartenders are on or when the other female bartenders are there. He seems to like it when Roxy is on her own behind the bar."

"She's not completely on her own though, right?"

"No. There is a chef in the kitchen and a couple of kitchen hands. I've watched them come and go from the bar."

"Is the *Rockstar* the only person who turns up when Roxy is on or are there more regulars?"

"I counted about twelve regulars, all older men. They don't hang around the bar area. Bit hard to see where they are but I think they're toward the front of the bar at tables."

"Now what? What's your take on this?"

"I think she's right. He's there watching her."

"Is there enough to get him trespassed or a protection order?"

"He's harassing her, but we'd have to prove it, and he'll say he's a patron sitting at the bar. Might be hard getting a protection order. We can have Roxy trespass him though."

"What about the emails and messages he's sent?"

"They show he's overzealous when it comes to Roxy but is that enough for a protection order?"

"If she feels threatened, I think yes."

"Maybe the first thing we should do is talk to this guy and get his story. Find out what he's up to. His attitude will tell us a lot."

"Good thinking."

Enzo stood and knocked on the door.

"Come on in," Crockett said.

We exchanged looks and went in. She was still in the chair.

"All good?" Enzo asked Crockett.

Crockett nodded. "Ms Costa doesn't have much to say. She apparently was *lost*."

"In the same place twice … unfortunate," I said.

Costa glared up at me. "People get lost."

"I'm sure they do. I'm also sure you didn't find yourself lost in the same place two days in a row. That implies a very poor sense of direction."

"Let me go," she replied. "You have no business holding me."

"You have no business at our friend's house," I countered. "You've had ample time to tell the truth, and it doesn't feel like you have."

Crockett and I made eye contact. My phone buzzed. It was Steph. The teams were in place and waiting for us to turn Costa loose. I showed Crockett the text. He took a knife from his desk drawer and moved toward Costa.

She squawked and tried to pull away.

"Keep still. I'm trying to cut you free," Crockett said. He carried on, cutting the tape free and cutting the cable ties.

She rubbed her wrists and stood. "Now what?"

I handed her the notebook we'd taken from her earlier.

"Get out of here," Crockett said. He grabbed her by the elbow and spun her to face the door then escorted her from the building. "Don't get lost."

I texted Steph and told her she was loose.

Chapter Three:
[Ronnie: What on earth?]

The drive into town was surprisingly void of idiots. Thursday started well. Now if we could roll that good start into a full-on good day, that'd be terrific. I uploaded all the photos I'd taken of Costa's notebook pages to my laptop intending to find someone to translate them.

"Ronnie?"

"Yeah," I replied, glancing over the top of my screen at Steph. "What do you need?"

"A reason to live," Steph replied absently.

I laughed. "Not sure that's in my wheelhouse."

"Fair enough. How about your latest time sheets and reports then?"

I emailed them right to her and shot her a smile. "You, okay?"

Steph pushed her chair back and came over to my desk. She plonked herself in my spare chair.

"Remember when you and Ben got engaged?"

"Uh oh."

She flashed her blue eyes at me. "Oh yes, uh oh."

"Nana?" I asked. I mean who else would it be?

"Jenn, and your Nana."

"I am sorry." I meant it.

"Not your fault, but wow they are doing my head in."

"Want something else to think about?"

"Sure, hit me with it."

"Bartender with a stalker."

"Let me at it."

"Brilliant. Enzo wants in on this too. You okay working with him?" I knew the answer already. It was yes.

"Sure."

"I think you'll enjoy this case. You might even like the client. Roxy is pretty cool."

Steph lifted her head and straightened up in the chair.

"Roxy the bartender from *The Tote*?"

I nodded. "You know her?"

Steph smiled. "It's Upper Hutt."

"Why do I think there is more to it than that?"

"No idea."

Far too innocent.

"Not buying it. Spill the tea."

"Our community isn't that big ..."

"You're not talking about Upper Hutt, are you?"

She shook her head. So, Roxy is gay.

"She's family," Steph said with a wink.

"Gay?"

"Yes, as I said, family."

"Do you really all know each other?"

Steph laughed. "Probably not so much now but it used to be the case."

I slid a manilla folder across the desk to her. "This is what we have so far."

She flipped the cover open and read the first page. "The guy is legit harassing her?"

That was an odd question. I waited. Had a feeling there was more to come on that front. Patience. She turned the page and continued reading. A minute later she closed the file.

"Does Mr Rockstar have a real first name and a surname?"

"He's not Cher, so I presume so."

"I've seen him somewhere."

"It's Upper Hutt!"

"Touché."

"Are you going to tell me?"

"I'm deciding."

I waited. My cell phone rang. Steph and I watched the picture on the screen. Neither of us spoke as the call rang out.

"She's going to ring back," Steph said.

The front desk phone rang, loud and incessant.

"It's her," I said. "It's her."

"Of course it is. You didn't answer your mobile."

I jumped to my feet and rushed to the front desk. I just got the phone to my ear in time to catch Nana.

"Ronnie Tracey speaking."

"Veronica, I do wish you would stop calling yourself Ronnie," Nana said with a punctuating sigh.

"How can I help Nana?"

"The girls and I ..."

That was never a good start to a sentence.

"Uh huh, you and the cronies what, Nana? How can I be of service?" I rammed a smile into my words.

"They're not crones, Veronica. That's quite rude."

I bit back a small laugh because I knew that would not help. "Sorry Nana. How can I be of service?"

"We have a slight problem with a case."

My stomach twisted. "A case, Nana?"

"Yes, dear. It looks like we have a missing client."

"Okay. How long has the client been missing?"

"Since last evening."

"What's the case, Nana."

I could almost hear Nana pursing her lips before deciding if she'd tell me. "I don't want to breach any confidentiality agreements."

Fair enough.

"Would you like me to take a look and see if your client is missing or just a bit forgetful?"

"If it's not too much trouble Veronica."

"Of course it isn't Nana."

"I shall expect you presently."

"I'll bring cakes for morning tea. Bye Nana."

"Bye, bye dear."

I hung up. Steph was watching me, having moved to perch on the edge of my desk, she wore a grin that would put the Cheshire Cat to shame.

"Have fun working for your Nana," she said.

I moved slowly toward her.

"And you and Enzo have fun with your old love-interest Roxy."

Steph's grin melted away. I was right. Ha!

I grabbed my bag off the floor by my desk. "You want

me to get cakes on my way back?"

Steph regained her composure. "Does Nana love tormenting you, and Donald?"

She sure does.

"It's because she loves us so much," I replied, smiling.

So much love.

Chapter Four:
[Ronnie: Okay, Nana]

Cake. Don't forget the cakes. If I repeated it enough times I might remember. Once upon a time the most requested sweet treat in our family, and at the office, was Squiggle Top biscuits but now they're a disappointing disappointment and none of us will go there again. Now, it's bakery treats for the win.

I stopped at Broadway shops and got a selection of cakes I knew would be well received by Nana and *The Cronies of Doom*. I had no problem providing Thursday's morning tea, it was whatever else they needed that could be a problem.

At the front desk of the retirement home, I set the box of deliciousness on the dividing counter and scanned for Margot. I couldn't see her. "Margot, are you in?" I called into the vacant space beyond the reception area.

A muffled voice responded, "One sec." She popped into view. "Good to see you, Ronnie."

She lifted the sign-in book up from the desk and handed me a pen. I took the pen and handed her a small paper bag with a cream donut in it. I signed the visitor book as Margot peeked into the bag.

"What's this for?" she asked smiling.

"Morning tea," I replied. "Get it down you before the cream turns nasty. Warmer than I thought outside."

"Thank you, that's very kind of you."

I smiled. "You deserve it. Enjoy. I'm off to help Nana and *The Cronies of Doom* with something mysterious."

Margot nodded. "They're very busy these days with all manner of mysteries. Good luck."

I had a feeling I'd need it. I lifted the box of cakes and made my way through the corridors, dodging elderly people with walking sticks, walkers, and those who shuffled along. As much as I tried not to breathe in the distinct aromas of the home, I couldn't quite make the whole walk with a single breath.

I hoped that the delicious smells from the bakery box countered the less pleasant aromas of institutional room freshener, hospital-grade disinfectant, and creeping death. I knocked once on the interior door to Nana's apartment, steeled myself for what would come next, and opened the door.

"Is the jug on Nana?" I asked, closing the door with my foot.

"Of course, dear," she replied. "I'm in the kitchenette."

I followed her voice with the box of cakes. I didn't see any cronies in the living area. Guess they weren't here yet.

Nana smiled, stretching her taut thin lips over her teeth.

"That teal top looks lovely on you, Veronica," she said, offering up a papery old cheek for me to kiss.

"Thank you, Nana." I plated the cakes. "Are Frankie and Ester joining us?"

"Yes, dear."

I took four side plates and the plate of cakes out to the living area and put them on the coffee table.

"I thought they would've been here already," I said rejoining Nana in the kitchen area.

"They're gathering intelligence and are due to check in presently," Nana said glancing at her watch.

They're doing what now? Smile, Ronnie. Just smile. This is probably some sort of nightmare and you're still asleep at home with Ben. Safe. I blinked.

"Tea?" I asked.

"It's steeping. Would you bring the tray through for me, dear?"

I hadn't noticed that Nana had left the kitchen.

I poked my head around the dividing wall and saw Nana comfortably in her favourite chair with a notebook and her cell phone on her knee. I fetched a tray laden with the Royal Albert teapot, milk jug, sugar bowl, and teaspoons then went back for the teacups and saucers.

Nana smiled at me as I moved everything off the tray.

"It's lovely having you here Veronica." Her faded blue eyes twinkled with mischief. "Ben's ring suits your finger."

I sat down. "Less sparkly ring talk, Nana. What's this intelligence gathering bizzo?"

She tapped the side of her nose with her index finger. That was not an answer.

"Didn't you say you needed my help?"

"I did. We have a missing client."

"Are you sure your client hasn't got mixed up and forgotten an appointment?"

"She's definitely missing."

"Okay. If you'd like my help I'm going to need more information."

A name would help.

Voices outside the interior door alerted us to incoming cronies. A quiet knock was followed by the door opening. In came Ester and Frankie chattering away.

"Ladies," I said. "Teas made."

The door closed. Frankie smiled at me. "Lovely to see you dear."

"You too," I replied.

Nana gestured to the laden coffee table.

"Marvellous spread June." Ester clapped her hands with unreserved glee. Nana and *The Cronies of Doom* settled in. Frankie poured the tea. I waited for the general chatter to subside. Once everyone had a cup of tea and a cake in front of them, I spoke.

"Nana tells me you have a missing client. Maybe you all could fill me in?"

Frankie and Ester looked at Nana. She nodded. How kind of her to allow *The Cronies of Doom* to speak with me. So generous.

Ester placed her teacup on the saucer with a rattle. She whipped out a notebook from the folds in her trousers. She licked her forefinger and turned the pages with a flourish.

"Our new client stopped answering calls yesterday

afternoon and we haven't seen her."

She could be dodging calls. Not unheard of.

"What was she doing yesterday afternoon? Do you know?"

"We don't know."

"Can I have a name, photo, more details about this person?

"Her name is Ms Costa."

I sighed. Of course, it is. Why would it be someone I've never heard of?

"How did you meet this Costa person?"

"She'd heard about us from the newspaper."

"Getting some good mileage out of that Nana." Then an awful thought fell from my lips. "Oh, sweet baby Jesus. Was there another story?"

Frankie smacked her hands on her thighs. "Another story!" she crowed.

"There's no need for blasphemy, Veronica."

"Really because I think there might be." How did I miss it? I crossed my fingers. If there's a God, it won't be true.

"Just a mention really, in *The Leader*," Nana said with a false-teeth-defying smile.

And we're back in the nightmare of far too much fame and notoriety. Buggery bollocks.

"What were you doing for this client?"

Nana rattled her teacup on its saucer. "I don't think we should get into particulars."

"If you want my help you need to give me particulars."

"Just find her Veronica," Nana said tutting.

We had her under surveillance, but I was loath to give Nana that information. Technically I knew where she was or, at least, could find out very quickly.

"Sure Nana, I'll wave my magic wand and conjure her right up."

"Don't be like that dear. Snippy doesn't suit you."

"Not even in my teal top?"

"Veronica. I don't know what's got into you this morning." Nana shot me a look that said I was in deep trouble if I carried on in the same vein.

Frankie giggled. Ester picked up another cake.

"It is a pretty colour on you," Frankie said.

"Can we stay on topic please?" So, I don't get myself in any more hot water with Nana. I finished my tea and looked at Ester. "What did you discover while you were gathering intelligence?"

"That she was last seen in Wallaceville."

"On foot or was there a vehicle involved?"

She licked crumbs off her fingers before she consulted her notebook. "Mrs Harris saw her walking on Martin Street toward town."

"And this was when?"

She consulted her notes. "Quarter past three in the afternoon."

"She could've gone shopping," I said. "What makes you think she's been missing?"

"She didn't answer her phone when I rang her." Nana's reply was a tad curt and implied that surely no one would dodge a phone call from her.

I left that alone.

"Anything else?"

"She didn't answer any of our calls last night or this morning."

"Do you have a photo?"

Nana reached for a manilla folder tucked beside her chair. She flipped it open. It looked like one of our case files. I waited. She produced a photo and handed it to me. It was definitely the same Kerrin Costa. That was awkward.

"Okay," I said and snapped a photo with my phone before handing the picture back. It was expected that I would take a photo. They didn't know I already had one on my phone. "So, are you going to tell me what you were doing for this woman?"

The three of them exchanged glances but said nothing. I picked up a fruit slice and bit into it. Grandad called them fly-cemeteries. I'm pretty sure that should've put me off as a kid, but I think I grew to love them more. I concentrated on the pastry and fruit filling, savouring each mouthful. As I enjoyed my slice of deliciousness, I became aware of eyes on me. I swallowed.

"Can I help you all?"

"No, dear. It just does us good to see a young lady like you with a healthy appetite."

I scanned their wrinkled faces to see if that was a judgemental observation or not. Nothing hinted at judgement, surprisingly.

Just as I wondered what alternate reality I'd stumbled into, Nana reached out and patted my hand.

"Not too many cakes Veronica or that wedding dress will be a little snug."

I smiled sweetly. And we're back. "Thank you, Nana."

"Wouldn't like to prove your dear departed Grandad wrong now, would you?"

Frankie's lips moved into a quick tight smile. "What was it he used to say, June?"

"You can't fatten a thoroughbred," I said before Nana could answer.

Frankie snickered.

"I don't think Veronica needs to worry," Ester replied. "She's long of limb."

Did that old cop just call me gangly? I filed the comment away to run it past Donald later.

"Ladies, I need to know what's really going on so I can find that woman."

Frankie frowned. "Whatever you think it is, it isn't."

"Of course." I didn't know what I expected. "You know what? Perhaps you could just say yes or no, as you're not comfortable giving me details."

"Go on," Nana said. The three of them leaned in, all ears. Literally. Old people have big ears. I guess they grow forever. I shoved that aside.

"I think, ladies, that the woman who hired you is up to something nefarious and has dragged you into that something." I sat back to see what that dislodged.

"She's just looking for someone she lost touch with, a

cousin," Frankie said. "Surely that isn't bad."

And we have a winner.

"A cousin? How about that! Oh well, perhaps I'm wrong. What's the cousin's name?"

"Sandra Solway," Frankie replied despite the look Nana shot her.

"And have you found her?"

Frankie shook her head.

"She doesn't seem to be in the region," Ester said.

Nana looked daggers at both of them. "You're going to have to sign a nondisclosure agreement, Veronica."

She flipped through pages in the folder and handed me a piece of paper with her pen. Buggery bollocks this is ridiculous.

"We cannot go on until you sign the paper," Nana said, with a frosty glare at *The Cronies of Doom*.

"Fine." I grabbed the piece of paper, gave it a quick read, then signed the bottom before handing it back. "Happy?"

"Yes, thank you," Nana said.

"I have a question for you three." I took a breath and let it out. "Any reason why your client would be by Emily's house?"

"None," Ester said. "She hasn't asked about anyone but the cousin."

How odd.

"Why would you ask that?" Nana picked up a piece of raspberry slice.

I opened photos on my phone and flicked to the photo

I took of Kerrin Costa in Crockett's office and restrained in a chair. I zoomed in so no one could see her restraints and showed it to Nana, and then Ester and Frankie.

"That's her?"

Nana's brow wrinkled as she nodded.

"Why do you have a photo of our client?" Ester asked.

Before I could answer Nana piped up, "Do you have her?"

"No, but we did. Picked her up snooping around Emily's yesterday morning. It was the second time she was seen snooping there, by the way."

"Makes no sense," Frankie said. "She only talked about her long-lost cousin and how much she missed her."

"And she found you three to help her." Not at all sus. "What did you talk about?"

"She talked about her cousin," Frankie repeated brushing crumbs off her dark blue twinset.

"You said that," I replied. "But what did you three talk about in front of her?"

Frankie sucked in her thin lips as she frowned.

Ester folded her hands into her lap.

"I do not remember any conversation per se, but if I recall correctly there was a thank you card on the coffee table from Emily and Crockett," Ester said.

"How was it delivered?" I directed my question to Nana.

"By post."

"Was the envelope on the table?"

Nana nodded. "I think so, I wanted to save the stamps.

They're scarce as hen's teeth these days."

"And Emily had her name and address on the back of the envelope, am I right?"

"Of course she did. That's what one does when addressing an envelope," Nana responded. "If you used the post, you'd know that dear, wouldn't you?"

"Yes, Nana."

Usually, I used the post to mail things to myself. Sometimes I posted things I wanted out of the way and inaccessible for a few days.

Next question. "Did any of you see the woman touch the card or envelope?"

They all denied any knowledge.

Talk about pulling teeth. This could've gone a lot better and a lot faster.

"Was she left alone in here at any time?"

Ester spoke. She'd flipped open her trusty notebook. "Unfortunately, yes, she was. We had a short conference in June's bedroom, deciding if we'd take the case."

All right, I'll play.

"Knowing what I just told you and how she possibly came across Emily's address, what do you make of your client now?"

If anyone had an opinion it would be Ester, the retired police officer. I waited to see if she'd share her insight.

I didn't have to wait long.

"She was calm, polite, had an accent that I couldn't recognise, but was barely there."

"Anything else?"

"She said she saw an article about us. The one that The Guardian ran a wee while ago. She thought she'd see if we could help her while she was here on holiday."

"Do you know how long she'd been here?"

"She didn't say."

I eased my phone from my pocket and rang Crockett.

"What's up, Ronnie?"

"We need to scrub all the CCTV footage from the bookshop. Let's see if our new friend visited there."

"I'll get on it from here. Let's get Emily into a safe house after she finishes work today."

She'd be safest at my place. "My place."

"That's a great idea."

I hung up then rang Jenn at the office. I stood and walked to the ranch slider while I waited for her to answer.

"How can I help Ronnie?"

"Can you hang downstairs with Emily until I get there?"

"Sure. What do I need to know?"

I could hear her running down the stairs.

"Someone is snooping around her life ... don't know why yet but I doubt it's good."

I heard Emily greet Jenn. "I'm here," Jenn replied.

"Thank you." I hung up and turned around. All the old eyes were on me. I looked at the dishes on the coffee table, then at the elderly women. I said nothing as I cleared the dishes and stacked everything on the bench for washing.

Back in the lounge, I bent down and kissed Nana's papery cheek. "I'll be off. Please try and stay out of trouble."

"Will you find our client?" Frankie asked.

"Yes. I will. If you hear anything let me know." I let myself out via the ranch slider to the garden and made my way to the bookshop. Determined to make it my business to find that woman and have another chat. This time it wouldn't be friendly, and I was absolutely fine with using Enzo and his enhanced interrogation techniques. I also wanted to know what she'd written in her notebook because that might hold some clues to the whole situation. Best if I sent those to someone who could help interpret them A-SAP.

Chapter Five:
[Emily Jones: That is not me.]

"Who are you?" Emily watched the man with dark hair unlock a red car. They were in the Woolworths car park not far from the bookshop. Sun beat down upon them. Emily could feel the heat radiating from the ground.

"I am a friend," he replied, and motioned to the car door.

"I don't know you, so how can you be my friend?" Emily's eyes narrowed as she tried to find stashed memories of the man with dark hair. Nothing came. "What's your name?"

"Lucas."

"What's his name?" Emily pointed to the other man.

"Stefan."

"He looks mean."

Stefan grumbled and said, "This is taking too long."

Lucas silenced him with a frosty look, then turned his attention to Emily. "You do know me. Simone, you do know me."

"Who is Simone?"

"You are."

"I am Emily Jones."

"You are Simone."

"That is not my name." Emily squared her shoulders and clenched her jaw. "I *am* Emily Jones."

"Get in the car, Simone."

"No."

The other man stepped up behind her, reached around, and opened the back passenger door. A wave of heat hit her. "Get in."

"No." Emily moved sideways avoiding the man, then took a step back, and turned. "You get in the car. I'm going back to my bookshop and Jenn. She's, *my* friend."

The dark-haired man met her by the boot. "You can't go back in there. Now get in the car." He placed his hands on her shoulders and spun her around. "Now, Simone."

"Stop calling me that. I am not that person. You are wrong." Emily's voice crumbled leaving a panicked raw edge. "Stop it!" Her eyes darted around the car park. There was no one near enough to help her.

The men stood on each side of Emily. Neither man touched her.

"Get in the car," the dark-haired man, who called himself Lucas, said. "Just do it. Emily."

She did as he asked and watched them from the back seat as they exchanged looks. Emily didn't know what the looks meant. She was relieved they'd stopped calling her Simone. As the car drove out of the Woolworths car park toward Geange Street, she looked over her shoulder and thought she saw Ronnie's car stop outside the bookshop. She hoped it was Ronnie. Ronnie would help Jenn. Ronnie would get Crockett. Ronnie could find her, anywhere. That's what Ronnie did. The car pulled out of Princes Street and onto Fergusson Drive leaving the

43

bookshop and Ronnie in the distance. Emily leaned her head against the back of the seat and closed her eyes. Over and over in her mind, she told herself that Ronnie would find her because that's what Ronnie did. Lucas and Stefan could not keep her hidden.

Emily's eyes opened and she looked out the window. Houses, playgrounds, more houses, bus stops, people walking with dogs or children, and sometimes both. She tried to see street signs so she could keep track of where they were. When they turned into Shakespeare Ave, she knew they were in Poet's Block. Lucas turned left into Thackeray Street, passed the kindergarten, then turned right into Moore Street and popped out on Moonshine Road.

Then he turned right and drove back to Shakespeare. This time he turned left off Thackeray onto Sheridan Crescent. Emily was familiar with the area. Crockett didn't live that far away from where the car stopped. A few streets maybe. If she could get away, then she could get to Crockett. Lucas backed the car up a driveway on Sheridan Crescent.

"Where is this?" Emily asked, looking at the house next to the car.

"A safe place," Lucas replied.

"Why am I here?"

"You don't need to know," Stefan said. "Less questions and more compliance."

The men exited the vehicle. Lucas opened the door for her to do the same. Emily sat staring straight ahead.

"Out," Lucas said.

"No," Emily replied.

"Fucks sake," Stefan muttered. "We're doing this again?"

"Don't be a pain in the arse, get out."

"No." Emily refused to look at either man. She remained staring out the windscreen. As she sat, she wondered how long she needed to be at a location for it to register on Ronnie's radar.

"Get out of the car." Stefan grabbed her arm, just above her elbow, and tugged.

Emily pulled her arm from his grip. "No!"

"I'm not doing this all day," Stefan growled. "Get out."

"No."

"Please, Emily, get out of the car," Lucas said.

She sat still for the longest twenty seconds either man had experienced then carefully got out of the car. Emily looked around. It was a regular house, in a regular street. There was nothing remarkable from the outside at all. It sat back from the road with a manicured lawn from the house to the footpath. It was a red brick house with white painted trim around the windows. A matching garage was at the end of the driveway and not attached to the house.

"Where are we?" she asked.

"Again, a safe place," Lucas answered, escorting her up the path to the front door.

She looked over her shoulder as the car started. "Where is he going?"

"Nowhere. Moving the car into the garage, that's all."

He keyed the door lock then swung the door open. "Come in. I'll make us a coffee."

"I'd prefer Milo," Emily said, as Lucas led the way to the kitchen.

"What is Milo?" he asked with a pinch of surprise.

"Like hot chocolate, but nicer," she said.

"Since when did you like hot chocolate?"

"I don't know," she said.

He pointed to a kitchen table and four chairs. "Sit anywhere over there."

She did. She sat so she could see out the kitchen window into a garden. The window reminded her of something. There was some wire mesh inside the glass. School. That's what it reminded her of. Classroom doors sometimes had glass with wire mesh. She ignored the mesh and gazed beyond it into the garden. There seemed to be a high fence around that part of the property.

"Who does this house belong to?"

Lucas filled the jug and turned it on. "You sure about the Milo?"

"Yes."

He opened various cupboards and eventually came up with a small green tin of Milo.

"The house is a rental," he said.

A door opened, then closed. Stefan appeared. "Coffee. Good idea," he said. Stefan turned to face Emily as she sat at the table. "Have you remembered anything yet?"

She frowned. "About what?"

"Yourself."

"I am Emily Jones. I was a police officer. I run a bookshop. What else do you expect me to tell you?"

Stefan slid into a chair opposite her. "What's that scar from?" He leaned over and tried to trace the line down her face. She slapped his hand away.

"An accident. Don't touch me."

Lucas placed a mug of Milo in front of Emily. He gave Stefan a warning look before going back to the bench for their mugs of coffee.

Chapter Six:
[Ronnie: Bugger me!]

I pulled up out front of the bookshop ten minutes after leaving Nana's. There was a bit of unexpected traffic. From the car, I could see that the lights in the shop were on, but the door was closed. Funny to have that shut on a warm day. But then, it does get very noisy on high-traffic days so that might've been the problem.

I tried the door, and it slid open. Couldn't see anyone.

"Hello!" I called inside.

A low groan came from the back of the shop. I tugged my phone from my pocket and dialled 1-1-1 as I moved faster toward the noise.

Jenn was on the floor behind the desk.

A voice in my ear asked which emergency service I wanted.

"Ambulance," I replied and gave them the shop address before hanging up.

"What happened?" I crouched down by Jenn as she tried to struggle into a sitting position. I put my hand out to steady her and help her sit.

"Someone whacked me across the back of the head." She tried to stand.

I pressed down on her shoulder as sirens wound through the air. "Don't move. Ambo is almost here."

"Don't make a fuss, it's just a bump."

"Where's Emily?"

"She was shelving books." Jenn turned her head toward the back of the shop. She grimaced and touched her hand to her head. "There. She was right there and there was a customer with her."

A flash of green outside told me the paramedics were about to enter the shop.

I stood and spun around. No Emily. "She isn't here." I waved the paramedics over. "Jenn was hit across the back of her head. I think she was knocked out," I said and hurried into the room next door, then into the kitchen. No sign of Emily. I checked the bathroom. There was no sign of her. She wasn't anywhere.

In the shop, I opened the cupboard under the counter. Her backpack was there.

Breathe.

In. Out.

Breathe.

In. Out.

My phone was in my hand. One glance across the shop told me the paramedics were still with Jenn. I tapped on Crockett's phone number. He didn't answer. I was about to send him our emergency word when I had a better idea. I opened our group iMessage.

And texted Ben, Enzo, and Crockett: Red roses. Afternoon tea.

A paramedic spoke. "We're going to transport Jenn to

Hutt Hospital."

Jenn was not best pleased.

"I'll have Steph meet you there," I said. "Do as you're told."

"She better hurry up," Jenn said as they escorted her out to the waiting ambulance.

I rang Steph. She picked up on the fourth ring. There was a lot of background noise. "What's up?"

"Steph, Jenn is on the way to Hutt Hospital. She was knocked out in the bookshop."

"Shit. How bad?"

"Not sure. She was annoyed at having to go to hospital."

"She's fine then," Steph replied with a small laugh.

"I'd say concussion, but she'll be right."

"I'll head to the Emergency Department and wait. I'm in Queensgate."

"Text Ange and see if she's working today, then you can go through the ED and wait for the ambulance."

"Good idea. I'll do that now."

"Good luck. Keep me posted."

The phone call ended as the familiar throb of a Harley roared up the street. Then a car pulled in right behind mine. A car door slammed. Crockett stormed in the door with a face like thunder, followed by Enzo wearing leathers.

Crockett's eyes scanned the shop before landing on me. "Where's Milo?"

"I don't know." I grabbed his arm as he tried to go into

the next room. "I've searched the shop. She's not here. We should go upstairs and check the cameras."

Crockett stopped moving and breathed out. "I was checking the cameras. I've been looking through footage since you rang me earlier." Of course, he was. He would've missed any alerts because he was already in the system scrubbing older footage. Shit.

Enzo dropped a hand on Crockett's upper arm. "Come on, mate. You couldn't have known what was going to happen here."

Enzo put his other hand out, palm up. I dropped my keys into it. He took Crockett out of the shop and along to my offices. I checked for anything out of place. Any hint of something that Emily could've left to give us a clue as to what happened. I looked around the counter area, moving things carefully. There was nothing.

In the middle of the shop, I stopped and breathed.

Just breathe.

In. Out.

Slowly, I turned in a circle. If she had the chance to leave something, where would it be?

Her favourite books. I spun back to the kids' books. One was upside down. I picked it up and fanned the pages. A bookmark fell out.

Enzo burst through the door. "She put something in a book!"

I held up the bookmark I'd retrieved from the floor. "This."

"A bookmark?"

"For a book set in Wellington, not a kid's book." I handed it to him. "Find that book."

Crockett strode in. "You need to see this surveillance video from the bookshop." He thrust one of my iPads into my hands, reached over, and pressed play. On the screen, I watched two men walk into the shop, so I paused it for a second to take note of their height. On one side of the front door there was a height chart of sorts. I grabbed a pen off the counter and wrote their heights on a memo pad. Both were over six feet tall, but not much over. I pressed play, again. One approached Emily at the counter and the other browsed. I turned the sound up a bit. The one who approached the counter smiled and asked for a book recommendation.

"He's sounds almost American," I said more to myself than Crockett. "What the hell is going on?"

The male followed Emily to the back of the shop. He was interested in spy/thriller-type books. Emily must've felt that something was off. She watched him browse for a moment then flicked through the bookmark display stand on the desk before picking one out. She turned and slipped the bookmark into a kid's book then tipped the book upside down. She turned back in time to see Jenn hit. "The Jaded Spy," I said. "Why did she choose that bookmark?"

"A message?" Crockett replied. "Has to be something about those blokes."

"Okay, so while we had surveillance teams on the Argentinian woman, two men abducted Emily. We've missed something big."

Enzo pushed a copy of *The Jaded Spy* into my hands. I flipped the book over and read the blurb. "Listen to this: Alexander, the curator, is sent to Auckland to escort Captain James Cook to the Auckland Art Gallery. On opening night, the priceless portrait is stolen. Alexander has to find the painting to save his career, but he also has to deal with a Soviet spy whom he has been clandestinely photographing." I smiled. "I'm paraphrasing, there's a woman involved."

Crockett and I made eye contact. He voiced what I was thinking, "Not another Alex situation."

I shrugged. "She was a Russian spy. We're not going back there! At least one of the men who took Emily was maybe American."

Enzo leaned in and read over my arm. "A Māori Land Rights group claims to have kidnapped Captain Cook." He frowned and nudged me. "Ransom?"

"Not so far."

"I don't see anything that tells us why Emily chose this book," Crockett said. "Unless it's a ransom situation?"

I took the next piece, "There's a boyfriend and some missing scientific notebooks. This part is interesting ... the notebooks are wanted by the FBI and the KGB." I let that settle. "So now we have the Security Service and the New Zealand police as well as the FBI and KGB."

"Sounds like a great book," Crockett said. "What was Emily trying to tell us?"

"We're not finished," Enzo replied and continued

reading aloud. "The main character is this Alexander dude, and he has to come to terms with being a spy, betraying his friends and deciding how far he will go in his new government job. He struggles to discover who he has become and what he has lost."

"Now, that could make sense if Emily was a spy, but she was a cop and PI," I said. "She does struggle with what she's lost - memory-wise."

"It's getting complicated," Crockett said. "We've got Russians, spies, art theft, missing scientific notebooks, kidnapping and land rights. Jesus H Christ."

"No mention of Jesus," I said with a grin. "This is the last bit. Set in 1976, *The Jaded Spy* is the middle story of *The Jaded Trilogy* and is a window into a vibrant changing New Zealand, with the growing Māori Land Rights movement, student riots, the Soviet spy scandal and a political party that will do anything to stay in power and destroy its enemies."

The three of us digested the information. My attention caught on the political party that will do anything to stay in power. National were in power then and they are now. Fair assessment of their tactics.

"Same political party in the Beehive then as now," I said.

"And they're ripping the country apart by overturning everything Labour accomplished," Enzo said.

He wasn't wrong, but it was the first time I'd heard him express a political opinion.

"What are we supposed to be focusing on?" I asked,

passing the book to Crockett when he held his hand out.

"All right, she chose this book quickly. Why this book?" Crockett turned it over and over in his hands, studying the front cover and the back blurb. "This is a stretch because Emily doesn't know much about herself prior to the accident. This book has FBI, KGB, Secret Service, and New Zealand Police. We know there is one American, or we think there is."

"And you think the other guy is Russian? If he is he'd be FSB not KGB these days. Unless you know something, we don't." I said to Crockett.

"I think she's trying to tell us something about the situation behind the abduction," he said.

"Māori land rights?" I asked, knowing that wasn't going to be it.

"Could be terrorism. Perhaps something was stolen? But I doubt it was a painting of Captain Cook," Crockett said. "There's a reason for the book. I know there is."

"It could be anything at this point, Crockett. Let's keep all of that in mind though."

"Good idea," Enzo said. "Shall we take this party up to your office Ronnie?"

"Go ahead. I'll close up and put a sign on the door."

"We'll all go together," he said.

I found some yellow cardboard in the credenza and wrote a sign that said: Shop Closed Due To Illness. I taped it to the glass door. If Emily did find her way back, she'd go upstairs and find us. I turned the lights out and locked the front door. Crockett and Enzo waited on the footpath. Together we went up to my offices above the bookshop.

Crockett swung the main office door open and held it for me and Enzo. He had the book in his hand and Enzo carried the iPad.

I headed to my computer and fired it up. Enzo and Crockett dragged chairs over to my desk and sat. It didn't take long before I was in the CCTV account and viewing this morning's events. What I wanted was a clear image of their faces.

I took a screenshot of one man's face, the one that didn't hit Jenn. The other guy kept his face away from all the cameras. Guess he was the brains of the outfit. I was pleased one of them was stupid. I dropped the image into the Facial Recognition App I had. We all watched the program flick through images. No match.

"Buggery bollocks, no wonder he didn't care about the cameras! He knew we wouldn't find him in a database," I said.

"Can you phone a friend and get help?" Crockett asked.

At least he didn't mention *Genesis* in front of Enzo. "Of course."

I chose *Uncle George* from my phone contacts and called the number. The call rang out. I hung up and my phone rang: unknown number.

"Uncle George?" I asked. Enzo shot me a curious look and I ignored it.

"Yes. What do you need?"

His voice sounded slightly European this time. I knew

he or she used voice-changing software and that was about all I knew for sure.

"Resources. Emily was grabbed from work and Jenn was hospitalised."

"Tom and Ginny are at your disposal. Reach out to Bill Bailey at Army; he owes us a favour."

"What about Dane Wesson?" I was pushing it to ask about Dane. But he was once a super special FBI agent, and I suspected *Genesis* would have a use for him, so I assumed he'd been brought into the organisation.

"Expect a chopper later this afternoon. He'll be on it. Where and when will be in a text message. More than likely, it'll be the Army Camp."

I froze and smiled. I was right. Good old *Uncle George* did have access to Dane Wesson.

My voice returned, "How?"

"He's *Genesis*."

"Since when?"

"That's several jumps above your pay grade."

"I'll expect a text."

The call dropped or whoever the mystery person that I called *Uncle George*, hung up.

Crockett tapped my arm. "What?"

"We're getting Dane Wesson," I said. "He's your mate, right?" Crockett took him south to stay with his mate Mitch after the Charlie Indigo Alphas and the Foxtrot Bravo Indigos got too close. Man, I wish I could just think of them as alphabet companies or how other people think of them.

I turned to see Crockett's face. "Yeah. He is. How was he offered up?"

I shrugged. "No clue. He was suggested by a friend is all I know."

A frown darkened Crockett's features but he said nothing. Well, well, well, if Dane being offered up isn't a clue as to who runs *Genesis*, I don't know what is. I decided to keep that to myself.

"We've got Tom and Ginny at our disposal and apparently Bill Bailey owes a favour so we can reach out to him."

Crockett nodded. I could see thoughts roaming around Enzo's face and I knew what was coming.

"Uncle George?" he queried. "Donald hasn't mentioned an Uncle George."

"It's kind of a codename for an old friend, not a real uncle," I replied.

He didn't believe me, I could tell by the look in his eyes. A beat passed and he moved on.

"Police?" Enzo asked.

"Who do you know? Ideally, we want every cop to have her picture and the photo we managed to get of that guy in the shop. Can you make that happen without mentioning a kidnapping or abduction or anything that would excite them into wanting to know more?"

Enzo nodded. "Crockett and I've got a couple of mates who are cops. They'll get the photos out without too much fuss." Enzo shifted in his chair as he tugged his phone from his jacket pocket. "Is this a national security issue? Maybe that's what Emily meant with the book?"

I shook my head. "We don't know enough to make that determination." It could be one of many things if she chose that book on purpose.

"Text me that image of the guy in the shop," Enzo said.

I did as he asked. "Have you got one of Emily?"

"I do. That photo of all of us from last week. I'll trim it so it's just Emily."

A heavy silence dropped like a weighted blanket over the room.

I knew I needed to find out what was written in that notebook.

Chapter Seven:
[Ronnie: Now what?]

"What does your gut say?" Enzo asked.

"She was snatched for a reason. Could be national security, although I don't know how. Could be money, could be a pissed-off spouse, and it could be something to do with *Wherefore Art Thou* and not our extracurricular pursuits. Could be something else entirely."

"Chatty your gut," Enzo said. Our eyes met. "Donald."

"Go get him — use one of the safe houses. I'll get Nana."

Enzo's hand grabbed mine. "You set up a base here and I'll get Nana and Donald to safety." He looked thoughtful for a moment. "Home. They're safest at home. Okay if I take a couple of drones with me?"

"Yes. Good idea. Make sure the perimeter alarm is activated and for sanity's sake, keep Nana off the deck."

Nana. I pondered on her and her mystery-solving business for a moment and wondered if this could have something to do with Nana's missing client, the woman we grabbed. It'd be quite a coincidence if it wasn't. Payback started to feel like a good reason to snatch Emily.

Enzo left. Leaving Crockett staring at me.

"Can I help you?"

"Can you do your woo-woo thing?" He held his hand in

front of him and circled it.

For once I didn't shoot him a filthy look for calling dowsing woo-woo.

"Yes. You contact Ben and find out how far away he is. I'll ring Ginny and Tom and get them working on the city CCTV cameras."

Once everyone was contacted and either working toward finding Emily or close to joining us, I stood and stretched.

"Let's do it," I said and led the way to my preferred dowsing room. Crockett had seen me dowse so many times he knew the drill. He opened the window for me and took down the smoke alarm before sitting on the chair near the door.

I lit two blue candles and spread a map of Upper Hutt on the big table in the middle of the room. I keep most of my pendulums hanging inside a cupboard with candles, incense, and other semi-precious stones. I opened the cupboard and looked at the row of hanging pendulums. They shook gently and then one circled. Smoky quartz. I took that pendulum and went back to the table and the map.

I had a quiet word to my spirit guides. Holding the pendulum by the chain with my arm bent at the elbow and wrist relaxed I said, "Show me yes."

The pendulum swung out from my body.

"Stop."

It stopped dead.

"Show me no."

The pendulum swung across my body.

"Stop."

Again, it stopped dead.

I asked spirit three questions that I already knew the answer to. A test. Just to make sure there wouldn't be any nonsense.

No one wants nonsense when they dowse, and spirit sometimes plays games. I guess you get your jollies where you can on the other side.

I started at the bottom of the map right around the demarcation line between Lower Hutt and Upper Hutt. Circles swung as I carefully moved my hand while making sure I didn't move my fingers. It takes practise and I've had a lot. The first hint of Emily began in Pinehaven. There was a weak tug toward Ginny and Tom's house. The next small nuance of a tug was near the hills that Fendalton Crescent backed onto, Art's place. Then nothing until Wallaceville. Her house gave a much stronger reading, as did the bookshop, and the hall she went to every week for a group therapy session. I got as far as Kaitoke with minimal tugs and alerts. Where the hell was Emily? I started from the Remutaka hills and worked my way back down the valley toward the bookshop and my offices again. There was something around the back of Upper Hutt and in toward Poet's Block. That was also a bus route. The biggest readings were expected ones: the bookshop and her home. Then the weak bus route twinge. Was it something? I couldn't decide. It was no stronger than any readings of travel into the CBD proper, not around the bookshop.

"It doesn't look like she's in Upper Hutt," I said and dropped the pendulum on the map. From the cupboard, I took another map, this time a regional map. "I'm trying again."

Crockett said nothing. His jaw clenched.

I started from Upper Hutt. By the time I'd done a complete circuit of the map, I knew two things. One, if she was anywhere, she was shielded, and two, if she was shielded then someone knew I could track people. Perhaps they knew there was a hidden tracker somewhere on her or in her arm or something. Most people wouldn't automatically leap to dowsing or anything else people saw as paranormal or a sixth sense. Unless they knew and how could they?

I glanced at Crockett. His jaw muscles clenched and unclenched.

"You'll get a headache if you don't relax your jaw a bit," I said. It was more an observation than anything requiring a response.

"Why can't you find her?" He stood and stepped closer to the table. "Why?"

Last time I couldn't find someone, it was Ben I couldn't find. I wondered if maybe it was because I was too close then dismissed that idea. He was behind a thin foil shield which was just enough to prevent me locking onto his signature.

"Someone has prevented me or anyone tracking her, Crockett, but from the very beginning. As soon as she left the building." I breathed out to relax my shoulders. "There's no directional information apart from along a bus route." Alternately, I could be losing my secret skill. That didn't sit well with me.

"That's something."

"It probably isn't. She's a regular bus user."

When it was Ben missing, I knew so much more than I did now. Frustration built.

"If they'd taken her backpack then the AirTag would help us," Crockett said with a shake of his head.

That was the first time I'd heard about an AirTag on her backpack.

"Why did you tag her backpack?"

"I didn't. I presumed you did." His head swivelled slowly until his eyes met mine. "Did Jenn or Steph tag her?"

I already had my phone in my hand and was calling Steph. Three rings and then she said, "Jenn's fine. They'll keep her overnight though. Looks like concussion."

"Good, she's fine. Tell her I'm sorry about her head. Did you or Jenn tag Emily's backpack?"

"Hold on." I could hear her talking to Jenn. "No. Have you got the backpack?"

"Yeah."

"See if you can pull information from the tag." She paused then said, "I'll be there in an hour."

"Thanks." I hung up.

Crockett jammed his hands into his jeans pockets. "And?"

"Wasn't them. Where's the backpack?"

"In the main office," he said. Crockett left the room. I finished putting everything away, blowing out the candles, shutting the window, and putting the smoke alarm back. It wasn't as easy for me to do that as it was for Crockett, I had to drag a chair over and climb on it.

I locked the door on my way out and found Crockett in the main office searching Emily's bag.

He tipped the contents of the backpack onto the coffee table by the windows and searched through everything. It wasn't obvious. Then he unzipped what looked like a change purse and withdrew an AirTag.

"When did you know it was there?"

"I found it when I snooped through her bag after she'd disappeared."

"It's not snooping when someone is missing, Crockett. It's for her."

I'd opened Find My on my phone and looked under the items tab. I could see the AirTag but there was no information. It was just there on the map at my office address.

"They're separated from it, right?" Crockett nodded. "So, it should've sent an alert to them, and we would be able to hear it because the tag has an audible alert."

"Did you hear it?"

"Nope."

"And there isn't a name, or anything attached to it?"

I shook my head. "Guess they're not stupid enough to leave information for us to find."

Crockett removed the battery from the AirTag then put it back in the purse and put all of Emily's things back in her bag. He slumped onto the couch. "How long were they watching her movements? When did they add the tracker to her backpack and where did they do it?"

I made a call to a couple of our investigators and asked them to come into the office then slipped my phone into my pocket.

"Reinforcements," I said. "I'll get them to scrub all the CCTV footage of the bookshop cameras from the last three months."

"You think they've been in before?"

"They put that tag in somewhere and it could've easily been here."

"Easily?"

"Okay maybe not easily, but if someone distracted Emily enough, someone else could drop something like that in her bag." I closed the app on my phone.

"They'd have to know where she kept her backpack. They'd need time, it wasn't just dropped into it," he said.

"Where else could someone get to her backpack undetected?"

"Maybe at group." Crockett's jaw clenched again. "I'm usually there though and everyone has their bags under or beside their chairs. The circle is almost in the middle of the hall." He lifted to eyes to meet mine. "No new people in group, either."

"It's her traumatic brain injury support group?"

"Yes."

"We'll figure it out, Crockett. We will find her." I tried a reassuring smile but suspected I failed. "I took a notebook off Costa. I think we need to get the pages translated."

"Can you do that?"

I sat behind my desk and uploaded all the images from the notebook to an email and sent it to an old friend, Serena Martin.

"How long do you think it will take?"

"Not long." To speed the process up I sent a text message to Serena and told her I'd emailed her some images to translate.

Crockett paced the room, pausing occasionally to look out the window at the railway station and the street.

My email pinged. Crockett hurried to my desk. "And?"

"It's a travel journal," I said. "She's been to Antwerp and said there was no sign of Simone, she stayed in their usual hotel for three days. Then she went to Germany. Nothing. She got notified of a sighting in Germany, but it was a false alarm."

"Who is the Simone chick?"

"No idea. So far, she hasn't said." I read on then paraphrased. "France. Weather was bad. She went to Paris. Simone had not registered at the hotel where she said she'd be staying. Concierge very helpful. He gave Costa access to registered guests over the last seven years. No Simone, not even her aliases."

"She's been all over the map trying to find this Simone chick," Crockett said. "How does that track with what we know?"

"Not sure, Nana said she was hired by Costa to find a cousin, Sandra Solway. No mention of a Simone." I read some more. "She went to London next. Nothing and no more sightings. There's a lot of travel talk, restaurant's, and so forth. Stuff we don't care about."

"Filler stuff to make anyone looking think she's on holiday," Crockett said.

"That's what it looks like." I read on and then paraphrased some more. "Next stop Australia. Sydney. Again nothing. Lots of touristy things. She checked out hotels Simone used to like staying at and managed to get into the airport cameras."

"Resourceful."

"Very. Here we go. She got a hot tip. Simone was seen in Wellington, New Zealand."

"That explains why she's here," Crockett said and sat on the chair near me.

"Right, she starts looking in Wellington. No sign. She writes that she might hire a PI to help with the search. Then ..." I took a breath. "Now it gets interesting. Simone was seen in Upper Hutt. The Genoas are hunting her. She might be working in a bookshop. Looks different but not that different."

Crockett and I stared at each other for a long time and finally, Crockett said, "Emily works in a bookshop."

And I said, "There are only two bookshops in Upper Hutt."

"Who the hell are the Genoa's?"

I shook my head. "No idea but I'll bet you a pottle of ghost chips that they're the people who took Emily."

Chapter Eight:
[Ronnie: A delivery?]

Thursday marched on. Steph peered around the office door before entering.

"I have arrived," Steph announced with a wave of her hand. "Where's that AirTag?"

Crockett took the purse from the backpack and handed it to her. "Battery is in there too."

Steph turned her computer on, then put the battery back in the device.

"We couldn't find anything," I said, as I gathered case notes from my desk, added them to a folder and slid it into my desk drawer.

"Were you working a case before this interruption?" Crockett asked.

"Yeah. It can wait." No one will die if I don't turn in the final report for a theft case.

Steph cleared her throat and caught my attention. "How much work is there in that report before I can bill the client?"

"A couple of hours," I replied. "I'll get it done, but not right now."

Steph nodded but didn't comment.

My phone rang. Donald's picture flashed onto the screen. I answered. "What's up?"

"There is a grocery delivery truck outside our house,

and someone knocked on the door."

"We don't order groceries." We don't even have courier packages delivered to the house. We don't order takeaways for delivery to the house either. There are strict rules to keep my family safe.

"What do I do?" Donald asked.

"Do not open the door. Do not use the doorbell camera or microphone. Just ignore it."

"Anything else?"

"Nana's with you?"

"She is."

"Check she didn't order anything."

In a perfect world, my Nana wouldn't know how to order groceries online, but someone gave her a smartphone and the world is not perfect.

I touched the speaker icon and placed my phone on my desk. We could all hear Donald talking to Nana. She denied ordering groceries.

"Did you hear?" Donald asked, his voice louder now that he was speaking into the phone.

"Yes. It's probably just a mix up but don't go outside. Ben should be there soon. He'll deal with it."

"Okay. Any news?"

Crockett spoke, "Not yet."

"Are you coming home?"

"Yes. Don't know when though. Be safe."

"Don't die," Donald said.

"I'll try not to."

I hung up.

Crockett rose from the chair and stretched. "It's got to be something to do with that sheila who was snooping around her place."

"Bit too much of a coincidence, isn't it?"

"We need to find her and talk to her again."

Steph waved a hand towards me. "I may have something."

We joined her at her desk, one on each side of her, looking over her shoulder. "How'd you get that?" It was an electronic sales receipt for a pack of three AirTags sold by Noel Lemmings.

"Sometimes it's not what you know. It's who you know," she replied, tapping her index finger on the side of her nose. "The serial number was helpful."

"They paid cash," Crockett said. "No name. It's a dead end again."

Then I realised what Steph was doing. "It's time stamped and they have cameras pointing to the tills."

"Can we see the feed, or do you have to go down there?" Crockett asked.

A link popped up in an iMessage, and another message followed with login information.

"We can see it," Steph replied, and clicked the link then logged in. She glanced at notes on her memo pad, then added times to the footage. She added ten minutes on either side of the sale in the perimeter search box. A new tab opened with the requested video.

We watched.

A woman approached the counter and spoke to a

salesperson. Another woman approached the counter and spoke with a different salesperson. Two men waited then one of them placed boxes on the counter. I kept one eye on the time at the bottom of the video screen.

"It's her," Crockett said, pointing to a woman. The camera showed a clear image of her face.

"The Argentinian," I muttered. The time flicked to the time of the sale of the AirTags. It was her who bought them. "What the hell is that chick up to, buying AirTags and tagging Emily?"

"We need to pick her up," Crockett said, straightening up. "Thanks, Steph. You're a corker."

"She's under surveillance. We can get her whenever," I said. "She's under surveillance, Crockett. She may have tagged Emily's bag and snooped around her house, but she didn't knock Jenn out or grab Emily today."

He paused and stared at me. "Do you know something I don't know?"

"Nope. Well, not really. Costa asked Nana to find a woman called Sandra Solway and may have seen Emily's address on an envelope at Nana's." I may have inadvertently implied Nana and *The Cronies of Doom* were responsible for giving out Emily's address. "But we know Costa bought the AirTags so she did not need to get an address off an envelope. Did she?"

He shook his head. "Who is the Solway sheila?"

"Don't know. Nana drew a blank. This happened." I swept my arm around the office. "And I haven't had a chance to see what I can find out about the Solway woman."

"Okay. And that's it? You don't know anything else?"

"Cross my heart and hope to die." We knew the same things. Costa was looking for someone called Simone. Costa tagged Emily. Costa's notebook said the Genoas were hunting Simone.

"Let's make like a kangaroo and bounce."

Steph interrupted us, "I'll copy this section of the video, so we have it."

"Thank you," I replied. "Can you hold down the fort?"

"Of course."

From my desk, I grabbed my bag and phone. Crockett was already waiting at the door, car keys in his hand. I waved to Steph, and we ran down the stairs. No one walks any more.

Chapter Nine:
[Ronnie: What is this about?]

"Do you know where we are going?" I asked as I clicked my seat belt into place.

"First we're going to Emily's place."

Okay. I had nothing to add so I watched the scenery as Crockett drove. Part of me hoped I'd see Emily walking down the street on her way home.

I didn't.

Crockett pulled up the driveway and turned off the car. I knew he had a key to Emily's house because I gave him one at Emily's suggestion. Emily had improved so much since meeting Crockett that she was almost the Emily I used to know. Her confidence came back in leaps and bounds, some memory returned, but a lot of muscle memory never left. She just didn't know she had it. Emily's accident robbed her of more than half a leg. It took her memory, her identity, everything that made her Emily Jones. Emily Jones left the police to become a PI with my company, then almost two years later she had a car accident. Her life as she knew it, ceased to exist. Her life as I knew it, ceased to exist.

Crockett's voice interrupted my thoughts of Emily. "You coming?"

I nodded. "Yep."

"Where were you?" Crockett closed his door as I

opened mine.

"Miles away, thinking about how much Emily has changed since you came into our lives." I gave him a smile, but I knew it was weak.

He approached the front door. As Crockett went to put the key in the lock, the door creaked open.

It wasn't locked or closed properly.

He shot me a 'stay there' look, unholstered his weapon, and gingerly opened the door wide.

There were no sounds of movement. Crockett entered the hallway and reminded me to stay put with a hand signal. I wasn't going anywhere. I was more than happy to let him clear the house since he was armed, and I was not.

He walked towards me. "All clear. But someone has been here. Come and see." Crockett turned around and went into the lounge.

I closed the door behind me and joined Crockett in the room. It was a mess. Couch cushions were ripped up. Scatter pillows were in pieces and furniture upended. Pictures were off the walls. Broken glass was scattered amongst the stuffing from the couch and cushions.

"They didn't just toss the place, they destroyed it," I said, picking where I stepped with care. "Just this room or all the others?"

"It looks like this throughout." He moved a broken picture frame out of the way. "I can't tell if anything is missing."

I surveyed the damage, then moved into the kitchen to

see what that looked like. The oven was in the middle of the room. The cupboards were emptied on the floor. The table was tipped over, and drawers were empty and on the ground. Someone moved the fridge out from its usual place. It was still plugged in and working. I opened the fridge door. I saw milk, bread, butter, cheese, vegetables, all still fine. I pulled the freezer drawer open. It still contained frozen foods and ice-cream. It didn't look like anyone had bothered with the fridge or freezer drawer too much, which was odd considering the rest of the room.

"What were they looking for?" I didn't expect an answer and pushed the fridge back where it should be so I could get to the laundry door. All the kitchen cupboards were open. Pots and pans were scattered across the floor with broken crockery, glasses, and free-range cutlery. "Why?"

"I don't know," Crockett said. "The bathroom looks like this too and her bedroom."

I opened the door to the laundry. The washing machine was halfway across the floor. The cupboard under the tub was open, and cleaning products were strewn all over the floor. Thankfully, they were still in their bottles with the lids shut.

"Ronnie!" Crockett called from somewhere down the hall.

"Coming."

He was in Emily's spare room.

"What's up?" I said from the doorway.

He pointed to a series of holes in an interior wall and the lining of the exterior wall about a metre from the floor. I couldn't see daylight, so they didn't go right through.

"Someone was looking for something," I said. "Why only knock holes in this room?"

"Because whoever it is, was of the opinion that the thing they were looking for was in this room. Or they were interrupted mid-destruction." Crockett picked up a blanket and put it on the bed. "No sign of whatever they used to knock the holes."

"And the only way they'd think something was in the walls was if Emily told them." I looked around the room. It'd been tossed like the rest of the house. "They could've done most of the damage before they grabbed her. Then come back to knock the holes or like you said, they were interrupted."

"Interrupted ..."

"Unless they found something in the wall."

"The cameras," Crockett said. He pulled his phone from his back pocket and opened the camera application.

"Shouldn't we have gotten alerts when we entered the house?"

He glanced from the screen to me. "Yes."

"When was the last alert?"

"When Emily left for the bookshop this morning."

I could see his finger moving as he scrolled. Not satisfied watching, I used my phone and did the same. I definitely had no alerts. Not since eight thirty when

Emily left the house. I scrolled back. I saw her go inside the evening before. More scrolling revealed the Argentinian woman wandering around the property the day before that.

She knew about the cameras. She knew how long it took us to respond. That's why she was there twice. Buggery bollocks.

Crockett showed me his screen. He was in the same place I was.

"Snap," I said. "She'd been lurking for two days. She knew how long it took for us to respond."

"And where the cameras are."

I pulled up the live feed. "They're still working," I said as I watched a cat walk down the path. "Why didn't we get alerts?"

"Someone jammed the feed," Crockett replied. "That's the only thing I can think of."

"How close would they need to be?"

"On the street I guess."

I scrolled to when Emily left the house and carefully moved forward hoping to see a car out the front or someone on the path near the house. Nothing.

"They didn't just jam it, they stopped it recording," I said. "There's maybe an hour of nothing really happening. I saw the postie on the footpath out the front of the house then nothing for a good hour. Then it seems to record again. Not much happening. A mum pushing a stroller, people walking dogs and then the postie was back in his red and yellow electric postie cart."

"Why would the postie come twice?" Crockett showed me his phone screen and I showed him mine. Same, same.

"He wouldn't."

I scrolled back to the first time I saw the postie. "It looks like a postie golf cart."

"Yeah," Crockett replied. "How can we find out who delivers to this area?"

"I don't know. I'd say we could call NZ Post, but we'd need a decent reason and even then I doubt they'd tell us," I said. "And then we'd need police help."

"We need someone who can get access to their system."

Genesis might have a way in or a person within that could help us.

"Or someone who is a postie ..." I smiled at Crockett. "I'll make a phone call."

I chose Uncle George from my recent calls list and rang him/her/them. The call rang out. As my screen darkened an incoming call was announced by Siri. "Unknown caller."

I answered. Crockett shook his head.

"Ronnie, how can I help?" Uncle George sounded more like *Auntie* George this time.

"Do you have anyone inside the postal service?"

"Yes. What do you need?"

"To find out who delivers mail to the Miro Street area and why there were two deliveries today."

"Will I need the times?"

"Probably."

Crockett checked the footage and gave the times. I relayed them to Uncle George.

"I'll get back to you."

"Another question. When do we expect Dane Wesson? Haven't had a text."

"Sorry. Got busy. You should see the helicopter coming up the valley any minute."

"Where are they landing?"

"Trentham Camp."

"Thanks. We'll head over and pick him up."

"While you are there go see Bill Bailey. He might have something for you."

"Thanks."

I hung up.

Crockett opened the front door and took care to lock it after us.

"There aren't any tool marks on the door," he said. "Either they're really good at breaking and entering, or they had a key."

I filed that away for later. Did they have Emily's key or was she with them? Now, we needed to get to the Camp.

Chapter Ten:
[Ronnie: Now what?]

By the time we parked outside the Messine Centre, I could hear the helicopter in the distance and see its dark shape getting ever closer in the sky. I've long since stopped wondering how *Genesis* can commandeer military vehicles. I knew I was looking at an incoming Air Force helicopter. Whoever is running *Genesis* has some deep pockets and a long reach. It was heading for rush hour so flying directly into Trentham was a smart move.

"You reckon that's Dane?" Crockett asked with a nod toward the noisy helicopter that was coming into land.

"I'd say so."

"Do you want to split up?"

I nodded. "I'll go see what Bill has for us. You go get Dane."

"See you soon."

I hopped out of the car and watched Crockett drive toward the main entrance of the Camp. My phone rang.

It was Uncle George.

"Is this about the postie?"

"Yes," said the robotic female voice. "There was one postal delivery. Whatever you saw that matched the first time stamp was not a post office worker or a postal delivery cart on legitimate business."

"Thanks." I hung up and strolled up to the Messine

Centre main entrance and rang Bill.

"I'm out front," I said and hung up.

Thirty seconds later I could see him walking towards the glass door from wherever he'd been. He opened the door and ushered me into a room just off the hallway. I'd been in the room before. It was a comfortable room that was used to speak to anyone they didn't want wandering freely through the building.

"I heard you might have something for me?" I asked as I sank into a big leather armchair.

"Potentially," Bill replied, sitting in the opposing armchair. "We've got some interesting people in the country who don't want us to know what they're up to, and they appear to be up to whatever it is, together."

"Argentinian by any chance?"

"One is. The other is from Belgium."

"State Security Service?"

"Yes."

"What do the VSSE want in New Zealand?"

"That we don't know yet. We just know they're here."

"Aren't overseas security agencies supposed to declare their operation in whatever country they land in?"

"And they did. They just didn't tell the truth. One is here on holiday and the other is here on consulate business."

I don't suppose that's a surprise.

"Two operatives from two different countries are working together?" Not unheard of. I mean, I work for *Genesis,* and we have operatives from all agencies worldwide. We work for the good of all. That's not usually how security service agencies operate. They tend to be working for a particular country.

"It appears that way. I'm not convinced."

"What do you think they're doing here?"

"I don't know what they're doing here." Half a smile touched his lips. "The only current chatter I'm aware of is about a heist eight years ago."

"Why is that important now?" My mind wandered to the book that Emily pointed out. Was it about art? Was this all about a painting?

"Maybe they've had a lead. All I can tell you is there is chatter, but it's dregs of old news."

"Heist? Art?"

"No, well not entirely; art and diamonds." He studied me for a moment. "The Argentinian, you've met?"

I nodded. "She was snooping around a friend's place. We scooped her up but didn't find out much."

"What aren't you saying?"

I took a couple of beats to consider my words.

"The friend is Emily. Someone snatched her from the bookshop today. Her place was ransacked. They even smashed holes in a few walls." And now that he'd said diamonds maybe someone believed she had them or had something to do with it.

"Do you need help?"

"Are you offering?"

"Of course." Half a smile edged onto his lips. "Always liked Emily."

That was news.

"I didn't know you knew her."

"How could you, she probably doesn't know she knows me."

Back up a bit.

"Hang on. How do you know Emily?"

"For starters, I didn't know her as Emily originally."

What the actual frying-pan-out-the-window is this? The secret life of Emily? I knew I'd lost my animation but was powerless to pick up my thought thread. I don't know how long I sat there in stunned silence. Eventually, my brain kicked back in. Emily was a cop, then a PI, that was Emily. Our Emily. We met when I left the service. She was a cop. She was wasted as a cop and brilliant as a private investigator.

"What?" That was all I could manage.

Bill smiled like he was enjoying himself. "If I read you in, this stays between us. This is not information for Crockett, Ben, or Enzo. This is classified."

I stared at him for a beat. "We all hold high-security clearances."

"I know, and this is still above all your pay grades."

"I hold Top Secret clearance. How can this be above our pay grades or clearances?" You can't get higher than Top Secret. Not in New Zealand, anyway.

"Piper doesn't know about this, that's how."

Oh, something that the head of New Zealand Security Intelligence Service doesn't know.

"So, who does?"

He smiled and pointed to himself. "You're looking at him."

Air hissed through my teeth. "Just you?"

He nodded.

I looked around the small room. "How secure are we here?"

"Let's find out."

He took his phone from his pocket and asked me to turn mine off. I did. Bill placed his phone on the coffee table. There was an App open.

"What is that?"

"Something the techs have just perfected. A digital scanner. It looks for transmitters."

A green light swirled on the screen for about ten seconds then blinked solid green.

"No bugs. Keep your phone off though." Bill switched his off as well.

"Coffee would be nice."

"It'll have to wait; I don't want anyone coming in here."

"Talk," I said, getting comfortable in the chair.

Bill checked his watch. "That helicopter? Was that for you?"

He knew it was, he probably knew who was on it, as well. "Yep."

"Better make this fast then. Long story short," Bill said. "Emily was my asset."

"Since when?"

"Since we put her inside the Police College to become a

cop."

Holy moly.

"Why?"

"In a country like New Zealand, you can't just build a legend and make someone a cop because they will come across other cops from the same Wing they graduated with, at some stage. One police college means the legend has to start at the beginning."

Well, that made sense. Proper deep cover. Bloody hell. "Okay. Continue."

"She did really well, which was not a surprise. Her chosen city was Upper Hutt. And Emily Jones became a serving police officer and a damn good one at that."

"But why?"

"Because sometimes we need to know what police are doing and they don't always play ball. She was our insider. She was going to stay in as long we needed her, building relationships, working, being a good cop."

"And then?"

"I think you know. You retired from the Service, and I had a feeling you weren't out of the game completely."

"So, you engineered a meeting with Emily, and you knew we'd get on and that I'd offer her a position with my company." I glared at him. "You utter wanker. You infiltrated my company. You were spying on me."

"I needed to know what you were up to, Ronnie. National Security and all that jazz."

"I'm still standing so how much dirt did you really get?" I paused and looked right into his eyes. "You are defence, not national security. What did you really want?"

"To know what you were up to and who you were working with. Ben Reynolds' appearance made me curious, and you weren't coughing up any answers."

I thought back to when Ben first appeared in my life. Emily wasn't with me then. It was just me, Jenn, and Steph but we were doing very well, thank you. Emily appeared right after the operation with Ben. Within days, of the resolution. I ran into her at the supermarket, she was in uniform. That was when it began. Sneaky bastard.

"So, Reynolds appeared, and days later I met Emily." How did I not see that as a set-up? Because I wasn't looking. The job was over. We survived. I collected on a big fat payday and pushed everything aside. Life moved on. *And Emily was a cop.*

Bill waited in case I had something else to say. I didn't. Anger mounted.

"I backed off and let Emily run the operation however she saw fit."

"Operation? You mean spying on me. It wasn't an operation it was infiltration."

He didn't deny it. "Every few weeks I'd meet Emily at a bar in Wellington and buy her a drink. She'd tell me what you were working on. When she realised she wasn't going to get anything good as a cop, she left the force and joined you full-time."

I took a deep breath and let it out slowly as I considered all the jobs I did and how many included

Emily. She was great at surveillance. No wonder.

The company grew. She was involved in almost everything. Except for anything involving outside agencies. That must've pissed Bill off. A small laugh dropped off my tongue. She did know who I was working with sometimes though. Pretty hard to hide Ben and his famous face. We worked together a lot.

"Must've been annoying when she couldn't report on agency work."

Bill nodded. "Somewhat. I always knew after the fact if it was something you had a hand in, but I couldn't prove it, and you didn't let anything slip."

"Maybe you underestimated me, Bill."

"I know I did."

"Emily worked for me for almost two years before the ..." I air quoted. "Accident." I thought back over that time. She was a friend. She was an employee. She was Emily Jones, former cop. I tried to haul in details about any visitors she had, or any times she'd mentioned family or seen her family. "You and I met a few times over those years."

"Yes, we did."

"How big is the dossier you have on me?"

His lip twisted into a smirk. "About as big as the one you have on me."

Touché.

"You may as well tell me about that night, Bill."

He considered my request for a split second before making his decision.

"You're right. That night, we met in Wellington, and she said she had something, but I considered it was more a gut feeling, to be honest, about a situation at the labs in Wallaceville. It wasn't corroborated so when she thought something was up, she started watching the place at night."

"God. She was on a surveillance job in Ward Street for one of our cases."

"I know. That's how she was able to watch the research centre. She had a rough idea that whatever was going to happen would happen in a short time frame."

"Her car accident was Day Three of the job she was on."

That job was handy, as it turned out, but also dangerous for her.

"We knew we had Russians working with Americans and Kiwi cops. There were scientists involved. Someone from the CDC was at a conference in Auckland and made contact with the FBI team who were in Wellington. We weren't bothered about the Kiwis until we found out one of them had worked with CIA previously and then she became interesting. We uncovered a relationship with an FBI unit as well. We didn't know if she was a spy or legit. And it all came together that night in Wallaceville when a drone sent a missile across the night sky and into the lab. The thing is, that also happened in Australia and Germany. It was simultaneous. No one admitted responsibility. And there was no one left alive to question here. An operation conducted in secrecy on our shore by more than one foreign power, but we couldn't prove it."

Everything swirled around and sounded like the plot of a novel.

"I remember I was pulled in and debriefed by NZSIS, just in case I knew something. The extent of my knowledge was Emily had a car accident. I suppose you were behind that story?"

"I was."

"How the hell did the drone and its missile get covered up so well?"

"A snow job. Grab a couple of people and ask them if they saw a UFO flying across the sky. The trick is to create more of a conspiracy than the conspiracy nuts. We went UFO and drowned out their missile. When they got louder, we added the possibility that it was the remains of a satellite or a meteor tracking with the UFO."

I'd heard all those stories from random people. And he was right, they were louder than the truth. No one wanted to believe what had really happened. As long as you provide alternatives for people, they'll adapt what they saw to fit one of the offered narratives.

"It was a ghost strike. All we had were remnants of a missile. It was American, we thought. So, we dug around and discovered those particular missiles were fired from an Iverson drone. That was it. Iverson Industries had US government contracts and gave us nothing. The Americans denied all knowledge. The Russians were outraged that we even suggested they were involved. Australia shook their heads in horror at the implication that they had something to do with it. They had a similar event so declared it definitely wasn't them. Anyone who knew anything was dead or taken from New Zealand very quickly."

"So, you had nothing, and Emily nearly died. That about sums it up, yes?"

"Yes."

"Where does this leave us now?" I rammed any annoyance deep down. Emily was missing and he clearly didn't have her, and I couldn't see a connection from that particular piece of history, to today.

"I'm offering my help."

"Good to know. I better go find Crockett and see who was on that helicopter."

"Dane Wesson," Bill replied. "You didn't think I wouldn't know who was on an Air Force chopper landing at Trentham Camp?"

I smiled. "I'll call you if I need you," I said. "How come you didn't use Crockett to find out what was going on before the lab exploded?"

"I tried. He didn't take the bait. And afterwards, ASIO declared he had no knowledge and was in the vicinity by accident not by design."

"Wesson?"

"You know as well as I do, he was not capable of answering any questions for years."

"So, you knew he survived but kept it quiet?"

"I knew because I kept an eye on Emily. It was unfortunate that the FBI finally twigged."

"What's going to happen if she remembers who she really is?"

He shrugged. "No idea. But it's not likely."

"Not with you giving her such a comprehensive legend and the rest of us reinforcing that she is Emily Jones, former PI, and retired cop." Reinforcing it while absolutely believing it made for a convincing cover story. "Who is Emily Jones?"

A half a smile flickered on his lips. "Emily Jones is Emily Jones."

Bullshit.

I stood and offered him my hand. I'm an adult. I'm an espionage officer. This is how life goes. Everyone watching everyone. Everyone lying to protect their interests. No hard feelings. We all have jobs to do.

We shook and then I asked the question I wanted the answer to.

"Why do you think the Argentinian secret service and the Belgium security agency have an interest in Emily?"

"I don't know. Emily was Army Intelligence and worked in Europe for a few years. Maybe she came across them there."

"It has the makings of a bad joke. Army Intelligence, SIDE, and the VSSE walk into a bar ..."

Something flashed across his face.

"What was that?" I pointed at him. "You know something?"

"It probably wasn't a bar they walked into."

"If you know what they want with Emily, you need to

find a way to share that. It might make all the difference."

He shut down. "I hope you get her back. As far as I'm concerned, she is Emily Jones, your friend, a former cop, and a former PI. That's all that's left." Bill opened the door and escorted me out the main doors. "Best of luck."

I stopped in the doorway. "Who is she really?"

He shook his head. "It doesn't matter now. Let me know if and how I can help bring her home."

"Who is Simone?"

"I don't what you are talking about."

I nodded, turned and left. Liar, liar, pants on fire.

Emily was a plant, and she didn't know it. This world we operate in is shitty to the extreme. And he knew who Simone was.

Chapter Eleven:
[Crockett: Get a wriggle on]

Dane was sitting in the car while I leaned over the roof looking for Ronnie. She'd been a lot longer than I thought she'd be, and I hoped that was a good thing. I finally saw her leave the building and waved from across the car park. The sun was setting casting orange and red onto a few long clouds. The heat from the day would begin to dissipate soon.

She hurried over.

"All good?" she asked with a strained smile on her face.

"I think so. Dane is good, he's in the car. He called shotgun."

Ronnie's face cleared and she smiled all the way to her eyes. "Siri called shotgun," she said opening the left-hand back passenger door and sliding across the seat. I hopped in the driver's seat.

"Hey, Dane," she said.

Siri said, "Hi, Ronnie. I'm sorry about Emily."

"Me too," she replied.

I glanced in the rearview mirror at her. She smiled back. "Where to?"

"Enzo wants us back at the house," I told her.

"Okay, home then."

I adjusted the mirror. It was a quiet trip to Ronnie's. Not the sort of silence that I was accustomed to with her.

This was a silence that felt like she was trying to make sense of something. Almost a confused silence, if silence can be anything other than silent.

I parked on the road. Ben's car was in the driveway. Dane and I exited the car. Ronnie didn't move. I swung her door open.

"Are you all right?"

"Yep," she replied. "Let's get inside."

The front door opened before we got to it.

In the entranceway, I saw grocery bags as Donald opened the door wider.

"Since when?" I asked Donald, pointing to the bags.

He shrugged. "No one knows who ordered them."

"Where's Ben? I thought he'd deal with this a few hours ago," Ronnie muttered.

Donald tossed his fringe out of his eyes. "Busy. Enzo put up a drone to make sure there was no one watching the house."

I scanned the bags and saw a label. "It says right there." I pointed. "Who is Terry White and why did he give your address?"

"I don't know," Donald said with a huff. "Some very strange things are happening today."

Ronnie stepped up next to me. "Guess we may as well take these bags upstairs and enjoy the free groceries."

"I tried to get the supermarket to pick them up, but they said they wouldn't," Donald said. "Wouldn't hurt to see what's in the bags."

"Hopefully, nothing that should've been in the

freezer," Ronnie said, picking up a bag and walking up the stairs ahead of us.

Donald picked up two bags; Dane and I followed suit with the remaining groceries.

"Would've cost a bit to send six bags of groceries," I mumbled to myself. Donald was right about something strange going on. I was dying to know what Ronnie found out from Bill Bailey. Whatever it was it clearly required processing. Whatever she knew was going to rock boats. I knew enough to know when Ronnie goes quiet, shit is going down. I mentally prepared for a brown tsunami.

Ronnie was in the kitchen unpacking a bag of groceries. She didn't look up when we entered the room. I placed the bags I carried on the bench by hers. Dane and Donald did the same. Ronnie peered into the bags, then began unpacking them and setting the contents on the bench.

"Quite a haul," she said. "Many packets of biscuits and I count four bags of Robert Harris Italian Roast plunger grind coffee."

"You drink that," I said. "Do you think someone has worked out where you really live?"

She shrugged. "A lot of people drink Robert Harris."

"It was bound to happen one day," I said, watching her closely.

"Yes, I suppose it was." She added more groceries to the piles and flattened the bags. Donald took the pile of bags and put them in the recycling.

I grabbed the jug and filled it with water. Coffee was

my plan. Plenty of it. May as well drink some of the free coffee.

"Where's Ben?" Siri asked as Dane poked his head around the corner to the lounge.

"I don't know," Ronnie replied. "He'll be around somewhere."

Enzo strolled into the kitchen with a smile on his face. "Ben is in your room," he said to Ronnie. "Nana is in the lounge. She would like a coffee." He turned to Dane and stuck his hand out. "You must be the famous Dane Wesson. I'm Enzo. Donald's husband."

They shook hands.

"Jug's on," Ronnie replied. "I'll be back. Crockett can make the coffee."

Ronnie vanished out the door before I could comment.

Dane tapped my arm to get my attention then Siri spoke, "What's wrong?"

I shook my head. "I don't know."

Enzo shot me a look. "With Ronnie?"

I nodded.

Donald piped up, "Obviously she's concerned about Emily and Jenn, and as always, Nana." Donald flapped a hand at the three of us. "I'll be in the lounge with Nana. Someone, please bring our coffees through." He stalked away, but over his shoulder, he said, "We're going to need to organise dinner."

"Is that it?" Siri asked before Enzo could.

"I don't think so," I replied. "Let's get the coffee underway. Maybe she needed to see Ben."

All of a sudden.

I knew her. I knew she'd found something out from Bailey and whatever it was she didn't like it much. Or maybe she needed some processing space. I also knew that if she couldn't share it she wouldn't.

"We're going to need both French presses," I said just as Enzo set them on the bench in front of me. "Thanks."

He smiled and spooned ground coffee into them.

I got the mugs out of the cupboard. Dane meandered away with his iPad. By the time he came back, we'd put mugs, sugar, milk, teaspoons and a packet of biscuits on a large tray. Enzo took the tray. I went ahead of him to make sure the coffee table was clear.

Enzo placed the tray on the table. "I'll be right back with the coffee," he said.

"This looks very nice," June said. "Well done boys."

"Thanks, June," I said. "Have you met Dane?"

June nodded. "I have. Isn't it great, the technology today?" She gestured to Dane's iPad.

"It certainly makes communication easier for me," Siri said while Dane smiled.

"Where did Ronnie get off to?" June asked.

"To find Ben, I think," I replied. "I'm sure they'll appear soon."

Enzo placed both French presses on the table and plunged the plungers.

"Go give them the hurry up," Donald said to me. "Coffee will be cold at this rate."

There was a little reluctance on my part. They had to

be in Ronnie's bedroom, and I didn't want to interrupt anything. Unless they were in the bat cave, of course.

"I'll be right back," I said and ambled my way down the hall to Ronnie's room.

I knocked twice.

No answer.

"Ronnie?" I said. "Coffee's made."

I gave another rap on the door. "Ben! Ronnie! Quit whatever you're doing, I'm coming in."

I opened the door a crack. "Are you decent?"

Not a peep.

I blew air through my teeth and opened the door properly. There was no one in the room. That meant they'd left or were in the bat cave. I pushed aside a couple of shirts so I could see better and knocked quietly on the back wall of the wardrobe. The door slid open.

"Glad that was you and not Donald," Ronnie said. "What do you need?"

"Coffee is made. I was sent to get you." That wasn't a lie. "What's going on?"

Ben stood and pushed his chair in. "Trying to work something out," Ben said.

"Would that be something to do with whatever info Bill Bailey had?" I asked.

Ronnie stood and pushed her chair in. "No. Wedding details. Nana's here and she will start the interrogation any minute." Ronnie smiled. "We had to get our stories straight."

She lied right to my face, and I could've easily believed

her if they weren't in the bat cave.

"Well, I hope you have. Get a move on before Donald comes looking for all of us."

We left the secret room. Ronnie closed the door and waited to check it had locked. She moved everything in her wardrobe back where it should be. The clothes hanging on the rail fully concealed the secret door and biometric lock. I found it hard to believe that Donald didn't know about it but maybe he didn't. Not my business anyway.

June greeted Ronnie when she arrived in the lounge. Ronnie kissed June's cheek and sat next to her.

"Is everything all right, Veronica?"

"No. It's not," Ronnie said.

Maybe we'll get some information, I thought.

"I imagine you are concerned about Emily," Nana said. "Dreadful business."

"Yes. I am" she replied and picked up a cup of coffee.

She was still not keen to talk. Whatever she knew couldn't be good. I checked my phone. There were no messages from Emily. Not that there would be. Her phone was in her backpack. I didn't know if she was able to remember phone numbers. Most people lost that ability with the advent of smartphones, and she'd had a serious brain injury to boot.

Enzo noticed my movement.

"Anything?" he asked.

"No."

"She's been gone a while now and there hasn't been

any contact," Enzo mused. "What is it they want?"

I shrugged. "No idea." I looked at Ronnie. "What do you think?"

Her head shook slightly. Her phone rang.

My gut twisted. She showed me the screen. Ginny. Ronnie answered the call and put it on speaker.

"Ginny. You're on speaker. We're all here."

"Hellaire, my lovelies."

A chorus of hellos came from the room.

"We've scrubbed all the CCTV from the CBD, paying special attention to the area around the bookshop," Ginny said.

"Anything?" Ronnie asked.

"They parked in the Woolworths car park, in the parks closest to Fergusson Drive. Couldn't get a license plate. The cameras aren't that good there. It's a deep red Toyota Camry."

"Did you get faces?" I asked.

"We'll find her, Crockett," Ginny said. "We will."

"Sooner rather than later would be great. Any faces?"

"One, that one guy. Lucas Genoa. Tom is running him through everything we can think of to find out who he is and how he is involved. The other wore a baseball cap and kept his head down. He knew there were cameras in the bookshop. He walked in behind the other guy."

"Okay, so one of them is actively avoiding cameras, and the other doesn't care." I leaned on the wall. "Mr Avoidance must be someone we can easily ID."

"I'd say so," Ronnie replied.

"So would I," Ginny said. "The problem is we don't have anything to go on as far as he's concerned."

"Definitely a bloke?"

"As far as I can tell," Ginny said. "Ninety-five percent sure."

"Good enough." I felt the chair behind my back as I pressed into it. We didn't have anything more to go on. Why? "Did you see Emily getting into the Camry?"

"Yes."

"Was she under duress?"

"It did not look like it, but there was a discussion prior to her getting into the vehicle."

"I need to see the footage." I launched to my feet. "Can you send it, or should I come to you?"

"Come here. Run an SDR. Don't bring the Harley it draws too much attention."

"I'm not new to this." I snapped without meaning to. "Sorry."

"You're under stress," Ginny replied, then added calmly, "Don't do it again."

Ronnie hung up then looked at me. "Drink your coffee. Then we'll all go."

I nodded. Sat down and picked up the mug nearest me.

June cleared her throat so quietly I almost missed it, but I didn't. I zeroed in on her.

"June, what do you have to say?"

She pursed her lips and did not look pleased.

"Nana?" Ronnie asked. "If you know something ..."

"All right Veronica," Nana said. She was snippy. "The

name Genoa is not unknown to me."

I saw Ronnie roll her eyes and stepped in before she exploded at her Nana. "June?"

"I've heard that name before."

"Where?"

"It was a conversation in the dining room at the rest home."

I played poker with June and her cronies; I knew a bluff when I saw one.

"Nana!" Ronnie exclaimed. "Do you know something?"

"Don't be dramatic, Veronica"

Ronnie jumped to her feet and stormed from the room.

I eyed June for a few seconds. She was holding something back.

Chapter Twelve:
[Ronnie: Random?]

Crockett wasn't handling the lack of information regarding Emily's disappearance at all well. But he didn't yell at Nana. That was on me.

I didn't blame him for not handling this lack of direction well, but still he needed to get his head in the game. We didn't even know what the game was and who the players were. Apart from that one guy. Lucas Genoa. And we already knew from the notebook that the Genoas were hunting someone. I watched Crockett without really watching him. Was easy to do from the back seat of Ben's car. I positioned myself behind Ben so I could see Crockett's profile. Ben drove. Crockett rode shotgun. Enzo and Dane stayed at home to keep an eye on Donald and Nana, and to run the drones looking for anyone surveilling our neighbourhood. I couldn't decide if the groceries meant someone finally figured out where I lived, or if it was a mistake. But how would anyone mistakenly write my address on their Woolworths account for delivery? They wouldn't. Terry White, the mystery man, will have to wait. We've got two other mystery men before him.

Ben pulled me out of my thoughts by opening the back door.

"You coming in?"

"I guess I should," I replied with a smile, then I followed him and Crockett through the gate and up the back steps. They left their shoes outside; I left mine in the laundry.

Ginny greeted us with her usual warmth as we lurked in the doorway.

"Hellaire. Tom is making coffee," she said from the kitchen. "Come on in properly."

"Where can I see the footage?" Crockett asked.

Ginny pointed to the dining room table and her iPad. "It's ready to go. Just press play."

Crockett strode past us, picked up the iPad, and continued into the lounge. Two cats followed. He was a cat magnet. I peered at him from the dining room. He'd sat on one of the couches, and the two cats that followed him were now on either side of him. He sat in silence watching the screen in his hands.

Tom gave me a mug of coffee. "Are you going in?" he asked.

"No. I'll sit at the table." I placed the mug on a coaster and pulled out a chair. Ben was already seated and so was Ginny.

"What else did you find?" I asked Ginny.

"Just the video. Couldn't find either man prior to them parking the car in the Woolies car park."

"How far did you go back?"

"Two days."

That was reasonable. "What do you know about a SIDE officer named Kerrin Costa?"

"Ah, now," Tom said. "A wee while back she was whispered to be involved in a heist in Belgium."

"Kerrin Costa?"

"Yes. I remember there was a lot of chatter, but as far as I know, it was gossip, not real talk. She was in the city when the heist went down. If I remember correctly, she was making noises about diamonds and art, and worried about security prior to the incident."

"It was diamonds?" I asked. "Definitely diamonds?"

"Belgium is renowned for diamond trading," Tom said. "Makes sense it would be a diamond heist."

I gave him a look. "You're sure about the diamonds?"

"Yes."

"Anything else taken?"

"Two paintings, but the diamonds were the thing everyone focused on, from memory."

"Any way to dig that gossip up?" Ben asked. "It might be relevant."

"We can try, but it really was just in-house gossip."

"In-house?"

"I was stationed at an embassy at the time," Tom replied. "An attaché doing a quick job."

So, he wasn't always at home. I cast my mind back. What did I know? That *I* was in Europe during *a* diamond heist. The newspapers ran stories about a second-story man being involved and there was a massive security shake-up. Shit was that it?

"Any other gossip at the time?" I asked. Crockett joined us in the dining room and placed the iPad on the table.

"Not that I recall. Everyone was talking about the heist. You were in Europe then, Ronnie?"

I nodded. "Mostly in the UK though. I heard gossip about foreigners being, behind the heist, and it was hinted maybe someone from the intelligence community had an involvement, but there was nothing substantial. No one could prove anything." From memory, it was an auction house that was robbed. Security was heavy yet three people managed to remove diamonds and replace them with zircons. I let memories surface. The whole thing was a little too Pink Panther meets Cat Woman, and rumour had it that someone in a cat suit was seen rappelling from a four-story window. But I knew how easily false information was spread and assimilated by the all too eager public.

"Interesting," Crockett said. "What does this all have to do with Emily, and finding Emily?"

I shook my head. "No idea. If this was a ransom situation we'd have heard by now. I think whoever grabbed her did so because she has something they want."

"Diamonds," Ben said quietly. "Maybe paintings."

A deep frown spread across Crockett's forehead. "Are you serious?"

"Someone was looking for something, right? She's gone. Kerrin Costa is wandering about Upper Hutt trying to find a cousin yet is seen twice at Emily's place. What are the odds?"

"Not very good," I added. "What if Emily was in Belgium during the heist?"

His frown deepened. "On holiday?" Crockett asked. "She was a cop."

I nodded. Yes, she was, but only because Army wanted her inside the Police for whatever reason, and inside my company doing a bit of spying for them. Who knew my life was so interesting? Bloody Bill. Yet another person who should've been called Richard.

Crockett stared at me for a beat. "You know something."

Yep.

"I don't know any more than you."

Crockett picked up a spare coaster and flipped it through his fingers. I watched him. It was awful not being able to tell him what Bill told me. I needed a way to drop hints.

His eyes darkened as thunderclouds rolled across his face. "This is bullshit."

Ginny swooped in with a jangle of her bracelets and a waft of perfume. "It's never easy when someone we care about is in trouble, Crockett." She patted his shoulder. Bracelets tinkled. "Clear heads will prevail."

He dragged his eyes from mine, then refocused with an accusatory stare. "Why can't you find her?"

"She's shielded."

"How would someone know to shield her?"

"No idea. The people who know about my special skill are all in this room, except Donald, of course."

"You're positive no one else knows? Not even Emily?"

"Not even Emily," I confirmed.

"Didn't she wonder how you found people so quickly before her accident?"

"I'm pretty good at covering my tracks and making sure the narrative fits with what I find, Crockett. I haven't been doing this for five minutes."

"Sorry," he grumbled. "I just thought maybe Emily knew and whoever has her now knows."

"Unless you told her, she doesn't know."

He shook his head. "Not my place to tell your story."

That's right and it's not my place to tell Emily's story even though she probably has no idea what her real story is, now.

"We're not getting anywhere," Crockett said. "We have two men and only one we can clearly see. It didn't look like Emily was forced into the car, and that bothers me. We have run into Kerrin Costa snooping around Emily's, but she didn't give us anything. The person who was posing as a postal worker must've jammed the cameras so they didn't record anything at Emily's house. You can't find her. And we have nothing but gossip." His fingers thrummed on the dining room table. "How is this not related to you, Ronnie?"

"We can't rule it out," I said. "I don't think it is, I think this is something from the past."

"You do know something," Crockett said. "Otherwise, why would it be related to her past? Her past as a cop? Can't be her life as a PI if you don't think this is anything to do with you, and *Wherefore Art Thou*."

I blew air out and sucked air in.

"I can't tell her story," I said.

"Can't or won't?" Crockett asked as his blue eyes met mine. "Can't or won't?"

"Jesus H Christ." I sucked in another breath. "She was in Belgium when the heist happened."

You could've heard a slug fart.

Silence continued for what felt like a full minute.

Crockett closed his eyes and breathed. "So, were you?"

"Europe, yes, but I was working out of the UK and only heard about the heist via newspapers. And Tom was in Belgium."

"Did you all meet up and steal diamonds?" Ben asked with a small smile on his lips. Perhaps he wasn't sure if he was joking or not.

"No, we did not," I replied. "We did not meet at all. I had no idea Emily or Tom were there."

"All three of you," Crockett said. "Quite a coincidence."

"It's a smaller world than most people think," Tom said. "I did not meet Emily or Ronnie in Belgium. I was there as an attaché working a short job. That was it."

"Okay."

"Who is Lucas Genoa? Have you dug up any background?" I asked, looking at Ginny, hoping to move the subject to something other than diamonds and Belgium.

"He's interesting," Ginny replied. "Very interesting." She picked up the iPad on the table and touched the screen a few times before opening the stand on the back of the case and standing the iPad on the table. "Watch."

We crowded around the device and watched.

Lucas Genoa was walking through Wellington Airport. When he disappeared from one camera, he popped up on another. The feed continued like that until he stood by baggage claim and a man met him.

"That's Peter Piper," I said, letting air whistle through my teeth. "Peter fucking Piper."

Crockett flashed his eyes from the screen to me. "Why would the head of NZSIS meet Genoa at the airport?"

"I don't know," I replied.

Ginny reached over and tapped the screen. "Genoa is definitely his name, but his file is locked down. We can't get access. And he clearly knows Piper."

"You were right about him being interesting," I said. "Someone must be able to access his file." I thought for a minute. I could access a lot more than anyone realised because of the link the former head of *Genesis*, MacKinnon, gave me, and also my old mate Justin's flash drive of handy tools. "I might be able to find something."

Ginny gave me a questioning look. "It's above all our pay grades."

I smiled. "Yeah, we'll see."

"Where to?" Crockett asked.

"Home," I replied.

Ben and Tom stood and moved into the kitchen together talking in hushed voices. Crockett looked from me to them. I smiled and shrugged.

"Let's go," Crockett said, standing and pushing his chair in. He followed Ben out the back door.

"Stay safe," Ginny said, giving me a hug. "Eat, sleep, all of you. None of you will do anyone any good if you all fall over."

"We will. Keep looking for sightings?"

"You know we will. We'll be in touch."

I pulled my shoes on and hurried out the back door into the night to catch Crockett and Ben.

Chapter Thirteen: [Ronnie: Why?]

No one said anything on the way home. Clouds covered the moon giving the night an eerie feel and somehow making the world quieter. We all had things to think about. I was going over and over the meeting of Lucas Genoa and Peter Piper. It was strange. Life is strange but that was super strange. As soon as we got home, I jumped out of the car and hurried upstairs. Crockett and Ben followed. I heard the front door close and lock behind them. A hint of toast lingered in the kitchen. A saucepan in the sink bore the tell-tale red of spaghetti sauce. Donald must've made spaghetti on toast for everyone.

I entered the lounge to find Donald entertaining Nana. Enzo wasn't in view. A dark shape out on the balcony moved; the sliding door opened. Enzo entered carrying a drone. Dane came in after him.

"Anything?" I asked.

"Not nearby. I don't think anyone knows where you live."

"Not nearby?"

"Fergusson Drive. There's a car parked by the Tawai Street corner facing south. It moved when you came through."

"Someone followed us home?"

"No, they tried to follow you home. Ben's SDR was

thorough."

I looked at Ben. "I didn't even notice what way we came home."

"You were deep in thought," Ben replied. "We've been all over the area, twice."

I turned back to Enzo. "If they saw the car then they'll be looking for it."

Ben was already heading out the door. Enzo and Dane went back to the balcony with the drone. I heard Ben's ringtone echo in the stairwell.

Nana spoke, "What's happening Veronica?"

"Enzo is checking for a car that might have tried to follow us. Ben is moving cars downstairs."

Crockett had vanished.

"Where's Crockett?" Nana asked, looking around the lounge.

"Probably helping Ben switch the cars around so Ben's is in the garage."

A few minutes later everyone was back.

"We put my car in the garage, your car in the carport across the road, Crockett's car up your driveway."

"Not-neighbours?"

"Uh-huh."

Good idea. No one lives there.

Enzo and Dane came in from the balcony. Dane carried the drone.

"All looking good," Enzo said.

Dane placed the drone on the coffee table, then typed on his iPad. Siri said, "Might pay to have someone look for surveillance by your office and the bookshop, Ronnie."

I nodded. Pulled my phone from my jeans, chose a contact, and paced as I waited for Andy to answer.

"Ronnie, how can I help?"

"I need surveillance on my offices and the bookshop."

"What happened this morning?"

"Emily was grabbed. Jenn was knocked out."

"Shit. I'm wrapping up that supermarket job. Quite pleased that I pinged the produce manager stealing meat."

I looked at my watch. Overtime. Steph hated paying overtime, but I knew she'd be fine with it for Emily's sake.

"Wrap it up quick. Steph will bill them once your report is in. Surveillance is top priority."

"I'm on it."

He hung up.

I stopped moving. Just stopped.

Breathe in.

Breathe out.

Repeat.

Ben's voice bounced across the room. "Ronnie? You, okay?"

My eyes met his. "Why Emily?"

"Leverage?"

"For?"

"That's the million-dollar question. What is it they want that they think Emily has or can get them?"

"Maybe a case of yours. Common knowledge that you're close to Emily."

"Surely that would be a deterrent to nonsense ..."

"Of course. Unless they're stupid."

"Obviously," A smile edged onto my lips. "Pretty stupid to take us on."

Ben's arms circled me. "If we rule out bad guys so stupid they'd get a Darwin Award, what's left?"

"Ransom."

"Has there been any contact?"

I shook my head. "Not a squeak."

"If we rule out ransom?"

"Information," I said. "She knows something, or we know something."

"That's possible. How long has it been?"

"Six hours and thirty-two minutes."

"BOLO?"

"Yes. Sort of. Enzo reached out to a few cop mates."

"Get her photo out via social media?" Ben was thinking better than I was.

"We should put Donald on that, his reach is phenomenal after the saga of the not-neighbours."

"Not a bad idea to keep him occupied. I noticed a new glue gun and a mega number of rhinestones."

"Oh dear, he's discovered Temu, hasn't he?" I asked.

"That makes sense." Fear flickered through his pale blue eyes. "It's not for our wedding, is it?"

"Hell no!" But it could be. Now was not the time to worry about rhinestones and hot glue. Also, Ben and I had a secret. They'd all be pissed off with us when they found out what we were going to do, but it saved us from rhinestones and hot glue.

Ben whispered in my ear, "*Genesis.*"

"Someone connected invisible dots."

"Or a play to see if they can flush a *Genesis* operative out?" Ben suggested. "How many of us do you think there are?"

"Hard to say. We have nothing to base guesswork on." We know of four including us.

"What do we know right now?" Ben moved so we could still talk but he was angled to see the whole room. "I think we need to go old school. Moscow rules."

"You think we should scatter? Get our feet on the ground? Live drops and dead drops?"

"It can't hurt."

"You that sure we have surveillance on us? I've seen no sign of it." I took a beat and revised that. We had groceries arrive without ordering them. Enzo said he potentially saw someone taking too much interest in us with the drone. There were signs.

"Yes."

"All right then. We find them and run some counter-surveillance. If they're watching us, then they're watching for a reason. Let's find out what it is," I said. "I don't think we need to ditch our cell phones and go fully old school."

Ben called Crockett over. "We're going almost old school."

"Ronnie's Rules it is."

"Rude."

They laughed. Nana looked up.

"I need to see if I can get more info on Lucas Genoa," I said. "I'll be digging into whatever I can find."

Nana piped up, "Did you say Lucas *Genoa*?"

"Yes, I did. It's not the first time that name's come up, is it Nana?" A ball of cold dread formed. "Now are you going to tell me what you know?"

"Our client was looking for a cousin."

We all turned to Nana in stunned silence. "Ester told me the cousin was Sandra Solway."

"We might have been mistaken."

"I'm sorry, you were what?"

"Veronica, it's our case. We can't just bandy names about."

"You had me sign an NDA! Were you looking for Sandra Solway?" I asked slowly and deliberately. "Kerrin Costa is looking for Sandra Solway?"

Nana's head shook ever so slightly. "I'm sorry, Veronica. That is precisely what Ester said. And I allowed it. Kerrin Costa wanted us to find her cousin. That was correct. But her name is Simone Genoa." She lowered her eyes and gathered herself. "Why are you looking for a Genoa?"

Holy moly. Simone.

"He kidnapped Emily."

Nana shifted uneasily in her chair. "Can't be the same family."

"It can, Nana. And it probably is. And I doubt that either Genoa is related to your client."

I now had two names to play with. Crockett glanced at me, gave me half a look that said get to it, then settled himself next to Nana.

I took the opportunity to skedaddle to my room and the bat cave with Ben hot on my heels.

Ben sat down and watched as I opened a drawer, then opened a locked box with a key I kept in a box at the back of the middle monitor on the desk. I plugged Justin's flash drive into the computer.

"Bill said a VSSE officer was working with someone from SIDE."

"Costa is SIDE?"

"Yep, so who is she working with to find this Simone person?"

"No idea. So far, we have Lucas Genoa and an unknown male. Maybe him?"

"Maybe."

"What are you looking for?" Ben asked as I scrolled through the contents of the drive.

"A back door. A way to circumvent any security clearance."

"You have that?"

"I hope I have that," I replied, as a folder caught my eye. "Could be something." I hovered the mouse pointer over a folder called 'The Book of Enoch'.

Ben nodded. "There's no book of Enoch in the Bible."

"Nor in the Torah. Perhaps the whole angels bonking

120

humans and creating Nephilim was too much for people to cope with," I said, opening the folder to reveal more folders. "Which one do you think we should try first?"

Ben scooted his chair closer. "What are our choices."

I clicked on Book One. Seemed like a good place to start and lo and behold I found more folders. "It's a rabbit warren."

Ben read out loud the folders on the screen. "The blessing of Enoch, The Creation, Fallen Angels, Intercession of Angels, Book of the Words of Righteousness, Taken by Angels, The Holy Angels."

I was about to eeny-meany-miney-moe it, when my hand was drawn to Taken by Angels. "Here this is where we look." I opened the folder. The folder contained two images. I ran the mouse over the first one and looked at the properties. "That's a pretty big file for an image that isn't that great." I double-clicked to see what would happen. A browser opened and then another window.

Ben nudged me. "Where are we?"

"I don't know. Let's have a look around and see if we can find out."

Instead of files and documents, the window contained an image, an old hunting cabin. It took up the entire screen. There was a telephone book on the table. I hadn't seen a telephone book in years, but I still knew what one was. As I moved the mouse around, various things on the screen jittered. An old chair wobbled as I passed over it. There were more books in a bookcase. Some of them jiggled as I passed over them. I went back to the phone book and clicked. It opened in a new screen and asked for a password. I used the password Justin and I used to use years ago when we were in college. And just like that the screen changed to reveal a list of names.

"Is that a search button?" Ben asked, pointing to a small question mark in the top right-hand corner.

I tapped it and then put Sandra Solway into the search bar. I wanted to rule that name out as anything we needed to worry about.

We watched in silence as a little coloured wheel spun and then stopped. Nothing.

"At least we don't have anyone else to worry about," I said on an exhale. I added Lucas Genoa to the search bar. The spinning wheel returned. Colours blurred as it twirled. All of a sudden there was a ding, and we had a result. A photo of Lucas Genoa popped onto the screen.

Tapping the photo got his entire work history and life.

"He's a spook," Ben said. "Argentinian."

"Why could no one else get this info," I mused out loud, "Why is his secret life so much more secret than everyone else's?" I scrolled down the document. And then what could be an answer popped up. "He was in Belgium and so was Peter Piper."

"This is getting really interesting now," Ben said. "So, they were both in Belgium, but why is it so highly classified? A lot of people were in Belgium. Emily, you, and Tom were in the vicinity."

"I don't know why his presence was so highly classified. That's what we need to find out."

Another window opened. *Genesis.*

"I think I just got snapped snooping by the boss," I said, as I watched and waited for whatever it was that *Genesis* needed to tell me.

Three dots sprang to life.

Genesis: Have you found Emily?

Me: No.

Genesis: What are you doing, and how did you get into classified files?

Me: fluke

I shrugged and looked at Ben.

"That's as good as anything," he said, his eyes on the screen waiting for more dots to turn into words.

Genesis: You should not be in there. Leave now.

Me: We needed to know who Genoa is. It's about Emily.

Genesis: Has it helped?

Me: Yes

That wasn't even close to true. I had more questions than ever.

The pixels floated freely then the chat window vanished.

"That was weird," I said. Going back to reading the file on Genoa. "There is no mention of a sister."

"Did you really think he had one?"

"Part of me did," I replied. I suppose Costa would be interested in any 'family members', or it's a coincidence that Lucas Genoa is here at the same time as Costa asked Nana to find Simone Genoa. Nana would've said if she found any Genoas. I know she would.

"He's had an interesting career. Wonder how he met up with Peter Piper originally and what that connection is about?"

"No doubt we'll find out," I said. Just to see what would happen I typed Simone Genoa into the search bar.

The coloured wheel spun then up popped a file with no photograph. That was strange. Usually, personal files had a photo attached.

Ben and I read the information on screen. Then leaned back in our chairs and stared at each other.

"She was in Belgium," Ben said, not taking his eyes off me. "She's not Argentinian."

"No, she's not, is she?" I flicked my eyes back to the screen. "Dual citizenship. New Zealand and the United States."

"Plenty of people have dual citizenship," Ben said.

He was right. They do. It felt like another layer of secrets.

"So, the surname is just a coincidence," I mumbled. "Doesn't seem right." I hit print.

I printed everything we had on Simone Genoa, Lucas Genoa, and his known associates. Then went through a complicated shutdown process and put everything back where I kept it. I gave some thought to how quickly

Genesis knew I had accessed the system. When I opened a link there must be an alert fired off to *Genesis*. Makes sense.

Ben piled up the papers that shot out of the printer. We left my cave, paper in hand, and returned to the lounge.

Crockett looked up expectantly as we entered the room. "And?"

"Got snapped being nosy," I told him and thrust the papers into his hand. "Something odd is going on."

Crockett read the papers. "It's not odd, Ronnie. It's fishy as fuck."

My brain was spinning. What if Simone Genoa was Emily? What if she wasn't solely Army Intelligence back in the day? What if she was *Genesis*? Could that be why *Genesis* is interested in her disappearance? I stopped the nonsense. I had no idea when *Genesis* was formed.

Crockett interrupted my thought process. "Lucas Genoa and his associates aren't nice people."

"Say what?"

"I've come across his mates before. They are not nice people and if the Genoa bloke is keeping their company, then he is not a nice person. If they have Emily, then we need to try fucking harder to find her." He jumped to his feet and strode into the kitchen.

Enzo motioned for me to stay put as he went after Crockett.

Nana tutted.

I looked at her.

"Problem Nana?"

"Crockett's language, Veronica. Far too rough."

"I think we can excuse his language in the circumstances, Nana, don't you?"

Ben added, "This is an unusual situation, June. He's worried about Emily."

"We're all worried, dear, but we don't need to sink into the gutter."

I threw a warning glance in Nana's direction. She pursed her lips but said nothing more.

"Donald?" I caught his attention. "Did you get Nana to pack an overnight bag?"

"Yes," he replied.

"Let's get some sleep. Show Nana to the guest room. You did make up the beds?"

"Yes, Ronnie," he said. "Both spare rooms. Dane and Crockett can take the room with twin beds."

Dane tapped on his iPad then Siri said, "Don't worry about me and Crockett." He typed some more. "We'll go to his place."

"Okay," I replied. "See if you can get him to get some sleep."

Dane nodded.

Chapter Fourteen:
[Emily Jones: Not me!]

The night wore on. Moonlight occasionally found its way through parting clouds in the inky sky. Emily sat at the formica table and traced the gold in the fake grey and white marble pattern. Her index finger was running across the tabletop until Lucas spoke.

Her hand paused as she looked up.

"Do you know who I am?"

"Yes. You told me your name is Lucas." She covered her mouth as she yawned.

"That's right. Do you remember meeting me before?"

"No. Only today when you came into the bookshop." She flashed her eyes at Stefan. "Is Jenn all right?"

"Probably," Stefan replied. "I didn't kill her."

"Why did you hurt her?" Emily asked. She pulled her hand back from the table and into her lap.

Stefan made direct eye contact with her. If intimidation was his goal, he knew he'd failed. Emily's tired eyes stared back, unblinking for what felt like a minute.

"Why?" Emily demanded.

"She was in the way."

"No. She was behind the desk, working, and *out* of the way."

Stefan motioned to Lucas. "Is she for real?"

Emily scowled. "Of course, I am real."

A smile tweaked the edge of Lucas's mouth, but he controlled it. "He knows you are real Emily. It's an expression used by people when they don't think a person is being serious or maybe they are joking."

Her scowl remained. "I am serious. Jenn was not in anyone's way." The scowl softened. "Why would someone joke about that?"

"You're right of course, they wouldn't. It was a stupid thing for Stefan to say. He should choose his words with more care."

Stefan shook his head slowly. "We're getting nowhere."

"It's not a race," Lucas said quietly. "Why don't you go check the perimeter." Stefan didn't move. "Now."

He hauled himself to his feet and left the kitchen. Lucas waited until he was gone before speaking to Emily again.

"How long have you been in New Zealand?" he asked.

"I was born here."

"Oh, whereabouts?"

Emily shook her head. "I don't remember."

He nodded a little. "How long have you worked in the bookshop?"

"I can't remember," she said. "I think it might say on our website."

Lucas looked at his phone, then back at Emily. "I didn't see anything on the website. There was a biography of two staff members. You and another woman who works part-time, I think her name is Sandra."

"Yes. Sandra works there sometimes. Hopefully, she can take over until I get back there."

"What did you do before you worked in the bookshop?"

Emily watched him before answering, unsure if she should tell him what she knew about her past. She shrugged. "I don't remember." Emily traced the gold lines in the fake marble some more. Lucas watched her.

"I need to use the bathroom," Emily said.

"Do you remember where it is?"

She shook her head. Her eyes watered as she tried to suppress another yawn. He rose and beckoned to her to follow. Lucas led her down the hallway and pointed to a door on the left. "Toilet is in there, and the bathroom is the next left. Come back to the kitchen when you are finished."

"Okay."

She stepped into the toilet room and closed the door. There was a privacy lock, and she used it. Emily stood on the toilet and tried to see out the small fanlight window. It didn't open far due to a security stay. She was quite thin but even so she didn't think she could squeeze through the opening. All she could see was darkness through a small gap. The frosted glass pane embedded with wire gave nothing away. Carefully she stepped down and used the toilet. A voice, she didn't recognise, in her mind, said 'pee when you can'.

She did.

She washed up in the bathroom and inspected the

window while she dried her hands on a thick beige hand towel. It was the same as the toilet, no room for her to slip through. There was a big windowpane, but it didn't open, and once again it contained wire mesh. Emily hoped that Ronnie would find her soon and bring Crockett when she did.

Why would these two men take her away from the bookshop she wondered. It didn't make any sense to her and Lucas calling her Simone to start with was annoying and strange. She stared at her reflection in the bathroom mirror.

"I am Emily Jones," she said. "I wish Crockett would find me."

Someone knocked on the door.

"Emily?" Lucas called out.

She opened the door. "Yes."

He escorted her into another room. Not the kitchen. A lounge room. She sat in a big brown velvet armchair. He sat across from her.

"It's more comfortable in here," he said.

She nodded. "I'd like to go home."

Lucas smiled. "I suppose you would."

"Now, please. I want to make sure Jenn is all right and stop everyone worrying about me."

"That's not going to happen. We are looking for something and you know where it is."

Emily frowned at him. "I don't know where anything is that belongs to you."

"We think you do. And I think you will tell me."

Emily sighed. "I cannot tell you something I do not know."

"Tell me what you know about Belgium," he directed firmly.

"It's a country in Europe. I remember because Ronnie told me about it when there was something in the newspaper."

"What was in the newspaper?"

Emily thought back to when she asked Ronnie where Belgium was. Pieces of the afternoon cobbled themselves together. "It was a story about diamonds. Yes, that's what it was. I asked Ronnie about Belgium because she said that's where the most diamonds are sold."

"Anything else?"

She shook her head. "No."

"Have you been there?"

"No. I haven't been there."

Emily didn't know if she'd been there or not, but no one had ever told her about going to Europe, so she didn't think she had. She was a police officer, then a private investigator, and now she ran a bookshop. There was no room there for trips to Europe. She thought about Ronnie's engagement ring.

"Diamonds are used for engagement rings," she said. "Ronnie and Ben are engaged. Ronnie has a diamond ring."

"Do you have any diamonds?"

She shook her head. "I am not engaged."

"You can have diamonds for other reasons," Lucas said

with a smile. This was not going as well as he expected. Simone wasn't coming to the party. The Emily thing was stuck. "When did you dye your hair?"

Emily looked surprised at his question. "Dye it?"

He nodded. "When did you dye your hair? You must have to do it often."

"I don't dye my hair," she said. She picked up a handful of her hair that hung down her shoulder. "This light brown or dark blonde or whatever it is, is the colour I have always been." She flicked it behind her.

"Are you sure?"

An abrupt laugh from Emily made him jump. She laughed more and then found her voice. "I would know if I dyed my hair or if it used to be a different colour."

Lucas smiled. "I'm sure you would."

"I go to the hairdresser every six weeks for a trim," Emily said. "Sometimes Donald does a special deep conditioning mask on my hair, but he doesn't colour it."

She wouldn't choose mouse brown if she did colour it, Emily decided. Who would even choose a dull colour? She would quite like to have blonde hair with bright, blue streaks.

"Okay, I just thought you used to have dark hair. Like mine."

"Why would you think that? We haven't met before. Do you think you saw me somewhere?"

"I suppose I might have you confused with someone else."

"Is that person called Simone?"

"She is."

"I am Emily Jones."

"And you haven't seen me before?"

"I saw you the first time this morning when you made me get in the car."

Emily clenched her teeth. Why hadn't anyone found her yet? She knew she wasn't far away from Crockett's house. She needed to leave. She could get to Crockett's if she could just get away from Lucas and Stefan.

"I am tired."

"Come with me," Lucas said.

Emily stood and followed him. He opened a door and ushered her into a room with a single bed. There was bedding folded at the end.

"Get some sleep," he said and left.

She heard a bolt slide after Lucas closed the door. There was no use trying to escape that way with the door bolted. She opened the curtains and checked the windows.

Emily jumped when a face appeared from the dark. Stefan.

She pulled the curtains closed and lay on the bed.

Chapter Fifteen:
[Ronnie: What now?]

Friday morning arrived with a fanfare. My phone rang on my bedside table. Liam's name and photo popped up.

"Can I help you, Liam?"

"A Black Notice arrived from INTERPOL this morning. It might interest you."

"They're for identifying deceased persons ... and you think I'd be interested. That can't be good."

"It's come from Belgium. They found the body eight years ago and haven't managed to ID the person."

Belgium again.

"And now they send out a black notice."

"They had no fingerprints or dental record matches. Now they've done digital facial reconstruction. I've found the person to be familiar and I need you to take a look."

"Okay. Why no prints or dental?"

"No fingers or teeth. DNA is on file but so far it hasn't matched anyone."

"Do you want to drop the picture in a message?"

"No, I'd sooner see you in person for this one. You and Ben. Don't bring Crockett or Enzo."

"All right." I looked at my watch. "We'll be at your office in an hour, is that okay."

"Perfect."

I hung up. Ben was sitting on the bed, waiting.

"We're going to meet with Liam," he said.

"Yeah. Without Crockett or Enzo."

Ben narrowed his eyes, licked his lips, and nodded. "Let's go."

We went in search of my Nana. She was in the lounge looking out the ranch slider to the balcony. I saw her smile as she viewed me as a reflection in the window. She turned to greet me. "Good morning, Veronica. I think today will be the day that you all will find our sweet Emily and bring her home."

"I hope so." I smiled at her. "Nana, can you please stay here with Enzo and Donald? Dane and Crockett are here as well," I said, as I noticed a glint in her faded blue eyes. "No nonsense."

"Goodness, Veronica, you'd think we got into mischief constantly the way you talk."

"You do," I replied. "Please, just stay here."

Donald piped up as he entered the lounge, "She'll be here with me. You go do what you need to do."

Ben and I smiled at Donald. Bless him for still thinking he could contain Nana and the cronies once they got an idea in their heads.

"Right, we're gone," Ben said.

We hurried to the stairs.

Dane was sitting at the dining room table reading something on his iPad. Crockett was making coffee in the kitchen. Enzo was nowhere to be seen.

"Where are you going?" Crockett asked.

"Need to check something. Back soon," I said with a

small smile and followed Ben down the stairs.

It was an okay drive into the city. Took just under forty minutes. It wasn't bad going. We parked down the road from Police Headquarters in Victoria Street, Wellington. A few minutes after that we were escorted through the building to Liam's office.

He greeted us at the door and closed the door as we sat in the chairs in front of his desk.

"You made good time." Liam sat at his desk and pulled a file out of a drawer. "I printed the information for you."

"Thanks," I said.

He passed a police-issued manilla folder across the desk to me. "Take a look."

I opened the folder to find the Black Notice front and foremost. The next page held a surprising photo. Bloody hell. Ben whistled through his teeth. I flashed my eyes up to Liam.

"You look as stunned as I did when that photo came through."

"It can't be right," I mumbled. "How could it be right?"

Ben took the photograph and stared at it. "It can't be."

"Why today?" I asked. "They've had eight years and the reconstruction arrives today."

Liam frowned. "Maybe it took that long to get through the unidentified bodies and do the reconstruction. And what's so strange about now?"

"Someone grabbed Emily Jones from the bookshop yesterday."

"Shit."

"You should've had a missing person's report come through," Ben said, as Liam typed on his keyboard.

"Yep, here it is." He spun his screen to face us. There on the screen was the missing person's report for Emily as filed by Enzo.

"I don't know what to make of this photo, Liam," Ben said.

"Nor do I. Doesn't seem possible," Liam replied.

And I sat there thinking it was not only possible but probable. There was a lot they didn't know about Emily's past and still a lot I didn't know. The urge to ring Bill and demand real answers was high. So was the desire to talk to Peter Piper. Secrets begat secrets. And the boss seemed to be harbouring some that directly impacted us, or at least Emily. When I emerged from my thoughts, I found Liam and Ben waiting.

"Anything you'd like to add, Ronnie?" Liam asked.

"No, don't think so," I replied with a smile.

"What do we think about the dead body?" Liam asked.

"We think the impossible. We think it is Emily Jones," I said. "It can't be. But it certainly looks like her."

"Remember this was a reconstruction," Liam cautioned. "And if Emily was grabbed yesterday, she couldn't be dead in Belgium eight years ago. Could she?"

Ben agreed with a nod.

"I don't suppose so, no. It's just ..." I put the photo on the desk face up. Scrolled through my photos and found one of Emily. I left that screen open and placed my phone next to the photo on the desk. "It's uncanny."

Ben leaned in closer. "First glance, it's the same person, but if you look carefully, you can see some clear differences."

I followed his finger as he pointed out Emily's jawline and cheekbones. Different enough in the right places so it wouldn't trigger facial recognition databases and pop the woman on everyone's radar as Emily Jones.

"It's not her," I said on an exhale. "It is someone very similar though."

I locked eyes with Ben. "Similar enough to get Emily grabbed by someone thinking she is the woman from Belgium, especially if none of the players involved know that woman was killed in Belgium."

"Possibly."

"Where are you on the abduction?" Liam asked.

"Nowhere."

"We have an ID on one of the males," Ben said. "So not quite nowhere."

"Who?"

"Lucas Genoa," I told him. "There is also someone from the Argentinian secret service, a Kerrin Costa, who was trying to find a cousin. She was snooping around Emily's. We had information from a source that said she was looking for a cousin, Sandra Solway. Potentially Costa is involved in the Emily situation." I couldn't believe I called Nana a source. We now knew that Sandra Solway didn't exist or at least wasn't the person Costa was looking for. Oh, no, she was looking for Simone Genoa.

"Yep."

"It's more than a situation Ronnie. Time to name it and knuckle down," Liam said. "Do you want my help?"

"Yours or INTERPOL's?"

"Both if required."

"That would be great. And for an operating name. Operation Milo."

Liam typed on his keyboard while he spoke. "I am alerting all branches of Police about the Operation. Henceforth, all communication about Emily will be coded Operation Milo."

"Tip line?"

"Do we have a job number?" Liam asked, but I saw him checking his email. "Never mind, I see someone in the Upper Hutt Police Station has set one up. I can put out a media release stating the job number and asking anyone with information to phone 105 and mention the number."

"Thank you," I said. "The more eyes on this the better."

It almost went against everything for me to want police involvement, but this was Emily and we needed eyes. Lots of eyes. Thoughts crammed together. None of them were helpful.

"We really should add information about Lucas Genoa. Do you have anything usable?" Liam gave me an inquiring look.

"Let's say no, shall we?" I said. "Best if I don't muddy the waters any more than I have already."

He folded his arms and leaned back in his chair. "What

does that mean?"

"It means it's above everyone's pay grade, and we need to find him without using what I may or may not know."

Ben tapped his fingertips on the edge of Liam's desk.

"Do you have something to add?" Liam asked him.

"No. I concur with Ronnie. We can't use anything we might or might not have come across in a slightly off-beat data search."

"Off-beat," Liam said. "Bet there is another word for that. One that starts with I and ends with -egal."

Ben laughed. "I can neither confirm nor deny."

"How about an image?"

"That we have," I said, picking up my phone from his desk and locating an image that Ginny found for us. I AirDropped it to his phone.

A few seconds later, Liam looked puzzled. "Do you see what I see?" He spun his screen to face us. He'd added Lucas Genoa's image to his screen along with the image of the dead chick from Belgium.

"Possible family resemblance," Ben and I said together.

"Look at this then," Liam said, and added another image to the set. The same dead woman but with dark hair instead of blonde.

"Well, shit," I said. "They could be siblings."

We thanked Liam. I shoved a copy of the file under my jacket, and we left.

Chapter Sixteen:
[Ronnie: Who is Emily Jones?]

"Are we going back to your place?" Ben asked as we followed late morning traffic onto the motorway north.

"I'd like to talk to Bill Bailey again."

"Okay. Trentham Camp it is."

"I need to see him somewhere else."

I texted Bill: Meet me at Briscoes in twenty minutes.

Three dots appeared on my screen as Bill typed. Then they disappeared. Then they came back and finally, his message followed.

Bill: I need a new dinner set.

Me: Farmers?

Bill: Yes, upstairs in The Mall.

"Drop me at The Mall please," I said to Ben.

"Do you want me to wait?"

"That would be nice. It won't take long. I can't imagine Bill wanting to give me anything usable."

I could be wrong. And I would quite like to be wrong. We'll see.

Twenty minutes later I jumped out of the car and hurried into The Mall via the Logan Street entrance. Ben would find a park outside and wait. Along with most of Upper Hutt, we preferred to park outside rather than pay for the privilege of parking under The Mall.

I side-stepped slow shoppers and hurried past Muffin Break. Someone called out my name. I glanced over to see Nana's friend, Pat waving. I waved hello and kept going. No time for chit-chat.

I used the internal stairs in Farmers and arrived on the top floor without seeing anyone else. I scanned the departments looking for Bill. Sure enough, he was looking at crockery. I perused the other side of the stand. I held up a plate so he could see it.

"Why?" Bill asked, picking up a plate and weighing it in his hands before replacing it on the stand.

"Because it's a nice pattern," I replied and put it down again.

He picked up a milk jug and put it down, then inspected one with a different design.

"What do you need?"

"An answer to a puzzle," I said and showed him a plate I quite liked. Reds, oranges, and yellows in an abstract blocky pattern with a gold border.

"That looks like a puzzle," he replied.

"Could Emily's disappearance be a case of mistaken identity?"

"I'm sure it could."

I put the plate down and chose one with dark blues and greens, still abstract and blocky, but no gold.

"Bill. Was there someone who looked very similar to her in Belgium when she was?"

"I don't know." He toyed with a mug before appearing

to change his mind and put it down.

"I need an answer. I need to know if Emily was there because she looked like someone who was a target." There I said it. "Was she supposed to take someone's place?"

"It's possible."

He held a bowl in his hands. It was shit brown and fitting.

"Yeah, that design," I replied.

"It's dirt brown," he said.

"Uh-huh." I walked away.

It didn't take me long to hurry down the internal stairs and slip out the underground parking exit. I spotted the car parked along Queen Street just before the Logan Street corner.

The front passenger door opened as I approached.

"Thanks," I said with a smile and got in.

"How'd it go?"

I buckled my seat belt before telling Ben what happened with Bill and how I thought it went. "He's not giving up much, but he didn't deny Emily was in Belgium at the same time as someone who looked very like her, or who she looked very like."

Ben checked his mirrors, then pulled out. "What do you make of that?"

I smiled. "Same thing you do. Someone was murdered and Emily took her place in whatever it was that was happening."

"It certainly looks that way from where we are

standing."

"Did the men who took Emily know she was a ringer, or do they believe she is whoever the hell was murdered?"

"And there we have the million-dollar question."

"Is the million-dollar question really millions of dollars in diamonds?"

"Could be."

Yeah, it could. They're tradable, transportable, and easily concealed. I remembered hearing that diamonds were smuggled out of certain countries back in the day inside toothpaste tubes. They could be inside anything.

"If that's the case then why wait eight years to come for them?"

"There must be a reason the others involved couldn't come sooner." Ben indicated and turned down Tararua Street. "We've got a tail."

I glanced at the wing mirror. "Silver SUV." I grabbed a pen from my bag and wrote the plate number on my hand.

Ben indicated left. We weren't going home. I used my phone and logged into the Waka Kotahi database. The plates came back to a rental company. Omega. I rang the Wellington office. Ben took another left and we were on Brentwood heading toward Fergusson. By the time someone answered we were across Fergusson and down Tawai Street.

"Hi, I have a query about a rental."

"Are you a current customer?"

"No. It's being driven erratically. Plate number is:

Indigo Romeo Lima Five-Six-Seven."

"I can't help you, ma'am. Please notify police."

"Just give me the name on the rental agreement."

"Ma'am, I'm not allowed."

"I am Officer Emily Jones. Badge number seven-four-nine-zero."

I could hear the person breathing and then typing. "You need a warrant."

"By the time I get one, this person will have killed someone. Be a decent human being."

"It was signed out by a Mr Tony Robinson."

"Robinson. Address?"

"I only have his home address. It's in Virginia, in the United States."

"Great. Thanks."

I hung up.

Ben had turned into Ararino Street and then into the railway station car park. He parked down The Tote end. We watched the silver SUV cruise past us, then do a U-turn. Ben and I watched the car enter the car park and creep toward us. Ben glanced at the glovebox. I reached forward and opened it. Inside was a Glock. I took it out and did a press check to confirm there was a round in the chamber. I switched the gun to my left hand and moved my hand down between the door and seat, so it was partially concealed. The car parked one space away. His door opened. He got out of the car and walked towards us with his arms raised from the elbow. He approached Ben. Ben zapped his window down. I moved my hand to bring the Glock into my lap.

The man nodded at me then spoke to Ben, "That's not very friendly. I'd always considered New Zealand was a friendly place with gun control laws."

"We don't know you and you were following us," Ben replied. "State your business, pal."

"I want to talk to you," he said and started to drop his hands.

"Keep them up," Ben said. I opened my door, shoved the Glock in my waistband and scooted around the car to the male.

"Hold still," I said and frisked him quickly. I took his wallet and dropped it into Ben's lap. I removed an M9 from his waistband holster and kept hold of it. "Go around the car bonnet and get into the front passenger seat."

"You mean the hood."

"Just walk."

I didn't want him walking behind me. As soon as he was situated, I climbed in the back righthand side. It was much easier to hold a gun on him from my chosen seat.

"Okay, Mr Robinson, what are doing following us?" Ben asked. He'd angled toward the man.

"You know who I am. Great. I'm hoping you'd lead me to a woman I'm looking for," he said. He turned his head to look at me. "You don't need the weapon. I'm not a threat."

"Not that keen on taking your word for it, yet" I replied. "Who are you looking for?"

"A woman," he replied.

"You're a long way from Virginia," Ben said. "Long way to come for a woman."

I smiled. "Pretty sure you have women in your state."

"I do, but not this particular one."

"Does she have a name?" Ben asked.

"She does."

"Would you like to share with the class?" I asked. "Can't help you if we don't know who you're looking for."

"Amanda Walton."

Ben moved in his seat. "Like the Walmart Walton family?"

"Spelled the same but I don't believe there is a family connection."

"What makes you think Amanda Walton is in New Zealand?" I asked. "It's a long way from Virginia. If she's from Virginia."

"I don't know where she is from," he said. "Maybe she's from here."

"Why are you here?" Ben asked. "Why are you here, now?"

"There was a sighting. I'm here to confirm."

"A sighting in New Zealand?" I asked. There seem to be a lot of people looking for people all of a sudden.

"It's a good place to get lost."

"I suppose it is but we're picky who we let in," I replied.

"Can't be that picky, Mr Reynolds got in," Robinson said. I noted his smile.

"We like actors," I retorted. "They're entertaining."

Robinson laughed. "Have you got a problem with me being here?"

"Yeah, maybe I do," I replied. "You're not the first person to drop from the sky looking for someone in the last few days."

"Other people are looking for Walton?"

Ben shook his head. "The first time we heard that name was right here from you."

"Can you help me?" Robinson asked.

"Perhaps. It'll cost," I replied. "I'm a private investigator and I don't work for free. One other thing; why not just give me a ring or pop into my office? What's this following us nonsense?"

"Curiosity. I wanted to see where you were going."

"We live in New Zealand, trust me when I say there is plenty of cow poop here. We do not need imported poo."

"I'm sorry. I didn't mean any offence."

"Why did you follow us? Why are you carrying a handgun? What is the nature of your visit to Aotearoa? Who do you work for?"

He held his hands up. "Stop. You Kiwis talk too fast."

"So, you're slow, okay."

Ben adjusted his position again. "Let's take this somewhere else."

"The office," I replied.

Robinson started to protest but Ben cut him off. "Your car will be fine where it is."

The engine fired into life. I tapped Robinson on the

shoulder. "Buckle up."

Chapter Seventeen:
[Emily Jones: This makes no sense]

Friday afternoon arrived with brilliant sunlight and a light wind chased the clouds across the sky. Lucas put a mug of hot chocolate on the coffee table by Emily's chair. "There's no more Milo," he said.

She didn't respond. Stefan sat across the room from her. He also had a mug of something hot. Lucas sat on the sofa about sixty centimetres from Emily.

"I have some photos I'd like to show you," Lucas said.

"What of?"

"You. They're of you."

A frown creased her forehead, knitting her brows together. "How do you have photos of me?"

Stefan slammed his hand into the armrest of his chair. Emily jumped; her drink sloshed in the cup.

"This is taking far too long. Let me do what I do." His voice sounded low and menacing.

Emily closed her eyes and wished Crockett would burst into the house before whatever Stefan wanted to do to her happened.

"Show me the photos," she said.

Lucas took his phone from his shirt pocket and opened the photos. He typed then scrolled until he found what he wanted to show her. He passed her the phone. "Swipe left," he said. "There are more."

Emily stared at the first image. The woman had dark hair like Lucas's. She looked a lot like Lucas. Emily did not recognise her. "I don't know who that is," she said.

"Swipe and look at another photo. Look at all of them, Emily."

She studied the next photo. The same woman with dark hair standing near a fountain. She swiped again. It was another photo of the woman with dark hair but this time she was with Lucas and a woman.

"I don't know who she is." Emily stared at yet another photo of the mystery woman, Lucas, and the other woman. In the background of the image. she saw something. Emily touched the screen and zoomed in on the background. There was a man who looked a lot like Tom sitting at a table outside a cafe.

"What did you see?" Lucas asked, appearing right next to her. He took the phone. "Who is he?"

Emily shook her head. "I don't know. I thought he looked familiar, but he didn't."

"Do you know who the other woman in these photos is?"

"No."

"It's Kerrin Costa," Lucas said. He watched her face as he said it again. "Kerrin Costa."

Emily showed no sign of recognition at the name. She shrugged. He wasn't asking the right questions. That much she knew. She didn't know who the people were, but she knew he was asking her the wrong questions.

Emily's thoughts turned to Crockett and Ronnie. Then she realised what the mesh in the glass could be used for, it was probably through the exterior walls as well. The house was a low-level Faraday cage. She needed to get outside. Out of the house. She needed to get to Crockett.

"Can I go for a walk?" she asked. "I need to move. It helps my brain."

Stefan glared at her. "You're staying right where you are."

Lucas shook his head at Stefan. Emily watched their silent exchange. She wondered why Stefan was there. He wasn't in any of the photos she'd seen. He wasn't involved. She heard the words in her head again: 'He wasn't involved.' Involved in what she wondered. And how would I know?

"Please, Lucas. Just in the backyard. Fresh air helps." Emily observed his thought process in his eyes. He wasn't like Stefan. This was personal for him. She could work with that. He caved.

"You and I will go into the backyard for ten minutes," he said. "Come on."

Stefan jumped to his feet. "Don't be stupid."

Lucas held his hand out to Emily. "Come on." She took his hand and rose from the chair. "We will be in the backyard," Lucas said to Stefan. "You can stay here."

Stefan kicked the coffee table. Hot chocolate and coffee spilled. Lucas pulled Emily by the hand and dragged her behind him until he was shielding her from Stefan's temper. Stefan kicked the table again, upending it with a crash.

"Clean up the mess and get your shit together," Lucas said quietly. "We will be outside."

The minute she got outside the house, Emily scoped the yard looking for a weak point while smelling flowers and admiring the many plants.

"We can't be out here too long," Lucas said from where he sat on the back step watching her.

"Just a few minutes. It's so nice out here."

He smiled but she didn't see it. "Do you like flowers?"

"I suppose so," Emily replied. "I don't know what any of them are called except the roses though."

"I'm not very good with flower names," Lucas said. "My mother knew flowers."

Emily paused near a rose with red edges on the yellow flowers. "This is pretty, and it smells nice." She bent down and sniffed the rose while looking for a gap in the fence or a weak point. The perimeter fence was over six feet high. Not easy to scale without a jumping point. She spotted something behind the large overgrown rose bush. It was a bench like she'd seen in parks but with decorative metal legs and a latticed metal back.

"Come on, back inside."

"Can I pick a rose?"

"Go ahead."

Emily bent a stalk with an almost open bud on it, but it didn't break. She tried another and snapped it off. The bent stalk with a heavy bud dangled. It would be a little signpost to remind her where she saw the bench. If she could get out without an escort, she might just make it over the fence.

As she entered through the back door of the house, her artificial foot caught on the door sill. She stumbled. Lucas grabbed her arm before she fell.

"All right?"

"Yes," she replied. "Didn't lift my foot high enough. Sometimes, when I'm tired, it happens." She limped a little as she righted her footing.

"People do tend to trip more when they're tired," he said, closing the door behind them. "Is your foot all right?"

Emily laughed. "It's not real so of course it's all right."

Confusion settled on Lucas's face. "What do you mean?"

Emily pulled the leg of her jeans up to mid-calf. "It's not real, see?"

"How?"

"A car accident," she replied. "Are we going to the lounge or kitchen?"

"Kitchen."

She turned toward the kitchen door. Stefan strode down the hall towards them and caught a hand signal from Lucas.

"Wait for me in the kitchen, Emily," he said.

"Okay."

She wandered through the room and sat at the kitchen table with the grey and white fake marble top and the small threads of gold. She sat where she could see down the hallway. They didn't close the door. There was an exchange between the men. Emily could not tell if it was amicable or not. She could only see their backs. Emily traced the gold on the tabletop just like she had earlier.

Chapter Eighteen:
[Crockett: Just find her!]

"I don't understand why this is so hard." I rinsed my empty coffee mug and tipped it upside down on the draining rack.

Enzo stacked plates into the sink. "I'll wash these. You can dry."

Busy work. Sure, why not?

Hot water ran as he squirted detergent into the sink. Bubbles and foam formed almost instantly.

"Why do they want Emily?" I said, pulling a tea towel off the rail at the end of the bench. "What could they possibly want with her?"

"We will find out."

"It's been thirty-six hours."

"I know."

I dried dishes and stacked them on the bench. Donald swooped in and put everything away - teamwork at its finest. Now if we could just take our teamwork capability and find Emily.

"Do you know where Ben and Ronnie are?"

"On their way back," Donald said showing me a text on his phone. "They ran into a situation."

"What the fuck does that mean?" I hung the tea towel up to dry.

"I don't know," Donald replied.

His phone pinged with a tune I recognised. It was another text from Ronnie. I peered over his shoulder.

"Rude!" Donald exclaimed and tried to move to read his text without me.

"It's Ronnie," I said. "What does she want?"

Donald huffed and puffed. Enzo shot him a warning look. I guess he was used to his bluster.

"She said they're going to your office."

I grabbed my keys from the dining room table and shot down the stairs. They were going to my office again.

I heard Donald protesting from the kitchen but ignored him. I was starting to feel as if I was being cut out of the investigation and that wasn't right. Not right at all. It was my Emily who was missing. Somewhere deep in the recesses of my mind, I heard Emily saying, 'Find me'. I charged down the stairs and shut the front door a little too firmly on my way out.

Didn't have to be a rocket scientist to know that Donald would be on the phone to Ronnie. I couldn't take the most direct route to my office, so I headed north for six minutes then doubled back down Alexander Road. A last-minute decision had me at home switching the car for the Harley. If I'm rocking around, I may as well have fun doing it. I rode River Road to Silverstream then Fergusson Drive to Sutherland Ave, then left into Gower and right onto Camp. I parked behind the office and had zero doubt that Ronnie and Ben heard me arrive. The Harley is a lot of things but subtle isn't one of them.

I opened the back door, set my helmet on the bench,

and went into the main office. My office door was open. Ben spun to face me.

"Glad you're here," he said. "Join the party."

I stepped into my office. Ronnie nodded at me. There was a man sitting in the same chair we had the Costa sheila in. That made sense it was my office, and I only had one chair on that side of my desk.

"Who do we have here?" I asked.

The male turned.

"Hello, Crockett."

"Jesus. What the hell, mate."

Ronnie and Ben stepped sideways and faced me with questions scrawled over their features.

Ronnie spoke, "You know this guy?"

"Yeah. Tony Robinson." I struggled to make sense of him being in New Zealand let alone being in my office with Ronnie and Ben.

Ben grinned. "Why am I not surprised?"

"I know people," I said with a matching grin. "What are you doing here?" I addressed Tony.

"There was a problem. I got sent to sort it out."

"And you managed to get grabbed by these two ..." I shook my head. "Thought you were better than that."

"Asshole," Tony said.

"That your love language?"

Tony laughed. "Maybe."

Ronnie folded her arms and perched on the edge of my desk. Ben leant on the wall. Tony was the centre of our triangle. I stayed behind him. Making him turn his head if he wanted to see me.

"We have a crapfest rolling out in front of us and now we have you," I said. "What's your story?"

"I was sent," Tony said. "The exact words were, 'Get to New Zealand and put the kibosh on the situation.'"

Ronnie straightened up. Ben stayed where he was. I could feel their demeanour change. They went from giving Tony the benefit of the doubt to no fucks given. If I was honest, I'd taken that short trip as well.

A quick internal pep talk followed, 'Reel it in Crockett. It won't help if you lose it now.'

I exhaled.

"You were sent. Who sent you?"

Tony turned his head until he could see my face. "You know who sent me. It's work, nothing more."

"And the job is?"

"I'm looking for a woman called Amanda Walton."

I flicked my eyes at Ronnie; she responded with a slight nod. He must've divulged the name earlier.

"And Amanda Walton is important?"

"Yes."

"Why?"

"I don't know why. I just have to pick her up and make her vanish."

"Vanish."

Ronnie opened her phone and handed it to me. The first photo was Kerrin Costa. I swiped across the screen. The very next photo looked like Emily with dark hair. The photo after that was Emily. One more swipe put the guy we identified as Lucas Genoa on the screen. The next swipe was our John Doe. I went back to the first photo.

"Do you know this woman?" I asked, showing him Costa's photo.

"Don't know her but I have seen her around."

"Around where?"

"Not here. She was tailing me in Argentina a few years ago. She's SIDE."

"And the next photo."

I watched his face for anything that told me he recognised her. If there was, he hid it well.

"Don't know her." He swiped across to Emily's picture. "Now her, I know." Tony smiled. "Met her in Caracas."

"Met her or worked with her?" Ronnie asked.

"Both."

"How long ago?" Ben asked.

"It would have to be ten years ago."

"Who did she work for?"

"*Leviticus.*"

I felt my innards fall. *Leviticus.* Holy smoke. That's a CIA game plan.

Ben took a step towards Tony. "Are you sure?"

"Yes," Tony said.

"That just threw a spanner in the works," Ronnie said under her breath.

Tony scrolled to the next photo. "Lucas Genoa," he said. "Major asshat." He scrolled again. "This dickhead is Stefan something he's with VSSE. Any more?"

I shook my head. "Stefan what?"

"Don't think he ever told me his family name."

I felt my jaw tense.

"How do you know him?" Ben asked.

"He and Genoa play together. South America somewhere."

I unclenched my jaw. "Caracas?"

"Could've been."

"Not Europe?" Ben asked.

"I don't work in Europe, so no."

"You've never worked in Europe?" I needed some clarity. What the hell was Emily doing in Caracas? And why is someone from VSSE in South America? Belgium is a long way from Caracas.

"No. I'm based in the Americas."

"This is a long way out of your operations base," Ronnie said. "Why did they send you?"

Ben walked around Tony's chair, motioned to me, then went into the outer office. Ronnie stayed put, keeping an eye on Tony.

"What?"

"*Leviticus*," Ben said, keeping his voice low and quiet. "I've worked for them."

"They're CIA or at least CIA owned," I added. "I haven't forgotten."

"Yeah."

I let that mull for a few seconds. "The arms deal," I said. That was where we came across *Leviticus* last.

"Yes. I can tap a source and find out what Tony does for *Leviticus*."

"Do it."

Ben strode out the back door, closing it behind him. I went back to Ronnie and Tony.

Ronnie glanced at me. I nodded. She shot me a small smile.

"Tony," I said. "We'd like to hang on to you for a little while."

He nodded. "I expected that."

"Coffee?" Ronnie offered.

"Sure," Tony replied.

She looked at me. "Yep."

Ronnie left the room, pulling the door closed behind her.

"Now it's just us," I said. "What do you know about her?" I showed him the photo of Emily on Ronnie's phone.

"She's good at what she does. Wicked sense of humour."

I could easily imagine her being good at whatever she was doing in Caracas. Her sense of humour wasn't something I'd seen much.

"What did she do?"

"That's not my story to tell. You'll have to ask her."

"What is her name?"

"You've got her photo, and you don't know her name. Christ Crockett. Thought you were better than that."

"Humour me."

He cracked a small smile. "What if I told you her name is Emily Jones."

"Then I'd say you know more than you're telling me. And our conversation is almost over." I strongly doubted she went by Emily Jones in Caracas.

"Really. That's interesting," Tony said. "Think, Crockett. You're blinded by what you think you know and not allowing truth to evolve."

"Truth? Our chosen profession does not rely too heavily on truth at any given time."

"Sure, it does. Your truth. My truth. What's actually real. We don't operate that far from the source."

"Fuck you."

He's not looking for anyone called Amanda Walton. He's a liar and an arsehole. I stormed out the door and slammed it behind me almost collecting an incoming Ronnie.

Chapter Nineteen:
[Ronnie: We need more.]

Crockett paced the room, clenching and unclenching his fists. I put the coffee mugs back on the bench in the kitchen. Ben was pacing outside in the parking area and talking on the phone. I imagined he reached out to someone he knows within *Leviticus*.

My thoughts were running rampant.

If Emily was *Leviticus* did Bill Bailey know that? Did *Genesis* know? Was she a cop then?

Is Emily older than we know or did she pack life into her thirty plus years? Was she Army Intelligence and did she infiltrate *Leviticus*? The more we found out the less we knew.

Then something potentially useful sprang to mind. *Leviticus* wasn't *Leviticus* ten years ago.

I grabbed Crockett's arm to stop him moving.

He shook my hand off. "What?" he snapped.

"Go ask your mate when *Leviticus* became *Leviticus*."

He frowned at me. "Why?"

"Humour me."

He shrugged, opened the door, and spoke to Tony. "Who were they prior?"

"Who were, what now?"

"*Leviticus*. Who were they? When did the name change?"

The silence that followed told me volumes. Crockett shut the door, quieter this time.

"So?" he said. "What now?"

"Do you think he can't answer because he doesn't know, or because he won't answer?"

"I don't know. But if he worked for them, he'd know about the name change. Even in a poorly constructed back story, he'd know about the name change." Crockett dropped onto the sofa in a seated position. "What's the story with *Leviticus*?"

"We already know they're a CIA company used for all manner of operations and some legit protection in nasty places," Ben said as he entered the room. He was no longer on the phone. "They've been around a few years now but not ten, and prior to becoming *Leviticus* they were known as *Exodus*."

"Did they operate in Caracas?"

"Not according to my source although I wouldn't have been surprised if they had been there. They are a paramilitary company. They could've easily been providing security for whoever needed it. Venezuela isn't somewhere I'd like to be without private security."

"Do you think he worked with Emily in any capacity in Venezuela ten years ago?" Crockett asked.

"I don't know. My source did not know of an Emily Jones working in South America. If she was there, she would've had a different name."

"He looked at her photo and said he knew her," I said, replaying the events in my mind. "He didn't recognise

Simone Genoa if that's even the other woman's name. Show him a different picture." I took my phone from Crockett's hand and found the photo I wanted Tony to see. "This one." I gave the phone back to Crockett.

"Shit, that looks a lot like Emily."

"Yeah, who knew hair colour made such a difference."

He opened the door and showed Tony the photo. Ben and I waited. Crockett returned.

"Yes. He said it was Emily."

"It's not though, Crockett. It's not. There is a good chance he didn't work with Emily, but he worked with that chick."

"And that sheila called herself Emily Jones?" He wasn't convinced.

"Maybe she did. Or maybe he saw Emily somewhere and thought it was the other chick." There was a fairly decent chance that he was as confused as we were.

Crockett went back to Tony; Ben and I followed him into the room.

"Who is this?" Crockett said handing him the phone so he could see the blonde version of the other woman.

"Emily Jones," he replied without hesitation.

"And you worked with this person?"

"Yes. We've covered that already. You losing your marbles, Crockett?"

"This person." He turned my phone to face him again. "Is not Emily Jones."

Tony stared at Crockett like he'd grown two heads and sprouted horns. "That's Emily Jones."

Crockett shook his head then swiped back to Emily's photo and showed it to him. "This is."

"Show me again."

He did.

"Shit! And you're convinced that they're different people. And one of them is Emily and the other is?"

"We don't know for sure who the other is, but it might be a sheila called Simone Genoa."

"Related to Lucas Genoa."

Ben left to take a phone call. I watched him through the open door. Whoever rang him caused more pacing.

"Quite possibly," I said as my focus returned to Tony.

Crockett turned to look at me. "What's up?"

"Don't know." I left and he followed.

Ben was no longer pacing but stretched out on the sofa. He looked comfortable. His phone was lying on his chest.

"You good?" Crockett asked, slapping his booted foot.

He sat up, placed both feet on the ground and nodded. "Tierney is in town."

"Why?" Crockett asked.

"This situation we are in the middle of," Ben replied. "He said there are people in New Zealand who don't particularly want anyone knowing they're here. And he's curious as to why."

"Did you tell him about Emily?" Crockett asked.

"No. I probably should have but I didn't. Now I need to go explain myself," Ben replied. "It's almost like being summoned to the principal's office."

"Why is he so interested?"

"I'm not thinking it's for a good reason," I interjected. "You okay here? We're going to bounce." Ben's boss was in town and that man only appeared when things went sideways in a handbasket.

"Yep. I'll let you know if I get anything usable from Tony."

Ben grinned. I smiled.

"Dane is on his way here. Backup, just in case," I said.

"A witness, you mean," Crockett replied. "I probably won't cause him harm. Don't need a witness."

"But if you do lose your shit and kill him you might need help with the cleanup," I said. "Meet you back at home?"

"Of course."

"Don't bring him," Ben said, tipping his thumb toward the inner office.

"We need to find her, Ronnie," Crockett said with a grim look on his face.

"We will." I gave him what I hoped was a reassuring smile.

"Try your woo-woo thing again?"

I let his woo-woo comment slide again. He was a man on the edge, and I wasn't going to be responsible for pushing him over. Not today anyway.

Ben nudged me as we left. "You didn't bite."

"I don't always bite. Today is not the day."

Ben chuckled. "Let's go home."

"What about Tierney," I whispered in his ear as he

closed the back door.

Chapter Twenty:
[Ronnie: Home?]

Friday was disappearing, late afternoon snuck up on us. "Is this a Surveillance Detection Route or are we going somewhere that isn't home?" I asked as Ben headed south on Fergusson Drive.

"It's all going well so far," he said, checking the rearview mirror. "Thought I'd run an SDR going south before we went home."

"Good idea."

"I have them sometimes."

"And Tierney?"

"He's coming to us."

Stone-cold dread hit me like a softball bat to the head.

"Say that again."

"He's coming to us."

"Home? My house? Where Nana is?"

"It'll be okay."

I could see his cheek dimple as he tried to contain a smile.

"I don't know what fantasy land you live in where Nana meeting Jonathon Tierney is an okay thing." I huffed air from my mouth. "Best you stop taking whatever drug you're on that caused that nonsense."

His dimple deepened. I whacked his arm.

Laughter trickled from him until he gave up on even

trying to hold himself in check and his merriment expanded to full-blown guffaw. He glanced my way, then focused on the road again as he drove over Silverstream Bridge but stayed in the left lane. He was definitely taking the long way home. Looked like we were going home via Lower Hutt. Ben's laughter subsided.

"It's not even remotely funny," I said. "What's he here for anyway?"

Ben cleared his throat. "He liked it so much last time he said he would be back. And he is."

We crossed the river on the Kennedy Good Bridge and made our way north again. My thoughts were running a chaotic and twirly cross-country as I tried to work out how to mitigate the potential fallout from Tierney meeting Nana and deciding where I could dowse for Emily again. Something might have changed. It wouldn't hurt to try again. I didn't want to do that with Tierney around. I knew I had a map in my bat cave but dowsing in there wouldn't work. The bat cave is shrouded just enough to prevent interference from outside or to make sending a signal out tricky. I needed to be in the open or just in my bedroom. A sigh escaped. I don't know why I'm so intent on making things hard for myself. My bedroom door shuts. Problem solved.

When I next took notice of our surroundings, we were going under the rail bridge and entering Silverstream. We would be home eventually and then I'd have to deal with Nana's joy at meeting Jonathon Tierney.

"You're very quiet," Ben said. "What's happening?"

"Not much. I need to be able to dowse for Emily again. Can't do that near Tierney."

Ben nodded.

He took several left turns, then wound us back toward home. If there was someone following, he was confident that he had lost them.

I hurried inside not waiting for Ben. Romeo greeted me with a happy tail wag. I gave him a pat on his bony head and went through to the lounge. Nana was chatting to Donald. Enzo was nowhere to be seen. Smart man. Nana looked up and smiled at me. Her thin lips stretched across her old teeth.

"I'm glad you are back Veronica. Have you any ideas about dinner?"

"I haven't really had time to think about anything except finding Emily," I replied and plopped down into an armchair. I took a cleansing breath. "Nana, Ben's grandfather is in town and he's coming over."

There was no hiding her delight. "That's excellent news. I didn't get to meet him last time he was here."

"I want you to promise to be on your best behaviour, Nana."

"What on earth does that mean, Veronica?"

"It means, Nana, behave. Maybe keep your mystery-solving to yourself."

"If the man asks, I will tell him," Nana said. "Us oldies need to stick together."

That's what I'm afraid of. That right there. Nana could pull him into her web.

Then I thought about Dane. Shit. Tierney cannot see him or hear about him.

"Donald, Nana, I have something I need to ask of you. It's very important." They waited. Ben walked in with Tierney. Bugger.

"Hello, Mr Tierney," I said, stepping forward to shake his hand. He pulled me closer to hug me.

"Veronica, it's delightful to see you again. Call me Grandfather, we're family. Now who do we have here?"

Buggery freaking bollocks.

"My Nana, June Tracey, and my cousin, Donald Henere-Tracey."

Tierney shook Donald's hand, then moved to sit next to Nana. "How wonderful to meet you Mrs Tracey. Your granddaughter is delightful."

"Thank you. It is a treat to meet you. What brings you back to New Zealand?"

"I decided I'd spend some more time with Benjamin and Veronica, after all, I'm not getting any younger and they haven't set a wedding date yet."

Good grief. Now he's going to start. I could easily forget who he really was as he played Ben's Grandfather to perfection.

Nana nodded wisely as old women do, then looked over to me. "Veronica, I think Mr Tierney should stay for dinner." Nana clapped her hands together. "A family dinner."

"Call me Jonathon, after all, we are family."

"Jonathon it is. Please call me June."

Buggery buggery, bollocking pancakes with shit sprinkles.

I smiled at Tierney. "What a great idea, Nana. How about staying for a meal, Grandfather?"

"If it's not any trouble, I would very much like that."

Ben's silence caught my attention. He was standing in the doorway looking at his phone.

"I'd better get the dinner prep started," I said, knowing full well that the oldies wouldn't expect anything less. The last thing I wanted was to leave Nana and Tierney alone to talk. I needed to find a way around that situation.

"Give me a hand Donald," I said, smiling.

"Just coming," he said, flapping a hand at me.

When he joined me in the kitchen I used a hushed tone. "I need you to make sure Dane's name doesn't leave Nana's lips. It's very important. This is your mission, Donald. I'm trusting you to help protect Dane."

He nodded. "Do I need to know why?"

I shook my head. "Best if you don't. Just keep the subject away from what's happening now and make sure Nana never mentions Dane."

"I will do my best." He saluted me.

"You have to succeed, not just do your best. If Ben's grandfather sees him or hears about him it will put Dane in danger." I was ramping up the mission to make sure he got the point. I didn't know if there was still a danger cloud swirling around Dane. But I did know that we were asked to find him once for Tierney and the subsequent knock-on effect wasn't fun.

"Who is Ben's grandfather and why would he care about Dane?"

"I can't tell you."

"To protect me?"

"Yes, Donald. To protect you. Get in there and monitor the conversation. I'm counting on you."

Donald nodded and hurried back to Nana. Ben appeared with his phone in his hand.

"I told Dane to stay away from here," he said.

"Good. I told Donald to make sure Nana doesn't mention Dane or the current situation."

"Okay then, let's get dinner prepped. What are we having?"

"Besides a stroke?"

Ben nudged me with his shoulder. "It'll be okay."

"What about some sort of baked potato thing?"

Ben grabbed the bag of spuds from the bottom of the pantry and started peeling. I found a dish big enough and got the rest of it organised. Ben layered sliced potatoes, grated cheese, and béchamel sauce in the dish.

"Did you hear your grandfather mention a wedding date to Nana?"

"No."

"He did. Tell me again how that in there is going to be all right." I pointed toward the lounge just as Donald hurried in with my phone in his hand. He thrust it at me.

"Thanks," I said, motioning him to go back.

I answered the ringing phone from an unknown New

Zealand cell phone number.

"Hello, Ronnie Tracey speaking."

"I'd like to meet with you," the male said.

"And you are?"

"Peter Piper."

"And why do you want to meet me, Mr Piper."

Ben moved closer so he could hear the conversation. I didn't want it on speaker.

"I believe you have a problem."

"How would you know that, and what makes you think I want you involved?"

"We might be able to help each other, Ronnie."

"Might we just? Where do you want to meet?"

"Middle ground. Boulcott Hospital foyer."

"When?"

"Eight in the morning. Don't be late."

He hung up.

Ben and I stood in silence for a moment. Then carried on and put the potato bake in the oven.

"We've got salad fixings in the fridge, so that'll work with the potatoes," I said after inspecting the contents of the refrigerator. "Oh, there's steaks in here too." I did a quick count. "We've got enough." I looked at Ben. "Enzo cooks a good steak."

"I'll go check on the *family*," Ben said. "Was there something you wanted to do?"

I nodded. "I'll be in my room."

Ben kissed me lightly. "We can do this."

I kept my thoughts to myself and went to my room.

Chapter Twenty-one: [Crockett: Crazy Town]

I checked Tony Robinson's story and let him go as the afternoon slipped away. He didn't know more than us. I knew how to get hold of him and he genuinely seemed to be looking for the same people we were. If he found Emily first, he'd let us know or we'd track him down and shoot him. I blew a long breath out, picked up my cell phone, and rang Art.

As soon as he answered I said, "I need you to keep an eye on someone for me."

"Sure. Send a pic. Gimme a name. How's it going?"

I sent the picture and the name via text.

"It's slow. It's frustrating. Just keep an eye on him. He left my office two minutes ago."

"On it. I'll run him through everything we have, find out what he had for breakfast, and settle in for a surveillance job. Covert or overt?"

"You know what ... I don't give a shit if he knows he's under surveillance." Fuck him.

"Overt it is then."

Art hung up.

My phone rang before I could put it in my pocket. One of my mates in blue calling.

"Grant?"

"Yep. Hey, got a male in the interview room who might

have seen Emily."

"Shit. I'm on my way."

"Tell the desk sergeant to buzz you through because you're meeting me."

"Will do."

Ten minutes later I was at the police station, buzzed through the security door, and in an interview room.

"What did they do?" I leaned on the wall and jammed my hands in my jeans pockets. The dishevelled male stared at an imaginary spot on the table between us.

He shook his head. "You're one of them."

"One of who?"

"Them, the ones who put a tracker in me."

All right. Nuttier than a jar of Pics peanut butter. The bloke held his head in his hands, giving me a good look at the blood-soaked left sleeve of his pale grey hoodie.

"The tracker," I said. He looked up. "Tell me more about the tracker; where is it?"

I found a tracker in Emily's backpack. Sometimes even lunatics have real information.

"You know where. After the lockdown. They did it to everyone."

"Riiiight."

"Those injections. The way we all had to have them. We had to." His eyes opened wider. "They're tracking you too."

"Hope they're enjoying it. Now that I know, I'll make sure they're bored."

"You'll be sorry if you don't get it out." He pulled up

his bloody sleeve and showed me a saturated bandage.

"Did you do that?"

He nodded. "It was too deep. I couldn't get it out."

"I think we should get you to the hospital. They'll be able to get it out there." Or get him medicated and stop him digging around in his own arm.

He violently shook his head. "No. No. NO!"

"Tell me where you saw my friend." I needed this bloke to tell me what he knew and then get him out of here.

His head wobbled on his neck almost like a tremor.

"She was with them."

"Them?"

"Lizard people."

"Lizard people?" I looked over at the mirrored wall and rolled my eyes. I knew Josh and Grant were watching from the other side, and running interference, so I wasn't interrupted.

"That's what I said. You don't have to believe me, but they're real."

"And what do they want with my friend?"

"To control her. Make her do things for them."

Someone knocked on the mirror.

"I'll be back in a minute. If you think of anything that might help us find my friend, yell out."

"It's too late. They have her."

I ducked out the door and closed it behind me. The two cops in the viewing room were doing their best to hold themselves in check. Josh was doing a better job than Grant.

"Do you think he knows anything?" Josh asked.

"Probably not," I replied. "Why is he here?"

Grant cleared his throat. "He was hanging around Upper Hutt College. We were called to move him along and I showed him a photo of Emily."

I nodded. Fair enough. The more people we get that image in front of the better. "And?"

"He was adamant that he'd seen her recently with two men."

"Okay." I pulled up photos of the kidnappers. "I'm going back in, if I get nothing you can do whatever you want with him."

Grant grinned.

Josh took a breath. "We'll be right here."

I opened the interview room door and stepped in. "I'd like you to look at some photos for me. Tell me if you've ever seen these people." I showed him the first photo.

"He's a lizard person." He pushed my hand away. "They'll know you have the photo. They'll get you."

"I don't think they will." I swiped for the next photo. "How about this one?"

His eyes flicked to the screen then away. "He's the other one. They have that woman."

"Where do they have her?"

"In a house."

"Okay. That's really good. Do you know where the house is?"

His face blanked. He shook his head.

"The police officers said they found you by Upper Hutt

College. Why were you there? Do you remember what you were doing there?"

"They train them there." He nodded. "That's a lizard person training school. They're not real teenagers. Those teachers aren't human. No one is human there." Panic edged into his voice. "I can't talk to you. They'll know."

I sat down opposite him and lowered my voice slightly as I said, "They can't find you here. The police station has a shield over it. Like a big invisible dome. We're safe here."

He looked around the room. Suspicion oozed from his pores or maybe it was a lack of deodorant.

"Are you sure?"

"Yes. I am."

"Do you trust the police officers?" he whispered.

"Yes."

"The lizard people were close to the high school. I thought they were patrolling to find people like me. You know, the ones who can see them for who they are."

I nodded. "I understand. Did those lizard people have this woman with them?" I showed him a photo of Emily again.

"Yes."

"Can you remember exactly where they were with her?"

I could see him thinking, so I waited. It would've been pretty easy to lose my cool and shake the truth out of him. The one person we think saw Emily and her abductors, has a kangaroo loose in the top paddock, and I didn't think that was the only thing he had loose somewhere.

He licked his lips.

"Can you remember?" I asked quietly.

"It wasn't the same road as the school," he said. "It was close though. I'm sure it was in Poet's Block." His hands shook as he ran them through his hair. "Do you know Poet's Block? I think they have a nest there somewhere."

"I know Poet's Block. Sounds like I need to take extermination equipment with me."

"Yeah, yeah. You should do that."

"Do you remember the house?"

"Not new," he said. "Didn't look different from most houses there. You know, older homes. Might've been red."

"Could it be a brick house?"

"Yeah."

"Were you walking or in a car?"

"Walking."

"How many corners from the house to the school?"

He shrugged. "I don't know. I had to run. If they saw me, they'd grab me too."

"Okay."

"It's too late for her. They have her. They'll turn her into one of them."

"I hope they don't," I said. "Sit tight. I'll get someone to drive you home."

"I won't be safe there."

"Maybe you could stay here for a little while. And I'll

ask the police to check out your street and house to make sure it's safe."

He nodded. "Thank you. But without the dome, they'll find me."

"Pretty sure one of my cop mates has a portable dome shield." I held my hands about ten centimetres apart. "They're small powerful units." I smiled at him. "I bet he won't mind putting it over your house to make sure you are safe."

"I'm sorry about your friend."

I left the room and popped into the adjoining viewing room.

"An invisible dome ...," Grant said. "That was actually pretty clever."

I grinned. "Took a chance. It could've gone down like a fat kid on a seesaw, I got lucky."

"Where are you headed now?" Josh asked.

"I'm going to go for a wander in Poet's Block."

"Do you think he really saw Emily?"

"I don't know, but it's the only lead we have."

"Yell if you need help."

"Will do. Thanks for that," I said, and tipped my thumb towards the window that enabled viewing of the interview room.

"We'll see if we can get him some medical help before his arm turns into something horrible," Grant said. "And perhaps a short stay in the mental health unit."

"Good idea." I smiled. "Wherever you put him though, make sure there is a dome."

"Hell yes. No lizard people will get him on our watch," Josh said. "I can guarantee it."

Chapter Twenty-two:
[Ronnie: Save yourself Emily]

I closed my bedroom door firmly, then snipped the lock. It was a privacy lock so not anything heavy-duty. It was just enough. The late afternoon sun bathed my room in gold.

I found my spare map in a drawer of my dresser; didn't even need to go into the bat cave. With the map spread on my bed I checked I could reach every corner from a kneeling position. It wasn't exactly the most comfortable way to dowse but it would work. There was no time for ritual today, so I jumped right into pendulum work. From the northernmost point of the city limits, I began a slow move south, watching the pendulum's movement and waiting for something, anything, to happen. Big circles became smaller tighter circles, again there was a trail that led around the back streets to west of the city from the CBD. It wasn't strong but when I honed in on it, I got a slightly more powerful sense of movement along that trail of energy. I moved my hand to the beginning of the energy and let the pendulum lead me again. Now there were smaller circles. I definitely felt something I hadn't felt the first time I'd tried to dowse for Emily. It wasn't strong but it was there and not far from Upper Hutt College. Everything else stayed the same. The usual high energy points at her home, the bookshop, Crockett's place, the hall where she went to her recovery group, and the lesser but familiar spikes near the scene of the *accident*. There was so much trauma around the site of the drone strike that the energy would never dissipate fully.

I took the pendulum back to the college just to confirm that the reading was not at the college. It wasn't but it was close. I got a bit of a twinge in a street near Cottle Kindergarten and then another in Sheridan Crescent. For the first time since Emily was grabbed, it felt like we had something to follow. I packed up and went in search of my phone so I could tell Crockett.

I strolled into the lounge with a smile planted firmly on my face. Nana and Tierney were deep in conversation. I glared at Donald who smiled back showing his beautiful, straight, gleaming teeth. Ben winked at me. I joined him on the sofa.

"Dinner smells good already," I said.

"Enzo checked on it a few minutes ago," Ben replied. "Did you get what you needed to do, done?"

"I did. We should take Romeo for a walk after dinner."

Romeo ambled over. He had his ears on and heard the word walk. I rubbed his head. Nana and Tierney were still chatting away, smiling and laughing. I threw up a little bit in my mouth. Romeo chose to go over to Nana and nudge her until she patted him. Then the conversation turned to greyhounds. He's a clever dog.

I whispered in Ben's ear, "Is Nana flirting with your grandfather?"

Ben laughed quietly. "You should've seen them before. It was worse."

"I can't even. I just can't." It was time I checked dinner or slit my wrists or something. "Kitchen." I got up and was noticed immediately.

"Veronica, dear," Nana said with far more perk in her voice than usual.

I turned to face her. "Yes?"

"Jonathon and I require a refill." She raised her sherry glass. "If you would be so kind."

"I'm just off to run an errand, Nana. Ben would be delighted to refresh your drinks."

"What could be important at this time of day? Is this something to do with Emily?" Nana's old eyes glinted.

"No. Just a supermarket run, something I forgot for dinner," I said with a smile before I followed Ben to the kitchen and pointed out Nana's sherry in the pantry. "Keep her off Emily as a topic, as best you can."

"Where are you really going?"

"I might've picked up on Emily, but it's not a strong reaction and I suspect it's pretty much a wild goose chase."

"Be careful and remember wild geese lay eggs too."

"Righto, that was an odd turn of phrase."

"Too much time with old people," Ben said then kissed me. "I'll keep a close eye on the conversation."

"Thank you," I said then ran down the stairs, car keys jangling in my hand and jumped in my car.

Chapter Twenty-three:
[Emily: What's taking so long?]

Emily sat at the same formica table, tracing gold through the grey and white faux marble with her finger. The last rays of afternoon sun made the gold sparkle.

Stefan was nowhere to be seen. Lucas sat opposite her, watching. She was used to his uncomfortable attention.

"How did you get the scar?" He pointed to her face.

"Car accident," she replied. "Same one that cost me half a leg."

"Must've been a terrible crash."

She shrugged and kept tracing gold wiggly lines.

"Not something you want to talk about. I get that."

She bit her lip to stop herself smiling. He didn't get it at all. She looked at him. "Why am I here?"

"We're looking for something."

"Why do you think I have it?"

"We know you had it," he replied. "And sooner or later you're going to tell us where it is."

"If you say so." Her attention was drawn to the kitchen window. A piwakawaka flitted around a bush that grew under the window. Emily stood up.

"Sit down," Lucas said.

"No." She walked to the window over the sink bench and watched the small bird.

"What are you looking at?"

"A bird," she replied.

"Tell me where it is …"

"I don't have anything of yours. I've never met you before. How could I have anything of yours?" She turned around and leaned a hip on the bench. "How?"

He frowned.

"We aren't letting you go until we find it. You may as well tell us where it is." He stood up. His tone changed. "Before Stefan uses other methods to get the information."

"Other methods?"

He nodded. "Ones I don't like, but I might have no choice."

"What does that mean?"

"He uses enhanced interrogation."

"What does that mean?" Emily looked him dead in the eye. "You're so sure I know what you're talking about. News flash. I do not."

"Stay where you are."

"Where would I go?" She glared at him when he turned away from her.

Lucas left the room and pulled the door closed after him. Emily waited, wondering, and wishing Crockett and Ronnie would hurry up. She couldn't hear anything outside the closed door. She leaned her ear to the door and heard muffled voices. Emily tuned everything out except the voices. She heard the name Tony Robinson and one of the men say he was looking for them. She smiled at the idea of more people out there trying to locate them. By the stressful crack in the voice, Tony Robinson wasn't someone they wanted to find them. Footsteps alerted Emily to movement. She hurried to the window; the piwakawaka was still catching tiny bugs on the wing. It was a busy bird. She tried the window latches. They were stuck fast. No one opened the kitchen door. So, she snooped a little. With care, she opened a drawer and found a pencil and notepad. There were no utensils to see. But a pencil would make an okay weapon and paper is always handy. She tore off a sheet and stuffed it in her jeans pocket.

The kitchen door creaked. She pushed the drawer in as she leaned closer to the window. The door opened. She looked over to see Lucas enter and beckon her.

She stayed where she was.

"We're leaving."

"I don't want to."

"It doesn't matter what you want. We are leaving and you are coming."

"Why?"

"Because we are moving."

"I don't want to go anywhere else!" Emily gripped the edge of the bench. "I'm not leaving!"

"You want to make this worse than it is now?"

"I am not leaving." In the back of her mind, something about a secondary location pinged in her brain. She couldn't remember what it was about a secondary location, but it wasn't good.

"We are leaving, and we are not done with you."

"I need to use the bathroom before we leave."

"Go," Lucas said.

She edged past him keeping her eyes on his.

Once in the bathroom, she wrote fast 'Emily Jones. Lucas. Stefan. Want something they think I have. Moving to new place.' She folded the paper carefully and placed it inside the toilet roll hanging on the wall. She took the opportunity to use the toilet. She pushed the pencil into her pocket, washed her hands and checked the note hadn't fallen from the toilet roll. She flushed and opened the door. Lucas was still near the kitchen. Stefan was gone.

"Come in here," Lucas said to her from the kitchen.

"Where are we going?"

"That's need to know, and you don't."

She entered the room. Her attention drawn by the piwakawaka flitting around the bush outside the window.

"I want to stay here," she said.

"It's time to move," Lucas said.

Before she could add another protest Stefan appeared with a syringe in his hand.

"No!" She yelled as loud as she could. He kept coming. "Help! I need help!"

"Shut her up," Stefan muttered.

Emily struggled against the hand over her mouth as she tried to pull her arm away from Stefan's grip and the needle. She bit the hand. Lucas yowled. Then a sharp prick in her neck was followed by Stefan's voice. "Don't move; I might nick an artery."

She froze.

They talked as if she wasn't there while they waited for whatever they'd given her to work.

"How did you find out about the Black Notice?" Lucas asked, watching Emily closely for signs of sedation.

"I know someone in INTERPOL," Stefan said. "Give me a hand. Grab a blanket. We don't want half the street seeing her unconscious."

"I'm curious." Lucas wrapped the blanket around the slumped body of Emily. "Took them a long time to finally do digital facial reconstruction to try and start looking for an identity. Why did it take so long?"

"You wouldn't think there'd be that many people killed in Antwerp in a year that would cause a cold case backlog that spanned years not months." Stefan dragged the printout from his back pocket and supported Emily with one arm against the bench. "Looks like her. It's crazy."

Lucas agreed, then asked, "What the fuck are we going to do about Robinson?"

Emily's world blurred into a soft soothing grey.

Chapter Twenty-four:
[Ronnie: Never have I ever]

The sun was low and almost setting when I parked on Moonshine Road near Upper Hutt College, and hurried across the road. I really wanted to make progress and find Emily, another night not knowing that she was safe, was untenable. I noted there wasn't much traffic around. That was a good thing. Moore Street was my starting point because it was right there, and it led to Thackeray Street and from Thackeray I could get to Sheridan Crescent. I plodded toward Cottle Kindergarten keeping my eyes open and head on swivel. Looking for anything at all that suggested Emily was nearby. Ahead and on the other side of the road walking towards me was a familiar tall figure - Crockett.

I waved and waited. It turned out I didn't need to text him, and I didn't need to beat myself up over not texting either.

Crockett picked up his pace and motioned me to cross the road to him.

"Did you get something?" he asked.

"Not much, but a bit of a twinge in this area again. Why are you here?"

"Police picked up a lurker on Moonshine and he said he saw Emily somewhere in Poet's Block."

"It's not a small area."

"It was near the school, he reckoned."

"As close as Moore Street?"

"I don't think so. Was thinking Thackeray but nothing jumped out."

"Didn't jump out for me either but I only came as far as Sheridan, could be further toward Shakespeare?"

"I've been from Shakespeare this way."

"Have you been down Sheridan?"

"Nope."

"What are we looking for?" I asked because all I had was a slight tug toward this general area and no specifics.

"An older style home."

I looked up and down Thackeray Street. Then down Sheridan as far as I could see. The taillights of what might've been a black SUV disappeared into the distance.

"What sort of car was it?"

"Red Toyota Camry."

Okay. There was no other traffic.

Poet's Block is an older area. "That's it? Older style?"

He shrugged. "The bloke was vague and also of the opinion that he had a tracker in his arm from the COVID jabs."

"Reliable then." I smiled at Crockett. "We're going to have to go door-to-door."

"Might be brick. He said it was red, but he also said he'd be captured if he talked to police because they're after him."

"Who is after him?"

"Doesn't matter."

"Okay, we knock on brick houses first then," I replied. "He sounds like a colourful guy."

"Yeah, colourful."

I pointed out a red brick house a few doors down. "Start there."

We strode up the driveway to the front door. I knocked. No sounds of movement. "Let's look around. Could be out back."

There was a garage at the end of the driveway and next to it a high solid wooden fence and gate. There was no way to easily see into the backyard. And no windows in the garage were accessible from the driveway.

"I'll give you a boost, see what's over there," Crockett said while lacing his fingers together and bending slightly.

I stepped into his hands and let him lift me. "It's a nice backyard. A lot of garden. Some trees. No people, no signs of children, or animals." I placed a hand on his head as he lowered me until I could step off his hands.

"Next house."

We strolled back down the driveway to the street. I noticed an older woman hurrying across the road towards us. "Wonder what this is?" I whispered to Crockett.

"Hello, can I help you?" the middle-aged woman said.

"We're looking for some friends of ours," I replied with a smile. "Forgot their street number."

"A young couple live there. They're at work," she said.

"Thank you, Mrs ... ?" I said and noticed Crockett had

his phone open to photos.

"Mrs Snell," she said.

Crockett showed her a picture of Emily. "You don't know which house she lives in do you?"

"Don't think she lives in this street. I know everyone. Never seen her."

He swiped to a photo of Lucas Genoa. "How about him?"

The woman inspected the photo closely. "No. Can't recall seeing him before."

"Thanks," I said, and we walked away.

"Good luck," she called after us. "I doubt you'll find your friend in Sheridan Crescent."

We changed our minds about brick houses and knocked on every door. Most people weren't home. By the time we were coming back the other way, my knuckles were almost raw and my hand ached.

"What have we learnt?" I muttered to Crockett at the driveway of the next house.

"That she's hard to find," he said. "Come on, let's get this one over with. It'll be dark soon."

"You can knock," I replied, shaking my hand out before putting it in my jacket pocket.

Crockett knocked. No reply. That was the theme. Either it was retired people, or no one was home. Most of the latter houses had evidence of children, and many had dogs or cats. We'd been barked at so often; it was obvious we were doing something in the street.

We were across the road from the first house again and

in front of the nosy neighbour's house. Crockett and I made eye contact. "Let's go ask her again. What was her name?"

"Mrs Snell."

We trundled up her front path. Crockett knocked. The door opened. She must've been watching us.

"You're back," she said. "No luck?"

"None," I replied. "Guess we'll try the next street."

Crockett smiled at the woman. "Just wanted to say goodbye and thank you for your help."

"Wish I could've been more help," she said. "It's a quiet place, Sheridan Crescent. Everyone knows everyone."

"You would've noticed a man running down the street this morning like his britches were on fire?"

Her head tipped slightly, and she tapped a finger on her lips as if thinking. "Yes, I would've noticed that."

"I suppose you would've noticed two men carrying a woman, as well. If you'd been looking outside?" I added.

More finger tapping. "Yes, I would've noticed."

"Thank you, anyway," Crockett said.

We walked down her path to the road and strode along to the Thackeray Street intersection.

"She saw them," I said.

Crockett pulled his phone from his pocket and made a call on speaker.

"Grant, can you find out who owns a house we think Emily was, or is, at?"

"I can. Text me the address."

He moved his phone to his other hand and sent a text.

"Hey Grant, it's Ronnie, want to come give us a hand?"

"Josh and I will be with you shortly. Stay put, see you in five."

Crockett nodded at me. "If we need a key?" he asked.

"Extenuating circumstances, that is your key. Wait for us."

"Party lights?"

"Any excuse to use the party lights, Ronnie, you know that."

Crockett hung up.

And we waited.

Chapter Twenty-five
[Ronnie: Now what?]

Josh and Grant arrived exactly five minutes after we hung up. Not bad going. No doubt the party lights would've alerted the street to something going down.

Crockett nudged me. "Old Nell Mangel will be twitching those curtains like a champ."

That's who she reminded me of. Bloody hell. Years ago, she was the nosy neighbour on Neighbours. Nana used to watch it when we were little kids.

Trust the Aussie to pick that.

Grant adjusted his belt. Josh smiled in our direction. The four of us tramped up the driveway to the front door.

Grant knocked and called out, "Police, anyone home?"

There was no answer.

Josh leaned closer to the door, listening to nothing.

"Did you hear that?" he said to Grant.

"Someone calling for help." Grant took a plastic card from his wallet and slipped it into the lock. It's terrifying how easily some locks open. The lock popped and the door opened.

I turned my head to see the woman across the road let her net curtain fall back over the window.

"We're being watched," I said to Crockett as the four of us entered the home one after the other.

My first impression of the house was not that a young couple lived there. There were minimal furnishings in the lounge room: a couch, two chairs, and a coffee table. There was no artwork, and nothing personal. The kitchen wasn't much better. I flicked on the kitchen light. Dusk was settling and it was darker inside than out.

There were three mugs in the kitchen sink. I opened cupboards. There was one white mug in a cupboard along with four side plates, four bowls, and four dinner plates. I tipped the mug to look at the bottom. As I assumed, it was a fifteen-dollar plain white dinner set from The Warehouse.

The men were searching the other rooms. I opened every drawer and cupboard. There were no signs of life or living apart from the three mugs in the sink. There was no proper cutlery, just a bunch of disposable bamboo knives, spoons, and forks. I was surprised the dinner set wasn't paper. One drawer contained a notepad. But that was it. A piece of paper had been torn from the pad, a ripped corner remained stuck to the top edge.

I sat at the formica kitchen table with a grey and white fake marble pattern and small rivers of gold. My index finger traced the trails of gold.

Josh spoke. I jumped.

"Have you got something?" he asked.

I shook my head. "You?"

He shook his head. "No one lives here. There is one single bed. It has been slept in."

"Maybe she got some sleep then." I hoped she got some sleep.

"You think Emily was here?"

"Yes. I have nothing to base that on. Nothing at all."

"Sometimes a hunch is all you get, Ronnie. Don't discount it." Josh looked around the room. "Did you find garage keys?"

I shook my head. "I found bugger all."

"I'm going to open that garage. Think I can get into the side door from the backyard. If I can't open the door, I'll go to plan B."

"You do that. I want to walk through the house."

I rose from the table, pushed the chair in, and took a deep breath. Crockett's voice echoed down the hallway. "Ronnie, come here."

"Where's here?"

"Third on your left."

Third on my left was the toilet. "What?"

My stomach lurched as glass shattered outside. I guessed that was plan B.

He handed me a note. It was the same kind of paper from the drawer, same torn corner. "Read."

I did. "She was here."

Josh shouted for us. Grant popped out from another room and headed for Josh's voice. We followed.

The backyard was nice. Fully fenced with a pretty garden. Emily would've liked it if she'd been allowed out there for some fresh air. Twists and knots in my gut told me time was running out. The side door to the garage stood open.

"Is this the car you're looking for?" Josh asked, motioning us to come in. "Mind the glass."

There it was. The red sedan. They had another car. Of course they did, they weren't amateurs. Here we go again, on the back foot. I still had the note in my hand. I showed it to Grant and Josh.

"Looks like proof," Grant said. "Can you confirm that is Emily's handwriting?"

Crockett took the note and put it in his jeans pocket. "Yes, that's her handwriting."

Josh pulled latex gloves from his vest and opened the car doors. "Might be something. This car has GPS. Let's see where they've been."

He looked under the driver's side visor and the keys fell out.

I got in the front passenger seat and watched Josh open the GPS and pull up a map.

As soon as I saw the map I knew it was a car I'd pinged going the western back roads of Upper Hutt, not a bus. Emily's house didn't show on the map as a point of interest. Maybe it wasn't them who tossed the house and smashed the walls.

"Where were they before they hit Upper Hutt?" They had to have a base somewhere.

Josh moved the map on the touch screen. "Wellington. They picked the car up from near the airport." He moved the map again. "They don't seem to have a base. They picked the car up and came straight out here."

"Shit." They weren't from here so where were they taking her now? "They have local help, they must do."

"That makes sense. I'll keep looking. We can put a

photo of the car on Emily's BOLO."

"Good thinking. You do know we can't have police taking point on this, right?"

He nodded and grinned at me. "We're an information resource. If we get you close, then that's awesome."

"How the hell are you going to make this work?"

"Don't worry about it. It's your mission but our case. We will provide backup when required. Like we did here."

"Josh, how is this going to work without you and Grant getting in the shit?"

"We've been assigned to you by the area commander," he said. "I don't have specifics."

Bill Bailey. It had to be Bill who got us a police team. Or maybe it was *Genesis*.

"All right, then. Can you two handle this situation?" I waved my hand around the car. "So, we can move on?"

"Yep. Go."

I checked my watch. Dinner would be ready. I'd been gone too long to use the supermarket as an alibi.

"Crockett?" I got out of the car.

"Let's go," he said, heading for the broken glass. "Mind where you step."

Glass crunched under his boots.

"Where's your car?" I asked him as we exited through the garden to the back door. The warm rays of the setting sun hit my back.

"Shakespeare," he replied.

"Mine's on Moonshine. We need to go home. Dinner.

But you also need to know Jonathon Tierney is there. Where's Dane?"

"He's at your office chasing something."

"Chasing something?"

"Something triggered a memory maybe, I don't know. Steph is with him."

"Can you make sure he stays there or at least doesn't come to my place until we can get rid of Tierney."

"Consider it done. I'll ring Steph. See you at home."

At Thackeray Street, I went left, and he went right.

My car was waiting exactly where I left it. It still had all its wheels, and the windows were intact. That felt like a positive. I guess it was too early in the looming night for idiots and thieves. I pulled a U-turn and headed for the traffic lights on the corner of Moonshine and Fergusson Drive. I could've taken a right just past the college, but something pulled me toward the lights.

I waited for the green. Across the road leaning against the stone fence of St Johns was a white-haired old man. He never once looked in my direction. That was odd. I turned right on the green light. Two streets down on the other side of the road was another elderly man lurking on the corner. And then I spotted another on the Tararua Street corner. Old men were zig-zagged down Fergusson Drive. I wondered how far they went in either direction. And that was a question I should ask Nana because old men don't usually stagger themselves down streets while trying to look nonchalant - not in my experience anyway. Admittedly I had limited experience with elderly men, but I knew a lot about interfering, old women.

I parked across the street from our house. Cheesy oniony potato goodness wafted down the stairs and met me when I opened the front door. My stomach rumbled. There was a sizzle and then the smell of seared beef.

Ben was in the kitchen checking on dinner. Enzo was already cooking the steaks. He had a list of everyone's preferences. I saw my name next to medium rare. Good job.

"That smells really good," I said.

"So does that potato dish you and Ben made," Enzo said. "Doing to well-done steaks first."

"It's ready." Ben said. He had the oven door open and was checking the potato bake. "We were waiting on you." He closed the door and switched off the oven. Then he wrapped his arms around me. "Crockett coming?"

"Yes."

"Find anything?"

"We found where they were, but no clue where they've gone." I leaned back in his arms so I could see his face. "I need to have a word with Nana."

"Before dinner?"

"Yes."

"Right, I'll get Donald to help me set the table. Enzo can finish up here. I'm sure Grandfather could do with a small rest."

That worked.

I kissed Ben. "Wish me luck."

"You got this," he replied, planting another warm kiss

on my lips.

I took a breath, straightened my shirt, ran my hands through my long hair and strolled into the lounge. "Nana. A word please," I said from a metre or so away from her and Jonathon Tierney, fully aware that I'd interrupted her conversation.

"Veronica, manners." She flashed her faded blue eyes in my direction.

"We all know that my lack of manners is a constant irritant for you. This is important. Join me in the laundry room please." It sounded like the laundry was a separate room. It wasn't. It was in the back of the garage and led to the backyard. She was going to have to go down the stairs.

I spun on my heels, ignored the tutting and carrying on coming from Nana, and ran downstairs to the laundry area. It gave me time to formulate my questions. Nana wasn't the fastest at stairs anymore. A smile tweaked my lips. She could be. It depended on the level of frailty she wanted to portray. I had a feeling that she wasn't playing the decrepit woman card today. She was far too busy having fun with Tierney. Would she use her walking stick or not? I perched on top of the washing machine and waited. A familiar clunk sounded on the stairs. She was using her walking stick. That was interesting. The cane donked and clunked on the concrete garage floor, announcing her presence.

"You were rude, Veronica. I expect you'll apologise to Jonathon."

"We're talking about you right now, Nana."

Nana step-clunked her way across the floor to me.

"Why were there elderly white-haired gentlemen stationed on corners along Fergusson Drive?"

"How on earth would I know?"

"Drop the act. What are they there for?"

A buzz came from Nana's person. She fished a phone out of a hidden pocket in the seam of her floral dress and checked the screen.

She read a text, then stabbed at the phone with her gnarled index finger. Once done she looked up at me. "They're on a mission."

Ben appeared at the perfect time.

"Mission? To what end?" I asked watching Ben silently cross the garage floor. A smile eased over his features. Nana couldn't see him. "Nana, the mission?"

"If you recall, Veronica, the girls and I were hired to find someone. We have a job to do."

Ben grinned. His shoulders shook ever so slightly.

"I could not find that woman, Nana, remember?"

"Yes dear, but we still have some avenues to check."

"And the old men are doing surveillance?"

"Veronica, dear. I know you were not at the supermarket."

I figured as much. "You had old men watch me."

"Consider it an insurance policy. I need to keep you safe. Donald and Ben would never forgive me if something happened to you while you were investigating someone for me."

Ben clamped his mouth shut. His shoulders shook.

"I was working a case," I said enunciating each word with precision. "A case. I do not need or want old men watching me."

Ben's whole body shook. He was about to explode.

Nana opened her phone and made a phone call. "Alpha One. Pull back the surveillance."

Ben doubled over.

Alpha One?

"Put that on speaker Nana, please."

She did as I asked. Ester's voice flowed from the phone, "I have Alpha Two with me. We haven't heard anything about Lighthouse since turning down Tararua Street."

Ben was almost on his knees proving that trying to control himself was a losing battle.

"Alpha One," I said without the least bit of humour in my tone. "This is Lighthouse. Please pull all surveillance and coordinate with Steph at *Wherefore Art Thou*."

"Roger that, Lighthouse."

Ben hit the ground, laughter exploded from deep within him, and it was all I could do to keep myself in check. Nana spun around, then turned back to me with a shake of her head.

"Alpha One, please ring Steph immediately," I said.

"Roger, Lighthouse. Control, is this also your wish?" Ester asked.

"Yes," said Nana. "Steph is the person you should liaise through. If anyone sees Emily, notify the whole team immediately."

I reached over and pressed the red button to end the call. "You have codenames ..."

Ben struggled to his feet while wrestling his mirth into submission.

"Of course, there are codenames, Veronica."

"Does Ben have one?"

She turned her head and Ben stepped up beside her, the struggle continuing.

"Pier," Nana said.

"And Crockett?"

"Watchtower."

The new scenario was equal parts hilarious and terrifying.

"Okay, right, what we're going to do now is erase this conversation from our conscious minds and pretend it never happened," I said. "You, Nana, are to step away from anything to do with Emily."

"Many hands, Veronica."

"I know, but this is dangerous. We don't exactly know who we are dealing with."

"I think you do know. And I think you need help. Eyes, Veronica, extra eyes."

"We have police help," I said hoping that would settle her down.

"That's good. We must get our Emily back safe and sound."

"I agree, but please, Nana. Please, leave it to us."

"I can't make that promise, dear. What if we find

something?"

"You won't be finding anything because you will be leaving this situation alone."

Nana huffed, turned around, and clunked back to the entrance way and the stairs.

Ben stood speechless. I'd never seen him like that before. At least he'd stopped laughing. We walked slowly across the garage and up the stairs.

In the kitchen he finally spoke, "She's getting worse."

"I didn't think it was possible."

Chapter Twenty-six
[Crockett: A dossier]

Dusk gave way to night. It felt awful not having Emily back and not knowing if she was all right. Another night without her felt like I'd failed her.

I hung back near the stairs and called Enzo over.

"What do you need?" he asked.

"Did you have a drone up this afternoon or this evening?"

He nodded. "I had two at various times."

"Did you record?"

"Of course. It's all in the cloud. What are we looking for?"

"A car leaving Poet's Block area."

Enzo arched an eyebrow. "Okay. We're going to go through all the footage from Moonshine lights south and north?"

"Yes. It's a long shot."

"Yes, it is. I'll send the access code to Ronnie's office. She's called the cavalry and already has her people scrubbing CCTV from everywhere in Upper Hutt."

"Do you know how Tom and Ginny got on?"

"Last I heard they were tapping into private cameras."

"Hmm, handy."

"Thing is Crockett, we don't know what we're looking for."

"Unless we get lucky with a camera angle and see who is driving ..."

"Red light cameras," Enzo said. "They don't just get number plates."

"Yeah, but we have what, one red light camera in Upper Hutt?"

"Pretty sure the lights near Totara Park on River Road have red light cameras."

"They're trying to find something. I don't think they're going north. If they think Emily hid whatever it is then they'll stay in the area." That felt better. My brain had kicked back in. They weren't leaving, not without whatever it was. Potentially diamonds. They're easy to conceal. Where would Emily put something like that?

"You good now?"

"Yeah. Thanks."

"I'll send the link and log in to Ronnie's team. We should eat with the family." Enzo pulled his phone from his pocket and sent a text. "Come on. Let's eat."

There was amicable chatter around the dining table. Tierney blew me away. He was nothing like I knew him to be. Once again, he really could've been Ben's grandfather. Ellie would've gotten a kick out of this. Him, Mr Congeniality. Ronnie passed me the potato dish. I scooped a helping onto my plate and passed it to Enzo. Salad came at me from Ben.

Was Emily eating? Were they taking care of her or torturing her?

Ronnie nudged my hand with hers. I looked at her. She

gave me a small smile. It was enough to make me focus on the here and now.

June was more animated than I'd ever seen her. She was quite at ease with Tierney. Would that be the case if she knew who he really was, and the things he'd done? I forced that thought away because the same could be said for me. That was not a good place to dwell.

Now had to be the focus. Food. Company. Let everything else go for half an hour. Just be present. June raised a glass toward me.

"Glad you made it for dinner, Crockett," she said.

"So am I," I replied. I was. It wasn't a lie or even a stretch. I needed to be with the family we'd created, especially with one of us missing.

"We will find her," June said. "Ronnie's very good at what she does and we're all pitching in."

Ronnie coughed. Ben patted her on the back.

"Sorry," she said. "Went down the wrong hole."

Enzo chuckled. "It's a design flaw."

He wasn't wrong.

Tierney placed his fork on his plate and picked up his glass. He held it toward the middle of the table. "I'd like to propose a toast." His beady eyes missed nothing. "To the missing and the lost. May we bring home the missing and always remember those we lost."

I looked him dead in his beady dark eyes and clinked my beer bottle with his wine glass. "For Emily and Delta A."

Ben followed suit with, "For Emily."

Ronnie picked up her glass and raised it to Tierney. "Does that mean we can count on your support, Grandfather?"

"Of course," he replied. "Your grandmother filled me in on the search so far."

My mind scrambled over what June could've told him and came up with not much. I said nothing and listened.

"I have some resources that might help," Tierney said. "June told me she had some operatives surveilling the main road out here."

Ronnie coughed and coughed. Ben hit her on the back, harder this time. "Design flaw," she croaked.

"Chew your food properly, Veronica," June said. "Goodness, what a fuss."

Ronnie gulped her wine.

I was still trying to wrap my head around June having operatives running surveillance. No wonder Ronnie choked. Christ on a cracker. That old Trout was trouble. But I admired the way she lived her life. She was all in.

Ronnie choked a few words out my way, "You are Watchtower."

"Say again."

"Watchtower." She pointed at me. She pointed at Ben and said, "Pier."

"And you?"

"Lighthouse." She picked up her glass and gulped another mouthful of wine.

"You're dreaming."

Ben shook his head at me. "You wish she was

dreaming."

"You three need to behave," June said. "This is unseemly and we're just offering our help."

Ben's lips twisted. I could see his struggle to control rising laughter. This was insane. There is no way a ninety-four-year-old woman was using codenames and running surveillance. There should also be no way a ninety-four-year-old woman was flirting with Tierney, but she was. Some sort of fucked up alternate universe situation flowed around us. Was it real? Was this happening? I hoped not.

"Nana." Ronnie started to speak then stopped and opted to eat instead.

Enzo and Donald were quiet. Donald looked horrified. Enzo was about as amused and bewildered as I was.

"Holy Smoke," I said, on an exhale. I took a few breaths just to make sure I was here and it was real. "This is a situation that I wasn't prepared for." I eyeballed Ben. "A heads up would've been good."

Ben took a big swallow of his beer and avoided looking at anyone. I didn't blame him.

Right then. We've got the old bloke offering help. We've got June using codenames and running some kind of surveillance gig with old men. You couldn't make this shit up.

"Before this turns into a humdinger of a crapfest, I'd like to propose some ground rules," I said. Everyone stopped what they were doing. "First, I appreciate you all and your help. The thing is, June, we don't know who these people are and what's behind them grabbing Emily and leaving Jenn unconscious. We do know they're dangerous." I could see a protest forming. "I would not be comfortable putting you or your friends in danger. I'm going to ask that you sit this one out. Please." I could feel Ronnie's relief at my words. "Jonathon, I'd like to ask you to do the same. Sit this one out. Let us do this, please."

Tierney pursed his lips but didn't speak.

"I'm not ungrateful and I do appreciate your offers. I may need to reach out for your help, but not yet."

Tierney relaxed his facial muscles and patted June's hand on the table. "I think that's very wise," he said. "We will stand down and wait for your call."

Tierney was playing Grandpa so well, *I* almost bought it.

June nodded. She wasn't happy but wasn't prepared to show it in front of Tierney.

"If you could please help by holding the fort and keeping Emily in your thoughts. Stay with Donald, June. Let us do the running around."

June bristled silently.

Thoughts and prayers. For fucks sake. How did I become that idiot?

"Of course," Jonathon said. "I'd be delighted to keep June and Donald company."

"Thank you."

For all, I really didn't like the man, I knew he wouldn't let anything happen to Donald or June.

Jonathon Tierney was happy to play doting

grandfather. Alternate universe was right. And it was FUBAR.

Tierney smiled at Ben then adjusted his lips into a grim line. "Grandson, I trust you have everything you need for this *mission*."

"I do."

"Let me know if you need extra resources."

"I will."

June's eyes met mine. "Leave the dishes to us. You all get on and find Emily. We'll be here. Holding down the fort."

"Donald, is Nana's room still made up? I think she should stay," Ronnie said.

"Yes it is." Donald smiled and looked at Tierney. "We have two spare rooms; shall I make the other up for you?"

"That's very kind of you," Tierney replied, then smiled at June. "What do you think June?"

"It's a very good idea. If it's as dangerous as Crockett says, then we should stay together and keep Donald safe."

"Ground rules ... no ordering anything using this address or our surname," Ronnie said. "We've already had unusual delivery activity, and it looks like it was an actual mistake but how someone mistakenly used our address who knows."

"Is that something I could look into for you?" Tierney asked, dabbing his lips with a napkin.

Ronnie smiled at him. "I don't mind if you do. Donald kept one of the bags with the person's name and order number on it. He can show you that later."

"You have looked into it?" Tierney asked.

"I did. Woolworths told me the address was the one given by the customer when he opened his account. It was his first order. They rang him, got his real address, and delivered the order again. Pretty sure there is a phone number on the label."

"They picked the bags up?" Tierney asked.

"No. They picked a new order. I tried to get them to pick it up, but they said no."

"I will see what I can find out about the man who placed the order." Tierney smiled as he folded his napkin and placed it on his plate. "That'll give me something useful to do."

It was June's turn to pat his hand. "We like to be useful," she said.

I rose from the table and pushed my chair in. "Time, I got going."

"Wait up," Ben said. "We're coming."

Enzo rose and pushed his chair in. He bent and kissed Donald on the cheek. "Don't look so worried, Lover, we'll bring her home."

Ben, Ronnie, Enzo, and I left the house to June, Tierney, and Donald. The alternate reality had taken hold, and did not sit well with me. Tierney was a nasty bloke who poured gasoline onto situations and June was playing with matches.

Chapter Twenty-seven
[Emily: This is silly]

Lucas opened the left-hand rear passenger door and called Emily's name. She woke groggy and found focusing difficult. It was dark but not that dark. The moon added an eerie glow to the night.

"We're here," Lucas said. "Come on."

She sat up slowly and took stock of her surroundings. She had no idea how far they'd driven. But it was night, and they were on an unremarkable moonlit suburban street. Could be anywhere. She looked up and saw hills. She looked across the car and out the window on the other side. There were hills there, too, but further away. She looked at the nearest hills again and saw barren areas from recent logging. They stood out in the moonlight. They were on the Eastern side of the valley. She could see the logging from her bedroom window. Her house was on the eastern side of the valley. Ronnie lived to the west. Fergusson Drive divided the east from the west.

"Come on," Lucas said to her. "What are you looking at anyway?"

"Nothing," she said. "Just looking at the hills. Where are we?"

"At a house," he replied.

As she climbed out of the car, she saw Stefan standing in porch light by the front door of an ordinary weatherboard house. The front garden was sparse. The occasional struggling plant poked a flower up amongst weeds along the fence line. Security lighting lit the area. There were concrete paths and a concrete driveway. The house had light grey weatherboards and a dark grey door. The grass in the front yard was short and had more weeds than grass.

She couldn't remember seeing the house before, or the street. Maybe in the daylight, it would look more familiar. The car beeped and lights flashed. Lucas held her by the arm and led her up the path to the front door.

"Inside," he said.

Stefan was gone.

Emily stepped over the threshold and hoped she could find a way out, or Ronnie would find a way to her. She peered into the first dimly lit room. The house was similar to the last one, as in, there wasn't a lot of furniture. There was nothing on the walls, and a plain brown couch and chairs in the lounge. She'd never liked brown as a furnishing colour. Beige and brown showed a lack of imagination as far as Emily was concerned. Lucas showed her around, pointing out the bathroom and kitchen.

He stopped in the doorway of a bedroom. There was one single bed with a mattress. It hadn't been made. There was a brown duvet folded at one end and a pillow on top of that.

"You can sleep there," he said.

"I'm fine," Emily replied. She wasn't fine. She needed

to take her prosthetic leg off and give the stump a rest, but without her crutches, she'd be next to useless at moving around. She was pretty good at hopping around her own house because it was her home. This was different. Without the leg, she felt vulnerable. What would stop one of them taking it away?

"How long are we going to be here?" Emily decided to keep the leg on and hope for the best. It fitted well and didn't rub anywhere so she decided it wouldn't cause any real issues. Once Ronnie and Crockett found her, she'd be able to take her leg off safely.

"Depends on you. Tell us where you stashed our goods, and we can take it from there." Lucas took her by the arm again and marched her into the lounge. He gave her a shove toward the fabric-covered couch. Emily stumbled before righting herself and sitting down. It was a mottled brown, uninspired but comfortable. She shuffled to the other end, so she faced the door, then swung her legs up. She adjusted the position of her artificial leg with her hand. Tiredness caused her leg muscles to become disobedient.

"Where's Stefan?"

Lucas sat in an armchair. "I don't know. Here somewhere."

"What is it you think I have?"

"I don't think it, I know it. You have our diamonds."

Emily burst out laughing. "I do not," she retorted. "How would I get diamonds when I do not have any recollection of meeting you before you grabbed me?"

"We pulled a job in Antwerp a long time ago then all went our separate ways."

"How long ago?" Emily asked.

"Eight years ago."

"Okay. I wasn't in Belgium; I was a cop here in Upper Hutt."

Lucas shook his head. "I don't know what you were doing here in New Zealand, but I do know you were in Belgium with me, Stefan, Pedro and Tomás."

She remembered Lucas showing her a photo.

"I don't know a Pedro or a Tomás," she said. "I don't know you or Stefan. I wasn't in Belgium. I don't have any diamonds."

"And the photo?"

"You must've created it with Photoshop or something." Frustration built. "I don't know."

"The thing is, Emily, we were all supposed to meet up two years after the job and split the take."

"Two years?" A frown tugged at her eyebrows. "Why?"

"We needed everything to die down. Two years we figured would be a good time to come together in Paris and divide the diamonds."

"Paris?"

"France."

"I know where Paris is," she snapped. "Are you saying you gave me all the diamonds?"

He nodded. "You had a way of getting them out of Europe and then back in a few years later."

"That's a nifty trick. Wonder how I was supposed to do

that?"

"Diplomatic pouch according to Tomás."

"I'm not a diplomat. I was a fucking cop. What the fuck?"

Lucas's eyes widened; for the first time since finding her, she sounded like Simone. He didn't know why he was so surprised. She was Simone.

"That's what we were told. Clearly, we believed it, so it must've been verified."

"Who is Tomás? How would he know I had access to a diplomatic pouch?"

"Tomás Genoa."

The frown on her forehead deepened. "What?"

"Tomás Genoa."

"That's your surname."

"That was the name we all used when we met up. That's how we recognised each other. That was how we knew each other. Safer than using real names."

"This is all very complicated and hard for me to make sense of," Emily said, resting her elbow on the back of the couch and her head in her hand. "I don't understand any of it."

"I'm getting that impression."

"Then let me go home. I can't help you."

"It's not just up to me. Stefan wants his cut. I'm sure Pedro and Tomás do as well."

"Where are they?"

He shrugged. "I don't know. They turned up in Paris. Haven't seen them since."

Somewhere beyond the lounge room, Emily heard a series of faint noises she couldn't place. Lucas didn't react so she discounted it as random house noise.

"Maybe they moved on and it's just you two who are still annoying innocent people."

"We know it was you. We know you were Simone Genoa."

"You don't know that at all."

Stefan staggered into the room with blood running down his face. "We ..." was all he managed to say before he keeled over, headfirst onto the carpet.

Lucas jumped to his feet. "What the hell!" He knelt and felt Stefan's neck for a pulse.

"Is he dead?" Emily asked, swinging her legs off the couch and ready to stand.

"No." Lucas glanced up at her. "Stay put."

He freed a sidearm from a holster under his jacket and vanished from the room. Stefan lay unconscious on the floor. Emily hurried to the lounge door. This was her chance. There was no sign of Lucas in the hallway. She got to the front door, opened it as quietly as possible and let herself out. She closed the door and moved away and onto the weed-filled fence line. There was a car idling three doors away. She slipped into the moonlit night and prayed for cloud cover so she could get away. Emily went in the opposite direction to the car, keeping as near as possible to trees in people's yards. Behind her, she heard a muffled pop. She kept going looking for a way out of the street. In her haste, she almost walked past an alleyway.

Emily faltered then ducked down the alley and tried to work out which way it ran. West or East. It went towards the nearest hills - east. She moved as fast as she could. The next street she came to felt just as unfamiliar. Before she knew it, she was on a street that did feel familiar. She'd popped out by the Army Camp. She hurried along to Alexander Road. Emily decided that if someone was trying to follow her and pick her up again, they'd head west because they'd expect her to head for home. She stayed on the Army Camp side of the road, hurrying along the rougher ground by the fence instead of the footpath on the other side of the road. She kept moving. She finally found a housing development. The whole time she was listening for trouble and trying to remember the names Lucas had told her. She jumped at every dog bark. Cats darted across the footpath and roads or met in the middle of the streets. Lights flicked on. Car engines had her melting into trees and fences. Now she considered it was safe to head west. Just go west. West is safety. Another street opened out in front of her then became a chain-link temporary fence. Beyond the fence, she saw a mess of weeds and mounds of earth. A security light flicked on giving her a fright. Emily found a gap in the fence and slipped through. The uneven ground challenged her balance and artificial leg. She had no idea what lay ahead. The light flicked off. Emily prayed the moon stayed or she'd never be able to cross the paddock. She knew she needed to slow down and be mindful of the ground. She couldn't afford to injure her only real foot.

Chapter Twenty-eight
[Ronnie: Come home]

"Where are we going?" I asked. "Where do we start?" We stood at the end of my driveway in the moonlight. The nearest street light didn't quite reach us. A slight hum alerted me to a drone, and I knew Enzo had put a night vision drone up to check the area.

"Good question," Ben replied. "You two found where they were, but where did they go?"

I shrugged. "Do we go to Emily's and start there?" If we think they've stayed close, then maybe we start at Emily's, then go street by street. Hoping we come across something?"

We had nothing. Despondence crept over me.

Steph rang. "Tell me you have something?" I was tempted to cross my fingers. Hope is all there is, and we needed to keep it close.

"Dane and I have watched the Moonshine light camera looking at cars that could've ..."

I interrupted, "Anything?"

"I'm getting there," Steph said. "Four cars left by way of the Moonshine Fergusson lights. Two were driven by men. One went south and one went north. Neither car went through any other cameras, so no other lights."

I weighed that for a second. They could've been avoiding lights so that wasn't helpful.

"Thanks."

"We'll keep looking."

"Send me the number plates and vehicle info on those two cars."

I had an idea. Steph did as I asked then said, "I need Enzo. The Roxy situation took a turn."

Shit. That meant Donald would be in charge of Nana and Tierney by himself.

"I'll send him; where?"

"Tell him to go to *The Tote*."

"You meeting him?"

"Yeah. Dane will stay with the CCTV footage."

I hung up.

Me to Enzo: You see anything? Also, Steph said, go to *The Tote*.

Three dots moved then stopped then moved again.

Enzo: You're all clear. Problem?

Me: Sounds like it.

Enzo: You okay with me leaving home?

Me: No choice.

Enzo: I'm on it.

Ben, Crockett, and I crossed the street to my car.

"Heads up!" Ben turned, I threw my keys to him and called shotgun.

Just before Ben backed out of the driveway across the road, we saw Enzo leave on his Harley. The throb of the engine vanished into the night.

"Emily's?" Ben asked.

"Yes," Crockett replied.

I settled into the seat and watched the night ahead of us. I was looking for a miracle. I had no idea what cruising around the streets was going to accomplish but it was better to be moving. It was a fairly quiet night for a Friday. I decided that most people were probably already where they were going. Bars, friend's houses, or restaurants. Fergusson Drive wasn't busy. Ben drove south on Fergusson to the Sutherland Avenue traffic lights and took a left onto Sutherland. As he drove, I watched for pedestrians that could be Emily and looked for black SUVs up every driveway we passed.

"You okay back there, Crockett?"

"Yep. Checking driveways on the other side of the road."

We crossed the train tracks and kept going, past the Racecourse, past HIBs. Trentham Camp's main entrance came and went, as did the turn-off for the prison. We were on Alexander Road heading north when I caught a glimpse of something.

"What was that?"

"Didn't see anything," Crockett replied.

"Might've been my imagination. Thought a light turned off. Maybe a security light."

"Maybe," Ben said. "There's a new subdivision just up here."

"And a car museum," Crockett added. "And sound stages for a movie company. And I don't know how many other businesses."

That meant a lot of places would have movement-sensitive security lighting.

"This is the longest way to get to Emily's ever," I said.

"Let's have a look in the new subdivision," Ben said, taking a left turn.

"Worth a look," Crockett said as we cruised slowly past houses. There were empty new builds, partially built houses, and newish houses with families living in them. Ben drove to the end of the subdivision. The car lights illuminated a field of dirt mounds and weeds beyond a high temporary hurricane fence.

"Wait," I said to Ben, as he put the car in reverse. "There's something out there."

He flicked the lights to full beam. I opened my door. The interior light filled the car. I closed the door quickly and stood next to the car, watching and listening.

A car engine revved behind us in the distance. Across the fenced field I saw something move.

I opened the door and poked my head in the car. "Cut the lights and the engine."

Silence fell as the darkness took over. Then I saw it again. Something was moving away from us and across the uneven ground. I considered where the undeveloped ground led. The back of the racecourse was almost straight ahead and the back of a retirement village to the right of the racecourse from our point of view.

A door clicked open. Crockett appeared next to me.

"What are you watching?"

Ben joined us in time to hear my instructions. "Look straight ahead then move your line of sight about five centimetres to the right."

There was another flash of movement. "I got it," Crockett said.

"Help me make a bigger gap in this fence," Ben replied.

Crockett leant a hand. Seconds later the three of us were stumbling over the uneven ground using our cell phone torches when we had had no choice, making sure to keep the beam directed at the ground. Not wanting to alert whoever was moving ahead of us. I hoped it was Emily, but there was a good chance it was a teenager or a couple of teenagers up to no good and looking for a way into the Racecourse buildings. It wasn't unheard of for teens to break into the main stand and party. A couple of kids were caught once because they had no idea the Police Dog School was conducting an exercise at the Racecourse. I imagine when the kids emerged to find dogs and handlers surrounding them, they would've shit themselves. Lesson learnt - perhaps. Maybe it wasn't those kids crossing what would be an add-on to the new housing development we'd driven through.

I pulled myself out of my thoughts. Ben, Crockett, and I were spaced out across the field about three metres away from each other. We didn't talk. It was mostly too dark for hand signals. We just kept going and gaining ground on the person, or persons, we were following. If we got out without sprained ankles we'd be doing well.

All of a sudden, there was an oof noise and the person

ahead of us vanished. I glanced to Ben on my left then Crockett on my right. I figured we'd all heard it. The three of us picked up our pace. I flicked on the torch on my phone. The last thing I wanted was to trip or fall, that wouldn't help anyone. I noted the men turned theirs on as well. Illuminating the field just in front of me, I kept going until a dark shape shot out and tripped me. My phone went flying. Tumbling to the ground, I rolled and clambered to my feet.

"Argghh," I growled. A leg swung across the ground at me. I jumped out of the way. "Jesus. Stop!"

Crockett and Ben charged towards me. Crockett grabbed the person from behind and lifted them. Feet kicked out. One collected my shin.

I grabbed my shin and hopped. "Ouch, are you wearing steel caps?"

At that moment, Ben said, "Emily?"

Crockett spun the person in his arms and tipped their head back. "Milo," he said, hugging her to him.

No wonder that kick felt like it came from steel caps. Must've been her bionic metal leg and foot. Even with sneakers on that thing was hard.

"You found me," Emily said and slumped against Crockett. "You didn't give up."

I hobbled closer and put my arms around them both. "We don't give up, Emily. We don't give up."

"I'm sorry about your leg," she said. "I didn't know it was you."

"It's okay. I'll live. Let's get back to the car and the hell away from here."

"Yes, please," Emily said.

Crockett scooped her into his arms and carried her. That was a smart move. She'd be exhausted from the last few days and the adrenaline from trying to escape us.

Ben put his arm around me. "Bit limpy," he whispered.

"I'm lucky I still have a leg," I replied with a sigh. It hurt. A lot. But we got Emily back, so it was worth it.

It was slow going until we came within the reach of the security lights, and they shone like a beacon leading us to the car. Ben opened the back passenger door enabling Crockett to put Emily on the seat and buckle her in.

"How far have you walked Emily?" I asked, swivelling in my seat to see her.

"I don't know. Through a few streets. I saw Defence Force signs when I got out of the first street. I got lost, then I went the wrong way. I thought if they were still coming after me, that they'd think I went towards home. Then I found more streets and one of them led to the fence and open ground."

"Defence Force," I said, glancing at Ben. "There are a lot of Defence Force signs around this side of Trentham and Heretaunga."

"Look for the first sign you see. That's where we'll start."

I checked with Emily. "You okay if we drive around and see if we can find where they held you?"

"Yes. As long as you're all with me."

"No one's leaving you," Crockett said.

"Emily, is there anything you can tell us?" I asked as we drove past the Trentham Camp Golf Club across the road from Trentham Camp. "Did you come this way?"

"Yes. It's the opposite way to home. I saw signs like that on the streets with houses," she said as we passed several warnings that this was a Defence area.

I didn't know of another way to get to the Defence Force Housing from where we found her. Most of the houses were around the camp, but not out by the golf course, gun range, or prison.

"That was good thinking to come out this way," Crockett said. "Too open though. You were lucky."

"Maybe," she said. "I was trying to get as far away as I could. I knew I was near the eastern hills, and I needed to be west, but not from where I started, or they would've grabbed me."

"Near, or you could see the eastern hills?"

"I could see where they've been logging."

I imagined she'd gotten herself turned around in the dark while trying to get away. Then worked it out by the time she got to the new subdivision. The racecourse was absolutely to the west of Alexander Road, and she went the long way to throw them off. Maybe she was going to go further down the road into Wallaceville but opted for a shortcut across the field at the back of the racecourse.

We were cruising up and down streets filled with Defence houses. I expected MP's to pull us over at any moment.

"What did the house look like?" I asked.

"Grey. No garden in the front just short grass."

Ben turned down another street.

"Anything else?"

"Something happened to Stefan. He came in with blood coming from his head and collapsed. When Lucas went to find out what happened. I escaped."

"Good job," I said. "Really good job."

"What else?"

"There was a big black ute-type vehicle three doors down from the house and it was idling." She took a breath. "Someone might've gotten shot."

That's definitely something.

I watched houses and driveways for anything that looked out of place or like a problem. Clouds scurried across the sky and blocked the moon.

"Do you think they were military?" Crockett asked.

"No," she said. "Their hair wasn't tidy enough. They had accents but not ones I could recognise. Not New Zealand ones."

"Good. That's important information, Emily," I said.

"Look at this place we're passing now," Ben said, indicating to his window as the car slowed to a crawl.

"That looks like it," Emily said quietly. "Their car is gone."

Ben pulled over two doors up. "Let's go have a look," he said. "You and me, Ronnie. Crockett and Emily should stay in the car."

"Also, no one lives in the house. It's like the first house. No one lived there either but that one was nicer and had a garden."

"We found that house. We found your note," Crockett said.

Ben and I got out of the car and ambled across the road together. He grabbed my left hand and pulled me closer to him.

"Let's have a look around and see what's what," I said, keeping my voice low.

We scouted around the front of the house, then edged our way around the back. There was a low gate dividing the backyard from the front. There was nothing much to see outside at all. The moon abandoned us. There was a good deal of reluctance to use the torches on our phones just in case someone was lurking or looking out from one of the nearby houses.

Ben tried the back door. It clicked open.

"Careful," he whispered, pushing it wider so we could get inside. It was a laundry. The door to the kitchen was open. "Do you smell that?"

"Yeah," I whispered back. It smelt like blood. You'd need a bit for us to notice the metallic tang.

Slowly, we edged our way along walls in the dark room until we were properly in the house's interior. I wiped dirt off my phone and turned my phone's torch on. We were in the lounge room. The drapes were closed. A brown lounge suite and a small coffee table were the only furnishings, and nothing hung on the walls.

"This is where the smell comes from," I said, poking a body on the floor with the toe of my shoe. He lay in a pool of blood. There was what looked like a gunshot wound in his back. Emily said he had blood coming from his head. I guess whoever did that came back to make sure he was deceased.

"Must be Stefan," Ben said, crouching down and putting two fingers under the man's chin looking for a pulse.

"Anything?"

"No."

"Bugger. Won't get anything out of him then."

We searched the rest of the house. There was no sign of Stefan's cohort.

I sent a message to Bill Bailey: Ping my phone. There is a body here for you. We didn't do it.

Seconds later he replied: What are you doing in a Defence Area?

Me: Leaving.

We did something I really didn't think we would manage. We went home with the intention to go to bed. And as far as I knew everyone needed sleep. Crockett took Emily to his place for the night. Dane met them there. I didn't see Enzo or his Harley. There was a good chance he had a late night with the Roxy situation. Emily was safe. I was exhausted.

Donald was waiting for us.

"I have to turn in, I'm quanked," I said. You could've heard a snail sneeze as Donald and Ben's jaws dropped.

Ben slid an arm around my waist. "Is that some kind of Kiwi slang for something?" He semi-whispered in my ear.

"Not at all."

"Too bad."

"What on earth does that word mean?" Donald asked. "It sounds nasty."

"Nana used it once months ago. It means overpowered by fatigue."

"That's not what it sounds like," Donald said, arching his right eyebrow.

"How long have you wanted to say quanked?" Ben asked.

"Months." I chuckled as we went up the hallway to my room, leaving Donald in the kitchen with a distasteful look on his face while he processed my new word.

Chapter Twenty-nine:
[Ronnie: Go home, stay home]

Sleep worked its magic and it almost felt like a regular Saturday morning. There's nothing like having everyone safe. Ben and I enjoyed a late start to the day. It wasn't late by most people's standards, but it also wasn't five and still dark. Then I remembered I was supposed to meet Peter Piper at Boulcott Hospital. Bugger. Missed that meeting. He hadn't rung to ask where I was so maybe it wasn't that important. Peter Piper wasn't a now problem.

Donald had the coffee on. Enzo was in the dining room with Tierney and Nana. Everyone playing happy families. Once again, I could easily forget Tierney wasn't really Ben's grandfather. What a weird world we live in. No wonder I had trouble when anyone asked me what retirement from the Service was like. And just like that, my mind ricocheted back to the problem at hand. Who killed Stefan? Where was Lucas? Who had the black truck that Emily saw idling on the street Then back to who killed Stefan because it probably wasn't his partner in crime. What did they want? Was this really about art and diamonds? I had a feeling we needed to hunt out some answers before something else happened. The last question that niggled and jiggled was about them using a Defence Force house as a safe house. What the hey diddly ho was that about?

My first actions of the day were to let Liam know we had Emily and to tell Bill we had Emily. I didn't think Bill would be a big fan of mine after he got dumped with clean-up duty last night. That was only fitting. The killing happened on Defence land, and someone let those guys use that house.

Ben nudged me. "What are you thinking about? That smile you're wearing is evil."

A grin took the place of whatever the evil smile was. I knew where it came from but not what it looked like on the outside. That was probably a good thing.

"I was thinking it's a shame Bill got clean-up duty," I said, hoping my voice was quiet enough so Nana wouldn't hear me.

"Who's Bill dear?" Nana said across the table. "What did he have to clean up?"

"Dishes Nana," I replied. "We left him with the dishes."

Nana tutted.

Jonathon Tierney gave me a smile and a small nod that told me he knew who Bill was and what Bill had to clean up. It's a small world.

"Have some breakfast," Donald said, flapping a hand at a pile of pancakes. "There's bacon, caramelised bananas, maple syrup."

"Are we Canadian now?" I asked forking two pancakes onto a plate.

"I made an executive decision and made a nice

breakfast. Just eat it."

"As opposed to?" I asked, scooping caramelised bananas onto my plate.

"The rushed *on the way out the door* piece of toast."

I nodded. It was a fair call. That's exactly what I did most days.

"Veronica, you need to eat a proper breakfast," Nana said. "Your cousin outdid himself with this spread."

"Yes, Nana. Donald did well."

I'm sure I had room for improvement.

"Now that Emily is back and safe, I suppose we can get back to normal," Donald said while dabbing syrup from the corners of his mouth with a napkin. "I've quite enjoyed having everyone here."

He was the host with the most. Our social butterfly.

"Not quite normal yet," Ben said. "You'll have us all for a bit longer."

Fine lines creased Donald's forehead. "Emily's back. Yes?"

"Yes. But we still don't know what the kidnappers wanted, and we need to find them." Ben replied. "We don't want them trying again."

"That's sensible," Donald replied while spooning more caramelised bananas onto his plate. "I do make great bananas."

"You really do," I said, helping myself to more. "They are really good."

I noted Tierney was quiet during the meal. He was taking it all in, I supposed, watching how we all interacted and how openly we talked, and listening for anything he could use. Not for one second did I think he was here for anything good. Tierney's reputation and Crockett's outright dislike for the man gelled. We needed to be extra careful.

My phone buzzed on the table. I flipped it over to see *'Uncle George'* on the lock screen. "I'll be right back," I said. "Work."

I didn't answer the call until I was in my bedroom. No way did I want Tierney overhearing whatever *Genesis* needed to tell me.

"Go ahead, Uncle George."

"Can you locate Kerrin Costa?" Uncle George sounded like a posh Brit this time. Probably went to Eton.

"Yes. We have her under surveillance."

"She knows more than she told you. Her surname just dropped in a report from Europe."

"About?"

"The dead woman in Belgium, Simone Genoa, is not Simone Genoa. She could be Simone Costa."

"A relative?"

"We cannot be sure, but it would make sense, with Costa turning up in New Zealand."

"That puts a new spin on things. Does she know she's dead?"

"That's unknown. She may have been in touch with her people. INTERPOL have not released an ID. Still no DNA match. We should be able to prove a familial match with Kerrin Costa, but her DNA isn't in any database we can get to."

Because she's a spook. Mine's not accessible either nor is Ben's. Our fingerprints aren't even our fingerprints. So, we needed to collect and run her DNA ourselves. Then match it, or not, to the dead woman.

"We'll scoop her up and see where she's at with her investigation. She might want to play ball she might not."

"Be persuasive, Ronnie. She has intel that we need."

"Will do. Anything else?"

"No. Good job getting Emily back. She needs a proper debrief. Not you, not Crockett."

"You are aware that Simone Costa is the dead spit of Emily, right?"

"Yes."

"We can't prove Emily is Emily and not Simone Costa."

"I'm aware."

Great. That's helpful. "Who do you want to debrief Emily?"

"Dane."

"They're friends."

"Trust me. He'll handle it. He's good at listening and seeing the whole picture. Let him work."

"Yes, Sir."

"Tell me when you have the Costa woman."

"Of course."

The screen went black. *Genesis* was gone.

I put my phone in my back pocket and rejoined the family breakfast with a smile on my face. I decided to go with the 'good job' part of the conversation and worry about the rest after breakfast.

Ben was chatting to Tierney and Nana. Donald and Enzo were eating. I opted to eat and say nothing.

Romeo eased his way between my chair and a table leg. I patted his old head. He'd need a walk after breakfast. It would be a good opportunity for Ben, Enzo, and me to talk and get out of dish duty. Donald wouldn't be pleased but he'd cope. It was mean but necessary.

The rest of the meal vanished in a haze of family chit-chat.

Chapter Thirty
[Ronnie: Here we go]

Romeo managed to hold his excitement at getting his walking gear on. A twinge of panic hit me. He was old, one day he'd be gone. I breathed in then let a long slow breath out. Not today.

Enzo and Ben walked ahead of us down the stairs. Enzo had already flown a drone a few times just to check no one had gotten close to home base and had given the all-clear. Saturday mornings were busy this close to Trentham Memorial Park. A lot of sports were played on the fields. Depending on the season it could be cricket or rugby, and sometimes there was dressage. The car park was full; horse floats everywhere. I scanned the fields as we entered the park from the Brentwood entrance. Horse floats were parked in two rows between the entrance to the children's playground. On our left were dressage arenas, created by temporary rope fences. There were horses, riders, judges, and spectators. It was busy. We took Romeo toward Barton's Bush. He wasn't a big fan of the bush walk but once on the other side, we could walk along the river trail. He liked that very much.

I waited until we were on the trail before handing Romeo's lead to Ben and making a phone call.

"Hey Steph, how's Jenn?"

"Annoying."

"Recovering then."

"She could've been quiet for longer," Steph replied. "What do you need?"

"Have the teams got eyes on Costa?"

"I'll send you their log sheets," she said.

"Thanks."

The screen darkened as the call ended. Moments later an email pinged on my phone. I opened the attached document and scanned the entries.

"They're sitting on her in Stokes Valley," I said to Ben and Enzo.

"What trail do you think she's on?" Ben asked.

"On the trail of Lucas Genoa, perhaps."

"So are we. What is it she knows that we don't?" Enzo kicked at a stone.

I shook my head. "No idea. What would Genoa be doing in Stokes Valley?"

Stokes Valley is the coldest hole in the entire valley. It always felt damp to me. I looked at the progression the surveillance entries showed us. Costa was in Poet's Block but after we were. She was lurking around the Army Camp as well. Maybe she'd spotted Genoa and followed him to Stokes Valley. It did look like she was doing what we were doing. She was definitely in places we'd been, but not at the right time. She could've followed us, but I doubted it; we hadn't been to Stokes Valley. I rolled my thoughts back to the part where I considered she was tracking or trying to track Lucas Genoa. We didn't know for sure she was, but we knew Lucas Genoa was

Argentinian and so was she. There was a good chance she was here for him the whole time. Stefan wasn't Argentinian. It took far longer than I wanted but we had an ID. He was a German who resided in Belgium. As usual, I had more questions than answers. Stefan was with Belgium State Security Service or as we called it, VSSE. Was he one of the burglars?

I scrolled through my photos and sent one of Lucas Genoa to the teams in a group message with an attached note asking for them to notify us if he was seen.

The reply came from Enzo's guys: Haven't seen him so far. We will stick with her. Maybe she'll lead us to him.

I showed Ben and Enzo the text.

Three dots moved under the message.

A reply came through: Looks like she's getting ready to move.

Me: Stick with her.

Them: Will do. No eyes on Genoa.

We came out of the bush and up the stop bank.

Something didn't sit right with me about Stokes Valley.

"Ben, why does Stokes Valley seem like something?"

He shook his head and shrugged.

My phone rang. It was Ginny.

"Hellaire my lovely."

"Good timing," I said.

"I aim to please," she said with a light laugh in her

words. "And if I miss, I'll reload and try again."

"What do you have?"

"Not much. We've been all over the airport security footage. Apart from Peter Piper meeting Lucas Genoa at Wellington Airport, we've got nothing from the airport at all."

"Where did Stefan join them?"

"We don't have him coming into the country. He may have arrived well before Lucas Genoa."

"I guess that's possible," I said. "The Costa woman is in Stokes Valley, does that mean anything?"

"Hmmm. Not really no."

My phone buzzed with a text message from the surveillance team.

"Talk soon," I said to Ginny, and hung up and opened the message.

Romeo bumped into me. I glanced at him before looking at the photo on my phone. He'd spotted another greyhound ahead of us and wanted us to hurry up. One of the funny things about greyhounds is that they only really like other greyhounds or maybe that was just a Romeo thing. When he spotted a hound, we always had to go say hello. I shoved my phone in my pocket.

"Come on then, Ben, let's go say hi to the hound up ahead."

We moved a little faster. The owner of the hound saw us and slowed down. The hounds greeted each other happily. Romeo clearly wanted to walk with the brindle hound. Who were we to stop him?

I introduced us to the woman walking the hound. Didn't want her concerned with two men approaching her. Enzo didn't look friendly most of the time. He had the best resting bitch face.

"Nice to meet you," she said. "I'm Sandy and this is Olive."

We tramped about ten metres before my phone blew up with messages. Ben grinned at me and said, "We'll carry on, you catch up. That sounds important."

I stopped walking and let them get out of earshot before looking at my phone.

I scrolled back a few messages to see the photo.

It was a picture of Tom.

Tom was coming out of a building and getting into his car.

What the hell?

I read the many messages that followed the photo.

They referred to Tom as an UnSub. I was not about to correct them. Rollicking rabbits, what the hell was going on?

Costa was following Tom? Our team was following her.

Tom headed toward Lower Hutt with Costa on his tail.

I messaged the teams: Stick with her. Let me know if you see Genoa.

Enzo, Ben, and Romeo were moving further into the distance, I hurried to catch up to them. Ben and Sandy were chatting about hounds when I slipped up between

Enzo and him, then wound my fingers with Ben's.

Both dogs looked at me. Sandy followed Olive's line of sight.

"You caught up," she said with a little something in her voice. I didn't know her well enough to say it was disappointment, but I knew my fiancé was always a hit with the ladies, so I figured that's what it was.

"Unfortunately, I'm going to have to steal Enzo, Ben, and Romeo away," I said with a smile. Far, far away.

"It was nice to meet you, Sandy," Ben said, as he gave Olive a pat on the head. "You too Olive."

Enzo waved to the woman. "Maybe we'll see you another day."

We turned around and started the walk home. Once Sandy and Olive disappeared around a bend, I slowed down a bit.

"Didn't like her?" Ben asked with a dimpled smile.

"She was fine. We have a problem."

"Uh oh, that sounds serious," Ben said.

"How bad?" Enzo asked.

I took the lead from him and handed Ben my phone. I knew messages were still open. He held the phone toward me. I glanced at it, and it unlocked. We plodded on. Enzo and Ben read the texts as we went.

"Tom," Ben whispered. "She's following Tom."

"It looks that way," I replied. "There's clearly things we don't know."

"Yeah."

He closed the message app and handed me back my

phone. I slid it into my back pocket. The rest of the walk was silent, bar the occasional 'Good boy' for Romeo.

I opened the front door and took Romeo's harness off him just inside. He bounded up the stairs with renewed vigour. Maybe he just needed to see another hound. Enzo wasn't far behind him. Enzo occasionally exhibited puppy-like qualities.

Ben and I walked more sedately up the stairs. The dishes were done and put away. All signs of breakfast were gone. There wasn't even a hint of bacon in the air. Voices came from the lounge.

Nana, Tierney, and Donald were chatting. Nana was patting Romeo while she talked.

Enzo wasn't there.

The conversation halted when I walked into the room.

"Are we having a nice day?" I enquired.

"Of course," Nana replied. "We've been talking about your wedding."

Ben nudged me. I smiled like the dutiful granddaughter I am. "That sounds fun."

"You're going to have to set a date, you know," Nana said. "Ben, what do you think of September?"

"I don't like or dislike September," he replied. "Nothing against it at all."

Nana pursed her lips. Ha. Ben was in trouble.

"You know what I mean," Nana said. "What's your schedule like?"

"I'll have to check," he replied. "Can I let you know tomorrow?"

"See that you do. Time is marching on." Nana gave me a look as if to say I'd best not object. She wanted great-grandchildren and the window was closing. I'm fine with a dog. The window could slam shut and I'd be fine with it.

I turned my attention to Donald. "Where's Enzo?"

"He came in, said hello, and disappeared." Donald arched an eyebrow at me. "You have him working a case. I think he's off getting ready to go to work."

Good.

There was a loud knock on the front door. Nana smiled.

"Someone for you is it, Nana?"

"Just the girls, nothing to worry about, Veronica."

Oh, good. *The Cronies of Doom* were assembling. "I'll get the door then, shall I?"

"Thank you, Veronica," Nana replied.

A few seconds later I swung the front door open and let Frankie and Ester inside. "She's in the lounge," I said as I waited for them both to start the climb up the stairs.

The stairs were quite the mountain for the cronies. Enzo ran down, deftly sidestepping oldies. He winked as he passed me. There was a bit of huffing and a lot of puffing as the cronies clung to the banister with one hand and their walking sticks with the other. I waited. There was no sense trying to get around them. I imagined they were here to meet Jonathon Tierney. How bad could that be? Nana's already flirting and revelling in her delight of meeting Ben's 'Grandfather'. Was I ready to watch three old ducks vie for his attention? It was three old ducks and a man who'd been CIA since the dawn of time.

No. I was not ready to witness that catastrophe.

I decided it would be wise to leave them in Donald's capable hands while Ben and I caught up with Crockett, Dane, and Emily. I needed to ask Dane to debrief Emily and keep Crockett out of the way during that process. I also wanted to find out what was happening with Roxy and what happened last night. Something must've gone down for Steph to pull Enzo away from our dilemma.

And that reminded me I hadn't had a call from Peter Piper.

The old ducks were finally at the top of the stairs. I hung back until they clunked their way across the kitchen floor to the lounge and were suitably introduced to Tierney. Never did I see the day coming that I would be even slightly pleased Tierney was here with Nana. Apart from the horror of what could creep out of their mouths, having them here with Tierney could be a blessing. At least they weren't out running surveillance. And there we were, the ancient Scooby Gang was complete. We had old folk in all directions.

I beckoned to Ben from the doorway then waved to Nana. "We've got things to do, Nana."

"Righto dear, be safe," she replied with a thin-lipped smile that reached her eyes.

She was having far too much of a good time with Tierney.

Ben joined me in the kitchen.

"We need to get to Crockett's and get Dane doing the

debrief."

"I thought that's what you wanted. Let's go then." He glanced over his shoulder. "They're in their element."

"And that is absolutely terrifying." Nana was acting as though she was the bee's knees and the cat's pyjamas. I recognised the phrase as one Grandad used to use. I smiled to myself.

"What's the smile about?" Ben asked.

"Nothing just something Grandad used to say. Ben, once the debrief is underway I need to go meet Peter Piper at Boulcott Hospital."

"Do you want backup?"

"I can handle him on my own."

Chapter Thirty-one
[Emily: So many questions]

Dappled light filtered through the net curtains over the windows. Birds twittered outside. Emily liked birds. She was happy to be at Crockett's. In some ways, it felt like a normal Saturday morning. Emily sat on the couch in Crockett's lounge room. There was a steaming mug of coffee on the end table on her left. Dane pulled up an armchair, so he was closer. He held his iPad in one hand and typed with the other.

"Are you comfortable?" Siri asked.

"Yes, Dane," Emily replied. "It is funny calling you Dane and not Dean."

He nodded and smiled. Siri spoke, "I'm still getting used to my real name."

"What do you want to know?" Emily asked.

"We're going to talk about Lucas and Stefan," Siri said. "Had you seen them before they came into the bookshop?"

"No," she said. "I had not seen them before."

"Did they say how they knew you?"

"They cannot have known me," she said. "I had never met them before."

Dane typed. "Did they know your name?" Siri asked.

Emily shook her head. "No. They called me Simone."

"Do you know who Simone is?"

She shook her head again. "No."

"What did they do when you told them you were Emily?"

"Stefan got annoyed with me. He did not like me. He was impatient. Lucas ..." she paused for a breath. "Lucas was nicer. When I said I was Emily, he called me Emily."

Dane nodded. "Did they hurt you?"

Emily shook her head. "They drugged me."

"When?"

"Before they moved me to the second house."

Dane typed then paused, then typed some more. "What did they want?"

"They said I had something that belonged to them."

"Do you?"

"No. I do not know them, so how could I have something of theirs?"

Typing, pausing, typing.

"Did they tell you what they think you had, or have?"

"Diamonds."

"Diamonds?"

Emily nodded. "They said I had their diamonds."

"And?"

"That I had hidden them somewhere."

"How did they think you got the diamonds?"

"They gave them to me in Belgium. They said I had a way of getting the diamonds out of the country and into New Zealand. They said I brought them here with me."

"From Belgium?"

"Yes."

"Did they tell you why they came for you now?"

She nodded. Emily pulled the conversations she'd had with Lucas and Stefan together. "They said, I was supposed to take them to New Zealand and then in two years we were all supposed to meet somewhere, I cannot remember where. Not here. Then they said I did not turn up with the diamonds, so they started looking for me."

Dane typed. "They? Just Lucas and Stefan?"

She shook her head. "Two other people, someone called Pedro, and someone called Tomás."

"Where do they come from?"

Her head shook. "I do not know."

"Did they say you knew them?"

"Yes. They said I was part of the group. How could I have been, Dane? I was a police officer here. I was not in Europe."

Dane smiled reassuringly as he typed. "Anything else you can remember?"

"They said their surname was the same as his. Lucas said everyone used Genoa as a surname. That is how they identified each other."

Dane typed. "Lucas Genoa, Stefan Genoa, Tomás Genoa, Pedro Genoa and ... ?"

"Simone Genoa."

"Okay."

Emily sighed. "I do not know them. I never did."

"What happened at the last house?"

"Lucas was going on and on again about me being Simone and wanting to know where the diamonds were."

"And?"

"Stefan went out of the room. I do not know where to. I was glad he was gone. He was threatening. I felt like he would hurt me if I did not start telling them what they wanted." She took a deep breath. "I could not, Dane, I did not know the answers they wanted."

Stress reverted Emily to a time when her speech sounded more formal. Contractions waned.

"Close your eyes."

Emily shut her eyes.

Siri told her to breathe in through her nose and hold it for three seconds then breathe out from her mouth, and to let all the tension go with that breath. She did as she was asked. She opened her eyes.

Dane noted she was visibly more relaxed.

"Good. Now, did you hear anything while Stefan was gone?"

"Yes. There was some noise, but it was muffled, and I was not even sure that it was anything. Lucas didn't react."

"And then what happened?"

"Stefan came back in. He was stumbling, there was blood running down his face from his head. He fell over."

"What did Lucas do?"

"He told me to stay put, then he took a gun from his holster, and left. He told me to stay there again."

"What did you do?"

"I went to the lounge door but could not see anyone, so I went to the front door and tried it. It opened. I left and closed the door as quietly as I could behind me."

"What did you see when you left?"

"A black ute idling a few houses away. So, I went the other direction and tried to get to a place where I could get home without going straight there. I imagined Lucas would be looking for me."

"Did you hear anything?"

"The ute idling. And a pop sound."

"A pop?"

"Like a quiet gunshot."

"Did you see that ute again?"

"No."

"Then what happened?"

"I kept going, did not look back, did not go toward home until I came to that new subdivision past the Army Camp. I got through the fence and went towards the retirement village."

"Is that where Ronnie, Crockett, and Ben found you?"

"Yes."

Dane nodded. He typed. "Is there anything else you can think of?"

Emily took another deep breath and let it out. She took a few more breaths and evaluated the things Lucas and Stefan said.

"Yes. They were worried about someone else. I think someone was looking for them."

"Do you know who?"

"They said the name ..." She searched her memory for the person. "Tony. Yes. They said his name was Tony

Robinson. They did not know I could hear them."

"When?"

"Just before they moved me to the second house. I think that he was the reason they moved me."

Dane smiled. "Okay. That's really good Emily."

Emily smiled. "I am glad you are here."

"Me too," Siri said. "I wish I could talk to you without Siri. Maybe one day."

She nodded. "I hope so."

"I have a few more questions."

"Okay."

"Did you see anyone with a gun, other than Lucas or Stefan?"

She shook her head.

"Did you see anyone else at the house?"

"No."

"We're done." He smiled at his friend. "Are you okay?"

"I am." Emily took a deep breath and visibly relaxed on the exhale. "How is Jenn?"

"She has a concussion, but she'll be okay. She needs rest."

Emily stood up using the arm of the couch to steady herself. She had taken her prosthetic leg off before she went to bed and hadn't put it back on. She wanted a rest from it. Dane stood up and reached her crutches from the other end of the couch. He handed them to her one at a time. Crockett had gone to Emily's and grabbed them first thing, so she had a choice.

"Can I see Jenn?"

"Yes," Dane said. "Crockett will take you over to her place, later."

"Good. I need to apologise. It is my fault she is injured."

Dane's head shook. He typed but Siri didn't speak. A few seconds later Crockett came in from the kitchen.

Emily smiled at him. He returned the smile.

"It's not your fault, Emily," he said. "None of this is at all your fault. What happened to Jenn is on Lucas and his sidekick."

Chapter Thirty-two
[Ronnie: Peter Piper tells lies]

It was early afternoon when I ambled up the ramp and into the reception area of Boulcott Hospital on High Street. Boulcott was a private hospital next door to Hutt Hospital. There was a receptionist at the desk with a welcoming smile.

"How can I help?"

"Peter Piper's room, please."

"I'll take you through," she said and pushed a visitor book and a pen in my direction. I filled in the required sections, then handed it back. She popped a sign on the desk saying she'd be back in five minutes. "Come on."

I followed her along the corridors. She went into Piper's room first and checked he was ready for a visitor.

"He's in here," she said with a smile. "Have a lovely visit."

"Thank you," I said. I stood half in the doorway and watched her leave before entering the room properly.

Peter Piper was sitting up in his hospital bed. He didn't look too bad for someone who'd had surgery a few hours prior.

"I'm here. What is so important that the head of the Security Intelligence Service wanted to see me while in a hospital bed?"

"Lucas Genoa," he said with no expression in his voice.

"What about him?" I kept my voice even and low. Not wanting anyone to casually overhear the conversation while walking past. "I haven't met him, yet."

"I assumed you had." His eyes met mine. "My mistake."

"So, this was a waste of my time ..." I turned to leave his room.

"Not necessarily," he said. "I know Mr Genoa."

"Do you know where he is?"

"I do not."

"Then this is a waste of my time." I smiled. "Lovely to see you again, Peter. Heal well." I tapped my fingers on his tray table.

"I thought we could chat for a minute," he said.

"Desperate for visitors?"

"How's business?"

"Seriously? What'd you have? A frontal lobotomy? Since when does the head of NZSIS give a rat's arse about my PI gig?"

"Humour me."

He must be desperate. All right, I'll play.

"Pretty good, thanks. Just employed another set of hands." Who happens to be an enhanced interrogation expert. I hoped he'd take me up on my offer. Enzo was a good fit for our little firm.

"And the family?"

Twilight Zone music played in my head.

"They are well."

"I see that your Nana has quite a thriving mystery-solving business at her retirement village."

"So, the newspapers say."

"It's very enterprising of her."

"Not the word I'd use."

He smiled. "I imagine she's challenging."

"Yes."

I waited to see what came next. He sipped his water. When he was done, he placed the glass on the tray and looked at me.

"This is a custodial position. At the most, it will be two years while they find a permanent head."

Did I need to know that? Was he looking for a job? It was a very odd thing to tell me. We're not friends. We're barely acquaintances. I chose to leave it alone on the grounds that I didn't know what he expected me to say.

"I can help you," he said.

"With what?"

"The Genoa affair."

Oh, right, it's an affair now. "How?"

"I know Lucas Genoa. I have a certain amount of insight and I'm willing to help."

"Why? Why do you want to help me?"

"It's a small world. We need to look out for each other."

"Do we? Because that's not been my experience with NZSIS. Not the hierarchy anyway."

"High time we put that to rights."

"Really, so altruistic of you." Yeah, I'm not buying his brand of doo-doo. "Carry on and share this wonderful insight you have."

"He's here because of an incident in Europe."

"New Zealand is a long way from Europe."

He nodded. "He is here to retrieve something."

"Is that why you met with him at Wellington Airport?"

All animation froze for a beat then pinged back to life. "You don't meet friends at airports?"

"So, he's a friend?"

Piper shrugged. "We know each other."

"Apparently well enough to meet him at an airport." In a public place. Hiding in plain sight?

"Some people are best met in the open."

I smiled. "Of course. You wanted everyone to see and not care, whereas a clandestine meeting would raise a red flag."

Piper's eyebrows rose. "That's not what I said."

"Whatever floats your boat. I have a question."

"Go ahead."

"What does Lucas Genoa want with Emily Jones?"

His mouth twitched violently then settled in a grim line.

"What does Jonathon Tierney want with you?"

"Tell me about Genoa and Emily Jones."

He sighed and pushed his water glass around the tray table. "What does Tierney want?"

"Tierney is a friend."

"Don't kid a kidder, Ronnie. He's CIA and he's probably here because of Genoa."

"He's here to visit me and my fiancé."

"I don't think that's the whole truth."

"Where did you meet Genoa?" I smiled at him. "You may as well tell me." It appeared we were playing a game Nana called tit-for-tat.

Piper pressed his lips together for a beat then said, "At the airport."

"The first time," I said. "Where did you meet Genoa? Do you want me to help you? Shall I jog your memory for you?"

"If you know why ask?"

"Because I want to know if you'll tell the truth or not."

"Antwerp. We met for the first time in person in Antwerp." His eyes flicked to the door. He waited a moment then asked, "When did you meet Tierney?"

"Here, before the nuclear strike on Copenhagen." I lied.

He fumbled his glass, almost spilling the last of the water.

It was my turn again. "What is it that drew you and Genoa together?"

Would he say a common interest in stealing millions of euros worth of diamonds and art, or something lame like golf?

"You don't need to know the specifics."

Perhaps I already do know the specifics.

"All right, when did you meet Simone Genoa?"

All his facial muscles froze. He could've been injected with a heap of Botox he was that frozen. All of a sudden, animation returned, but just to his hand. He pressed the button to call a nurse. Beads of perspiration gathered on his blanched forehead.

A nurse hurried in. She looked at me and motioned to the door. "You need to leave. Mr Piper needs rest."

I showed myself out. Mentioning Simone Genoa really pushed his buttons. Fascinating. I'd have to find out more another way. On the way back home, I considered his reaction. Maybe he was the one who killed her. He reacted badly. Was he just tired or in pain so soon after surgery for his mystery whatever or did I hit a bunch of nerves with Simone's name?

"Hey Siri call Ben," I said, as I hit the motorway south.

"Calling Ben," my phone announced from the hands-free cradle on the dash.

"You, okay?" Ben asked.

"Yep. We need to dig into Peter Piper and his connection to Simone Genoa. I mentioned her and he reacted badly."

"I'll reach out through my channels. Do you want me to ask Grandfather?"

"Yes, good idea."

"How far away are you?"

"Twenty-five minutes."

"See you soon." Ben hung up.

Chapter Thirty-three
[Crockett: What do you know?]

Dane grinned at me as he walked into my kitchen slash dining area. He signed the word, "Coffee."

"Just made some, help yourself. Everything okay with Emily?"

He gave me a thumbs-up. Then he typed on his iPad and Siri spoke, "She has no idea who Lucas and Stefan are or why they think she has diamonds."

"I didn't expect her to," I replied. "Where is she?"

"Bathroom," he signed. I quite enjoyed the break from Siri's voice when Dane signed. We both knew American Sign Language. Dane's injuries sustained in an explosion left him unable to speak. He still finds it frustrating, but signing and Siri are his means of communication, right now. You take what you can get. He's alive. He's not a vegetable. More and more, he's the Dane I once knew, just without his own voice.

I sat up straighter at the table. "Has she got any idea where Lucas has gone?"

He shook his head.

Emily appeared in the kitchen doorway on crutches "I don't know them," she said. "I think they are confused."

I nodded and smiled at her. "So do I."

She joined me at the table. And leaned her crutches against a chair.

"Coffee?" Dane asked her via Siri.

"Yes, please."

He placed the mug he had in his hand in front of her and poured himself another. The three of us sat and drank our coffee. Birds chirped outside. Sun streamed in from the window above the kitchen sink. Thoughts rambled around in my head. Where would Lucas go? Who killed Stefan? Did that person take Lucas? Was that person Tony Robinson? There was only one way to find out. I picked up my cell phone and scrolled through my contacts and chose Tony's number. I put the call on speaker and placed the phone on the table.

"Who's this?" he said when he picked up the call.

"Crockett," I replied. "What did you do, Peckerhead?"

"Found your friend for you," he replied.

"Put her in more danger, idiot."

"Do you have her?"

"Yes."

"You're welcome."

"Where is Genoa?"

"Safe."

"I want to talk to him."

"I'm sure you do. You'll have a crack at him when I'm done."

"You're not helping, Robinson."

"I think I am. You're down one bad actor."

"You're dreaming if you think I'm going to thank you."

"You got your girl back. Let it go, Crockett. I have him. Your turn will come."

"Where's Lucas Genoa?" I looked at Dane while I spoke. "Do you know what they want?"

"They're looking for something."

"That's obvious, Einstein. What are they looking for?" I asked.

Dane touched my arm to get my attention when my gaze wandered. He signed: diamonds. I nodded.

"I think you know," Robinson said.

"I think you're full of shit and want a crack at it yourself."

"It's a job, Crockett. I'm not in it for me."

"Didn't realise you were for hire."

"That was a low blow." His voice tensed. "That's not what I meant, and you know it."

"What do they want?" I wanted him to say it because so far, we were just guessing. We had no proof the diamonds from the heist in Antwerp ended up in New Zealand. It didn't seem plausible. There was a tiddler of a notion that told me it didn't seem tenable, but it did happen. I'd seen far too much over the years to discount anything.

"They want diamonds, but you know that."

"And where are these imaginary diamonds?"

"Lucas thinks Emily has them."

Emily frowned at the phone. "I do not know where any diamonds are." She huffed air from her mouth. "People need to stop asking me about diamonds. I do not have the stupid diamonds. I never had the diamonds." Tears filled her eyes. "Are they going to take me again?"

I slid my arm around her shoulders, pulled her toward me, and hung up on Robinson.

"No one is going to take you away again," I whispered in her ear. "No one."

We needed to find the diamonds if they existed. That was the only way to ensure Emily's safety.

Dane tapped on his iPad. I waited for Siri to speak. "If you were going to put something somewhere safe, Emily, where would you put it?"

Dane was thinking the way I was. Her safety depended on us finding those stones.

"In Crockett's floor safe," she replied. "That's the safest place I know."

More typing from Dane lead to Siri speaking. "Where was your safe place before you met Crockett?"

"The bookshop," she replied.

"How about when you were a private investigator?" Siri asked.

"The cage in Ronnie's tech room."

That was specific.

"What about when you were a police officer?"

"I had a safety deposit box at a bank in Wellington." Emily's eyes widened; she looked surprised at what she'd said. I was surprised at what she'd said.

"What did you keep in the safety deposit box?" Siri asked.

Emily shook her head. "I don't remember. I didn't remember I had one until the words came out of my mouth."

"Damn," Siri said. "But we know more now than we did before. Good job Emily."

Emily smiled.

"Don't suppose you remember which bank it was?" I said, giving her shoulders a squeeze.

Dane was typing. He turned his iPad to face me and Emily. He'd looked up security deposit vaults in Wellington.

"Any of those look familiar?" I asked Emily as I scanned the list. It was a short list. Most banks had gotten out of the security deposit vault business. Only Westpac still had lockers, but they were in Auckland from the look of it. It looked like New Zealand Vault had the only safety deposit boxes in Wellington. They were at the bottom of Willis Street.

Emily reached out her finger and touched the New Zealand Vault. The link opened. She searched the page. "Maybe this one."

She went back to the search and opened the next link. Commonwealth Vault. They had branches in Auckland and Christchurch. She clicked the next on the list. Security Deposits Vault in Auckland. She shook her head and tried the last one. Westpac in Auckland.

"So, the first one?" I asked.

"I think so. But I thought it was at a bank."

"Okay, that's a starting point."

Emily leaned her head on my shoulder. "Why would I have diamonds?"

Dane carried on searching on his iPad for banks that

had safety deposit boxes. I picked up Emily's crutches that had slid to the floor. She was giving her leg a rest after wearing the prosthetic for far too long. Emily and I went into the lounge. We sat on the couch together.

"It was a bank," Emily said quietly.

"We'll find it," I whispered in her ear.

"It had a horse."

"The bank had a horse? A real horse?"

"No, a picture."

I tugged my phone from my jeans pocket and called Ronnie. She knew banks.

"Hey, question," I said when she answered. I could hear road noise.

"Yeah?"

"Bank with a horse?"

"National Bank," she replied.

"Great, thanks." I hung up.

"What did she say?" Emily asked.

"National Bank."

Dane had joined us and pulled up an armchair. He was typing on his iPad. He smiled at us and reached over to pass the iPad to me.

"Emily, look." I showed her the horse logo.

"That's it."

I read the story on the screen. "They did have safety deposit boxes in Wellington. A few years ago, they moved all the boxes, under armed guard, to New Zealand Vault."

"Can we get to it?" Emily asked relief wound through her words. "If we can get to it, then they will leave me alone."

I passed the iPad back to Dane.

"We'll need your key." I didn't add we'd also need to know what number the box was, what name it was under, and whatever photo ID she used to open it. Let's start with the key and worry about the rest later.

"I do not know where it would be?"

"Your keyring?" Siri asked.

Confusion clouded her eyes. "Where are my keys?"

"In your backpack," I replied.

"At the bookshop?"

"Ronnie's office."

"If it's not on my key ring, what do we do?"

"We search your house. Try and find where you would've put something small like a key," I said, wrapping my arm around her shoulders again and holding her close.

"Can you do that without me?"

"You'll be safe. Dane and I will be with you."

"Ronnie and Ben too?"

"Of course. Half the police force if that will help."

She breathed in deeply, then paused, then exhaled slowly. I could almost hear her mind counting. One-two-three-four on each inhale, pause, and exhale.

My phone rang. Ronnie's face lit the screen.

I answered. "Ronnie?"

"Your mate Josh the cop rang me."

"Something up?"

"He was following up on Emily." She paused for a beat.

"He mentioned lizard people ..." I heard a hitch in her voice. "Thought maybe you needed a hand capturing them."

"You're funny."

"Apparently Upper Hutt College is a breeding ground or training camp." She was struggling. "Would you use a net? Or do you think they'd wriggle through the holes?"

"Laugh it up, chuckles."

She choked back laughter then gave up and let it flow through her words. "Lizard people?"

"Don't worry about it."

Words ringed with amusement came at me from the phone, "Can't believe you didn't share that your hot lead was a conspiracy nut."

"They prefer theorists or truth seers."

"I guess we're the sheeple then," she said with a strangled laugh.

I felt a smile on my face. Emily was giggling. Even Dane laughed. Not Siri but Dane.

"Good to know I have everyone's support. The tip was still a good one."

"A lucky one," Ronnie spluttered. "See you soon."

Siri said, "How does she make that sound like a threat?"

"Gifted," I replied.

Emily picked up her crutches, stood, and limped away. At the hallway door, she looked back and said, "I'll just get my leg."

I nodded.

Chapter Thirty-four
[Ronnie: Nana and Tierney]

The house smelled like fresh coffee and scones when I opened the front door. Nice. Nana must've baked scones. I hoped they were cheese scones as I climbed the stairs. She made fantastic cheese scones.

Donald was in the kitchen.

"You're back, good timing too," he said with a dazzling smile.

"Are they cheese scones?"

"Yes."

"Did Nana bake them?"

"Also yes, but with help. She's passing the skill on to me!" Donald was chuffed with himself. "Scones are on the dining table with a dish of butter. Go help yourself. They're still warm."

I wandered into the dining room. It was suspiciously devoid of human occupants. Romeo was there though camped out and hoping for scones or a slice of cheese. The scones were wrapped in tea towels inside a large bowl, staying nice and warm, and soft. I opened the tea towels and removed a scone, then wrapped the rest. I put the scone on a side plate, then split it and added a generous slather of butter to both halves. The butter began melting. I took a bite. It was good, fluffy, and cheesy, with a bit of a kick. That'd be the cayenne pepper

I supposed. I scarfed the rest of the scone, wiped butter off my chin with a napkin, then poured myself a coffee from the French press sitting on a trivet next to the bundle of wrapped scones. With a coffee mug in hand, I went into the lounge.

Nana and Tierney were there entertaining each other.

"Perfect timing, Veronica," Nana said, with a smile that stretched her lips taut. "Your Auntie Barbara rang. The girls and I are going to Rarotonga! They'll be over shortly to discuss details."

I mustered joy. "Fabulous Nana. I'm sure you'll all have a wonderful time."

I couldn't see Ben or Enzo and was loathe to interrupt the oldies and their revelling in an upcoming trip. I slunk away to the kitchen with my coffee. Donald was doing dishes by hand. We'd both decided to do away with the dishwasher months ago. Now the gap under the bench held a temperature-controlled wine fridge. Priorities.

"Where's your husband?" I asked as Donald placed a large bowl on the dish rack.

"I think Steph called him about something so he's out working with her?"

"That sounds right," I said.

"Does it?" Donald asked. "Since when does he work with your lot?"

"Since he offered to work a new case for me, and work with Steph."

Donald flapped the dish brush around a plate in the bubble-filled sink. "It's the first I've heard of it." Then he scrubbed like he was trying to remove the pattern.

"Un-clutch your pearls, Donald. You know he doesn't talk about work."

He rolled his eyes while scrubbing the plate. Bubbles billowed from the sink and clung to the bench.

"What's the matter?" He didn't do anything that thoroughly unless there was a problem.

"Did you hear that Nana is going overseas?" He huffed and flapped at the bubbles. "The elderly cannot just hop on a plane!"

"Unfortunately, they can," I said. "They're old, not nuts."

"The jury is still out on that statement of sanity." He flipped bubbles around. "Can't we do something?"

"Nope. Not unless you want to go with them."

Donald's brown eyes flashed with gold. "That's a great idea! I knew you'd come up with something."

No, it wasn't. Chaperoning the ancient Scooby Gang in Rarotonga was a terrible idea. Terrible. I let it go. It was a problem for after our current disaster.

"Have you seen Ben?"

"In your room," he said. "Don't worry about drying up. I'll do that too. I need to keep myself busy."

I wrinkled my nose at him and took my coffee down the hallway to my room.

Ben was sitting on my bed with a laptop on his knee. He looked up and smiled when I swung through the door. "I'm glad you're back."

"So am I. Donald is playing martyr in the kitchen. Did

you hear the story of Nana going to Raro with Auntie Barbara?"

Ben nodded. "I just hope Tierney doesn't invite himself along."

"That would be a whole new ball of wax. We'll cross or burn the Raro bridge when we get to it." I sat next to Ben and looked at the screen he had open. "What are you doing?"

"Digging around to see if there are any images of Peter Piper with Simone Genoa."

"Find anything?"

"Not yet. There's bound to be something."

"Did you talk to Tierney?"

"No, haven't been able to prise him away from your Nana."

"Hold off on that. I don't want to tip him to anything to do with Kiwi intelligence. How about we slip into my bat cave and check *Genesis*?"

He grinned, closed his laptop, and stood up. "Let's do it."

I opened the secret panel in my wardrobe and in we went. The computer fired up when the lights flicked on. I wondered how long it would take before *Genesis* reached out once I fired up the flash drive that enabled me to access the *Genesis* system. This time I wanted to explore the other areas. We worked the Oceania sphere. I knew *Genesis* was worldwide, so Europe was where I wanted to start looking - if we didn't get booted out by the boss first.

I started looking through folders on the flash drive,

hoping to see something that would enable me to get into the European files. I ran the mouse pointer down the list of folders until I found Joshua 2:2.

Ben smiled. "The king of Jericho was told, "Some of the Israelites have come here tonight to spy out the land.""

"Guess we're the spies," I replied and clicked on the folder. "Lo and behold, here's a link to something." I clicked it. The link opened. Instead of Israelites spying we were inside a different *Genesis* to the one we were used to. It was similar but not the same. "Where now, I wonder," I mumbled as I allowed the mouse pointer to wander over the screen. It looked like a photo of a city, but I couldn't place it from the angle the photograph had been taken. "Where is this?"

Ben took a closer look. "I'm not sure. But it's somewhere in Europe. Maybe Poland or that vicinity."

"Let's figure out where we should look for images."

"How about that?" Ben asked, pointing to a large building in the background of the image. "Does that look like an art gallery?"

"Looks like an old building to me," I replied and clicked the mouse on the building. The building opened, revealing rows and rows of red folders all numbered. "What do the numbers look like to you?"

"They're too long for dates. Maybe, case numbers. Job numbers. Operational numbers?"

"And we think the heist was eight years ago." I scanned the numbers attached to the folders. "Wish we had some kind of key that would help." I scrolled and scrolled.

"There're hundreds of these folders. This page goes on and on."

"Jump to the middle," Ben said. "Hopefully there will be a date inside one of the folders then we'll know roughly how many we need to skip through."

The middle gave us direction. The direction was down - not to hell but down the page.

The numbers followed the same format on each folder. Now I knew I could jump folders as long as I was scrolling downwards. I could see a pattern, I just didn't know what it meant, and I felt like there was no time to mess around finding out. At any point we could be discovered, I could be discovered, and I had a feeling that would be very bad.

Each folder told us we weren't there yet.

I skipped about ten and tried again. Then jumped back into the middle of the ten and opened it. There were more folders and a year. All the documents inside a dated folder belonged to Operation Sidestep.

"Guess this is it." The first file contained an intelligence report from a *Genesis* operative in Europe. I grabbed a clean flash drive from my drawer and copied the documents from Operation Sidestep. I watched each file copy hoping we got them all before we were found.

A red warning popped up on the screen.

"Someone knows we are here."

I crossed my fingers.

Half a file to go.

Another pop-up warned an outside actor was pinging

my electronic trail to try and locate me. At the last second, I closed everything, removed both flash drives, and shut the system down.

Ben and I looked at each other for a beat.

"Do you think they traced us?"

I shook my head. "I think I killed the connection before they could figure out I was using a VPN. The IP thrown at them was Russian."

Ben smiled. "Nice."

I shrugged. Everyone expects Russia to get their mitts on everything. These days it's more likely to be China or maybe a Russian/Chinese collaboration. Next time I'd use China. It wouldn't stop them for long, but it would slow them down.

I wondered if I'd get a *Genesis* call asking if I knew anything about unauthorised access to Europe. It didn't usually take *Genesis* long.

"Let's get out of here and go to my office. We can read the files on the vault. Just in case something in them tries to ping back to home base, wherever that might be." I stood, stretched, and pocketed the flash drive. I then put the other drive back in its secure hiding place.

Once out of the bat cave, Ben and I headed for the kitchen. The smell of warm scones hung in the air. Maybe we should grab a couple to take with us. I paused in the kitchen and took a paper bag from the pantry. In the dining room, I dropped two scones into the bag. Ben passed me going into the lounge. I heard Nana's voice then Tierney's.

I joined Ben.

"We have a few things to do," I said to Nana. "Can you please stay here with Donald?"

"Yes, dear," Nana replied, a little too quickly for my liking. That was when I heard the doorbell and a chime from my pocket. The doorbell camera opened on my phone. *The Cronies of Doom* were at the door. I didn't think for one second that trouble would not follow.

Chapter Thirty-five
[Ronnie: Not in my office!]

The main office door was locked. Jenn was on sick leave. Steph and Enzo must've still been out working the Roxy case. We tried not to work weekends but sometimes that's how the cases rolled. I wriggled my keys from my pocket and let us in, then snipped the bolt open. Ben and I hurried up the stairs and I unlocked the main office door before pushing my keys back into my jacket pocket.

With the lights out and no one around the office felt eerie. Ben turned the lights on. I made my way down to the back of the spacious office to a computer that sat on a desk against the back wall. I pressed my index finger onto a key in the top right-hand corner of the keyboard. Everything whirred into life. Ben pulled up a chair next to mine.

"Let's do this," I mumbled and pushed the flash drive into the nearest computer port. It opened without fuss. I opened the first file in the list, and we read silently. Operation Sidestep was a *Genesis* operation from the beginning. They planned to disrupt a group intent on stealing diamonds to fund terror cells in South America. Each file detailed different parts of the operation and contained surveillance images. I scrolled through the images and found many of Stefan, Lucas, and Simone. They were all identified as Genoa. The files detailed meetings between the Genoas. There were images of them casing venues and auction houses that specialised in diamonds, and reports from operatives on what they'd witnessed and when they proposed the theft would take place. We read on. There was a report stating that two operatives from New Zealand were put into play. Both were fluent in Spanish. It identified them as Tomás Genoa and Pedro Genoa.

"Why Genoa?" I asked reading on hoping to find out why, Genoa. "Why New Zealanders?"

From the corner of my eye, I saw Ben shake his head slightly. "Are there photos of the two Kiwis? They might have already been close by, maybe that explains why two Kiwis were used."

"Not so far."

I opened the final file. It was an after-action report. Right there on the top of the page, it said the report was written and filed by Tom Smith.

"I think Tom knows far more than he was saying," I said quietly. "There are images attached."

I opened the attachments. The photos were of Tom Smith and Peter Piper, otherwise known as Tomás Genoa and Pedro Genoa.

"Well, that's just fucking fantastic," Ben said with a growl.

"Something is missing," I said, scrolling back up the page. They mentioned Simone Genoa, they mentioned that she was given all the diamonds and that they were to meet in two years to divvy them up. But no one mentioned Emily. We still didn't know when the switch was made. It would've had to have been early in the proceedings. Early enough that the Kiwis had the idea that she was part of the crew from the beginning.

There was no mention at all of a third Kiwi and no mention of why Simone was given the diamonds.

"Emily is not mentioned," I said. "Because she wasn't *Genesis*, she was Army Intelligence."

"She was, what now? Ronnie, what do you know that the rest of us don't?"

Oh, bugger. I took a breath and used the exhale to say, "Emily was Army Intelligence. That goes no further than us."

"Understood. That changes things from our perspective."

Just a little bit.

"So, no one inside the group knew that Simone was switched for Emily," I said slowly. "They didn't know." I looked at Ben. "Piper is *Genesis*, or he was *Genesis*."

"You think he's not now?"

I nodded. Although I bet they would've wanted to hold on to someone who is now head of NZSIS.

I scrolled back through all the files. I opened the search function and searched; nothing came back as Emily Jones. As far as *Genesis* was concerned, she wasn't there.

I shut everything down and removed the flash drive. From my desk, I grabbed a small, padded postage-paid postbag. I addressed it to my P.O. box, dropped the flash drive in it and sealed the top.

"Can you?" I said, handing it to Ben. He took it with a smile.

"I'll be right back. Okay to drop it into the nearest post box?"

"Absolutely."

He lightly kissed my lips and left. I moved to my desk and lifted the lid on my laptop. I had a quick look at the log sheets from our surveillance teams. The last entry said they'd lost Costa during the night. Shit. That wasn't good. I checked to see where Steph was by looking her phone up on Find My. She was on Totara Street.

I gave her a ring and she answered fast. "All, okay?"

"Yep. What's happening with you two?"

"Roxy had a brick through her window this morning. Cameras picked up that Rockstar person out front about the same time with something in his hand."

"Enzo with you?"

"Yep."

"Roxy, okay?"

"Yes. Shaken but not hurt."

"Turn it over to police?" An escalation like that meant we could hand it over and step away.

"That's just what I was going to do." Steph paused. I could hear Enzo's voice in the background. Steph came back. "Enzo wants to know if you need help."

"I think we do. Get Roxy sorted. Let police handle it from here on out. Then meet us at the office."

"Both of us?"

"Please."

"Right." Steph hung up.

I had the feeling she didn't expect me to want her to join our merry band of troublemakers. But I knew if I sent her home she'd come back because Jenn would be driving her spare without being able to work. Anyway, she's excellent at keeping tabs on our surveillance teams and tracking anything electronic. I wondered how Costa lost our surveillance. Maybe, I could do something about that.

Crockett texted me: Be there in ten minutes.

Noise outside on the stairs alerted me to company. I expected Ben. The door opened and much to my surprise, Tierney entered with Nana on his arm. Fantastic. Just what we needed.

I jumped to my feet and hurried across the room.

Tierney's dark beady eyes narrowed as he focused on me. "Veronica?"

"Sir."

"Where is my grandson?"

I heard the door downstairs close.

"Coming up the stairs ...," I said with a smile. "And you're both in my office."

Nana squeezed Tierney's arm. He escorted her to the sitting area. Ben walked in the door. He looked from me to Nana and Tierney.

"It must be Bring Your Grandparents to Work Day," he

said.

I looked at the door expecting *The Cronies of Doom* to appear. They didn't.

"What's happening here?" I asked looking at Nana.

"Jonathon had a feeling that you knew something about this awful situation with Emily."

"Did he?" I asked. "And that required you to be in my office?"

I held my phone in my hand. Ben moved to sit with the oldies.

I texted Crockett: Surprise party in my office.

It told Crockett there was an unfriendly ambush in my office. I needed to keep Dane away from here and that was the best way I could think of.

Crockett texted: We need Emily's backpack.

My keys were still in my pocket. That was handy. I knew the backpack was in the cage.

"Give me a minute," I said to the visitors and left the room shutting the door behind me. I hurried to the tech room. Unlocked the door, removed the backpack from the cage, locked everything, and texted Crockett from the hallway.

Me: Just you. I'm waiting on the stairs.

Ben poked his head around the door. "You, okay?"

"Waiting for someone for a pickup." I patted the backpack next to me and signed: Crockett is coming.

"I'll entertain the interlopers until you come back in."

"Thanks."

We'd be aces at the marriage thing. Teamwork makes the dream work. I shook my head. Corny, Ronnie. So corny.

The front door at the bottom of the stairs opened. Crockett bounded up the stairs two at a time. I chucked the backpack to him when he passed halfway. He caught it, spun on his heels, and vanished out the door.

I took a breath, plastered a smile on my face, and went back into my office.

"Now," I said. "What is it we can do for the pair of you?"

"I've been looking into the strange grocery delivery, Veronica," Tierney said. "It appears that someone signed up for the delivery service and purposely used your address. That person is not Terry White."

He was enjoying this about as much as Nana. "On purpose you say?"

"Yes, Veronica. Someone worked out where you really live."

Shit.

"Ronnie?" Ben said. "How big a problem is that?"

"Big enough," I replied.

It was bound to happen one day. We'd taken as many precautions as we could and still have a life.

"Who found me?" I addressed Tierney.

"A man named Tony Robinson." He watched me. "Do you know the name?"

"Yes."

"Do you know who he is?"

"I've heard the name." I blinked back memories. I pushed them into a little compartment that rarely saw the light of day. Not everyone I've come across in my life is worth talking about.

"Veronica, I can help you," Tierney said.

"I appreciate the offer."

He tipped his head in my direction. "Take me up on the offer, young lady." His lips stretched taut. "You don't want this Robinson fellow to talk and share his knowledge."

"You're right, I don't particularly want him to open his fat mouth and let more morons know where I live. And I don't want to have to move. Again."

But we have options. Donald and I owned several properties, all of which we rented out. We have in the past switched houses with one of our tenants when it looked like someone was getting a bit close for my liking. I didn't really want to upend people's lives again and it wasn't an easy job moving the bat cave to a new location.

Ben nudged me. "Ronnie ..."

I took a breath and nodded. "Yes. Please, help me with the Robinson issue."

Tierney smiled. "Very good."

Nana grasped his arm. I wasn't sure what was going on

with those two, but I didn't like it.

"Veronica," Nana said. "The girls are at home with Donald. He was worried about being alone."

"Donald was worried," I repeated. "Why would he be worried?"

"This Robinson nonsense, dear."

Oh, right, they talked about it in front of him. Excellent. He'll be frantic and pacing the lounge room, wearing out our new carpet. I pressed my lips together.

"Donald will be fine," Ben said more to me than Nana. "Speaking of Donald, isn't Enzo coming in?"

"Yes. They're turning the case over to police, then coming into the office." I looked at my watch. "Should be soon."

"Would you like to know where this Robinson fellow is?" Tierney asked.

"Yes, thank you." I can be polite.

Jonathon Tierney took his phone from his jacket pocket. He unlocked it with a glance, then opened something.

Coordinates arrived as a text message on both our phones. Ben looked first, then closed the text. Nana was fidgeting with a button on her cardigan. It wasn't like her to fidget.

"Nana, is something wrong?"

"No dear," she replied. "Not wrong exactly."

"Then what?"

"My surveillance teams."

Oh, dead flowers and early death. Not this again.

"Yes, Nana." It took all my concentration to keep my voice even. "Have they found something?"

"That client of ours." She fidgeted with the clasp on her handbag. "Kerrin Costa. They saw her. She was walking down Emily's street about an hour ago."

"Okay. Thanks." I took a breath and counted. "Nana, what did I say about surveillance?"

"I know, Veronica. It's just that we wanted to help find our sweet Emily and keep her safe."

I warned myself to be nice. She was trying to help. It's not the end of the world.

"Did you get a notification?" Ben asked me.

"Nope. Maybe she didn't go to Emily's after all." That made me wonder why she was on that street at all. It could be she's following someone. "Thanks for that Nana. I'm asking you again to let us deal with your client and this Emily situation. Please."

"I'll see to it, Veronica," Tierney said. "Now, if you don't mind, I will take your grandmother back to your house and see what I can do about this Robinson fellow."

"Thank you," I said. "We'd best get on with our next move."

"Best of luck," Tierney said, standing and helping Nana to her feet. I noted her cane was nowhere to be seen. I guess she didn't want to play the frail old lady card with Tierney around. He was older than Moses and quite happily using a cane. I was convinced that his cane concealed a sword.

I had planned on using my special skills to locate

Genoa and it still felt like a good idea. Tierney did not mention Robinson working with anyone or being with anyone. I wondered what happened to Genoa.

My mind was still running over the information we'd pulled from *Genesis*. Tom and Peter Piper were working for *Genesis* and wiggled their way into the diamond heist. Maybe we needed to talk to Tom again. Would it matter that we would be tipping our hand? Could we get him to tell us what he was doing in Belgium with Piper and why he was using Tomás as his name?

He kinda looked like he could pull it off, and clearly, he did. But what about Piper? I wasn't sure in what world that guy looked like a Pedro. He was the palest, most freckled, Pedro I'd ever come across. And surely, his acceptance of the leadership of NZSIS would've caused some red flags. I recognised him from the photo I saw from Belgium so the people he was working with would recognise him. I'm pretty sure there is a list somewhere with personnel photos of the directors of any security agency. He was a liability. They had to know.

I heard the door close at the bottom of the stairs. The oldies had left the building.

"You, okay?" Ben asked.

"Yeah. Just thinking about Piper. No wonder he's nervous. It wouldn't take much for him to be recognised as Pedro Genoa by Lucas."

"Yeah. Might be awkward for him to explain his association when he was working a *Genesis* job at the time."

"I'd imagine if it became public knowledge that he worked with terrorists that being fired would be the least of his problems."

I heard footsteps hurrying along the hallway outside the door, but I didn't hear the door downstairs.

"They must've used the back stairs," Ben said looking at me and referencing the footsteps.

We watched as the door opened.

Costa stepped inside and closed the door behind her.

That was not who we expected.

"Can I help you?" I asked.

"I think we can help each other," she replied, looking from me to Ben, then to the door. "We need to move quickly."

She slid the bolt across on the top of the door.

"Is someone following you?"

"I think so," she replied. "I hope I lost them."

Surely, she wouldn't be worried about elderly white-haired men?

"Who?"

A small smile crept from her mouth to her eyes. "Not those old men, your grandmother has out there doing God knows what."

So, she knew about them and their link to Nana.

That was good to know.

"Who?" Ben asked, peering out the blinds over the windows to the street below and across to the railway station.

"Lucas Genoa."

"We'd like to talk to him," I said.

"I think he and another man are following me."

Was that why she was on foot? It wasn't a bad idea really, unless they were in a vehicle and intent on grabbing her.

"Why?"

"I suppose we all want the same thing for different reasons."

"Diamonds?"

Costa moved her head a fraction. "Do you know where they are?"

"No. But now we know where you are, so thanks for that."

"Do you have your friend, Simone?"

"Simone is not our friend," Ben replied. "Simone is dead."

Costa slumped against the reception desk. Defeated or deflated, I wasn't sure which.

"Dead," she repeated. "Dead. When? Was it Genoa?"

"Quite some time ago. And we don't think Genoa had a hand in it. But maybe," I said.

She frowned. "How?"

"Murdered, we think," Ben said. "We saw the Black Notice from INTERPOL."

"INTERPOL?"

"Yes," Ben said.

"I haven't seen a Black Notice," she said, her voice cracking.

"Why don't you sit down." I stepped up next to her and

guided her to our seating area. I glanced at Ben. He whipped out the door. By the time she was settled, he was back with a glass of water.

"Thank you," she whispered taking the glass. She took a few sips.

Ben and I sat down. She didn't need us towering over her. She sighed as she placed the glass on the coffee table. The news of Simone's death seemed to hit her hard.

"You are sure it is Simone?"

"Not a hundred percent," Ben replied. "But we don't know who else it could be. They put time of death a few days before the diamond heist. It fits."

Yeah, we're not one hundred percent. Simone and Emily are very similar. Without a DNA swab, we wouldn't know for sure. Emily's DNA wasn't in any database, so we had nothing to compare her to except that of the dead woman. We knew the dead woman's DNA wasn't in any database. If we took a swab and the results ended up in an accessible database, Emily could find herself in more danger from her past. Was it a coincidence we couldn't verify their DNA or just the world we lived in? They say everyone has a doppelgänger. I really hoped it was a doppelgänger situation.

"You need to tell us what is going on here," I said, leaning forward. "We might be able to help."

Maybe she's not the enemy after all.

"Simone was a thief. A very good one." She picked the glass up and took several sips before placing it on the table. "I was here with the consulate on unrelated business. Someone had 'seen' her in New Zealand."

"Unrelatedly spying," I said with a smile. "Yeah, we know who you are."

She didn't return the smile. Instead, she made direct eye contact. "Do you?"

"Argentinian national with Secretaría de Inteligencia del Estado." We generally referred to it as SIDE.

She didn't refute that. We had had this discussion when we first found her snooping around Emily's.

"Genoa will not believe that Simone is dead," she said, her voice low. "He will not."

"Why?"

"The same reason I do not believe she is dead."

I fought to prevent a frown from creasing my forehead. No frown lines before our wedding.

"And that reason is?" Ben leaned forward to match me. We both had our elbows on our knees and hands dangling in front of our legs. "We've seen the reconstruction."

"Why did it take so long for INTERPOL to send out a Black Notice? Doesn't the timing seem suspicious to you?"

"A little bit," I replied. "But we've seen and compared the reconstruction to Emily. If that's where you are going with this."

"That is where I am going."

"Emily is not Simone."

"I don't think you can be as sure as you sound."

"I know Emily. She is not Simone." Except Emily was

Army Intelligence and we are going on Bill's word that Emily took Simone's place for the job. It could've been the other way around. Not everyone tells the truth. I almost laughed at that idea. These days no one told the truth. You can't even believe what you see. There are amazing deep fakes out there. We used them too for various things. Technology is terrific but the consequences of its use can be terrible.

Costa picked up on my train of thought. "Not so sure now?"

I circled back to her not getting a notification of the Black Notice. How unusual was that?

"Do you usually get INTERPOL notifications?" I asked.

She shook her head. "Not like law enforcement. Depending on where we're working, we might get relevant ones passed on. Doesn't hurt to know who they're looking for and what they think."

"Are the diamonds earmarked for funding a terror group?" I might as well just put it out there and see what bells ring.

"Yes. That is what we suspect. Our intelligence suggests that they are to fund South American terrorists set to disrupt various governments across South America."

"So, you want to make sure the diamonds never reach Genoa ..."

"Yes."

Or she wants the diamonds to fund a terror cell or two, or a drug cartel wants them.

No one tells the truth.

I could feel Ben looking at me. "What are you thinking?"

"Nothing much. Just wondering if anyone will ever find those diamonds and why they'd be in New Zealand at all."

And what do Tom and Piper have to do with it all? And is Emily really Emily? It was just the usual trust issues. Why would Emily bring them into New Zealand when Tom and Piper were part of the crew? Why wouldn't Tom take control of them and hand them over to whomever?

Costa spoke. "We didn't know who took them or where they went. Lucas and Stefan Genoa knew. So did the rest of that heist team. I went where Genoa went."

"You're not here for unrelated reasons at all," I said. "You're following a trail and now it's gone cold. That's why you're in my office now."

A small smile flittered before the look in her eyes cemented. "Lucas Genoa was grabbed by someone. That same someone killed Stefan. There was no sign of your friend Emily in the aftermath."

"How do you know that?" Ben enquired.

"I have my sources."

It must have been Bill bloody Bailey or one of his people. It was Defence property, so it stood to reason that Bailey or someone on his team was feeding intelligence to other players. Of course, it could've been Jonathon Tierney. Would he go as far as to say we had Emily back or would he leave that part out?

"Excuse me for a moment. Bathroom break." I stood. My phone was still in my pocket. A nasty idea emerged. I closed the door behind me and went straight to the tech room. I grabbed one of the alternate phones and left mine in its place. Then I hurried along the hallway and down the back stairs. I needed to get far enough away from the office that activating the phone wouldn't let anyone who could be monitoring for signals know that someone was sending messages. I ran down Princes Street and crossed Main. Then I turned left and moved as quickly as possible without being too obvious. I ducked down the pedestrian-only corner by the old courthouse. I walked straight passed CBD towers and into a car park. From the car park, I hurried to the Police Station. I took the long way around to make sure I wasn't followed directly from the office to the police station. If someone was trying to follow, I would've seen them. In the foyer, I fired the phone up and hauled phone numbers from my memory banks.

When I went to text Crockett, I noticed my name came up as Jonni. I'd fluked grabbing the alternate phone that I most often used. It was registered to Jonni Wright.

I texted Crockett: Make sure you answer my call and are NOT near Emily.

He texted back: Will do, Jonni.

I gave everyone two beats then made a FaceTime video call to Enzo, Steph, Crockett, and Dane. It's a good thing I can remember phone numbers.

One by one they answered.

"Get somewhere safe, I do not want this overheard," I said. A police officer opened a door behind the front desk. It was Josh. He waved and pointed to the security door. Josh let me in and showed me to a quiet room downstairs. "I'll be outside," he said.

"Thanks."

I checked the screen. Everyone was present.

"We have a problem," I said. "Costa is in my office. She thinks Simone is alive."

"She isn't," Crockett said, causing his picture to pop front and centre.

"Perhaps not," I replied.

"Shit," Crockett muttered.

"Someone is feeding her information. It's either someone from Army Intelligence or it's Tierney."

"What's our next move?" Enzo asked.

"We have to find those fucking diamonds," I said. "I'm not trusting anything that's coming from anyone but us."

"Nefarious?" Crockett said.

"Funding terrorism, about as nefarious as it gets," I said. "If that's true and it could be."

"When you say you're not trusting anyone ..." Enzo's face popped up.

"Just us," I replied. "God, I hope I can trust everyone in my circle." Could I trust Emily? "Keep a close eye on Emily, please."

"What the fuck, Ronnie?" Crockett was back in the

middle of my screen.

"Think about it, Crockett. We have no way to verify she is Emily. Just think about it." He didn't look pleased. "I've gotta go, I left Ben with Costa and said I was going to the bathroom."

Enzo chuckled. "The cop shop has bathrooms."

He must've recognised my backdrop or heard Josh's voice. "Say hey to Josh for us."

I winked then closed FaceTime and deleted the call log. I opened the door to find Josh waiting where he said he'd be.

"Everything okay?" he asked as we walked up the stairs.

"Not sure."

"Guess that's why you wanted that phone to ping its location as the Police Station."

"That's right."

He opened the door to the foyer and held it. "Enzo passed that job to us. We'll make sure that guy doesn't bother Roxy anymore. Looks like the prosecutor wants to charge him with several counts of vandalism, stalking, and breach of that restraining order Enzo and Steph secured to protect Roxy. We've locked him up for now. He goes before a judge tomorrow."

"Excellent." I switched the phone off and pushed it into my pocket. "Thanks, Josh, for ..." I waved a hand toward the stairs.

"Anytime. Yell if you need some party lights and sirens. My section is on this shift."

"Will do."

I quickly went back to work. This time I chose a more direct route down Fergusson Drive to Princes Street then ducked into the alleyway between a row of shops and Donald's hair salon and our offices and bookshop. I ran up the stairs and put the phone back into the tech room, picking up my own phone at the same time. I pushed it into my pocket. Took a deep breath, slowly released it, and went back into the office.

"All right?" Ben asked.

"Yes, thanks. Sorry about that." I smiled at Costa who looked suspicious. "Girl things."

She nodded but the suspicious look in her eyes took a few seconds to fade.

"I need to find Simone," Costa said. "She's the only one who can tell me where the diamonds are."

"Good luck with that," Ben said. "She's dead."

"Is Simone your cousin?" I asked. It would be nice if something was true.

"Yes. She is."

"How did you hear she was supposedly alive and in the Wellington Region?" I asked.

"A friend in the American embassy sent me a photo of her, very much alive."

"A friend?" I queried.

"Kirsten," she replied. "Kirsten. She was in France when I was. We became friendly."

"And this Kirsten woman sent you a photo of Simone?" Ben said. "Kirsten Knight?"

"Yes. Kirsten Knight."

I knew he was doing what I was doing and trying to remember where Kirsten and Emily could've crossed paths.

"How did she know what your cousin looked like?" I asked.

"I showed her a photograph after she went missing in Belgium."

That was a long time ago. And Kirsten managed to tie the real Simone to Emily and tell the grieving cousin that Simone was alive in New Zealand. I knew she was annoyed last time we met up because Crockett wouldn't fall for her charms and told her had a girlfriend. But setting Emily up was extreme. I don't suppose it would be too hard for Kirsten to find out who Crockett's girlfriend was and to get a picture. That's next-level nastiness.

Her eyes drifted to my engagement ring. "That's a beautiful ring. Congratulations. Who is the lucky man?"

"He's sitting right next to me," I said. Ben looped his fingers through mine.

"Marrying an actor. No doubt life will be exciting for you."

She did know who Ben was. It wasn't really a secret he'd been spying in plain sight for years. Gaining access to all sorts of situations and people because he was a well-known actor.

"I doubt it'll be boring, that's for sure," I replied. "I'm already having to get used to people wanting to have their pictures taken with him when we're out for dinner."

She nodded sympathetically. "Where is Simone?"

Nice try.

"Dead in Belgium," Ben said.

"We're going to have to get on. Our grandparents are expecting us to look at wedding venues with them today," I said with a smile. "If we find anything we'll be in touch."

Ben and I stood still holding hands.

She followed our lead, then pulled a wallet from her pocket. She handed me a card. I looked at it.

"Thanks. Follow me to the reception desk and I'll give you one of our cards. It's easier to text or call than run the risk that I'm not in the office if you show up."

I handed her a generic card with the office phone number.

She handed it back. "What is your mobile phone number?"

There was no harm in giving it to her. I wrote it on the back. "Sometimes it might take me a while to answer messages and if I'm working, I don't take phone calls."

"Understood," she said.

Ben opened the door for her. "Let me show you out," he said, with a charming smile that displayed his dimple. I didn't think that would work on Costa, but I guess he had to try.

"Not necessary, I found my way in, I can find my way out."

"Straight down the stairs in front of you," I said. "The back door is locked."

We watched her until she got to the bottom of the

stairs, and we saw the door open.

I waited just to make sure she wasn't coming back. It didn't look like she was, so I gave Ben my keys. "Can you go lock both doors please?"

"Of course. Meet you in the clean room when I'm done."

That's what we did, we anticipated the next step. And I was most definitely heading for the clean room. We had different names for that room. Jenn referred to it as *Interrogation Two*. Steph called it the *Black Site*. It was a clean room. No electronics allowed. The walls were shielded to prevent anyone eavesdropping with a directional microphone from anywhere outside. There were no windows. Fresh air came by a ducted system that was regularly swept for bugs and not the crawling variety.

From behind the reception desk, I took a pair of nitrile gloves, and with the gloves on I picked up the glass of water Ben had given to Costa. I doubted we'd get DNA, but it would have fingerprints. I took the glass into the kitchen and swabbed the rim where she'd sipped. I sealed the tube with the swab in it. Then I lifted prints off the glass surface and scanned them into the app on my phone.

Ben poked his head around the kitchen door. "Coming?"

"Yep." I left the swab and the glass on the bench.

"Lab for that?"

"Yes. I'll give the courier a ring."

I made the phone call. It would be picked up within

five minutes from a drop box outside our front door. I put the tube into a small courier bag. Ben took it downstairs because he still had the keys. My phone chirped. No matches for the fingerprints. I knew Ben's would be on the glass as well. No matches at all then.

Chapter Thirty-six
[Crockett: This is not kosher]

Dane and I watched Emily go through the contents of her backpack for the fourth time.

We'd gone back to my place for the search. She hadn't seen the state of her home yet. That might negatively impact the search for the key, if there is a key.

She held her key ring in her hand and went through them all while shaking her head.

"Not there?"

"No. I know all these keys. Shop, office, my front door, and my back door, and your front door."

She dropped the key ring on the floor and went back to searching every pocket of the backpack again. "There are not any other keys." Defeated, she pushed the backpack away and it fell off the table. Upending on the floor. "I do not know where the key is."

"We'll find it," I said. "Come on. Let's try your house." I held out my hand. Emily slipped her hand into mine. Dane was already at the door.

For safety's sake, I ran an SDR. I spotted June Tracey's old blokes stationed at irregular intervals down Fergusson Drive and Ward Street. Couldn't help myself and gave them all a wave. What was June thinking? I hoped Tierney managed to rein her in a bit.

"You are smiling," Emily said as I pulled into her

driveway.

"I was thinking about Tierney reining June in a bit."

Dane chuckled. Emily frowned for a moment.

"Come on," I said and climbed out of the car. While I waited for Dane and Emily to join me, I scanned the area. We weren't yet close enough to set the cameras off. There was no one around.

Emily checked the letterbox. She arrived on the front doorstep with her house key in hand and no mail. An alert sounded on my phone. That'd be the front door camera.

"Before you go in. The Genoas searched your house. They made a mess. There are holes in the wall of the spare room."

"Okay." She keyed the lock and pushed the door open before tentatively stepping over the threshold. Dane followed. I had one last look outside, and once I was sure there was no one lurking or watching, I locked the front door behind us.

Emily was gone from my sight. Dane was waiting near the spare room door.

"It could be anywhere," Siri said.

"Could be. I'm hoping something will jog her memory now that we're here and know what we're looking for." I poked my head into the spare room and looked at the holes. "It doesn't look as though Genoa was looking for a key."

"Yeah," Siri said as Dane moved down to the lounge room.

I followed, looking around as I walked. Where would a key be? I know where I'd put a key - in my floor safe and good luck getting it out without help from me.

Dane wasn't in the lounge. I followed the sound of movement to the kitchen. I paused to right tipped chairs in the dining room. In the kitchen, Emily and Dane were picking up the contents of the cupboards. They were dumping broken crockery in the sink as they came to it.

"It won't take long to get everything back to normal," I said when Emily turned to see me.

"I will need to go shopping. I do not think there are any unbroken plates and cups."

"I'll take you."

I reached for the radio and put it back on the bench then plugged it in. It still worked. I turned it off because I wanted to be sure to hear anyone outside even though my phone would tell me. It felt better to work in silence than allow music to distract the process.

"Be right back," I said and went out the back door. I grabbed the big red wheelie bin and dragged it up the steps and into the kitchen. "It'll be easy just dropping stuff straight in here."

Half an hour later we'd picked everything up and thrown a good deal away. I'd wrapped all the broken crockery and glass in newspaper and added the parcels to the big bin.

Emily leant on the kitchen bench.

"It can't be in here, can it?" she said.

"Probably not," Siri said. "We didn't come across a key

in the mess."

She tapped her fingers on the stainless-steel bench top. "Where would someone like you hide a key?" she asked me.

"My safe," I replied. That did not please her. "If I didn't have a safe. I'd use an empty tin in my pantry."

She turned to the cupboard where she kept her tinned food. "How would I know?"

"It'd be lighter and underneath it would look different."

"They were all over the floor," she said. "It is not the tins."

"Freezer," I said. I spun and looked at the fridge. I'd pushed it back when we found the mess, but it wasn't unplugged or ransacked, not like the cupboards anyway. They may have looked through the contents of the fridge and just not been dicks about it.

"Freezer," Emily repeated. "Just in there?"

"I would've put it inside something."

She crossed the room and pulled the freezer drawer open. I watched as she removed a loaf of bread from the tray at the top and inspected it. She shook her head and put it back. Then she shoved the tray out of her way and accessed the frozen foods. There were packets of chips, two boxes of fish cakes (she must really like fish cakes), a two-litre vanilla ice-cream container, and a much smaller container of Kāpiti ice-cream. Next were some bread rolls, and right at the bottom were two packets of frozen berries.

She inspected the chips. Both bags were sealed and hadn't been opened. She put those back. Neither of the boxes of fish cakes had been opened. They went back as well. The bread rolls were unopened. The ice-cream still had the safety seal on it. She shrugged and put it back. She did the same with the Kāpiti container. It all hinged on frozen berries.

Both had ziplock openings and both had been used.

I grabbed a plastic bowl, and she tipped the first bag into the bowl. No key. I poured the contents back into the ziplock bag and dropped it into the freezer. Emily tipped the second one into the bowl.

Again, there was no key. Poking out of the berries was a piece of paper - a folded piece of a memo cube or maybe a Post-it note. She unfolded the paper and showed me a number. It was seven-five-five-three.

"That has to mean something," I said. "Most people don't keep Post-it notes with numbers on it in their frozen smoothie fruit."

She put it in her pocket. "I was going to throw the fruit away," she said. "I do not like smoothies, and it has been there so long the fruit is probably ruined anyway."

I tipped the fruit into the bag and put it back. "Why didn't you chuck it?"

She shrugged. "I do not know. Never got around to it."

"Maybe your subconscious knew it was important to keep."

"A number," Emily said. "What is the number for?"

I shook my head. "Don't know. Could be the box

number."

Dane agreed with a nod.

"If it's the box number then I must have the key," Emily said. "Maybe I do have a key. Where else would someone like you hide a key?"

"Don't know that I'd put one anywhere else in the kitchen. Kitchens do hold a variety of hiding places, and we've looked in them all." I leaned on the bench next to her. "It's promising. That piece of paper." Unless it was for something else, I supposed. Think positive. It's probably a box number.

My phone alerted. I checked the screen.

"We've got company," I said and motioned to Dane to take Emily. Then signed: Bathroom. He nodded. I watched two men approach the front door. They had to walk past the car so there was a good chance they expected someone to be home.

There was a knock at the door. I opened the camera app properly so I could see the faces of the men at the door. I half expected to see Tony Robinson but that wasn't him and I didn't think it was Lucas Genoa either. That was interesting.

I took my time reaching the door. Without opening it I said, "Can I help you?"

"We're looking for Emily Jones," one of the men said.

"Afraid you've wasted your time. She doesn't live here anymore."

My phone screen caught my eye. One of the men pulled a gun from under his jacket. Nope. Not today.

I ran to the bathroom and signed: gun. Bad guys.

The gunman shot the door lock.

I hustled into the bedroom, pulled my gun from my holster, and positioned myself so whoever came down the hallway didn't get any further. I knew Dane would have Emily in the bathtub with her head down. He'd also use his iPad to alert Ronnie, Ben, and Enzo. They could get here before the cops.

A shadow fell across the hall. "Hand her over, and we'll leave."

I waited. I heard two more footfalls. I spun out the door and shot the first guy in the shoulder. The second guy grabbed for his mate's gun. I shot him in the hand.

No one died. No one would die. I swept the legs out from under the one I'd shot in the shoulder. The other one was squawking and holding his hand.

"Sit down. Hold pressure and elevate that hand."

The other one tried to stand. "Stay down." I picked up the loose gun and shoved it in my waistband.

Dane emerged. I nodded. He frisked the first bloke and threw a wallet on the ground near the bathroom door. From the second male, he took another wallet.

"Don't fucking move," I said.

Dane hustled into the kitchen and came back with tea towels. He folded one up and gave it to shoulder guy. Then wrapped the other one's hand in a tea towel.

There was no need to have blood everywhere.

I handed Dane my gun. He took over while I picked up the wallets and went through them. Both men carried

Defence Force ID cards. Idiots. It had to be Bill Bailey's stupidity on display, surely. But it sure felt wrong. He wasn't usually clumsy. I heard a Harley rumble outside. And car doors slammed just as I photographed the cards and sent the pictures to Ronnie.

My phone alerted saying people were approaching. It was Ronnie, Ben, and Enzo.

Enzo pushed the door wider and waltzed in with a grin on his face.

"Probably going to get a speeding ticket. Hope the SOS was worth it," he said, grinning wider. "Who are these bozos?"

"Army," I said.

Ronnie walked in looking at her phone. She sighed. "Why would the idiot send these fools? Did he think we'd let someone else take Emily?"

I rocked on my heels. "I'm starting to think we've been lied to and led down the garden path."

"Same," Ronnie replied.

"Who is who?" Ben asked the wounded men.

"Bradley Wickens," one said holding his uninjured hand up.

"Campbell Vega," said the other. He kept pressure on his shoulder.

"Are we expecting anyone else?" Ronnie asked.

"No," they replied in unison.

"Good. And in your opinion, was shooting your way inside this house a clever idea?" She shook her head. "Maybe they're not from the intelligence unit."

"We're not," Campbell said. "We need medical."

"You'll get medical attention back at the camp. Soon," I said. "What are you doing here?"

"Looking for Emily Jones."

"Why?"

"It's a job."

"You're moonlighting," Ronnie said on an exhale. "You really are stupid."

"Who is the job for?"

"Some rando. I don't know their name. They said it was a simple scoop and drop," Campbell replied. "Cash payday."

"So, you're the brains behind this mess, are you?" Ben asked, giving Campbell a nudge with his booted toe. "Don't quit your day job, pal. You are clearly not cut out for whatever the hell this is supposed to be."

"Don't rub it in," Campbell replied, wincing

"Right. Back to who hired you," Ronnie said as she scrolled on her phone. She held her phone so Campbell could see the screen. "This guy?" He shook his head. She flicked to another photo. "Him?"

"It was a woman."

"Fuck me!" I kicked at the wall. "Fucking Costa."

Chapter Thirty-seven
[Ronnie: You piece of work]

Crockett moved closer to me and grumbled in my ear. "Did you get that bitch's phone number?"

"I'm calling her any minute. You, Emily, and Dane keep looking for that bloody key. Enzo, Ben, and I will deliver these idiots to Bill Bailey. He can find the appropriate help for them."

"Might look like a court-martial," Crockett said.

"I imagine that is what it will look like."

"How much shit, is the shooting going to rain down on us?"

"I won't be tolerating anything coming back at us. Not our doing. You had to protect Emily, and I think Bill will agree. About time he was of real use."

It would work as long as we kept the police out of it. To my knowledge, no one had reported gunfire in the area. Enzo had texted Josh to confirm and there were no reports of gunfire. Perhaps things were finally swinging our way.

Right when I thought that a black sedan pulled up outside Emily's and a driver got out and hurried around the car to open the back passenger door onto the curb. I saw the cane before I saw the man. Tierney. That man is everywhere.

"Ben," I tapped his shoulder to get his attention.

"Grandfather alert."

"That can't be good."

"Looks like a *you,* problem," I said, pushing him towards the door. It's definitely not a *me,* problem.

My phone rang. It was an unknown caller. Had to be *Genesis.*

"I need to take this," I said to Crockett and Dane and walked into the lounge before I answered the phone. "Hello."

"Ronnie," the electronically modified voice said.

"Uncle George."

"Yes."

"What can I do for you?" Because I knew what he could do for me. Get me some information about this disaster.

"Do you have Emily Jones?"

"Yes."

"Keep hold of her."

"I'm planning on it." I concentrated on the background noises and tried to work out where the caller rang from. For a split second, I thought I heard a kid.

"Someone entered a restricted *Genesis* website and copied information."

"Are you saying it was a hack?"

"No. I'm saying someone had a way in that didn't involve breaching firewalls. The information taken was about an Operation in Belgium."

"That's funny," I said, lightening my voice. "We're in the middle of something that originated in Belgium." I listened to the background noise again. It wasn't traffic, but children playing. Maybe they rang from a park. Maybe I was on the right track suspecting Crockett's mate Mitch Iverson was *Genesis*. He had a couple of kids. Twin girls from memory.

"Be careful Ronnie," the robotic voice said, and the line went dead.

Bugger. I wanted to ask them a few questions. Maybe it was good that I didn't. It might've confirmed their suspicions.

I could hear Tierney's voice in the hallway. It wasn't raised but he had a particular tone about him. The type that said he didn't suffer fools well. With a cleansing breath, I went from the lounge to the hallway.

"Veronica," Tierney said. "What is happening here?"

"We are about to deposit these men back at the army camp," I replied. "Does that meet with your approval?" Not that I cared. I cared that Dane stayed out of sight. I cared that Tierney knew where we were and arrived. I looked past him. "No, Nana?"

He huffed in annoyance. "Veronica, I would not subject your wonderful Nana to this." He cast his free hand around the hallway and clung to his cane with the other.

Wonderful, Nana?

A cringe shivered its way down my spine. She was wonderful, but not like he said it, that bordered on creepy.

"We're off," I said to Ben then looked at Tierney. "And

you are here why?"

"This situation was brought to my attention."

It was my turn to huff with annoyance. "Nana's surveillance or your own?"

He suppressed a smile. "Your Nana's. You were seen coming this way far too fast for it to be anything good."

Fair enough.

"And you're here ..."

"To help Veronica, in case the police were involved. It seems they are not, so my driver will return me to your home."

"We'll be back as soon as we can get there," I replied. "Please keep Nana in the house."

"She is under my protection," he replied, then turned, leaning on his cane he doddered down the hall and out into the daylight.

My internal self-talk reminded me to keep calm. Don't let it rile you. There are extenuating circumstances.

"Enough piss-farting around," Crockett said. "Get these two out of my sight before I lose my cool."

Ben and Enzo dragged them to their feet and escorted them out the door to our waiting car. I said goodbye and followed. They were handcuffed and in the back seat. Enzo put his helmet on and jumped on his Harley. He waved a finger as he took off.

I sat in the front passenger seat and called Bill.

"Dropping something off to you in five minutes. Be ready."

I hung up before he could say anything. In the car park

of the Messine Centre, Ben helped our captives get out of the car.

"Do you need help?" he asked.

I shook my head and prodded one of the men. I'd already forgotten who was who. They were that memorable. I pushed them along to the big glass door. Bill was on the other side waiting. He waved an access card and opened the door.

"Go," I said to the men. "Get inside."

Bill looked from them to me. We were all inside the building. "What do we have here?"

"These idiots belong to someone's unit." I gave one a small shove. He stumbled. "I imagine they're going to be unfit for duty for a little while."

He glared at the men. "I will locate your commanding officer. You can expect a severe punishment."

"Yes, Sir," one of them said. "Sorry, Sir."

"You will be," he replied.

Bill shifted his attention to me. "Do we need to have a conversation?"

"Not right now." I started to leave. "You'll hear from me."

"Can it be less bloody next time?"

"That all depends on what we uncover next." I waved and left.

Ben fired up the car. As he drove back to the office, I rang Costa. It went to voicemail. I left a message telling her to contact me A-SAP then hung up.

She really annoyed me.

Tierney annoyed me.

Bill bloody Bailey annoyed me.

Robinson was on the list as well.

Lies were oxygen to all of them. We needed to cut off their supply. Find the truth and run with it, no matter what. Sometimes I wished life was a soap opera and we could get results from DNA testing within the hour. It would take weeks to get DNA results back and then it would take even longer to work out who was who. I doubted we could even find out. Then I considered genetic testing to find out where people come from. But we'd need to know where Emily was from and her family background, and the same for Simone. And just like that I was back in the never-ending circle of lies. The dead person in Belgium was either Simone or not. Emily was either Emily or not. If we got any DNA on the swab, I'd sent to the lab it would at least tell us if there was a familial match between Costa and Simone.

What was Simone's real surname? We knew they were not all Genoas. Tom and Peter Piper were definitely not Genoas, Emily is not a Genoa. Did everyone use the same surname for a reason? Maybe that's how they identified each other when they first met. So perhaps one of them was a Genoa. Lucas was the obvious answer to that riddle. So, who was Simone? Was she Simone Costa? If Emily took her place, then she knew about the Genoa thing.

We needed to break through the bullshit barrier.

All of a sudden, I realised we weren't moving, and Ben

was standing by my open car door, waiting for me. It took me a second to work out where we were. Ben had parked in the alley behind the bookshop. There was another car there.

"Who does that belong to?" I asked as I exited Ben's car. It wasn't a car I recognised as usually being in the alley. Warm still alleyway air surrounded me. It wasn't unpleasant. There was a hint of baking bread and fresh coffee from the café on the corner.

Ben wrote the plate number in his notebook. I pressed the car door closed. He pointed to the number plate surround. "It's a rental. Omega."

"Bugger, we've wrecked a few of their cars. They probably won't be the most helpful when we ask who rented that one."

"They might be pleased to hear from us."

"I guess we provided a certain amount of entertainment the times we've wrecked their cars and had to explain how it happened for their insurance."

Ben grinned. "I'll call them."

I didn't realise he meant right then. I leaned on his car and waited. He can be very charming with little effort. Sometimes it was disconcerting but today it was amusing. As soon as he said the car was parked near the offices of *Wherefore Art Thou,* he put the call on speaker so I could hear what happened next.

"That car was hired by Simone Genoa. Please don't destroy any more of our cars."

Excellent, just what we needed was another Simone

Genoa.

I cleared my throat. "Is that you John? Ronnie Tracey here. I can't make promises."

He spluttered then regained his composure. "It's me. Why do you want to know about that car?"

"Curiosity," I said. "Can you send me a photo of the ID from the person who rented the car?"

"I suppose so. Please don't wreck it." There was a little bit of a plea in his tone. Anyone would think we were death to cars. We weren't, but sometimes shit happens and I prefer it happens to a rental and not one of my cars. My phone buzzed in my pocket. I pulled it out and checked the screen. It was a photo of an international driver's license in the name of Simone Genoa. I'm not sure it was a good thing that John didn't have to ask for my cell phone number.

"When did the woman sign the car out and for how long?"

"Yesterday and a week," he replied. "I have to go." He hung up.

Ben put his phone away. "We block the car in?"

"Yep."

He slid behind the wheel of his car while I moved to the stairwell doorway and waited. He angled his car across the rear of the rental. It wasn't going anywhere. But where was the driver? No one had accessed our building. I knew that because the cameras would've told me. The cameras would've told me repeated in my mind. Would they? We already knew camera feeds were blocked at Emily's place. I tried the back door. It was locked. It can be locked from the inside. I checked for tool marks. Nothing. But then someone who knew what they were doing wouldn't leave marks. It was a deadbolt. A slip card wouldn't work. Ben noticed my attention to the door.

"You think whoever it is, could be upstairs waiting?"

I nodded. "Back door is the logical entry point." I lifted my keys from my pocket and slid the correct key into the lock. Quietly I pushed the door open. There was no door handle on the back door, just the lock. On the inside, there were also two sliding bolts. Once the door was closed and locked. I slid the top and bottom bolts across. Now if someone tried to escape that way they couldn't easily. They'd need to pick the lock on this side as well. It was key entry and exit.

I looked up at the camera that should've alerted me to our entry. The light was on, but I suspected it wasn't recording.

We quietly opened the stairwell door and waited for a beat. Listening for anything that said someone was in the building. There were no sounds of movement from the hallway. It would be harder to hear anyone in the main office or front stairwell.

I climbed the stairs keeping pace with Ben. At the top, we listened again. There was no noise. I smiled at my fiancé.

He knew what was about to happen and grinned.

I flung the main office door open and called out, "Simone, are you here?" Movement by Steph's desk caught my eye. "Get away from that desk. It's not your business."

I made out a pale blue hooded sweatshirt but couldn't see who was wearing it.

Slowly, the person stood.

Well, shit, she was a brunette version of Emily. She looked like a dead woman walking.

"Simone Genoa?" Ben asked, from beside me.

"Yes," she said.

How many of them were there? She stepped away from the desk. Once in the open, I could see exactly how similar she was to Emily. I pointed to the couch under the window. "Take a seat over there."

She did. Ben stood by the door then turned, pushed it closed, and locked it. That was good thinking. I didn't want anyone walking in on this, and just lately everyone's been appearing in my office.

"Who are you?" I said, opting to stand behind my preferred armchair, rather than sit.

"Simone Genoa." I listened to her voice. I couldn't say for certain if she had an accent or if her voice was as generic as Costa's.

"Why are you here?"

"For my diamonds."

"We don't have them," I said.

"You have someone who does have them," she replied.

"Who sent you?"

"No one. I came for what is mine."

"You're dead," Ben replied. He also opted to stand.

"So, who are you really?"

"I am very much alive."

"You're not Simone Genoa," I said. "What's your name?"

She smiled and suddenly looked nothing like Emily. "Simone Genoa."

"You're annoying me," I said. "What is your real name?"

The woman's lips curled into a snarl. "I came for what is mine."

"The problem with that is that the diamonds don't belong to you or anyone else who is trying to get their hands on them. They belong to the company in Belgium that they were stolen from," I said and smiled at her. "We could not give them to you even if we did have them."

"I'm over this Genoa horse shit," Ben said and snapped a photo of the woman with his phone. He leaned close to me and whispered in my ear, "I'm sending this to *Uncle George* for ID."

I nodded. That was a great idea. *Genesis* should be able to tell us something about the woman. I hauled in bits and pieces from the files we downloaded. There was zero mention of there being another woman involved. The heist was pulled off by one woman and four men. We knew two of the men and needed to get inside that situation and find out what the hell was going on. Then there was Lucas Genoa and the now-deceased, Stefan Genoa. And of course, Emily Jones or Simone Genoa. There were not three Simones, were there? We knew of two: one deceased and one alive. How the hell was there another one? I checked the photo John and Omega car rentals sent me. It was an International Driving Permit. The photo was the woman in front of me, but any driver's license photo is not that great. If you looked close enough then no one would question it. And she looked close enough. Close enough to Emily and close enough to Simone.

I opened a scanner on my phone. I had an idea and went with it. I walked over and stood in front of the latest Simone Genoa, held out my phone and told her to touch the screen with her fingers. She hesitated.

"Just do it," I said. "Don't make me force you."

Her lips again curled into a nasty snarl. "You're going to make me," she scoffed.

"Just do it. Unless of course, you aren't Simone Genoa and don't want us to know who you really are."

She balled her hands into fists in her lap. Ben moved into position. He grasped her right wrist and twisted. Grimacing and squeaking in pain, she let her fingers uncurl. I pressed them onto my screen. It took seconds to scan. Once it was done and the nice green tick appeared, Ben let her wrist go. She shook it out and rubbed it with the other hand. I stepped back to behind my favourite chair and started the database search. I also sent a copy of the fingerprints to *Uncle George*.

We waited to see where our answers came from first. Silence deepened around us. Minutes dragged by and then my phone pinged and a moment later, Ben's did the same.

We checked at the same time and smiled at each other before I shared our news with the Simone Genoa interloper.

"Shame you aren't Simone Genoa. Guess there are no diamonds in your future," I said. "Turns out you are not even a Genoa."

She fumed silently. Her face twisted in annoyance. "Don't be ridiculous," she muttered. "None of them are Genoas."

We knew that but we didn't know who they really were.

"No, they're not," Ben said. "It's nice to meet you Katerina Solkov, of the little-known South American country of Crimea."

I chuckled.

Katerina growled. "Stupid westerners. The Republic of Crimea is not in South America."

I rolled my eyes. Ben's joke was lost on her.

"No sense of humour. Perfect," I said.

She glared up at me. "The diamonds belong to Russia," she said.

We didn't have all the facts surrounding the case because we were too busy trying to keep people alive. Then it occurred to me that perhaps we did have all the facts and just didn't know it. They could be in the files we appropriated.

"Ben, I need to read something and then continue with this chat we're having with Katerina."

"You read, I'll watch her," he said.

I hurried to the 'vault' at the back of the room and fired it up. The files I'd downloaded were exactly where I'd left them. I started reading, looking for any mention of who owned the diamonds. I scrolled, read, scrolled, read, and then found it. The diamonds were up for auction and reportedly owned by a European company called Zelix. I wrote that on a piece of paper and powered down the 'vault'. Using my phone, I looked up Zelix. There wasn't a lot of information. Looked suspiciously like a shell company. I turned to my laptop and began a deeper dive into Zelix. It was a shell company; beyond that was an umbrella company, and beyond that an oligarch. I sent everything I found to *Uncle George* for verification.

My phone chimed with a verification text.

I crossed the room to where Ben and Katerina waited.

"I have confirmed that the diamonds belong to an oligarch. I imagine he would like them back, especially with all the sanctions due to the Ukraine war."

"That's an individual rather than Russia?" Ben queried.

"It is."

Katerina watched us, her eyes flicking back and forth.

"No one would want to hand over the property of an individual to a state, would they?" Ben asked.

"It would be rude, wouldn't it, to give someone's wealth away," I replied. Then looked directly at Katerina. "Do you work for Dimitri Aslanov?"

She dipped her head slightly.

"And he lives in London, better known as Londongrad, where the oligarchs and other wealthy Russians seem to have set themselves up?" Ben said.

I smiled. "I've heard it referred to as Moscow-on-Thames."

Katerina smirked. "He does. He wants his diamonds back."

"I'm sure he does. When you decided to be Simone, I guess, you didn't know that she was dead." I squeezed the back of the chair with my hands. "Why would you come to me pretending to be someone involved in the heist?"

"Costa is here looking for the diamonds. Lucas Genoa is here looking for the diamonds. Stefan is here. Do you understand?"

"Stefan is unfortunately dead."

"One down," she said.

"Simone is dead," Ben reminded her. "That's two down."

"You are a liar."

She didn't mention any familial link between Costa and Simone Genoa. Maybe our intelligence was wrong, and they weren't related like it appeared. Or maybe no one else knew. It felt like a long shot, but stranger things than that have happened. People think they know something, and it colours their world with bias. Was ours similarly coloured?

"Well, us liars are going to get back to work now," I said. "I don't want you running about town causing shit so we're going to need you to stay here."

I beckoned to her. She stood and moved towards me.

Ben smiled, and his most charming self emerged. "Follow me. We have somewhere a little more comfortable." I handed him my keys. By comfortable he meant our extra special sound proofed jail cell. As he walked away with her, I heard him ask if she had a cell phone. There was no fuss, so she probably didn't realise what was about to happen. When I heard Ben ask if she'd like a drink of water, I smiled. So considerate. If I were her, I wouldn't drink that water.

What a team!

I rang *Uncle George* and waited for the callback.

Chapter Thirty-eight
[Crockett: Where is the key?]

Ronnie texted and said they had a woman in custody at her office. We were still on the hunt for the key. People were coming out of the woodwork. Diamonds are a draw card for sure. We stayed at Emily's. It was quieter without the nonsense from earlier. Emily was quiet. She stood in the middle of the lounge.

"I do not know where I would hide a key," she said.

"We'll go room by room. We've searched the kitchen and dining room." I looked around the lounge. "Where could a key be in here?"

The furniture was moved by the Genoas and their search, but they weren't looking for a key they were looking for something a little bigger.

Emily shoved her hands down between the cushions and frame of an armchair and felt around. She produced a few coins.

Dane and I checked the couch. He found coins. I found an ice-block stick. Emily checked the remaining chair and found more coins. I picked up the coffee table and looked underneath it and found nothing. I placed it where it was supposed to go. Emily and Dane placed their coin haul on the table. It wasn't a bad haul: ten dollars' worth of ones and twos.

I took a painting off the wall and checked behind it for

anything that could've been taped or inserted into the frame. Another big fat nothing.

"Next room," I said. Then an idea manifested. "Emily, you left us a note at one of the houses, it was in a toilet roll. Maybe you hid something in the bathroom or toilet here."

Her eyes sparkled. "I might have." She hurried away to the bathroom, and I followed. Dane opted to try the spare room.

The bathroom cabinet was open. The contents were emptied into the basin. Shampoo and conditioner were tipped into the shower near the drain. There was only the slightest residual left from the bottles. The room smelt nice.

"Why did they have to empty everything?"

"They were looking for diamonds and diamonds are easily concealed in bathroom products," I said.

"At least the bath was not full of messy stuff," she replied. "Otherwise, it would have been yucky when Dane got me to hide in there."

I smiled. I knew he'd do that.

There were pill bottles strewn on the floor. The tops were off. I picked one up. "You're going to need all new medication."

"I have repeats at the chemist. I can pick them up." Emily started picking packets up off the floor and checking them for contents. She held a small dark jar in her hand. "They poked around in my moisturiser. I am going to need more everything." She dropped the jar on the bathmat. "I do not want any of this anymore."

Emily left the room. I watched her go then went back to picking up containers and checking them. She came back with a rubbish bag.

"Good idea," I said with a smile. "Chuck everything we've checked then we'll replace it all."

She nodded. Quietly she picked up containers, packets, pill bottles, empty bottles, squeezed out toothpaste tubes, and dumped them in the black plastic bag.

I did the same after checking they weren't harbouring anything key-shaped. Emily stood up with a small round container in her hand. She opened the lid and tipped the contents into the sink.

"Why did they smash up the bronzer powder?" She tossed it into the open rubbish bag.

"Arseholes, they're arseholes."

That was the only explanation. There was no need to destroy everything.

"My floor is filthy," she said adding more rubbish to the bin bag. "Do you think they found diamonds?"

"No. I don't think diamonds were ever here, Emily. I think you would've put them somewhere very safe."

"At the bank with the horse."

"Yes."

"What if they found the key?"

"They didn't find the box number. The key probably won't have any information on it."

"Okay."

We picked the last things up. I rinsed out the sink.

Emily took the rubbish bag and dropped it in the hallway then came back and turned the shower on to wash the last of the shampoo and conditioner away. I moved on to the bath and picked up empty bottles. Emily took a sponge from the cabinet and began to wipe up the powdery crap off the floor. By the time we were done, it didn't look too bad. It still needed a proper clean, but that could wait.

"Where next?" Emily asked from the doorway.

"You hid a note in a toilet roll so why don't you check the toilet? Make sure you look inside the cistern."

Anyone who watches telly knows that the toilet cistern is a handy place to hide drugs, guns, money, and anything else you want easily accessible, but hidden. They would've looked and Emily wouldn't put anything in such an obvious place.

By the time I finished washing out the bath, she was back at the door. "At least they didn't destroy all the toilet paper," she said holding a single wrapped roll in her hand.

"What have you got there?"

"A wrapped toilet roll," she said with a smile. "It is one of those novelty ones with a crossword printed on the paper."

"And they didn't unwrap it?"

She shook her head. "I do not know how long I have had it. But I do know I always keep it at the bottom of the basket with the other toilet rolls. They are not wrapped." Emily moved away from the door.

I followed her into the lounge. She sat on the couch. "Where is Dane?"

"I'll find him."

I ducked out and found him in the spare room. He was cleaning and tidying as he searched.

"Hey, Emily might've found something. Come on."

Back in the lounge, I watched Emily carefully unwrap the roll. It did have a crossword printed on it. She poked her fingers into the tube and pushed out something wrapped in more crossword toilet paper. Inside the paper was a key.

"We have it!" she said with glee. "I guess I do like hiding things inside toilet rolls."

I chuckled. "You sure do."

Dane grinned and typed on the iPad. "Good work, Emily. Now we just need to locate the box it fits."

"We need a little more than that. We need to know what form of identification Emily used to open the account. She'll need that to access it."

"I am Emily Jones," she said, firmly. "I would have used my ..." Words failed her. "What would I use?"

"You had a driver's license then Emily. You probably used that." Or maybe she used her passport. "Do you have that?"

"I do not know?"

"Okay, we need to find out before we go any further. Do you have an old wallet or purse that you used back then?"

I was thinking she might keep things from back then

for sentimental reasons.

"There is a box." She held her hands out and moved them to about thirty centimetres apart. "Like this."

"Shoebox?"

She nodded. "That size. In my room."

She shoved the key into her jeans pocket and led the way to her bedroom. She gasped at the shock of seeing the mess in her room. The wardrobe contents were pulled off coat hangers and dumped on the floor. Her dresser drawers were upended. Her bed covers were ripped off the bed and pillows torn open. Fluffy polyester stuffing covered the bed. Boxes from under her bed were emptied onto a pile of clothes.

This would take some time to sort through.

"Where was the box?" I asked, picking up the first box I saw.

Dane disappeared, then came back with the rubbish bag. I scooped pillow stuffing from the bed and shoved it in the bag. With that gone and the bedding folded at the end of the bed we had a surface to put things on as we picked up and tidied.

"It was on the shelf in the wardrobe, I think," Emily said. She tiptoed and reached her hand up to the shelf. She withdrew her hand empty. "Must be amongst this mess."

One by one she picked things up. Dane put the drawers back in the dressing tables. Emily hung clothes on the empty coat hangers. Together we made short work of the disaster. In the end, we were left with four colourful boxes, about shoe box size. Two were bigger plastic boxes with lids that fit under her bed. There was a pile of shoes, handbags, backpacks, and purses, books, notebooks, and pens scattered around.

"It is that box," she said pointing to an empty pink box.

"When we find homes for all this other stuff, that should help us find the things that belong in the pink box."

I set the empty boxes on the bed with their matching lids underneath them and Emily began directing where things lived. The shoes were easy. Shoes lived in one of the big plastic boxes under her bed and handbags went in the other. We searched through each handbag just in case.

Dane turned the light on as dusk moved across the room.

Chapter Thirty-nine
[Ronnie: Just tell the truth]

Ginny and Tom became all the more important as the day wore on. I knew Crockett and Dane were helping Emily find whatever was needed to locate the diamonds, or not, as the case might be. None of us actually knew if she had ever had them or what she could've done with them if she did. Were we supposed to take the word of international crooks and spies? That didn't sit well with me. I helped Donald make dinner to take my mind off my uselessness. Ben had managed a few quiet moments with Tierney out on the balcony. Nana was preoccupied with *The Cronies of Doom*. Maybe it was good having them here after all. I hoped they were planning their Raro adventure.

Snippets of conversation floated in the air from the lounge. I chose to ignore them all as I set the table. I couldn't handle much more chit-chat from old people about surveillance and one more code name was almost guaranteed to break my brain.

"Are we ready out there?" Donald called from the kitchen.

"Yes," I replied. "I'm coming."

I took the plates through to the dining room while Donald carried a huge platter of roasted vegetables. He scurried back for the carved lamb artfully arranged on another platter. There was nothing Donald enjoyed more than entertaining and dragging out all the fine family china that Nana had bestowed on us. The last dishes were covered serving bowls containing green beans and peas. I brought through the gravy boat.

Donald stood for a minute and surveyed the spread with a satisfied smile.

"The only thing missing is Enzo," he said wistfully.

"I doubt he'll be long," I said. "Wasn't he finishing up paperwork with Steph?"

Donald nodded and popped into the lounge. "Dinner is served."

All those over seventy shuffled and clunked into the dining room. Donald stood directing people to the seats he'd chosen for them. He really did love entertaining. I waited for Ben and Tierney to join us then sat in my assigned chair.

Table chatter praising Donald for his meal kept everyone occupied. It was bloody good lamb. The man can cook.

All of a sudden, I had the strongest feeling that now was a good time to see Ginny and Tom.

"They'll be home," I said jumping to my feet so fast my chair tumbled behind me.

"Veronica! Manners," Nana admonished.

I fixed my eyes on hers. "Thought we had previously established that I have none."

Her faded blue eyes flashed at me. "You do not behave like that at the dinner table. Now sit down."

Nope.

"I think you've forgotten whose table this is," I said softly. I knew there was nothing wrong with her hearing. Another flash of faded blue. I righted my chair and pushed it in.

"Are you coming?" I asked Ben.

"Of course," he replied, placing his knife and fork on his plate before standing. "I doubt we'll be gone long." He took my hand, and we left.

We left Nana fuming. I doubt she'd ever been as outraged as she had over the last few days. It wouldn't hurt her. Sometimes life doesn't wait for the niceties.

Ben and I sat in the car with the engine running.

"Where are we going?"

"To talk to Tom and Ginny."

Fifteen minutes later Ben parked at the top of their driveway, and we walked down. Tom's car was there. It felt rude to knock on the door of anyone's door at dinnertime and worse that it was Ginny's. I got over it pretty fast.

"Right, you knock," I said to Ben.

"Chicken," he whispered.

"Yep."

Before he could knock, the door opened revealing Ginny's welcoming smile. "Haven't seen you two in a few days. Come in. Have you eaten?"

"Yes," I lied. We're here for answers, not food.

"Come on. Get in here," Ginny hugged me and opened the laundry door so I could leave my shoes there. Ben left his on the top step, gave Ginny a hug, and then shut the back door on the warmish evening. Tom put his knife and fork down and looked up.

"What brings you two out at dinnertime?"

"Tomás Genoa," I said with a smile. If it meant anything to him, he hid it well. There was no reaction at all.

I pulled out my usual chair and sat down.

"That's a serious expression," Tom said.

"Serious problem," I replied.

"Emily?"

"In a roundabout kind of way," Ben said sitting down.

Ginny sat too.

"You can keep eating," I said. "No sense in your dinner going cold."

Hopefully, no one will choke.

"Come on, out with it," Tom said. "What's going on?"

"Circle back to you being in Belgium eight years ago." I chewed my lip and hoped Uncle George would come through with proof that Tom was also in Paris two years later.

"I remember the trip. What's this about?"

"Did you go to Paris five years ago?"

As I said it, I knew why Emily didn't go. She was busy losing her leg in that 'car accident'. Or maybe not. I didn't know when the Paris trip took place in relation to her 'accident'; could've been before, during, or after.

"When was that trip to Paris?" Ben asked.

"I didn't go to Paris," Tom said.

My phone buzzed. One glance told me it was a text

from Uncle George.

Uncle George: Five years ago, Peter Piper and Tom Smith travelled to Europe.

Me: Together?

Uncle George: No. Forty-eight hours apart. Different destinations.

Me: They travelled as themselves?

Uncle George: They did not.

This was like pulling teeth. I waited for a beat. All eyes were on me.

"Problem, Ronnie?" Tom asked.

"Looks that way," I replied.

I turned my attention back to my phone.

Me: Did they use their previous identities. Genoa?

Three dots moved then stopped. Then moved again.

Uncle George: Yes.

Me: Shit.

I put my phone away.

"Are you all right?" Ben asked, touching my arm.

"Yep." I looked at Tom. "Tom, Paris?"

"I did go to Europe five years ago. Remember, Ginny?"

She smiled. "Stockholm."

"Stockholm," I repeated. "Stockholm?"

"Not Paris," Ben added.

He shook his head. "I haven't been to Europe since."

"Any reason?"

"I decided not to spend too much time away from home."

Or he knew Emily was here and far more about her than he'd ever let on.

"Fair enough." I wasn't done yet. "And Stockholm, did you see Peter Piper?"

"No."

"You're sure, you didn't see him?" Ben asked with a friendly even tone.

"I'm getting tired of this Ben. And my dinner is getting cold," Tom said.

"Eat," I said.

Ginny's bracelets and bangles jangled as she lifted her laden fork to her mouth.

"Recapping, you didn't go to Paris five years ago with Peter Piper?"

"Correct," Tom said. "That okay with you?"

"It would be if it was the truth. I really want that to be true."

Everyone's cutlery dropped. Tom's eyes hardened. Ginny's glittered.

"All right," Tom said quietly. "You want the truth ..."

I sighed without meaning to. "It's way above our or my pay grade, especially considering no one is paying me. But without the truth, this mess will never end."

"Is Emily safe?" Ginny asked.

"For now."

"How about that truth, Tom. Or should I call you

Tomás?"

I had a feeling he was not *Genesis* back then or if he was, he wasn't Oceania.

Maybe he was under the European umbrella. Or maybe I was way off, and *Genesis* didn't want us to know, and Uncle George wasn't as forthcoming as usual?

"Tom, thanks," he said, before he took a big sip of wine from the glass in front of him.

"Okay, Tom. When Lucas and Stefan showed up why didn't you say you knew who they were? Why didn't you say you knew who Simone Genoa was?"

"Not my place, Ronnie. The Genoa thing could get me killed. I've kept my head down since finding out they were here."

"Not low enough," I said. "Kerrin Costa has been following you."

"I know. She was outside my office in Stokes Valley and followed me to Queensgate. I'm sure she enjoyed being dragged around the busy mall. I also know you have her under surveillance and therefore me as a by-product."

"You haven't met with any Genoas?"

"You know I haven't. If I had Costa they would know and so would you."

That was true.

"What's your relationship with Emily?"

"I don't have one, apart from friendship after you introduced us. Remember?"

I nodded. "I do. But the thing is, everyone thinks she's

346

Simone Genoa … and the two other people that no one could identify during the heist, and since, are you and Peter Piper." I breathed slowly then smiled at Tom. "So, you see, Tom. I think you knew the whole time who she was or at least the role she played. Maybe you didn't know she couldn't be in Paris for the designated meet-up to divvy up the diamonds."

"I recognised her when you brought her here some time ago," he said. "It didn't take me long to realise she had no idea who I was or any clue about our connected past."

"So, what happened in Paris?"

"I went to Paris via Stockholm. Booked myself into the hotel we'd agreed to meet at. I was using the name Tomás Genoa. The next day Peter Piper arrived using the name Pedro Genoa. Later that night Stefan and Lucas arrived. We met in the bar that night. We agreed to wait twenty-four hours for Simone to show. When she didn't, we split up and went our separate ways. Convinced that she'd either been caught or decided to keep the diamonds."

"Weren't there paintings too?"

"Yes. Lucas took those. He had a guy who could get a good price."

"Did he?"

"I believe the person paid for the paintings and returned them to their rightful owner. It was deemed better to let money change hands because they were worth far less than the diamonds. My orders were to recover the diamonds. No one gave a shit about the paintings except Lucas and Stefan."

"So, they got something out of the heist. Was that for their pleasure or to fund the terror cell?"

Tom nodded gently. "For themselves, I believe. I heard nothing of the cell receiving anything from that sale. They want the diamonds."

"They still want them. So, it's terrorists who are after Emily. They won't stop, will they?"

He shook his head. "Not likely. They could do a lot of damage with those diamonds and last I heard they needed some serious funds."

"Is there anyone else in the country wanting Emily?"

He shook his head. "Not as far as I know. I only know about the Genoas and Costa, who is here to stop the cartel that is funding the terrorists, getting their hands on the goods."

"I'm sorry, cartel?"

"You didn't hear about that?"

"No."

"It's South America." He shrugged. "Cartel is synonymous with terror group. It just is."

That much I figured but because we'd heard no mention of a cartel, in this instance, it was a little bit jarring. I don't know why the notion of terrorists after Emily felt better than a cartel after her. It just did. What a screwed up crazy world we live in where I'm all good with terrorists, but drug cartels are a step too bloody far.

"And do you know where the diamonds are?"

"I do not. The only person who does know is Emily."

"Our Emily knows very little," Ben replied.

"We could wait until the cows came home for her to remember where they are, if she did really have them and if she put them somewhere safe," I said. The other things that niggled at me popped up again. "Why did you all use the name Genoa? Did you all have passports and other ID to match the name?"

"It was called Operation Genoa but officially it was Operation Sidestep. No one in the group knew anyone else's real identity."

"You had an operational name for a gang of thieves. Nice." I watched Ginny eat the last of her dinner. "It feels like we're missing a big chunk of this operation. Who were you working for?"

"New Zealand," Tom replied. "We collected the intelligence that led to us infiltrating the gang of thieves."

"How did that happen?"

Surely, they didn't just rock up to Antwerp and announce they were looking for a high-paying cat burglary job. That had to be pre-arranged. They had to have met either in person or via FaceTime or some other encrypted video chat platform. Peter and Tom had to already have decent legends with shockproof backstories. It would've taken months to set it all up and give them the connections and skills that meant the Genoas couldn't go past their expertise and happily let them into the gang.

"It was all carefully curated. People like Lucas and Stefan do not put themselves at risk."

They did though. They were the only crooks on the team.

"Did you ever meet Simone?"

"Yes."

"Did you kill Simone?"

"No."

"Do you know who did?"

"I have my suspicions."

"Could Simone be Kerrin Costa's cousin?"

"Seems reasonable. That would account for Costa being so adamant that Simone is alive and here."

"Is Simone alive?" I watched his face carefully. "Is she?"

Tom's eyes met mine. "No."

"You're sure?"

"I am. But you don't look convinced," he said.

"Let's just say that when no one is who they seem to be, and the truth doesn't fit with the narrative we've been given ... it's hard to really believe anything."

"That makes sense."

"Are you absolutely sure that Emily is Emily?"

"As far as I am aware."

"But you did meet with her in Antwerp, and you'd already met Simone; did you notice the difference?"

"No. I met with Simone twice. I never knew Emily as Emily. Even now they could be the same person."

"Did you know who Simone worked for?"

"No. I thought she was a highly skilled cat burglar and worked for herself. But the job we pulled in Antwerp was orchestrated by someone in South America. Our intelligence said it was a terror group that was mostly funded by the cartels."

"Is a cat burglar really a thing? It's all so Pink Panther."

"It was Simone who climbed the outside of the building to gain entry via a non-alarmed window on the sixth floor. So, they exist all right."

"She scaled the outside of a building ..." That's a skill and a half. Emily the cop from Upper Hutt was a cat burglar. "Did she let the rest of you in?"

"She did. But she took the diamonds back out the window with her."

"Why?"

"She needed our experience to get into the vault and turn off the cameras and all that jazz, but she took the diamonds out. That way if we were caught, we had nothing but a few paintings."

Guess that was smart. But it's sounding more like Simone was the brains and Stefan, Lucas, Pedro, and Tomás were the backup.

I was no closer to anything that made sense. I had postulated that the leader or shot caller was Lucas Genoa and it did not look like that now. I didn't want to ask who did what when it came to alarms, cameras, and the vaults. My stomach grumbled loudly, and I remembered the roast lamb we'd left on the table at home.

"We should go. I'm sorry we interrupted your dinner. I'll try not to do that again," I said, as I stood up.

"This is an unusual situation, Ronnie," Tom said. "I'll chew it over and see if I can remember anything helpful."

"Thanks."

"Meanwhile, I hope Costa enjoys following me around."

"She's SIDE ... but does that mean she's not working for a cartel?"

He shook his head. "Her keenness is more than likely due to cartel influence. They can be very persuasive."

If Simone really was her cousin and they got word of her here in New Zealand and threatened Costa, or maybe a few family members, then she might not be the enemy. Or she was part of this whole mess and Simone's partner in crime. Or she was straight-up cartel.

I put my shoes on and waited for Ben outside. It was a nice night; warmish and calm. Costa could still be the enemy. Maybe I needed to have another chat with her. Maybe she'd be more open now. Why I had no clue. But if she can't get what she needs then maybe she'd like to talk.

Ben and I strode in step, and in silence, up the driveway to the car. I didn't have a lot to say on the way home either. Mostly I just hoped Donald had saved our dinner because I was starving. Ben took the longest way home possible while my stomach growled loud enough to wake the dead.

He eventually parked outside our place. I watched the street for a minute before getting out of the car and heading for the door. I could still smell roast lamb as I hurried up the stairs with Ben next to me. He opened the kitchen door for me. Donald and Enzo were doing the dishes.

"Your dinner is in the fridge," Donald said. "Nana is still annoyed with you."

I grimaced. "I expected she would be." I took our plates out of the fridge and nuked Ben's in the microwave first.

It wasn't long before we were sitting alone at the dining room table eating. Enzo came through with a glass of wine each for us then returned with the bottle.

"You might need more than a glass," he said with a smile.

"It's been that bad?" Ben asked.

Enzo nodded and vanished back to the kitchen.

Chapter Forty
[Crockett: Now we know.]

We grabbed a pizza for dinner once we'd cleaned up the house and put all the things back where they belonged. Hunger was real.

The pink box sat on Emily's bed. She thought it had everything in it but couldn't be sure because she didn't really remember what was in it to start with. Life is hard and sometimes unfair. Inside the box were two wallets. They were empty. She'd put them in there when they were found on the floor.

"There's nothing else that goes in here?" I asked as I checked the wallets one last time.

"I don't know," she said. Emily picked the box up. That was when I noticed the inside wasn't as deep as it should've been. Looking down on it, you couldn't really tell. It was painted in such a way to imply depth - clever.

"May I?" I said and indicated I wanted to pick the box up.

"Yes." Emily held it up to me.

I sat next to her with the box on my knee. I tapped the base on the inside.

"Hear that?"

Dane and Emily nodded.

"It's got a false bottom?" Emily queried.

I pressed parts of the base gently to see where it might

open. I felt some give in one corner. It was tight. That was probably why it survived being tossed around the room by the idiots. I glanced around.

"What do you need?" Siri asked.

"A knife or screwdriver."

Dane nodded and left the room. Ten seconds later he handed me a flathead screwdriver. I prised the bottom of the box open and showed Emily what was inside. A navy-blue passport and a wallet. She took the passport and opened it. A frown grew as her eyes darkened.

"What is it, Emily?"

"Looks like me but everything else is wrong. It says I am Simone Genoa." She handed me the passport. "I can't read anything except my name."

I flicked through it looking for customs stamps or entry visas. Something that showed travel. The passport was used to gain entry to New Zealand eight years ago. There was a stamp suggesting the passport holder arrived in France two weeks before the trip to New Zealand. There were no other stamps.

"It's an Argentinian passport. It's in Spanish."

"But I am from New Zealand," Emily said as her frown deepened.

I handed it to Dane. He inspected it with care. "Looks real. I don't think it's a forgery."

"Where is my passport?" Emily asked out loud while she pulled the big box of handbags and purses out from under her bed. She sat on the floor and went through every purse. We watched her.

Dane handed me the passport. "What else is there?"

"A wallet." I reached into the box and grabbed the wallet. Opening it revealed credit cards issued to Simone Genoa, an international driver's license and an Argentinian driver's license. Both were issued to Simone Genoa.

"That's interesting," I said showing Dane the license. "They went to digital licenses, didn't they?"

"I think so. I can see that being a problem though. If it's attached to your phone like our vaccine certificates were and you don't have a card in your wallet, what happens if your phone dies?"

"It was definitely an ambitious project."

"You'd need a paper or card version for travel?"

I shrugged. "Maybe that's what this is. It's with an international license."

"What?" Emily asked, shoving the box she was searching back under her bed. "Maybe I don't have one of my own."

"You probably do have one Emily. Maybe in the safety deposit box?"

"You think I put my stuff in there and kept this woman's things with me?" It didn't sound like she believed that. I couldn't say I blamed her.

She sat heavily on the bed. "Maybe I am Simone."

"You're Emily Jones," I said. "You are my girlfriend, Emily Jones."

"Why do I have a passport and driver's licenses that belong to Simone Genoa?"

"I don't know. We will find out. And it will be okay."

"What if I am Simone?"

"Can we put that aside for now? Let's find out what's in the safety deposit box first, okay?"

"What do I do with this stuff?" She threw the passport into the box with the wallet.

"That might be the ID information you need for the safety deposit box. That passport, the key, and the box number."

"I don't want to carry that around. What if someone sees it and they think that's proof that I am Simone?"

"No one is going to do anything to you, Emily. Dane and I will be with you."

Her head shook slowly. "I don't want to touch that."

"What if I take it, put it in my pocket, then you don't have it on you."

"I suppose."

"Tomorrow morning. We will go see if we can track down that box."

"I don't want to stay here," Emily said.

"Okay, pack some clothes and whatever you need, come back to my place with Dane."

I stood up and took a backpack from the wardrobe and handed it to her. "Here you go."

"Thank you," she said. "It won't take me long."

I scooped the passport and wallet up and jammed them in my back pocket then put the pink box back where it went. Emily threw clothes in the backpack faster than I'd ever seen her pack. She took the backpack down the hall to the bathroom. I checked all the windows, pulled the drapes, double checked the back door was locked. By the time I was satisfied that the cameras were working and everything was shut tight, Emily was waiting by the front door with Dane.

Chapter Forty-one
[Ronnie: Liars lie]

Morning crept in with ominous shadows that suggested rain. That seemed fitting, considering how the whole situation was going.

Nana had barely spoken to me once we got home last night. Tierney was doing his best to be a peace broker. He had his car take The *Cronies of Doom* home. I know he and Ben had a short conversation about Emily and the diamonds. I didn't know the particulars.

I was starting to think we all held part of the puzzle, and it wouldn't make sense until we laid it all out.

Crockett texted me early to say he was going into the city with Dane and Emily. He didn't say why, and I didn't ask. There was enough rolling around in my brain to let him work on whatever it was he was doing without my input. Ben was flying drones over our neighbourhood.

I opened my wardrobe door and then placed my palm on the biometric scanner on the back wall. The door slid open. It closed behind me. The computer spun into life. The screens glowed as they woke from their naps. A fan in the ceiling whirred stirring the air and stopping everything getting too warm. I sat down, took my flash drive from its safe hiding place and inserted it into the waiting USB port. I navigated across the screen to the drive and then chose the file that allowed me to access

Genesis. Once inside the secure system, I started poking around, looking for something that backed up Tom's story. If it was a Genesis operation, then that information would exist somewhere. I'd read the after-action report, and it certainly suggested it was *Genesis.* Normal people would accept that as the truth and leave the rest alone. I have never been 'normal' people. Something felt off about the report, about the whole bloody operation.

If Tom and Peter Piper were running a Genesis op in Belgium where were the intelligence reports that the operation was based on? They didn't just wake up one morning and decide to become jewel thieves. They didn't just crawl out of bed and create iron-clad legends for themselves. There was a trail of intelligence somewhere and I wanted to find it. I wanted to know what really happened to Simone Genoa/Costa, whoever-the-hell she was.

I wanted to know why Tom and Piper were involved - really know, not what Tom shared but the *real* truth, no matter how weird it was.

Nothing jumped out.

Then a chat window opened, and Uncle George started typing.

It amused me that *Genesis* had adopted the Uncle George moniker so it's not just how *Genesis* shows up on my phone.

I watched three dots moving on the screen.

Finally, words arrived.

Uncle George: What are you doing Ronnie?

Me: Looking for answers

Uncle George: That's dangerous.

Me: Is that a threat?

Uncle George: It could be.

Me: Operation Sidestep was Genesis?

Uncle George: There was no such operation.

Me: Operation Genoa then, was that Genesis?

Uncle George: You've talked to Tom?

Me: I have.

Uncle George: Then you have your answer.

Me: What was Operation Sidestep?

Uncle George: Leave it alone Ronnie.

The chat window vanished. Leave it alone. What are the chances? Zero. I went back to searching for proof. Intelligence reports, anything, that said why Tom and Peter Piper were put in play. A red exclamation mark leapt to the centre of my screen and flashed. Shit! I had a feeling Uncle George was trying to boot me out.

I shut the flash drive down and closed everything.

Maybe he was serious about me leaving it alone?

I left my bat cave and went looking for Ben. I spotted the drone on the dining table and decided Ben must've finished his aerial surveillance.

Maybe Tierney knew something. He was here for a reason, and it wasn't to visit his grandson. I found them in the lounge. Tierney was regaling Nana with a story from his and Ben's past. They were in France and had some fun at a fancy dance with movie types. I listened quietly. He sounded like he had a lot of fun with Ben. He sounded like a grandfather.

When the story drew to a close, I asked if I could speak with him.

"Of course, Veronica. Shall we walk in the back garden?" Tierney grasped his cane with his right hand. "I'm sure Ben can keep June company."

I wanted Ben to hear what I asked but I guessed Tierney and I would have our chat alone. Romeo ambled over.

"Come on, Ro. It's backyard time for you." He plodded along next to me down the stairs, across the garage through the laundry area and out the sliding door to the back yard. Tierney followed without any trouble. He smiled at me as he stepped out the door.

"This is lovely," he said. "Lovely."

Romeo sniffed around the garden. I watched him.

"Thank you, Jonathon. We like it. Private and just fine for an old greyhound who has no interest in running around."

"What concerns you?" Tierney asked, sitting on our garden bench. "Come and sit with me." He patted the seat next to him.

"What concerns me?" I chewed my bottom lip. "Everything I've found out about this Emily situation. Everything."

"Would you like to talk about that?"

"I think I would." I never imagined I'd say those words to Jonathon Tierney. "The confusion starts with these people arriving in New Zealand looking for someone called Simone Genoa. It looks as though she is dead and has been for eight years. Dead in Belgium and yet these people think she's alive."

And I'm not convinced that she isn't.

"It's weighing on you, isn't it Veronica."

"A little bit."

"I think it's time you joined us properly, not just when I need you for a job. It will give you much more access to tools."

"Or you and Ben could use that access for me." I was not in a hurry to sign up for permanent assignments and the red tape that would bring. I'd have to let *Genesis* know and I doubt they'd be happy with two of us working with the Charlie Indigo Alphas. It's all good being roped in for the odd assignment though.

He smiled. Tierney is one of those men whose faces change completely when they smile. He went from stern serious CIA to grandfatherly in a split second.

"I will do what I can for you. What is it that you suspect?"

"That the diamonds are Russian and there is a South American cartel after them. I suspect they funded the heist."

"You're sure about the cartel?"

"I'm not sure they funded the heist, but it works for the narrative. Because somebody did. This wasn't something for personal gain." I didn't think it was anyway.

"Do you trust your source?"

"It is, or was, a reputable source. At least I believed so."

"What does that mean?"

"It was someone known to me."

"All right. What do you know, Veronica? You may as well tell me."

"I know a lot, but I don't believe much of it." I didn't feel like sharing everything, just yet.

He nodded. "Trust takes time, my dear." His manner changed back to all work and no play. "Do you think *Genesis* could be involved?"

"I've never heard of *Genesis*."

"Oh, I felt sure you had."

"Sorry to disappoint. Who are they?"

"Supposedly a top-secret intelligence agency."

"From what country?"

"That's the thing, they supposedly have no country affiliation. They exist outside the bounds of rules and regulations."

I add disbelief to my tone, "What? For the greater good?"

"Yes, something like that." His eyes never left my face. He was scrutinising, probing, looking for gaps or cracks that would tell him I knew something of *Genesis*.

"How do you know about that top-secret agency if it's so secret?"

He smiled indulgently. "Once upon a time, there was a young woman who freelanced for all sorts of people, even us. She had a dear friend called MacKinnon who held secrets that eventually killed him." His smile remained.

Well, bugger. All of that was true.

"That's a nasty end to your story," I said returning his smile.

"It was for MacKinnon senior and junior. Secrets are only secrets if you never tell a soul," Tierney said. "Did you know MacKinnon?"

He obviously knew I knew him, so I made sure to tell the truth. "I did. He was a good man. He introduced me to Ben." That was all I was prepared to say about MacKinnon. "Are you here to help us with the Emily situation or pick at threads to see what unravels?"

"I am here to help. Put me to use. I can help you, Veronica."

His old thin hand patted mine.

"Can you find out who Emily Jones really is?"

"I'm sure I can."

"Will you?"

"Yes. Anything else?"

"There's a man looking for Lucas Genoa. He might already have him, I don't know. But he is also looking for Emily, even though he won't admit it. His name is Tony Robinson. Is he one of yours?"

"The name rings no bells."

It should, because he was the one behind the grocery delivery. Was Tierney losing it? Age had to play a factor at some point. I didn't want it to encroach now though. Not when he could be useful.

"He was behind the grocery delivery."

"Ah, yes, that person."

"I think he's American. Could he be *Leviticus*?"

"He could be, of course. I don't personally know every employee."

"I'd like to know who he's working for and why he is here."

I nearly told him we had a Russian sitting in my office cell. She was detained, which legally is illegal. She'd been detained against her will even though she did go quietly. That was another oddity.

"Veronica, your grandmother is a remarkable woman," Tierney said with a small smile on his old lips. "We must ensure her safety."

That almost felt like a threat, but I couldn't turn it into something full-on ominous.

"If she could be persuaded to play doting Nana and not amateur sleuth, she would always be safe," I replied, adding a smile for good measure.

His smile faded into wrinkles and age. "You don't give her enough credit."

"Perhaps I don't. She does need to step away from this though. Cartels and terrorists are far too dangerous."

"I agree. Perhaps giving her an assignment? Some busy work that won't cause issues but will help in some way?"

A smile played on my lips. I could feel *Uncle George* spinning out of control.

"What if … hear me out … what if I ask her to find a missing person?"

His dark eyes narrowed. "Who?"

"I'll make one up. Someone we believe is central to this Emily situation."

He nodded. "Go on."

"Give me a name and a brief description and I'll hand it over." That way, I'm not really lying, Tierney is. "I'll tell her we're stretched thin and perhaps she and the girls could track the person down. To help Emily."

He smiled. "Let's make it in keeping with the situation. She'll see right through it otherwise." He tapped a finger on his chin. "Ah, yes, Tomás Genoa."

I smiled. "Sounds made up."

"It does, I think the Genoa part will stop a fit of pique and interest her enough."

"Sounds like a good plan. I best get back inside and see what she's up to now."

"I'll be along shortly." He took a phone from an inner jacket pocket. "I'll make some calls and see what I can find out about Miss Jones and Mr Robinson."

"Thank you." My eyes searched the garden for Romeo. He was lying under a bush out of the sun. "Come on Ro, enough outside time."

He rose awkwardly, then stretched before ambling towards me. We walked together into the garage and up the stairs. Close, but not touching.

Chapter Forty-two
[Ronnie: Where do we go now?]

How much did he know about *Genesis*? Instead of going into the lounge, I went to my room. Something was off. Way off. I stood in my room and slowly turned around. Had he been in here? Had he heard me open the bat cave?

I texted Crockett: Do you have an RF detector, and can I borrow it?

Crockett: Don't you have one?

Me: Not good enough to detect what could be here.

Crockett: Charlie Indigo Alpha?

Me: Yeah.

Crockett: Be there in a few.

I shut messages down and put my phone in my pocket. Conversational noises floated in the air barely making it to my room. I ignored them and sat on my bed. What if he knew about the bat cave? I jumped to my feet and slid the wardrobe door open. What did it look like when I closed it earlier? I counted the shirts hanging on the left. I counted the dresses hanging on the right. I don't know why I considered the number would've changed. I couldn't imagine Tierney wearing my shirts or dresses. A shudder ran through me. That was too much. I moved the dresses to the right as far as they would go. The door was visible. The biometric lock was visible. I moved the dresses back again the way I usually did. And questioned what I saw when I opened the wardrobe. Did it look the same? Did I leave it the same way this morning?

I had no idea. I didn't usually worry too much. The only reason Donald ever ventured over my threshold was to borrow a phone charger and that hadn't happened since he married Enzo. My room was a sanctuary. I scratched that notion. *Genesis* had managed to get someone into my house and bug my room once upon a time. We found it and killed it. And that was the end of that chapter. This felt different. In some ways, *Genesis* felt like a benevolent uncle looking out for me hence I dubbed *Genesis,* Uncle George. Everyone needs an Uncle George who can track their movements via city CCTV cameras, traffic light cameras, and public transport cameras. No, that really was creepy. Good ol' Uncle George was far too nosy for his/her own good.

There was a quiet knock on my closed bedroom door.

I called out, "Come in."

The door opened and Ben stood there smiling. His smile slipped away when he saw my face.

"What's the matter?" He motioned to the door.

"Closed please."

He did as I asked. The smile on his face replaced by a frown.

I signed: Don't speak.

He nodded. I opened my bedside drawer and took out

a notepad and a pen. Signing was great, but I'm rusty and it would take me forever to work out how to tell him my room might be bugged by his 'grandfather'. I wrote and showed him.

He sat next to me and took the pen. He wrote: what are we doing about it? But said, "I wondered where you were. Anything I can help with?"

I took the pen and paper off him and wrote: Crockett is coming over with an RF detector. But said, "Just a bit of a headache. Probably haven't had enough water to drink."

"Where's your water bottle?" He motioned for the pad and pen: I'll go let Crockett in and then bring him down here.

"Can you get me more water, please?"

He handed me the pad and gave me a kiss. "I'll bring you more water."

"Thank you, my love," I said with a smile.

A mischievous glint sparked in his eyes. "We need to talk venues and dates."

"When you get back with my water. I promise." It was all I could do not to laugh. Venues and dates. We had a plan.

Ben chuckled and left my room, closing the door behind him.

Our plan was about to kick into gear. We just needed to settle this whole Emily, diamonds, Russian, South American cartel, terrorism, business. Then we were off, plan in gear, no-nonsense. As long as no one overheard our planning last week, but we should be okay because

Tierney wasn't here then. Lucky us.

One rap at my door told me Ben was back. He came in carrying a fresh bottle of water and grinned. A shadow followed him. "I found this guy in the kitchen," he said moving further into the room to allow Crockett to come in and close the door.

"Nice in here," he said, smiling and producing an RF detector from his leather jacket. "You need to drink more water."

I took the bottle off Ben and swigged from it. "Happy now, are we?"

Ben and I turned our phones off. I briefly wondered if anything in my bat cave would register if it was on, which it wasn't. Crockett fired up his toy, on silent. We didn't need to hear it squeal like a stuck pig if it detected something. The red and orange lights would be enough. It took him two minutes to sweep the entire room including my wardrobe. Twice he showed us red and orange lights. Ben pulled a tiny listening device from behind a painting on my wall and another from under my bedside table. The final one was discovered in my wardrobe, under the collar of a jacket. Someone really wanted to hear what I had to say. The only person who would be that interested was Tierney. Or at least, the only interested person who had access was Tierney. Crockett did another sweep to double check there weren't cameras anywhere. I felt quite ill at that notion.

My water bottle sat on my bedside table. I unscrewed the top and dropped the three tiny and expensive devices into the water. With a grin, I sauntered off to the kitchen holding my water bottle. I tipped the contents into the sink and turned on the waste disposal. There was a slight crunching then the nasty little devices were gone. I left my bottle on the bench and went back to my room.

Ben and Crockett were still in there.

"How do I stop that happening, again?"

Crockett opened his jack and pulled out a couple of small white devices.

"What are they?" I asked.

"I formulated a plan to make sure you didn't get bugged again. These, are that" he said, placing two devices on the bed. They were small. About the size of a twenty-cent piece. "They are tiny alarms."

"Cool," I said. "And they work how?"

He pulled two other little circles from his jacket. "I stick one of these on the edge of the door and one on the frame, in corresponding places. When the door opens the connection is broken and the alarm goes off."

"How do I turn it off?"

"Close the door," he said with a grin.

"Oh, okay. There are two?"

"Yep. We need to rig one for the bat cave or wardrobe."

"Wardrobe."

"Okay, I'll do it now."

"Is there a way I can turn them off when I'm here and in and out of the wardrobe or my room?"

"Yes, a tiny switch on one of them. I'll make it the one in the door frame."

"Thank you."

That would make anyone coming in, to place more bugs a bit obvious. Unless no one was home but the sneaky bugging person, then what?

"I need a camera," I said barely believing I said the words out loud. Because everyone wants a camera in their bedroom. Bloody hell. This was getting ridiculous.

"Are you serious?" Crockett asked.

"Yes. But only Ben and I need the code to view any alerts."

"Do you have any at the office?"

"Yes, in the tech room, there should be a new box of discreet surveillance cameras."

"I'll zip off and grab a couple. I think we should put one in the hallway outside your room too."

"Good thinking." I took the keys out of my bedside table and handed them to Crockett. "Green is the downstairs front door. Orange is the tech room." Then I remembered our guest. "We have a guest in the cell. Don't go in there."

"A guest?"

"She's sleeping," Ben said.

I knew what that meant. He'd slipped her some roofies in a water bottle.

"Okay, I'll leave whatever that is alone." Crockett grinned, turned, and left.

Chapter Forty-three
[Crockett: Asleep?]

It was quiet in Ronnie's offices. There were no sounds of life anywhere. Part of me wondered if I should check on the prisoner because there were no sounds.

Then I remembered the room that held the jail cell was soundproofed. A jet could take off in that room and no one would hear anything. I was pretty sure she had cameras in there too.

Best leave it alone. I let myself into the tech room. Every shelf had a sticker saying what went where. That made it easy to locate the spy cameras. Let's be serious, that's what they are. Nothing that tiny is used for legit reasons. You're not going to see a sign on a house saying surveillance cameras are in operation when you're using these tiddlers. I took a small plastic container with two cameras in it. Under the cameras in the box was a card that had the information required to monitor them. I secured the box in my jacket pocket and locked the door on my way out. I paused by the main office door. There was no noise. I tried the handle, and it opened.

Steph was at her desk.

"Hi, didn't think anyone was in," I said.

"Just getting some paperwork finished," she said, giving me a smile. "And it might be quieter and less like a loonie bin here."

"Jenn?"

"Oh yeah. She's driving me up the wall. She wants to be back at work. She's annoyed she can't spend longer than ten minutes on the iPad. Her Facebook followers will be missing her, apparently." Steph kept typing.

"Everything else okay up here?"

"If that means, do I know what's in the cell? Then yes, I do. And she's sleeping."

"Okay then, I'll go back to Ronnie's."

"I might bring Jenn down later. She could probably handle some company. Nana still there?"

"Yep. With Jonathon Tierney playacting at being Ben's grandad. It's the stuff nightmares are made of."

"And you're here why?"

"Had to pick up some of those tiny cameras."

"How many have you taken?" Steph used her mouse and did something. She wasn't typing any more.

"Two."

"Okay. I've noted that down in the outward goods spreadsheet."

Ah, that's what she was doing.

"See you later then?"

Steph waved. I pulled the door closed and ran down the stairs. My Harley was sitting patiently at the curb. I looked around. There was nothing untoward. No one seemed to give a shit that I'd just appeared on the street. I jammed my helmet on, zipped up my jacket and roared off, northwards. I'd do a big loop, maybe include some back roads. Eventually, I rumbled down Ronnie's street. I parked up the driveway and left my helmet sitting over the right-wing mirror and resting on the handlebars.

I went to open the front door, but Donald beat me to it.

"They're upstairs in their room," Donald said. "I'm assuming you want Ronnie and Ben?"

"Yes. Thanks."

Donald peered out the door before closing and locking it. "Can't be too careful. Where's Emily?"

"At my place with our friend."

Donald tapped the side of his nose. "Of course."

I took the stairs two at a time, let myself into the kitchen then down the hall and knocked on Ronnie's door. Ben opened it. I handed him the box.

"I'll get home. Don't want to be away from Emily too long."

Ben nodded. "Stay frosty."

"You, too."

Even after running another SDR, I was home within ten minutes. I spotted old geezers stationed on Fergusson Drive. So, June still had her surveillance running. I'm sure that would not please Ronnie and I decided to leave it alone.

I put the Harley in the garage and let myself in the back door. Emily and Dane were watching television.

"Anything good?" I asked.

"No," Emily replied. "Just something about a shipwreck."

I sat next to her. "Are you ready to go find that safety deposit box?"

"Yes."

"Righto, then, let's tool up and get on with it."

Dane typed then Siri said, "Tool up?"

"We're not going after diamonds without ways to protect ourselves from everybody else who wants the diamonds."

"If there are any diamonds," Emily said. "I don't believe there are."

"We're going to find out," I told her. "Go do whatever you need to do before we leave. Dane and I will open the floor safe."

"We're going to be armed?" Emily asked.

"Yes, Milo. What's your preference?"

"Glock 17 with a paddle holster." Surprise registered in her eyes. "I don't know where that came from."

"Don't worry about it, Milo. I'll make sure you have a Glock 17."

She went down the hall into the bathroom. I opened the gun safe which is in the hallway floor under the carpet. The carpet looks like it's laid properly but it unhooks and peels back quite nicely to reveal the safe and then hooks back into its normal spot so it's not loose. I don't want anyone I don't trust trying to get into my stuff. I extracted three handguns and holsters, plus three extra magazines. My guns are always loaded, ready to go, but I don't keep one in the chamber. That doesn't happen until they're in my hands.

By the time Emily came back to the lounge we were ready to roll. She'd picked up a jacket from the bedroom.

I handed Dane and Emily their weapons and holsters. Once everything was snuggly in place and jackets were covering it all we left.

The trip into the city wasn't bad. I'd had worse. I knew we were heading to the bottom of Willis Street, so I decided we'd park under the Cake Tin if there was any parking available, and walk it from there.

I fluked a park and it cost a small fortune. Crikey, parking in the city was a rort. But we got there. We trooped from the stadium parking to the bottom of Willis with our heads on swivel. Eventually, we found the building.

It was flash inside and security conscious as you'd expect. Emily walked up to the reception desk.

"I'd like to access my safety deposit box, thanks."

"We'll set that up for you," the receptionist said with a smile. "What was the name."

"Simone Genoa."

The woman typed on her computer.

"And your box number?"

Emily withdrew the note from her pocket and read the number out loud.

The woman typed.

"I just need to see your ID, please."

Emily passed her the passport we found in the fake bottomed box.

"Great, I'll buzz an escort to take you down to the vaults."

"Thank you," Emily said with a pleasant smile. "I'll

need to have my bodyguard with me." She pointed to me.

"Can I see some ID, Sir?" she asked, looking directly at me.

I pulled my wallet out and handed her my driver's license. "Is this, okay?"

"Yes. I just need a record of it. Protocol."

She looked at Dane. "Are you also a bodyguard?"

He shook his head.

I intervened so he wasn't memorable. Nothing stuck in someone's memory as well as someone who was different. And Dane using Siri to communicate was different. "He'll be staying up here with you."

"That's lovely then," she said and made the call to whoever she needed to escort Emily. "Have a seat over there while you wait." She pointed to a leather couch and armchairs arranged around a circular coffee table piled high with brochures.

Emily smiled and moved away from the desk to the seating area. We followed like good bodyguards. I sat facing the room beside Emily. Dane stood, also facing the room but making sure he could see the door as well. We were pretty sure no one had followed us, but you can never be one hundred percent. People are sneaky. We waited in silence until an elevator pinged and a man wearing a nice suit stepped out. He strolled to the desk. The woman must've told him we were the customers who wanted vault access because he came straight over.

"Ms Genoa, so nice to see you again," he said, stretching his arm out for a handshake. "I'm Toby

Cameron."

Emily obliged and shook his hand. "Thank you."

"As you know we moved all the boxes from the National Bank to our vault a few years ago. Your key still works. Your biometrics still work."

"Good," she said. "Shall we?"

He led the way to the elevator. I watched him press the down key. We were on the ground floor, so I guessed the vaults were underground. I wasn't sure how I felt about being underground in Wellington what with the number of earthquakes I'd experienced since arriving in New Zealand. Emily didn't look concerned. I know she experienced a big quake in Wellington a few years before but she still didn't look bothered. Maybe it's people who haven't always lived in an earthquake-prone country that are worried about being trapped.

We went down two floors. That did nothing to help my concerns over earthquakes. We were two floors below ground in a city partially built on reclaimed land and prone to earthquakes. I forced those thoughts out of my mind. There was no point thinking about earthquakes; that won't stop them.

Toby Cameron used a card to exit the elevator and then gain entry to a room. There were huge steel doors sitting open within the room. Beyond them were heavy glass doors and a biometric scanning panel.

"Are they always open?" I asked.

"No. They're closed at five and open again at eight in the morning. The last entry we allow is four PM. It gives people time to get in and out."

"Do you have to close the doors manually?"

"They're automatic."

That was good to know. "Is there a warning?"

"An alarm goes five minutes before the doors shut."

That was also good to know.

Chapter Forty-four
[Emily: Fingers crossed]

Emily watched and listened as Crockett asked questions about the vaults. She wasn't concerned about anything, just interested in what would happen and how things happened. She wasn't interested enough to ask her own questions, though.

She waited for Toby Cameron to ask her to step up to the biometric scanner.

Once Crockett had finished with his questions, Toby turned to Emily.

"Ms Genoa, if you could stand about ten centimetres away from the scanner. There's a yellow line on the floor to mark the ideal position."

"Does it scan my face?" Emily asked.

"Initially it's facial then your handprint."

She glanced at Crockett. He nodded and gave her a reassuring smile. Emily stood on the yellow line and looked at the screen on the glass door. It sprang to life. An AI robotic voice said, "Welcome Simone Genoa." The panel returned to a soft grey. A lock on the glass doors opened.

"Now, if you could press your palm against the glass above the door handle."

She moved over and did as he asked. A blue outline of her hand appeared in the glass. Then turned green and another lock opened.

So far so good. Toby Cameron pushed the doors open. "To get out you need to do the same."

"Does it matter which order?"

"No," he said. In his hand, he had a key.

Emily took her key from her pocket along with the piece of paper with the box number written on it.

"What number are we looking for?" Cameron asked. Emily handed him the paper. "That number is this way."

He moved towards the back wall. The room was surprisingly spacious. The walls were lined with safety deposit boxes or at least the face plates of boxes. You couldn't see the boxes themselves. In the middle of the room, there was a large table covered in some kind of felted fabric. There were two chairs. They walked past the table and watched Toby Cameron locate the box.

"This is it," he said.

It was a medium-sized box. Below it on the next row down were larger boxes and still larger below that. Above it, were more of the same size, and then a row of much smaller boxes.

He put his key in one lock. Emily put hers in the other. They turned them at the same time and the box door opened. Toby took his key out.

"I'll leave you to it. You don't need to use both keys to lock it. Just yours will work and the other lock with trigger automatically." Toby left the vault room.

Emily waited until she heard him walking away and the elevator ping. Crockett faced out into the room just to make sure. When he was satisfied they were alone, he watched Emily. Emily dragged the long-covered inner box out and placed it on the table. She keyed the lock on top of the box and took the lid off.

Inside were manilla envelopes. She opened the first one and tipped the contents onto the felted table: a red passport and a driver's license. Emily saw her face but did not recognise the name on the license: Eva Jarvis. Confusion settled on her features.

"Eva Jarvis?" she queried. "Why would I have a passport from Malta?"

"Looks like an alias," Crockett said. "I wouldn't worry about it."

"Why do I have an alias?" She put the passport and license back in the envelope and set it aside.

"I don't know." Crockett smiled at her. "What else is in there?"

"More manilla envelopes." She took the next one out, opened it, and tipped it on the table. "More identification." Emily touched the gold image on the front of a dark blue passport. "Elizabeth Jackson. She looks like me. We do not have the same birthday, but it is the same year." She turned the license over with her fingers. It matched the passport. "Elizabeth Jackson is American. She's from Virginia." When she flipped the passport, a credit card fell out. It belonged to First Century Bank and had Elizabeth Jackson embossed on it.

"There was not one for Eva Jarvis." Emily gathered the things up and put them back in the envelope. "No diamonds." She wrinkled her nose and picked up another envelope.

Again, she tipped the contents on the table. It was another blue passport but this time it was from the United Kingdom of Great Britain and Northern Ireland.

"Whose is it?" Crockett asked.

"Elle Jenkins." Emily opened the passport and flicked through the pages. "She travelled a lot."

Crockett pointed to the driver's license. "Does it match?"

"Yes." A credit card fell from the back of the passport. "This belongs to Elle Jenkins too."

Crockett studied her as she gathered the things together and put them back in the envelope. There were two envelopes left.

She carefully picked the next one up and gave it a shake. "I think it's more passport-y than diamond-y," she said and tipped the contents.

There was a black passport with half a silver fern depicted on the right-hand edge, a blue passport that said United States of America in gold, two driver's licenses, and two credit cards. One was a Mastercard, and one was a Visa. Emily stood staring at the photo on the licenses and the name on the credit cards. She couldn't bring herself to touch the passports.

"You look," she said to Crockett and pushed it towards him.

"Okay." He picked it up and opened to the first page. The all-important page containing the chip and information. "Emily Jones," he said. "This is yours."

"And the American one?"

He opened it. "This is also yours."

"Why are they in here with the aliases if they're mine?"

"I don't know. For safety reasons, maybe? You can't lose them if they're in a safety deposit box."

Emily stared at him for a second or two. "What if I'm not Emily Jones and that's another alias?"

"Does it matter?" He gave it some consideration. "You must be Emily Jones because you were a police officer, remember?"

"They call me Emily, the cops I used to work with." Her frown eased.

"See? You're Emily." Crockett hoped he was convincing because it really looked like perhaps, she wasn't Emily. Maybe she got stuck as Emily after the *accident.*

"Do I sound like an American?"

"No."

She nodded, put the stuff away and grabbed the last envelope. She shook it, something moved but it didn't feel like paper. Carefully Emily broke the seal and tipped the contents onto the deep green covered table. There was a key to something and a piece of paper with coordinates on it: three words each separated by a full stop. She recognised the format as directional information from What3words. There were no diamonds.

"We were wrong," she said. "Another key and a place."

"Perhaps that's where the diamonds are?"

"So, I put them somewhere less secure than a bank vault. That doesn't make sense. If I had this box, why wouldn't I put the diamonds in it?"

"I don't know. But you must've had a reason. And a good one."

She kept the key, and the piece of paper but put everything else back in the safety deposit box. She locked the lid, put the box back into the wall, and locked the faceplate.

Crockett checked the time.

"We need to go before the alarm goes off."

She nodded. At the locked glass door, she stood on the yellow line and waited for the AI voice. "Goodbye, Simone Genoa."

She pressed her palm to the glass above the door handle. It glowed blue then green and she pushed the door open. Crockett and Emily met Dane in reception. Emily shook her head at his questioning look.

Once back in the relative safety of the car, she asked Dane if he had What3Words on his iPad.

"I do," Siri replied. "Why?"

She passed him the piece of paper.

"Okay," Siri said. "I'll see where it is."

They waited a few seconds for Dane to get them the address. He passed the iPad to Crockett in the driver's seat.

"It couldn't be anything else?" Crockett asked, looking back at Dane.

Dane shook his head.

"What is it?" Emily asked. "Why are you both so strange about where it is?" She didn't think it could be any harder to get to than the bank vault.

"It's a P.O. box."

"Post office box. Simone really likes boxes," Emily said. "Where?"

"Upper Hutt outside the Mall."

"Oh, in that little room thing. I know where that is."

"The problem is they're not secure. Mail delivery people can access them from the back."

"Why would I put the diamonds there then?"

"I don't think you did," Crockett told her. "There might be something there, but it won't be the diamonds."

The trip to Upper Hutt was uneventful and quiet.

Crockett parked outside the P.O. Boxes. Dane opted to wait in the car. He handed the piece of paper back to Emily. She'd need the number.

Crockett and Emily found the box without any trouble, there was no one else in there collecting mail which was helpful. Inside the PO Box, Emily found a manilla envelope addressed to EJ. She locked the box, and they returned to the car.

"Where should we go?" Emily asked.

"My place," Crockett said. "You can open it there."

"Doesn't feel like diamonds," she said. "But I don't know what they feel like." A smile played in the corners of her mouth. None of it was straightforward but it was starting to feel like a treasure hunt and that amused her. What didn't amuse her was finding so many aliases. She had no idea who those people were or why a police officer would need different identities. Her smile vanished and was replaced with a tinge of fear. Fear that she wasn't Emily Jones and didn't know who she really was.

Crockett's words popped into her consciousness to remind her she was a police officer and that cops knew her, and they called her Emily. She thought about Ronnie and working for her in the bookshop, but she knew she didn't always work in the bookshop. Bits and pieces of what she assumed were memories or maybe they were fantasies came and went. She worked with Ronnie in the field. She was a private investigator. She could only remember small chunks of that life. Sitting in a car with Ronnie watching someone's house. That felt like a memory. But the intermittent flashes of gunfire and fast roping from a helicopter felt like a movie. But she could feel the rope through the gloves she wore. Maybe she remembered parts of a movie and put herself in it? Emily stopped thinking and puzzled over how she knew about fast roping.

"Crockett?"

"Yep," he said. "We'll be there soon; I just want to make sure no one is following us."

"Have you ever fast roped?"

"I have. It's a lot of fun."

She could see Crockett's smile. "I think I have fast roped from a helicopter."

"Maybe you have. Maybe it's a memory."

"Or from a movie and I'm imagining it," she said

quietly. "It could be a dream."

Dane tapped her shoulder from the back seat. She could hear him typing.

"I can remember things that make me think I dreamed it, or it was something from a movie." He typed some more. "But when I physically feel something, like the memory is in my hands. That's how I know it's real."

Emily was quiet for a split second. "I can feel the rope. The friction on my gloves."

Dane typed and Siri said, "Then you probably did fast rope from a helicopter."

"That's helpful Dane," Crockett said, turning down the street. "A pretty smart technique for knowing if something is a real memory or not."

"Why would I be fast roping from a helicopter?" Emily wondered out loud.

"Maybe you were training with AOS?" Crockett offered.

"I don't remember knowing anyone in the Armed Offenders Squads."

Crockett's smile was back. "Yes, you do, Ronnie's mate Liam is in AOS and my mate Josh."

"Oh," Emily replied. "Maybe they will know why I remember a helicopter and fast roping?"

"Maybe. Next time we see Josh, we'll ask him. Liam moved into Wellington, so Ronnie doesn't see much of him now."

Emily smiled. She let the memories go and settled back into her seat with the envelope on her knee.

Chapter Forty-five
[Ronnie: Live and learn]

Ben and I set up the cameras. They were tiny and hard to spot when positioned correctly. I had one in a painting in the hallway near my room and one on the top edge of my curtains. Thankfully the shades of green in the abstract pattern, that almost resembled foliage, but failed, hid the camera well. I needed to check with the app to see what they could see.

"Go down the hall and then come back," I said to Ben as I sat on my bed and opened the app specifically for the tiny cameras. I put the code in, and the screen opened. I watched as Ben went down the hall and came back. I could clearly see his face. When he opened the door and came into my room, I could once again clearly see who he was. I shut the app.

"We're in business," I said with a smile. "Anyone snooping or thinking they're going to plant surveillance gear in here again will be on camera." They were designed to record movement, and I made sure that function was enabled.

I went into the lounge to find Nana and Tierney deep in conversation, heads bowed, it did not bode well.

"Can I help?" Tierney asked when he eventually noticed me standing in front of them.

"Did you get very far with what we discussed earlier?"

"I have feelers out. No doubt I'll hear soon."

"Can you text me when you get something? Ben and I have to pop out."

"Yes. I will. Be careful."

I smiled. "See you two later." Or sooner if you happen into my bedroom.

"Yes, dear," Nana said. "Do you think you could you give some consideration to dinner?"

"Ask Donald," I said and waved as I walked away.

"He might not be home for dinner," Nana called after me.

"Let me know then and I'll come up with dinner."

We escaped to Ben's car and headed for Crockett's in a roundabout way. Everything was roundabout these days. There were no straight lines in our world anymore.

I knocked on Crockett's door and we waited.

The door opened.

"If it isn't Cary Grant and the unflappable Ronnie Tracey," Crockett said.

"Quite the welcome. Someone is in a good mood," I said. "Had a good day?"

"I think I'm beginning to understand pirates and their treasure maps," he said, ushering us in and scanning the backyard before locking the door.

"Hi Emily," I said as she popped her head around the corner of the kitchen doorway.

"Hi," she said back.

"She sounds better," I said quietly to Crockett.

"Yeah."

We sat down in the lounge. Dane joined us and so did Emily.

"What do we know?" I asked. Hoping they had something.

Emily held a small postbag in her lap.

"We know the diamonds are not in a safety deposit box," Crockett said. "Or at least not the one we found."

"Where are they?"

"That we don't yet know."

"Okay. Are we any closer to anything?"

"We are and we are not."

"Just what I need, more cryptic nonsense." A frown threatened.

"We found three aliases belonging to Emily."

"Four," Emily corrected.

Crockett gave her a look. "Three plus Emily's passports and credit cards."

"Interesting," Ben said. "Will the real Emily Jones please stand up?"

"Funny," Emily replied. "But what if I'm not me?"

"Oh, you're definitely you," Crockett said with a smile. "You're my Milo."

"And someone's Eva, Elizabeth, and Elle," she said. "And also, people think I'm Simone! I wish I could remember."

"You will," Crockett said.

I wasn't so sure. She'd been fed a life and a lie, or many lies. The 'accident' gave them the perfect opportunity. It was far easier letting her go and denying her previous life or lives than risking it all coming out and landing in a messy way. None of the architects of Emily Jones' life wanted to bring attention to the secrets that thrive in the dark.

"What do we have?" I asked.

"Not the diamonds," Crockett said with a shrug. "How about you?"

As if on cue my phone buzzed. I looked at the images now live streaming from my bedroom. Jonathon Tierney was planting new listening devices. I showed Ben. "Your grandfather is a snake in the grass."

He grinned. "He's nothing if not predictable."

"Ronnie's right," Crockett said. "He's a snake."

I turned my phone so Emily and Crockett could see.

"What's he doing?" Crockett asked.

"Why is he in your bedroom?" Emily asked.

"He's trying to find new places to hide listening devices," I said.

"Why would he do that?" Emily asked.

"He thinks I have information that he wants."

"Do you?"

I nodded. "Yes. I do."

Emily laughed. "Everyone is a comedian."

Dane asked to see the footage via Siri. I handed him my phone. He watched, then gave it back to me. He typed on his iPad. Then Siri said, "Is it wise to have Tierney in your home when he's CIA and obviously thinks you have something he wants?"

I shook my head slowly from side to side. "Not at all

smart but at least this way I know where he is."

"How much could he have gotten from you and Ben so far?" Siri asked.

"Not much. I don't think the devices had been in place long when I twigged something was up and got Crockett here to sweep my room." Or maybe he heard us talking about *Genesis* and now he knows way too much?

Dane nodded. "Good," Siri said.

"You might need to take my RF detector when you go home. You can make a show of doing a sweep of the house," Crockett said. "It'd be hilarious to see how stoney-faced that man can get."

Yes, it would. It might make Nana think twice about flirting with him if we showed her the footage of him in my room too. I wondered how Tierney got so close to us. Did he suspect when he first turned up to run Ben during the arms deal? Did he suspect Ben or just me?

"Hey, Dane," I said.

"Yes," Siri replied.

"You're one of us, right?"

He nodded. "This is my first outing as one of you."

"How did they get you?"

As far as we knew Dane was sent to live with Crockett's mate Mitch and his girls down in the Marlborough Sounds. Dane was typing. He typed then stopped. More typing followed.

Finally, Siri said, "Initial contact was via email but not an email address I'd used in a long time, so I took a while to see the email. After that, there were phone calls."

"You didn't get approached in person?"

"No," Siri said.

Dane knows something. I know he does. I let the thoughts spin in my mind for a split second. I knew in my gut I was on the right track.

"Bugger, was hoping you could shed some light on who's pulling the strings."

The closest I'd ever gotten was a place called Linkwater popping up when I traced a phone call. Linkwater is part of the Marlborough Sounds. I guess that was a dead end after all. He probably used a VPN. Uncle George could be anywhere in the world. I had a feeling he was in New Zealand and close. One day maybe I'd find out. I knew I would, one day. I'd make it my mission to find the head of *Genesis*.

"Ronnie, what did you mean that Dane is one of *us*?" Emily asked. "Did you mean a private investigator?"

"Sort of." I smiled at her.

"But you own *Wherefore Art Thou*." I could see her mind working. Dots were connecting. "You mean like Ben and Crockett. You mean a spy. You are retired."

"I'm mostly retired, Emily. *Mostly*."

Emily nodded. "We need to find out who I am."

"You're Emily Jones," Crockett said.

"What if I'm not her? What if I'm someone else?"

"It doesn't matter," I said. "You'll always be Emily Jones to us."

"Dane wasn't Dane. He was Dean. He had a different name and a different life."

"Yes, I did," Siri said. "But that was to protect me from my past."

"The same could be true for me," Emily replied.

She wasn't wrong. And Bill Bailey knew who she really was. That man wouldn't give us anything.

I pushed all those thoughts into the background. What we needed to find was the diamonds. And I should probably do something with Katerina Solkov. Sooner or later, she'd wake up and I imagined she'd be cross.

"What's the next step regarding the lost treasure?" Ben asked.

Emily picked up an envelope from the floor and took the contents out.

"Another key and another piece of paper with words on it," she said. "Dane said the words point to a square metre inside a bunker in Karori.

"Karori bunkers from World War Two?"

"I think so," she replied. "Are they there?"

"They certainly are. Wrights Hill Fortress is what they're called. The only problem is they're not open to the public except for four days a year."

"Is today one of them?" she asked.

"I wish." I pulled up the details on their website. "It's open ANZAC Day, Labour Day, King's Birthday, and Waitangi Day."

"It's a fortress," Emily whispered.

"It is. It's not going to be easy to gain access but it's not impossible," I said to her. "Where in the fort is the treasure?"

"Plotting room," said Siri. "Or at least that's what What3Words pointed us at."

"Okay." Not exactly okay. How accurate could it be through metres of concrete? I guessed we were going to find out.

We didn't have much day left.

"We do it now?" Ben asked.

"May as well," I replied. "We're going to need a pry bar, torches, and a padlock to replace the one we're going to break."

"Mitre 10 for the lock," Crockett said. "I'll go grab that. What size do you reckon?"

"Go with large and sturdy. Get two. Just in case we need to leave via a different door."

"Okay. Are you staying here?"

"No, I'm going to the office to tool up," I said. "Also, we have a guest in the cell, so I really need to do something with her."

Emily laughed and took me by surprise. "People don't put guests in cells, Ronnie."

"Not usually," I said with a grin. "This guest isn't a very nice person."

"Dane, can you stay here with Emily?" Crockett asked.

He nodded.

Ben and I left for the office and Crockett followed us on his Harley, disappearing from our rearview mirrors at H2O.

Ben went past the office and parked in the car park on the other side of Woolworths. We strolled hand in hand into the supermarket via the Russell Street entrance. We grabbed a trolley, and Ben pushed it to the other door that led to their big car park. We looked out the glass doors. There was no one lurking who looked suspicious. The car park was mostly empty for a change. We left the trolley with the row of other trolleys by the store entrance and hurried down Geange Street and onto Princes then ducked down the alleyway. I unlocked the back door and ran up the stairs.

I walked past all the doors in our long hallway and checked the main office. Steph was gone. Everything was closed down. I unlocked the tech room and gave Ben the keys so he could check on the guest.

In the tech room I took five Ledlenser torches from their charging stations and checked their transport locks were on before placing them in a backpack from the top shelf. We had several pry bars on hand. I took one and propped it near the door. From the armoury safe, I grabbed two Glock G17's, Gen 4, and extra, full magazines. I preferred to have the same weapon that all three of our armed forces used. I figured we'd all need sidearms and that Crockett would provide arms for himself, Dane, and Emily.

I glanced around the room while thinking about what else would be useful. A door alarm would be useful. I took one from a box. It had two parts to it, similar to the ones Crockett put in my bedroom. We could set them across the tunnel behind the door we would be using, one piece on each side. When the laser beam was broken by the door opening it would send a signal to my phone as well as an audible oscillating alarm. It would be the early warning that we'd need to move our arses back to safety.

Chapter Forty-six
[Ronnie: Field trips are fun]

Nana rang to say Donald would be home for dinner. I told her we wouldn't be, and they should fend for themselves. Tierney was still there. He hadn't been back to my room so hopefully he'd finished snooping or he only wanted to snoop to the extent of listening devices not searching. It'd be bad for him if Nana caught him searching my room so maybe that was enough to stop him. Part of me wanted him to snoop in my room and get caught, the other part of me did not want to risk him seeing the biometric scanner on the back wall of my wardrobe.

Life is tricky.

Enzo met us at Crockett's and opted to come on the field trip. I wasn't altogether thrilled with the idea of Donald on his own with Nana and Tierney.

Enzo was sure he'd be fine, so I let it go. More hands with us was helpful.

We took two cars to Karori. Once we were on the motorway there was no way of eluding anyone following us, so we just had to hope we'd lose them in the twisted labyrinth that was the streets of Wellington. We didn't take a direct route to Wrights Hill Fortress. But once we were on Wrights Hill Road there was no way of disguising our destination. We parked just off the road on the shoulder and hiked up to the entrance.

It didn't look like much from the outside: there were a few warnings about trespassing and a couple of signs that said the fort was off-limits apart from the open days. They'd done a lot of restoration work on the bunkers. We weren't about to mess anything up except the padlock on the metal main entrance door. It reminded me a bit of a door on a ship. I didn't much like it. Crockett smashed the pry bar down onto the padlock. It opened. Things usually do when met with Crockett wielding a pry bar.

I glanced at Emily. "You'll need your torch on Emily, the lights won't be going."

We traipsed in the door to the first tunnel. There was a light switch. I flicked it and nothing happened. I suppose they use a generator and as it's not an open day, and there's no one here working, there'd be no power. Enzo pushed the door closed behind us. When we got what we came for and made it out, we'd put the new lock on and post them the key. There's a restoration society. They have a Post office box. I peeled the backing off the laser alarms and stuck one on each side of the tunnel making sure the beam would break if the door was opened.

In single file, we trudged down concrete steps. I was trying my best to haul in information about the floor plan. I'd been to the fort a few times. Did I know how far and what turns to take? Sort of. We were going to find out.

"I think it's about thirty metres to a crossroads of sorts. Tunnels run off the left and the right. We want to stay in this one. Keep going forward."

Crockett was in front. He acknowledged my directions with a thumbs up. Our torches were doing a great job illuminating the tunnel we were in. The air was still and not as damp as I expected. It wasn't unpleasant being down in the tunnels, just a bit nervy. Always in the back of my mind is an earthquake scenario. Knowing we've had some big ones in Wellington and these tunnels didn't cave in or fall apart was somewhat comforting, but not entirely. Our footsteps echoed around us.

"Coming up to the two other tunnels," Crockett said. "There are arrows on the wall saying where they lead."

"Keep going."

When Emily and I came to the two tunnels I read the arrows. The right-hand tunnel said, 'Gun Pit 2'. The left-hand tunnels said, 'Gun Pit 1'.

On we went.

Until Crockett said, "There's a bit of a bend here."

"Wait for us!" I called. "Don't want anyone out of line of sight."

Enzo looked back over his shoulder and said, "Look sharp you're dragging your feet back there."

I flipped him off. "I think it's the tunnel about thirty metres from the bend," I said loudly.

We caught up. Crockett, Ben, Enzo, Emily, Dane, and I stood at the entrance to a tunnel off the right of the main tunnel.

"Fingers crossed that it's just down here on the right," I said.

"Ladies first," Ben said and stepped back so Emily and I could lead the way. I opened a wooden door next to a sign that said, 'Plotting Room'. Inside was a large table. It was for plotting, I supposed. On the walls were framed maps. There were other maps on the table, a desk with a lamp on it, and some wooden cupboards that looked ancient.

"Where Emily?" I asked.

She moved to the cupboard in the far corner, opened the doors and couched down. She reached right into the back and brought out a tattered box. It was mottled greyish cardboard with faded green lettering about the size of a five-hundred-gram block of butter. She pulled out two more identical boxes and sat them on the ground. Emily almost crawled into the cupboard to reach something else: another box. This time it was a creamy, faded, water-stained box. It was the same size as the others. She set it aside, put everything else away, and stood up with the creamy-coloured box in her hand.

"Is that it?" I asked.

"I think so," she replied giving the box a gentle shake. "This must be it."

We checked that everything was where it should be.

Enzo grinned at me. "I expected a box of diamonds would be fancier."

"Donald would be bitterly disappointed," I said. "He can never find out about the diamonds. We'd never hear the end of it."

Chapter Forty-seven
[Ronnie: Moving right along]

An alert went off on my phone. In the distance and through a few twists and turns of solid concrete, I could hear the alarm I'd set at the main door. Someone was coming.

"We've got company," I said to Ben.

We were leaving but our egress was now dodgy. Not knowing who was coming down the steps and tunnels made it a little hairy. Crockett pulled his weapon from his holster and adjusted his grip on his torch. Enzo did the same. Dane shoved his iPad into the messenger bag he was carrying, replacing the iPad with a Glock. I fished around in my messenger bag looking for earpieces and a mic box. I handed Crockett and Enzo earpieces and clipped the mics on their collars. "Noise activated," I said. "You don't have to tap them."

I handed out the rest, so we all had mics and earpieces.

Emily held her tatty box in her hands. It seemed heavy. She looked momentarily lost. I held out my hand, took the box from her, and placed it in my messenger bag, making sure the inner zip was closed, and the outer flap was secured. I grabbed Emily's hand and moved back against the tunnel wall so Crockett and Enzo could pass us.

"Give me a two," Crockett said. Enzo came up behind

him and tapped his shoulder. "Stay liquid."

"Copy that," Enzo said. They moved into the dark tunnel. Crockett's torch the only illumination ahead of them.

I held back a snort of laughter. Seriously. Who did they sound like? S.W.A.T ... Nana loved Hondo or as Donald called him Sergeant Obvious. Good grief, now our lives resembled a show on the telly. Enzo obviously spent too much time with his husband, and Nana. I had no idea what Crockett was playing at, but I was enjoying it.

It was entertainment gold.

I was thankful we didn't have SWAT here. AOS were one hundred percent cooler.

The more I heard from my earpiece the more pleased I was that I didn't go down the law enforcement route. It was far too stressful and not at all like spying. I chewed my bottom lip: there was nothing stressful in my high-stakes former occupation that wasn't going quietly into the night as it was supposed to. I thought about retirement, and I rolled my eyes. Retirement is for the weak.

A sharp noise in my ear pulled me back to the present. I looked at Ben. He moved behind Emily; Dane moved up to be my two. There was another way out, but I couldn't remember where. Then it came to me. Down. We had to go down. There was a lower door to the parade ground outside.

"We're going for the lower door," I whispered.

Crockett responded with, "Copy that."

I moved to the next corner and headed down the tunnel. I saw an arrow on the wall and kept going the way it pointed. There were dark steep stairs. Down we went.

Ben whispered, "What if they covered the bottom door?"

"We'll cross that bridge when we find the door," I said. At a fork, Dane tapped my shoulder, and we kept moving down. Shining my torch on the walls ahead illuminated another arrow.

From my earpiece, I could hear Enzo and Crockett. They were still moving toward the front door. The alarm stopped fairly quickly after it started. Guess the baddies worked it out and shut the door. I was glad it stopped because I didn't want the alarm coming through our earpieces. That would be a headache and a half.

We kept moving at a good pace. I finally saw a sign that said, 'Parade Ground'.

"This way," I pointed. Dane tapped my shoulder. "Nearly there."

"Roger," Crockett said. "Meet you down there when we've neutralised the threat."

At the end of the tunnel we were in, was a heavy door. We'd meet them if we could get the bloody door open. My torch beam played up the wall by the door. Wetas. A freaking colony of wetas. No!

I quickly moved the light beam to the floor. I don't do wetas. Nope. Dane tapped me and pointed. I shook my head. I wasn't about to make a noise and wake those bastards up. Nope. Ben moved past us to the door. He scrutinised it and then pulled the pry bar from his backpack and jammed it into the edge of the rusty metal door. It creaked and groaned as it gave way. We could finally see daylight through the gap he'd created. He moved the bar and tried again. The door moved. He pulled on the edge and managed to open it enough for us to squeeze through. He sent Dane first to do a reconnaissance of the area. I could feel the wetas moving about. But that could've been my imagination.

It felt like forever until Dane came back and signed that it was clear.

One by one we left the dark, weta-filled tunnel. Ben and Dane pulled the door closed as much as they could. I brushed my shoulders, arms, legs, and shook my hair out, to make sure nothing creepy had hitched a ride.

"I can't see anything moving," Ben said, inspecting my back and hair.

"Good."

A gunshot nearly deafened us all. Simultaneously we pulled our earpieces out and shoved them in our pockets. Ben and Dane took off at a run up the hill from the parade ground that led to the car parking area and the front door. Emily and I ran behind them. Dane signalled for me and Emily to stay back near the trees. From our position in the trees, we could see a black car parked near the door.

"That's like the car Lucas and Stefan drove," Emily whispered to me. The mics were still working so Ben and Dane would've heard her. I wasn't game to put the earpiece back in, my ears were still ringing from the gunshot.

Ben and Dane cautiously approached the main door. They kicked it open. The alarm blared. Dane chucked one-half of the alarm system out the door. Once they were out of range from each other they no longer worked. I was glad he didn't shut the door. I wanted to be able to get in easily if needed and see anyone trying to exit.

I dug into my messenger bag and came out with a knife.

"What are you doing?" Emily asked quietly.

"Willful damage," I said. "Stay here, I'll be right back."

I crept across the open ground to the black sedan and jammed the knife into a back tyre then gave it a twist, just to make sure. I did the same to one of the front tyres.

Then because I was on a roll, I did the other front tyre and gave the final back tyre a slash and a stab. It felt quite good to jam a knife into tyres. I doubt they had four spares so that car wouldn't be going far and it's a bit of a walk down to civilisation from up on the hills of Karori.

I scuttled back to Emily in the tree line and hunkered down to wait. The box in my bag weighed heavily on my mind. We didn't yet know if it was the mysterious missing diamonds or another clue. Now was not the time to find out. That would happen when we were safe and in a secure location.

The sun slipped behind clouds casting a big shadow over the ground in front of us. Waiting became unbearable and yet we waited. I pushed an earpiece back into my ear. Wanting to hear our friends and get an idea if I should get Emily to our car and out of here.

Crockett's voice whispered in my ear, "Coming to you, Ronnie. Stay put and don't shoot me."

I smiled at Emily who looked terrified. "Crockett is coming out."

We waited. I waited to hear Ben's voice and to hear from Enzo. If something had happened to him Donald would never forgive me and nor would Nana.

Minutes felt like hours.

Finally, I heard a whisper that sounded like Ben. "Parade ground door."

Then there was another, Enzo, "Don't shoot, I'm with Ben."

Did they all think I'd fire without knowing who my target was? What the hell? That's a vote of confidence. At least Ben didn't think I'd shoot him.

"Emily, Ben and Enzo are coming out the door we used. Down there." I pointed back the way we came. "Watch for them. I'll watch the top door."

She turned around so she could see the parade ground. I stayed focused on the door near the black sedan. I judged the distance to be about fifteen metres. I wondered where Dane was. Maybe he was with Crockett. They must've all met at some point.

The door opened. Sunlight filled the gap. I had my Glock in my hand. Just in case. Crockett exited then behind him Dane pushed someone through the door ahead of him. The person didn't look wounded. Dane and

Crockett weren't leaking.

"We're out," Crockett said in my ear.

I rose slowly from the undergrowth beneath the trees and waved.

"Coming to you," I said, knowing he could hear me via his earpiece.

Emily was watching the grounds below us. "I see them," she said. "They do not have anyone with them."

I turned to look. No one appeared to be leaking as they ran across the parade ground and up the small hill to our position.

I moved out of the trees completely and to Crockett and Dane. Ben and Enzo gathered Emily and followed. There was a bit of huffing and puffing in my ear from the men that'd run up the hill.

When I was close to Crockett, I could see it was a man they had with them. As they got closer I saw a resemblance to the man Piper met at the airport. Lucas Genoa. I was pretty sure it was him.

"Who is this?" I asked, taking my earpiece out and switching the mic off. I put the tiny things in my pocket and buttoned it securely.

"Lucas Genoa," Crockett said with a small smile.

"And he was by himself?"

"No, he had a friend. Tony Robinson."

"He wasn't a friend," Genoa said.

"Where is he?"

"Dead. Genoa shot him."

"Bugger, I think he could've been helpful," I said. Ben,

Enzo, and Emily appeared on my right. "How did Robinson get here?"

"They carpooled," Crockett said. "Then he shot him about two metres from the radio room."

"So, he wasn't useful any more then." I turned to Ben. "Let's go?"

"Yes," he agreed. "Nice job on those tyres."

"Thank you."

Genoa grunted as Dane pushed him to get him walking. Genoa's hands were cable-tied behind him.

I watched Dane shove Genoa a few times to get him walking faster. I hung back with Ben. Emily, Crockett, and Enzo were right behind Dane and Genoa.

"How did they find us?" I asked. "We had the advantage not them."

Ben removed his mic, switched it off, and took the earpiece from his ear. I held my hand out for them then added them to my pocket with mine.

"Someone has a GPS tracker on them," Ben said. "That's the only answer that makes sense."

"Someone meaning Emily?"

"Has to be, doesn't it?"

We stopped walking and looked at each other for a beat. "It could be Enzo," we said in unison.

"Robinson might've still been working for *Leviticus,*" Ben said.

"Tierney would neither confirm nor deny when he was asked about Robinson. All he really said was that Robinson was behind the grocery order and that he didn't know every employee."

"Tierney planted a fucking device on Enzo. He had the opportunity and the motivation to make sure he knew where we were."

Ben sprinted ahead to catch up with everyone. I walked. Running seemed excessive. If Enzo was carrying a tracker. Tierney knew where we were. And he could strike whenever he wanted. I caught up just as Enzo began shedding his clothing. Ben was searching every inch of his jacket.

Crockett had stopped moving.

"Put Genoa in your car and get him away from us," I called out. "We think there's a Charlie Indigo tracker on Enzo."

Crockett waved in acknowledgement and double-timed his group to his car at the bottom of the hill.

We stayed together. Enzo and I joined the search for a tiny little tracking device. Ben turned his belt over and there it was: a little dot that measured about four millimetres in diameter stuck to the outside of his belt. No one would've noticed it because his jacket covered his belt. It could've been there a couple of days or Tierney could've planted it this morning when he was having a fun time putting new bugs in my bedroom.

Ben flicked the tiny dot off the belt and onto the grass. "Dress fast, we gotta go," Ben said.

We moved faster than before, almost running down the hill to our car. Crockett's was gone. We jumped in the car and took off. There was no other way out of Wrights

Hill Fortress, but down Wrights Hill Road. We followed the road to Campbell Street. Then took that until we found Karori Road. We wound our way through the suburb until we found Kelburn. Eventually, we found Kelburn Road and then Salamanca Road. That took us to The Terrace. It took a wee while to negotiate the city and get to Aotea Quay and the motorway north.

"Stay in the left lane," I said. "Head for Porirua and we can take Haywards Hill to Melling."

"The long way home," Enzo said. "Scenery is nicer I suppose."

"I suppose it is," I said. "I'd really like to avoid anything nasty, and Tierney was tracking you for a reason."

"Where is the box?" Ben asked, indicating to take the Ngauranga exit onto Centennial Highway.

"In my bag by my feet," I said and hooked the bag up, so it was on my knee. I checked the box was still there. And it was.

"Have you looked in it?" Enzo asked.

"Nope. We need to be somewhere secure before we do that."

"Good thinking."

I settled into my seat and relaxed a bit. We were moving. Ben hadn't commented on a tail or taken any evasive actions. We had breathing room.

"What are we going to do about Tierney?" Enzo asked.

"Good question," I replied. "We can't trust him. He's already bugged my room and tracked you. There must be something he wants. Could just be the diamonds but I have a feeling he's after more than that."

"How much more is there?" Enzo asked.

"Why is he listening in on conversations in my bedroom?" I asked. "That to me says he wants to find out if Ben is up to something, not just me."

"Apart from the creep aspect ..." Enzo said. "What does he think you'll lead him to?"

Ben glanced at me.

"Have you heard of *Genesis*?" I asked.

"I'm not a total heathen," Enzo said. "Do you mean the power company or the band?"

"None of the above," Ben said.

"What?"

"Tierney told me about it," I said wishing I wasn't lying to the man I considered to be my brother-in-law, not cousin-in-law. "It's a top-secret organisation, so he said."

"That does what?"

"Gathers intelligence, so he said." I'll just keep adding 'so he said' until I'm sure Enzo won't connect me with *Genesis*.

"Spies?"

"Apparently, according to Tierney. And we all know he's reputable."

"What country is using this *Genesis* thing?" Enzo asked.

"Tierney says, it's no particular country but an organisation with members from all over the world."

"And he wants information about them?" I could hear

the struggle in Enzo's voice as he came to grips with Tierney bugging us for intelligence about a secret organisation. "Why would you and Ben know anything about it?"

"Exactly," I said. "He's grasping at straws."

"The paper kind that fall apart in water," Enzo added. "We need to get him away from Nana."

Yes, we did.

Chapter Forty-eight
[Crockett: In Real Life]

I parked my car in the alleyway behind Ronnie's offices. I texted Steph to ask if she was upstairs. She was. She came down and unlocked the back door. Dane and Emily followed her up the stairs. I took our unwilling guest. I remembered Ronnie saying the cell was occupied, so I took Genoa into the main office and sat him on the couch. Lucky him he got a comfy seat.

One look cautioned Dane and Emily. I did not want them talking. Especially Dane showing his special way of talking. We didn't know enough about Lucas Genoa and what I did know, I did not like.

Steph was typing on her keyboard. She looked up now and then but went straight back to work. That was not a bad thing.

She knew we couldn't have any type of conversation with our guest in the room. The silence was a never-ending void. Thoughts collapsed into it and vanished.

Forever crawled by before Ronnie, Ben, and Enzo arrived.

"We're here," she called out before she opened the door.

"So are we," Emily replied.

Enzo smiled at Emily. He was last man through the door.

417

"Give me a sec," Ronnie said, taking her messenger bag off her shoulder and sitting on her desk at the back of the room. The floor plan was rectangular. Steph and Jenn had desks toward the reception desk at the front but along the wall opposite the door and reception. Under the front windows was a comfortable seating area with a sofa, two armchairs, and a coffee table in between. At the left-hand side, almost at the very back of the room was Ronnie's desk. On the back wall was a computer they called the vault. There was no internet access at all on that machine.

It was a good set-up. Today the spacious office felt crowded.

Ronnie checked her phone a few times before motioning for me to follow her out the door and into a room down the hall. There was a box on the wall beside the door with a lid. We placed our phones in the box and went into the room. With the door closed behind us, we could talk without being overheard. Right now, that was important.

"What's up?"

"Enzo was carrying a GPS tracker on his belt," Ronnie said.

"That sounds like a wanking Tierney move."

"I can't see who else would get that close," Ronnie replied. "That's how Genoa and Robinson found us at the fort."

"He was feeding them intelligence ..." Holy shit that changed things considerably. "He's been playing us all."

"Exactly my thoughts," Ronnie said. She chose a big armchair and plonked into it. "He bugged my room."

"This is turning into a dog's breakfast."

"Turning?" Ronnie questioned with half a smile. "Only turning?"

"It's not good, that's for real."

"We need to know how involved the Charlie Indigo Alpha crowd are in the heist and the aftermath."

"What are you thinking?"

"I'm thinking the cartel talk and the terrorist talk is a smoke screen. I'm thinking ..."

"That Charlie Indigo planned this whole crapfest and it's them who want the diamonds."

Ronnie nodded. "That is what I'm thinking. Robinson was *Leviticus* or so he implied."

"That would fit. Shame we can't ask him any more questions."

"Is it, though?"

"Na, he was a nasty bastard."

"I think Tierney was feeding Robinson but not Genoa," Ronnie said. "Genoa is out for himself. He wants the diamonds. I suspect he took and sold the paintings. If that's the case, then he might've done the job for a cartel initially, then decided to screw them over and keep the spoils."

"Pretty stupid to screw a cartel," I said. "This whole thing isn't the cleverest."

"Robinson's body is in the tunnels?" Ronnie asked but I knew she knew it was.

"Bet it isn't there now. Tierney knew we were there. His minions didn't report back so he would've sent a clean-up crew. Either to clean up or pin the death on one of us."

"Slow down, Trev." Ronnie did not look pleased. "You really think he'd turn this around on us?"

"If he's going to throw one of us under a bus it won't be someone who can bargain their way out."

"Emily."

"We can't let that happen."

I knew I needed help from people who were not involved in the crapfest. "I'll be right back." I let myself out of the room, grabbed my phone from the box and went halfway down the back stairs before I rang Art. "I got a problem."

"I'm your solver, where?"

"Wrights Hill Fortress."

"Okay. I have a cleanup crew in the city. They can go straight there." I could hear him texting as he talked. "Anything they need to know?"

"Yeah, someone is going to try and pin the death on Emily."

"My team are on their way. They were already in Karori taking care of another little problem."

"Thanks, Art."

"No worries."

I watched the phone screen go dark. I left my phone in the box outside the clean room and joined Ronnie.

"What'd you do?" she asked.

"Asked a friend to lend a hand." I didn't feel much like smiling. This was a disaster. A manufactured disaster. "Why?"

"That would be the multi-million-dollar question," Ronnie replied. "It's a puzzle."

"What is it you like to say ... puzzle wrapped in an enigma?"

"Yeah. That's it." She looked thoughtful. "We've got bad actors coming out of the woodwork. I just want to find out who is really behind this bullshit."

"Same. What do we do with Genoa? And the person you have in the jail cell? And the diamonds, if that's what we have in the box and not another clue."

Ronnie smiled. "So, we have a hand to deal. We have two people we can use as bait."

"That we do."

"Where are we going to put Genoa? He can't stay there in the office. We need him locked up. We also need to talk to him and find out if he knows who fed him the intelligence about Wrights Hill Fortress."

"We'll keep him on ice," I said reaching for the door. "I'll lock him up at Art's, and bright and early tomorrow, I'll bring him here and we can have a chat with him. Then I can lock him back up at Art's so we can figure how to use him to our benefit."

"Sounds good," Ronnie said.

Chapter Forty-nine
[Ronnie: Someone needs to talk]

I gave Genoa my best smile. He'd spent the night in a delightful prison cell at the back of Art's garage. I can be nice. I sat in the armchair in front of the sofa. Genoa was sitting on the sofa with Dane on one side and Ben on the other. Emily was sitting in Steph's visitor chair next to her desk. Enzo sat in a chair he'd brought over from another desk. It was a red straight-backed dining room chair, so it was from Jenn's desk. Crockett took the other armchair.

"Lucas Genoa, is it?" I asked.

"Yes."

"Okay. And why are you in our fair country?"

"I think you know."

"I think you need to answer my questions," I said keeping my voice light. I will be nice until it's time not to be nice.

"I'm looking for something. Simone has it." He turned his head toward Emily. "Ask her."

"I'm talking to you, right now. So, let's keep this between us." I smiled. "You're looking for something. Okay. Who has been helping you find this something?"

"No one." He looked directly into my eyes. "You've been a pain in my side from the beginning."

I smiled. "I'm delighted to have been of service."

"No one helped."

"Right, so you and what was his name?" I paused. "Stefan. You and Stefan did this all by yourselves." I shook my head. "Why do I feel that Robinson helped you?"

He stared straight ahead.

Ben nudged him in the ribs. "Talk," he said.

"Robinson was after the same thing as us. He wasn't helping me. He was trying to get what we wanted before us."

"Fascinating. And Kerrin Costa? Was she after the same thing too?"

His head shook slightly. "She's SIDE."

"We know what she is. What does she want from you?"

"Diamonds," Genoa replied in a soft whisper.

"Sorry didn't quite hear that."

"Diamonds," he said again.

"She wants them so she can return them to their owner?" I asked. I had a feeling she was working for someone, and it wasn't Argentina.

"I don't think that's what she intends," Genoa said.

"This is taking too long. Just get on with it and tell me what's going on here." I moved in the chair to get more comfortable. "The longer this takes the worse it's going to go for you."

His face blanked.

"Hello! Anyone home?" Crockett pushed Genoa's foot with the toe of his boot.

Genoa focused again.

"Glad you're back, now get on with talking."

A resigned look spread across his features. "You people don't give up, do you?"

"No. You threatened a friend of ours. We cannot let that go," I said. "I'm willing to listen and maybe we can find some common ground and maybe we will send you packing." My smile was not the sincerest. I knew that. Let him go? Ha!

"Nine years ago, I met a woman named Simone. She was teaching ESL."

"English as a second language, interesting job," I said. "Tell me more about Simone."

Suddenly he animated. "She was intelligent, picked things up quickly. I got to know her and discovered she was also a thief. She was what they call a cat-burglar or second-story woman. She liked the thrill of scaling buildings and entering from high windows. No one expected that."

I could see how her skill set would be attractive to someone like Genoa.

"We put together a team of specialised thieves. We did work everywhere. Taking any job offered, anything that would hone our skills for the ultimate heist."

"And that was?"

"Hijacked by a cartel." He didn't sound happy. "Simone and I wanted to steal diamonds from an auction house. Someone talked. I still don't know who. A cartel found out and told me we were going to hand the diamonds to them. We could keep the paintings."

The likely cartel rat was Stefan in my opinion, and I knew nothing about the man. "And what happened next?"

"I planned the job. It was me and Simone. Then they said we needed to take Stefan with us to ensure the diamonds were for them."

I silently patted myself on the back for the Stefan/ cartel link. "Just the three of you?"

He shook his head. "I wasn't allowed to bring the other two members with me. I had to find a safe cracker and an alarm guy in Europe."

Enter Tom Smith aka Tomás Genoa and Peter Piper aka Pedro Genoa.

"There were five of you?" Crockett asked. "One was cartel to keep you in line."

Genoa nodded. "That is correct. Stefan did not take part in the actual heist. He was the driver. He did not possess skills I needed beyond that."

I held my hand up to stop Genoa. "Stefan was German and resided in Belgium, he worked for their secret service. How did the cartel get him?"

"The same way they get anyone; you're foolish to think they only operate in South America."

"Fair enough," I said. "I wouldn't want Stefan inside with me if he had no relevant skills. No guarantee he wouldn't kill you all and take the diamonds. So why didn't he?"

"He was greedy," Genoa said.

"He wanted the diamonds for himself." Of course. "So,

he happily let them leave the country, knowing he could get them later?" And that made no sense to me but then I'm not a man, or stupid.

Genoa nodded. "He was stupid. The cartel wasn't going to let that happen."

"But it did happen. The diamonds left Europe and were not under Stefan's control."

He nodded slowly. "We had one way to get them out. Simone was the only person who could get them into a diplomatic pouch. Even the cartel couldn't get them out of that, especially a New Zealand pouch."

"Why did they let this go for years?"

"Because Simone vanished. They couldn't find her. I couldn't find her. She disappeared and as far as we knew she did so with the diamonds."

She kinda did.

"What was Stefan's real name?"

"Romero."

"And yours?"

"Genoa."

"Simone's?"

"Torres."

"How about the rest of your European crew?" I asked.

"Tomás Silva and Pedro Diaz."

"And who vouched for them? How did you find them? Did they spring up by magic?"

"An old friend suggested they might be able to help. He knew I wasn't able to bring my own crew."

"Trustworthy, I take it. You wouldn't have let two spies

in without someone you trusted vouching for them."

His face froze. The thing with our business is, it's a long game. And you have to be prepared to play a long game. Nothing happens by chance or quickly. It's set up, fed, built, until one day, it's go time.

And he was back. "Spies?"

I shrugged. "Possibly."

He shook his head. "No. They were Spanish speaking from Europe somewhere and well-known to my friend. Not spies."

"Whew, bet you're relieved."

A frown drew his eyebrows together. "What else do you want?"

"The name of the friend who found your European helpers for you," Ben said.

Just then a knock rang out on the office door.

Steph got up to deal with it. Sometimes we get walk-ins. She opened the door. A male voice said, "I'm here to see Ronnie, Ben, Crockett, and Dane."

Dane stood up and met the man at the door. They shook hands. Dane showed him in. What on earth was going on, I wondered. But not for long.

Crockett stood when he saw our visitor. "Mitch Iverson, what brings you to town?"

So, this was the infamous Mitch Iverson and potentially our *Genesis* boss.

"Business in Wellington thought I'd pop out and see you all."

"Not the best timing," I said. We were all standing

now, except for Lucas. He sat in silence. Studying his hands. I turned and shook hands with Mitch. "Good to finally meet you."

"You as well," he said with a grin. "Crockett has told me good things."

He turned to Ben. "You must be the famous actor, Ben Reynolds." They shook.

Then Mitch turned to Enzo. "Enzo, right? Donald's husband?" He stuck his hand out.

Enzo smiled. "Right on both counts." They shook.

Emily hung back by Steph's desk. There was something about Mitch she wasn't sure about, I could tell by the expression on her face. I let it go and didn't introduce her right away.

"Who's the guy on the couch?" Mitch asked.

"No one," I replied. "Maybe Steph could take you to the kitchen and get you a coffee while we finish up here."

Mitch's eyes found Emily. For the briefest millisecond, he looked like he'd seen a ghost. His eyes flashed to Crockett then back to Emily. Crockett caught the look and gave an almost imperceptible nod.

"Come on Mitch, let's get the coffee on," Steph said, holding the door for him.

"Sounds great," he replied, dragging his eyes off Emily and following Steph from the room.

All I wanted to do was ring *Uncle George* and see what happened next. We turned to the business at hand. Lucas Genoa.

"You got anything else to say?" I asked him.

"Your friend Emily is my friend Simone," he said. "She knows where the diamonds are, and only she knows."

"Your friend Simone died in Belgium eight years ago."

"No," he shook his head.

"I'm sorry about your friend, but she is dead," I said with as much kindness as I could muster. "Her body was discovered but identification wasn't possible. It's since been identified as Simone Genoa."

He blinked as if clearly a fog from his eyes. "Dead."

"Yes."

"Who killed her?"

"We don't know." I had a few working theories, but they were not for him to know. "We know she died before the theft. The person who scaled the building and climbed in that window was not Simone Genoa or Simone Torres. She was someone who looked very similar. She had everything to enable her to take Simone's place. Neither you nor Stefan knew the change was made."

"Why?"

"I don't know. We are not the people who were involved." I was damn sure it wasn't only Bill Bailey involved but also Tierney. I also knew we'd never be able to prove that. But I had a feeling ... a bad one.

"What now? I presume I'm not getting the diamonds, and the cartel will eventually hear of Stefan's death. I cannot go back."

"I suggest you ask for asylum. Pick a country go to their embassy and ask for asylum."

"I have no bargaining power. I'm a thief."

"Might be a skill that's more useful than you think," Crockett said. "We need to get you somewhere safe because there is someone after you and the diamonds, and it's not just the cartel that you've pissed off."

"Where?"

"Australia," Crockett said with a grin. "I'll take you now."

"To Australia?"

"Next best thing, the embassy. You'll be safe there until we can work out what to do with you."

"Not the American embassy?"

"Hell no," Crockett said. "That'd be out of the frying pan and into the fire big time."

Genoa swallowed hard. "Okay."

Crockett hauled Genoa to his feet and cut the cable ties off his wrist with a knife from his pocket. Crockett looked at me. "You okay with this?"

"Yep. Get him safe. We can talk to him again later if we need to."

Crockett nodded. Checked he had his keys in his pocket, and waved goodbye to Emily who was still sitting by Steph's desk.

I had a second, so I went down to my desk and rang *Uncle George*. As usual, it rang out. I don't know what I was expecting, perhaps to hear a phone ring through the kitchen wall but he'd have to be smarter than that. I waited for the usual call back, but my phone didn't ring. Was that because *Uncle George* was in our kitchen?

Chapter Fifty
[Emily: Who is he?]

Emily stayed where she'd been sitting. She had no interest in getting any closer to the man who was visiting Ronnie's offices. There was something about him she didn't trust or maybe it was something familiar, but she didn't know why.

Crockett left with Genoa. She knew why but wished she could've gone with them. It didn't feel as safe without Crockett there. Down deep in her gut, she knew that was wrong. Ronnie, Ben, and Enzo would never let anything bad happen to her. Nor would Steph. The new man, Mitch, made her stomach feel strange.

Ronnie, Enzo, and Ben sat with Mitch and drank coffee. Steph sat back at her desk. She placed a cup near Emily. "Here you go, Emily."

"Thank you."

"Why don't you go sit with the others?"

"I don't think I want to be near that man," Emily replied quietly.

"Okay. Is there a reason?"

She shook her head. "If there is I don't know what the reason is."

"Okay. Stay with me then. I'm happy for the company and you can listen to the conversation from here."

Emily nodded. She sipped her hot coffee and watched

what went on across the room.

"Hope you don't mind me calling in unannounced," Mitch said to Ronnie.

"No, not at all. It's nice to put a face to the man Crockett talks about."

"He's a good guy. Keeps in touch and comes down for fishing trips when he can." Mitch grinned at Dane. "How are you doing?"

Dane typed; Siri spoke, "Good. Didn't know you were coming to Wellington."

"Nor did I. A company wanted to see their prototypes early so I brought them up. Easier for me to come up then to explain to people how to get to my place in the Sounds."

"The ones you were working on last week?" Siri asked.

"Yes."

"Cool."

"Are you here for long?" Ronnie asked.

"No. Just the day. I'm flying back this evening."

"There seem to be a lot of Americans around all of a sudden," Ronnie said.

Mitch laughed. "There are only three of us in this room."

"And I've got one camped out at home," Ronnie said. "He's less welcome."

"Overstayed their welcome?" Mitch asked.

Ronnie smiled and nodded. "House guests can be tiring."

"I quite enjoy the company of mine," Mitch said. "I'm

sure Dane finds the girls tiring though."

Siri spoke, "They're fun."

"I've taken up enough of your time. No doubt you have things to do. I'll catch up with Crockett on his next fishing trip." Mitch stood to leave.

"Was nice meeting you, Mitch," Ronnie said. "One day we might come down and check out the fishing ourselves."

"You should. You'd be welcome," Mitch said.

He waved to Emily and Steph. And left. Ronnie joined Emily at Steph's desk. "Are you all right?"

"Yes."

"You didn't want to come over and say hello?"

"No. There was something about him. I don't think I like him."

Ronnie smiled. "Gut feeling Emily. That's what that is."

"Well, my gut feeling is that I've met him before, but I don't know where or why I think that."

"He's gone, so we don't need to worry about it now, do we?"

"No."

"Are we going to look in the box?"

"Yes, we are. Not in here though. Steph, you want to come?"

"I do."

"Go lock the downstairs door. Crockett will be gone for at least an hour."

"Righto," Steph said, taking keys from her desk

drawer. She hurried away. Ben and Enzo were talking by the reception desk.

"Hey," Ronnie called. "Leave your phones in here. We're going to do something."

Emily took her phone from her pocket and put it on Steph's desk. Ben and Enzo left theirs on the reception desk. Ronnie put hers with Emily's. Steph came back.

"Where's your phone?" Ronnie asked.

"In my desk," Steph replied.

"Okay, let's go."

Ronnie hurried to her own desk and took a small box from her messenger bag. She then led the way to the clean room. Once everyone was inside, she shut the door. There was a table in the middle of the room and chairs around it. From a cupboard, she took a cloth and spread it on the table. Everyone took a seat. Ronnie opened the box. Inside was a velvet bag. She took the bag out, weighing it in her hand.

"Definitely something that feels like gems in this bag," she said and carefully loosened the strings holding it closed. She tipped the contents onto the cloth on the table.

All eyes were on the pile of diamonds that glittered in the light.

"That looks a lot like diamonds," Enzo said. "Of course, Donald and his diamond tester and jeweller's loupe would be able to confirm that they are diamonds."

Ronnie pushed the pile and watched them spread out as they fell. "Wow."

"I think we found the diamonds," Ben said.

"Why did I have diamonds?" Emily asked. "Why did I hide them in the Wrights Hill tunnels?"

Ronnie took a breath. "Because Emily, you were Simone Genoa for a brief amount of time, eight years ago."

Emily shook her head slowly. "I can't have been her. I was a police officer. I was a police officer in New Zealand."

"I know," Ronnie said. "I also know that you were Simone Genoa."

"How?"

"The person who can answer that best is Bill Bailey."

She frowned, her eyes remained on the glittering diamonds. "I don't know anyone called Bill Bailey."

"Not now, but you did," Ronnie said. "You did."

Emily remembered something Lucas Genoa had shown her. A photo and she saw Tom in the picture. "When you say I was Simone Genoa and I was in Belgium," she started then faltered. "Lucas showed me pictures of me, but I didn't recognise myself, but in one, in the background, I saw Tom. Tom was there."

Ronnie nodded. "Yes, he was. He was there. You worked with him."

Her frown deepened. "But he didn't tell me he already knew me when you introduced us."

"No, he didn't," Ben said. "Sometimes people don't say things that maybe they should or that they think will upset someone."

"Would it upset me, Ben?"

"Probably, you have no memory of working with him, so why would he bring it up?"

Emily looked at the people at the table who were looking back at her. "Did I know all of you before?"

Ben and Enzo shook their heads. Ronnie and Steph nodded.

"You knew me and Steph. You were a cop and then you became a private investigator, and you worked with us." Ronnie pointed to Steph and herself. "We knew you. We did."

"And I was a thief," Emily said, her voice falling flat.

"A pretty bloody good one by the looks of things," said Steph with a smile. "Stealing those would not have been easy."

"There were paintings stolen as well," Ronnie said. "So yes, a very good thief."

Emily sat back in the chair and analysed her life; the parts she knew and the reality she lived. She wondered what sort of person she used to be. What was she like when she was a thief and a criminal? It didn't sit well with the truth she knew: Emily Jones, police officer; Emily Jones, private investigator; Emily Jones, bookshop manager.

Ronnie spoke and broke the spell cast on the room by the pile of diamonds. She scooped them back into the bag as she said, "Emily, right before you were grabbed by Lucas and Stefan. You knew something was going to happen. You put a bookmark into a kids' book."

Emily looked at Ronnie. "I put a bookmark for The Jaded Spy in the upside-down children's book for you to find."

"I know. We found it."

"Do you know why you chose that bookmark?"

"Yes, I do." Emily said. She smiled at her friends around the table. "When Jenn was injured, the man who said he was Stefan reminded me of someone. Someone bad."

"Okay, but why that *book*?"

Emily let images fill her mind. "The Russians want the diamonds. Paintings were stolen. I stole them. Tomás and Pedro are spies. That was the only book that I knew of in the shop that was about spies, Russians, and stolen art."

"How did you know the Russians want the diamonds?"

"Because I stole them from a Russian," she said quietly. "I stole them from an auction house, but they belonged to a Russian. He's very rich."

"And Tomás and Pedro, how do you know they're spies?" Ben asked.

"Because Tomás is your friend Tom, and I know him. He's not a thief. He's not Spanish. He opened the safe."

"But how do you know he's a spy?" Ben persisted.

"I don't know. I just know. I can't explain it."

"What about Pedro?" Ronnie asked.

"He worked with Tom. I know he wasn't really an alarm guy, but he was good at it. Someone probably told him how to disable the alarm system."

"Do you know who he is?" Ronnie asked.

She shook her head.

"Would you recognise him again?" Ben asked. They needed to know if Piper would pose a problem or make an attempt on Emily's life.

"No," she said. "I didn't see a photo with him in it, I don't think. I can't remember what he looks like. Just that he was the alarm guy."

"You remember a lot more than you used to," Enzo said. "You're coming back."

"I don't know if I want to come back," Emily said. "I don't know what sort of person Simone was. I don't know if I want to be someone like her."

Ronnie reached out and took her hand. "You're Emily Jones. Our friend. That's all you need to know. Emily Jones is a good person."

Dane had been quietly listening and absorbing the conversation around him. "Emily," Siri said.

"Yes, Dane," she replied.

"It doesn't matter who you were before. Like me, it doesn't matter who I was either."

"But you remember."

"Not everything which is probably good. We're lucky, we get to be whoever we want to be. Clean slate. We got to find our real selves in a way most people never do."

She listened, taking his words and letting them fill her.

"What happens now though?" she said. "I know some things. I know I'm a thief, so I broke the law. I could go to prison. I was a cop, and I broke the law."

Ronnie sensed an escalation and squeezed Emily's hand. "No, Emily, no. That's not going to happen. You're going to stay here with us."

"Are you sure?" Emily asked.

"Very sure," Ben, Ronnie, and Siri said simultaneously.

Emily smiled. It was okay to have friends like hers, she decided. Friends who didn't care what she might've been before no matter what that was.

Chapter Fifty-one
[Ronnie: Getting it done.]

I spun in my desk chair. We had the diamonds. I'd put them in the safe for now. None of us really knew what to do with them. I still had a Russian in the cell, and I knew we had to let her out sooner or later. Genoa was out of the way at the Australian embassy. They'd take care of him until they could get him out of the country completely. Now he was safe on Australian soil albeit still in New Zealand.

Stefan and Robinson were dead. Simone was dead. Tierney was still at my house. Probably snooping. Piper wasn't talking and he sure as hell would not be telling anyone about his foray as an alarm man on a heist. Tom and Ginny were solid. Tom wasn't about to talk about his role in the heist either. Interesting that he was the safe cracker. Could be handy one day. And I'm quite sure I met the head of *Genesis,* and that it's Mitch, which would explain how Dane was sent, the kids I heard in the background of a phone call, why I've pinged his phone in Linkwater Marlborough, and why Crockett isn't *Genesis.* Ha! Cracked that mystery right open. It was probably best if I kept that to myself though. I didn't want a repeat of what happened to MacKinnon. And I didn't want to be responsible for children being orphaned.

We just had Costa floating about convinced that Emily

was her cousin Simone Costa. I am not sure she's wrong. But I needed to convince her she was wrong and to leave without the diamonds. I couldn't risk them going to a cartel to fund terrorism. We couldn't keep them so what would we do with them?

Hand them to Tierney for *Leviticus* to use to fund their black ops? Give them to the Russian so she can take them back to her boss? Give them to Piper? Give them to Bill Bailey to do something with?

None of the options I came up with were good enough. They really weren't. Whoever got them could and would use them for nefarious deeds. That's the way life is. The more money people have the more they want and the more they screw things up for other people. The last option was, give them to *Genesis*. Could I do that? Could I?

Maybe I should find a charity that doesn't spend most of its money on paying the figureheads and administrators. I almost laughed. I was back thinking about getting them to *Genesis*. Laughter edged in when I imagined giving the diamonds to Mitch to take to Marlborough. He'd absolutely know I knew then. I stopped thinking and jumped to my feet. Dane was sitting on the sofa. Ben was nowhere to be seen. Steph was working. Emily was reading a book in an armchair.

"Where's Ben?" I asked.

"Making coffee," Steph said.

I went to the kitchen and there he was.

"We have to do something about Katerina Sokolov."

"What do you suggest? Ben asked, adding water to the big French press.

"She's roofied, right?"

"Correct."

"So, she won't remember seeing us."

"True."

"And she's suggestible?"

"Yes. Where are you going with this?"

"Up the dose. Let's take her to the South Coast and drop her off."

"Seriously?"

"We need her gone. Coffee first then errands." To be honest, I thought she needed to go to the beach via the Akatarawas, Crockett's favourite way to take someone to the beach. It was hard to find a body in those gullies.

That would just leave Tierney as a problem. He was going to pose a challenge. But I felt we had a good shot at sorting him.

I checked that Steph could take Dane and Emily to Crockett's. I knew Emily had a key. They'd be fine there.

An hour later Ben and I lifted Katerina's dead weight out of the boot of the car and lay her among the rocks on the south coast. We made sure the rocks were wet. Ben gave her a higher dose of Rhohypnol. She'd be dead before the tide carried her out to sea. The tide was coming in when we drove away. I felt a bit stink but I did not need her coming back to cause more shit, or worse tell her boss what she found here. It's best if some people just disappear. The sea does a good job making people and things vanish.

Half an hour later we climbed the stairs into my home. I could hear Nana and Tierney talking in the lounge. I avoided that and we went to my room knowing full well that Tierney could hear everything we talked about.

I winked at Ben.

"What happened in Antwerp? Why did the case and the body get buried?" I asked.

Ben leaned back against the pillows, laced his fingers behind his head and smiled slightly.

"What do you think happened?"

"I think someone did it on purpose."

"Why would anyone do that?"

"I don't know. Just a theory." I shrugged. "Just feels off. And it wasn't a coincidence that the body turned up now."

"Okay. I'll play. Someone knew the Genoas were coming to New Zealand and about the heist. Someone worked out it was all coming together. And then Tierney arrived. If I was watching, that'd make me very interested."

"Could someone have orchestrated this whole disaster?"

"Yeah. The most vindictive person I've ever met is Kirsten Knight."

I tried hard not to laugh. He really disliked her.

"No one likes her but that's a long way from pulling strings in Europe and getting a body buried," I said giving the voice of reason a shot.

"If they had buried her then there wouldn't be a problem now. Most of this would've gone a different way."

"Without a reconstruction, Emily would've been out on a limb. Not two women who look very similar, just Emily," I let a little fear linger in my words. No doubt Tierney would enjoy that.

"It probably wasn't ever supposed to happen," Ben said.

I nodded. "Eight years. People come and go. Maybe someone stumbled over the cold case and decided they'd have a crack at solving it. For all the right reasons, giving the parents closure. Everyone has them."

"I'm sure Crockett is grateful that person did."

"Was Kirsten in Europe back then?" If anyone would know it's Ben.

"Yes. She was."

"So, it could've been her."

Ben shook his head and smiled. He texted me.

Ben: Don't try too hard to throw her under the bus.
Me: Okay. You think he'll act on it?
Ben: Yes.

I stood up and pointed at the places we knew the bugs were. Ben joined me and we removed them, dropping the tiny things in a glass of water next to the bed. They were destined for the gobbler in the sink just like the last ones.

"Speaking of parents," I said. "I've never heard Emily mention parents."

"Maybe they're not in New Zealand. She's a dual citizen remember," Ben said.

"Maybe." He had a good point. "I haven't met your parents and I'm fairly certain you didn't hatch from an egg."

Ben grinned. "I might be a lizard."

"Don't think you are." I touched his face with my fingers. "Warm. Just as I thought."

Ben sat forward and snaked his arm around me. He pulled me close and planted a kiss on my lips.

"That secret we have ..." Ben said in a whisper.

"Tomorrow good for you?"

"Yes."

"You're sure you don't want to change your mind?"

"I'm sure."

Chapter Fifty-two
[Ronnie: some secrets are good secrets]

"Nana!" I called down the hall hoping she was still here. I hadn't seen her since late last night.

Donald poked his head out of his bedroom. "She's in the dining room with Romeo."

"Do you mean the dog or the old man?"

"The dog. I don't think Ben's Grandfather is still here."

"Oh, okay." I hurried into the dining room. Sure enough, Nana was there feeding Romeo tidbits of her breakfast. There was no Tierney to be seen.

"Good morning, Veronica."

"Morning, Nana," I said with a smile and a kiss on the proffered papery cheek. "Can I get you anything while I'm up?"

"More tea, dear. That would be lovely."

I filled the kettle in the kitchen and turned it on before joining her at the table. "Where's Ben's grandfather?"

"He's turned out to be a bit of a disappointment, I'm afraid."

This was news. I was all ears. "You don't say, Nana. What happened?"

She tutted. "I'm not one to tattle, Veronica. Gossip is so unbecoming."

I felt a 'but' coming. It wouldn't take much to nudge it

over the edge. "But, Nana?"

"Well, you really wouldn't believe it, but I caught him snooping in my things."

"Wow! Didn't think he was the snooping type. I'm sorry he let you down like that. It seemed that you two were getting on like a wildfire."

"So did I, until I caught him red-handed in my room."

"You sure he wasn't confused? He's quite elderly." I can throw a lifeline when warranted. This time it wasn't but I didn't want Nana to catch on that there was more to Tierney than she'd managed to wheedle out of him.

"Yes, that's probably why I caught him coming out of your room too."

"Oh, did you Nana?" I smiled at her. "I hope you gave him an earful."

"I'm a lady Veronica, but that man got the sharp end of my tongue. I'll not tolerate snooping into people's private spaces."

"Thank you, Nana."

"I hope his grandson is better behaved when he's a guest."

"They're nothing alike, Nana. You wouldn't know they were related."

I heard the jug boiling. "I'll fill the teapot."

Nana went back to sharing crusts with Romeo. I made her a pot of tea and found some of her favourite biscuits in the pantry. It's never too early for a Chocolate Thin. A wave of guilt hit me right in the face. Today was the day. And no one knew. I looked at my Nana sitting at the table

447

feeding my equally ancient dog from her plate.

Nope. No. No. I got up from my chair and hurried back to my bedroom. Ben was just getting up.

"We can't do it!" I said as I flung the door open. "We cannot do it without Nana and Donald and Steph and Jenn ..."

He pulled me into a massive hug. "I know," he said and kissed my forehead. "And we won't. Go tell them all to meet us at the courthouse at eleven."

"Everyone?"

"Yes."

I kissed him and shot off to find my phone and ring everyone.

Fifteen minutes later eloping was over, but we still got to surprise everyone by announcing our wedding was at eleven at the Lower Hutt Courthouse.

Donald went into a flat panic because there wasn't time for the rhinestoned-whatever he wanted to make. Crockett arrived surprisingly quickly after my text.

He grinned at me as he came up the stairs.

"Today then?"

"Yep."

"Emily's choosing a dress, I'll pick her up soon," he said. "She's excited." Crockett looked around the room. "Where's Cary Grant?"

"In our room."

Steph came over with Jenn. They bustled into the lounge before I vanished to get ready.

"I don't know if she's staying," Steph said tipping her

head toward Jenn. "She's not bloody right in the head."

I pressed my lips together to stop myself making any comment until I considered I had my smart arse under control. "No problem. How are you feeling Jenn?"

"Good. Don't know why I can't come back to work. And of course, I'm going to be at your wedding."

Steph smiled or at least her lips attempted a smile. "Nope. No work for you. And we'll see how the next ten minutes go, before we say yes or no to the wedding."

"I could've helped find Emily," Jenn said. "I bet no one checked the letterbox."

I felt my eyes widen. "No."

Crockett looked at Jenn like she'd just escaped from a circus. "She wasn't in a letterbox Jenn. She was abducted," he said.

"I bet she was, and you just don't want to say." She spun around and found Steph behind her. "It's the rules. You know the rules, Steph."

Steph grabbed Jenn by the arm and pushed her toward the kitchen. "We'll be leaving now. Congrats. Have a lovely wedding."

"Letterbox Olympics," Jenn said. "She could've been there."

The door to the stairs closed. I could still hear her voice and Steph chastising her. Jenn was not ready to come to work. Nope.

"What was that?" Crockett asked.

"She has a concussion," I replied. "That's just the ramblings of an injured brain. We will speak no more of it."

Crockett gave me a weird look and shook his head.

Nana and *The Cronies of Doom* took over the lounge. Enzo folded a paper bag and put it in his pocket, on hand just in case Donald hyperventilated during the ceremony what with the lack of rhinestones and other sparkly things.

Ben asked Crockett to be his best man, or as I liked to call him, Witness One. Donald was my best man slash Witness Two. Enzo and Emily were in charge of the golden oldies.

I didn't think for one minute that our wedding would not be an unmitigated disaster. But then again, nothing could set us up better for married life.

"Veronica, are you going to wear your dress?" Nana's voice rang out. There was no feebleness today.

"I was planning on wearing it Nana, yes."

"Well then hadn't you better hurry up and change? What are you going to do with your hair?"

"Leave it on my head, Nana. I've decided that my hair looks best on my head."

Nana tutted. "You're not taking this seriously."

I'm surrounded by clowns; how could I possibly take anything seriously?

"Nana, it's our wedding. It's fifteen minutes in a courthouse with a Justice of the Peace. Don't worry."

"Donald and I are feeling cheated." Her faded eyes narrowed at me. "Is there a reason that you are in a rush to be married?"

"Certainly not!" I told her. "You can take that to the bank."

Ben took my hand and encouraged me to follow him to our room. It felt better thinking of it as our room rather than my room.

"Put your dress on. I'll get my tux on. Let's go get married."

"You're going to have to zip me up," I said. "Isn't it bad luck for the groom to see the bride in her dress before the ceremony?"

Ben smiled all the way to his sparkling eyes. "No such thing as bad luck. We'll be fine."

Ten minutes later we made our entrance to the lounge to see our friends gathered there. I wished Steph and Jenn were coming.

Ben smiled at me and took my hand. "Let's go get married, Ms Tracey."

"After you, Mr Reynolds."

Waiting at the curb was a black Town Car. Ben smiled at me. "Thought this might be nicer than driving ourselves."

He was right. Crockett, Dane, and Emily followed us in Crockett's car. Donald drove Enzo and Nana. Frankie had driven Ester over, so they were good to go.

We met outside the courthouse in Lower Hutt at five minutes to eleven. I don't like waiting around. Ben knows that. Everything was timed for the least amount of waiting possible.

We filed inside the courthouse and were met by one of

the registrars. "Reynolds and Tracey?" The woman asked.

"Yes."

"I'm Janet, I'll be officiating your ceremony this morning. Follow me, your guests are welcome."

We followed her into a room. There were flowers, chairs, and a desk for signing the most important piece of paper: our marriage license. I paused for a split second halfway toward the front and all the flowers. I took a breath inhaling the carnation and rose scents.

"You, okay?" Ben asked from my elbow.

"Never better," I replied. "It's a bit surreal though, right?"

"Yep. Come on, almost wife. They're waiting."

Donald waited for me with a brilliant smile on his face. He linked his arm with mine.

"You look glorious. We could've added some stunning rhinestones to really flash you up," he whispered. "Hope Ben appreciates you always."

That glue gun and those rhinestones will find another use.

Donald stood next to me. Janet was in the middle. Ben and Crockett were on the other side of Janet.

Nana was making noises of approval from the seats in front.

She patted Emily on the knee. "You and Crockett next," she said with joy. "We can do something fabulous for you two, I'm sure."

I was giving 'hurry up' hand signals to Janet. Nana and Donald can only keep themselves in check for so long.

Our ceremony was short. We basically agreed not to be dicks to each other and always communicate openly. There was a little 'in sickness and health' bit in there as well. We exchanged rings.

I heard familiar voices calling their congratulations from the back of the room. I looked over and Steph was there with Jenn.

Our wedding was perfect. No one died.

The end.

Acknowledgements

Writing is mostly done in solitude, but it's not done in a vacuum. This book is no different to any that I've written, in as much as I don't talk about what I'm working on beyond a couple of taglines and the odd logline.

Welcome to Fight Club.

Some days it is a fight. Other days it's easy and breezy.

Not talking about what I'm working on doesn't mean there aren't some people that are necessary during the process.

Margot Kinberg is my favourite American author and also a good friend who makes sure my Americans are still American because she is awesome like that.

Bex is always my first reader. We find plenty to laugh about in the unedited raw words she's sent!

Nicky (my wonderful long-time friend and editor) is a proper God-send.

Geoff for his patient listening to bits and pieces that I share about the story (especially when I have questions that only he can answer).

Diesel knows everything there is to know about this story ... he will never tell a soul.

Special thanks to Robbie for being such a great character and for asking me to keep Tom in the Veronica Tracey Spy/PI series. I can't imagine the series without either of you.

Big thanks to Chrissy for keeping me sane (ish) during

the writing process.

Kids: thanks for being you.

Dad: for his steadfast encouragement, always.

Mark Valley: turns out I'm a tad competitive when it comes to words on the page. I didn't see that coming but thanks for spurring me over the line.

About the author:

Cat Connor is a prolific crime thriller author hailing from New Zealand. Her expertise in the genre is reflected in her engaging and suspenseful narratives, which have garnered a loyal following. Her work is known for its intricate plots, dynamic characters, and relentless pace, keeping readers on the edge of their seats until the very end. She has authored multiple books, including the popular "Byte" series, which follows the exploits of an FBI unit that investigates serial crime.

Cat's passion for crime and espionage is evident in her writing, as she strives to create a world that is both authentic and thrilling. Her meticulous attention to detail and extensive research, have won her critical acclaim and accolades from readers and peers alike. In addition to writing, Cat enjoys speaking on topics related to writing and publishing. Her talks are known for their candidness, humour, and practical advice. With her unique blend of talent, expertise, and passion, Cat Connor has established herself as one of the most exciting and accomplished authors in the crime thriller genre.

Her other passions include music, reading, tequila, wine, coffee, and chocolate. When she's not writing she can be found binge-watching TV shows, or listening to music. Cat is never far from her much-adored animals; Diesel the mastador, Patrick the tuxedo cat, and Dallas the tortie Birman.

You can follow and contact Cat at the following places:

Website: www.catconnor.com
Twitter: @catconnor
Facebook: @cat.connor
Instagram: @catconnorauthor
Bluesky: @catconnor.bsky.social
Threads: @catconnorauthor

Also by Cat Connor:

The Kiwi set Veronica Tracey Spy/PI series:
[Nothing happens here] -2020
[Lure the lie] - 2021
[Leave a message] - 2022
[Whiskey Tango Foxtrot] - 2023
[Foxtrot Mike Lima] - 2024

The FBI based Byte Series:
Killerbyte - 2009
Terrorbyte - 2010
Exacerbyte - 2011
Flashbyte - 2012
Soundbyte - 2013
Snakebyte - 2013 (novella)
Databyte - 2014
Eraserbyte - 2015
Psychobyte - 2016
Metabyte - 2017
Qubyte - 2018
Cryptobyte - 2019
Vaporbyte - 2020
Raidbyte - 2021 (collection of long bytes)
Cachebyte-2024 (collection of short bytes)

Fates Entwined: The Spellbound Bookshop Trilogy

Written in Leaves - 2023

Scattered on Cloth - 2024

Drawn from Cards -2024

Fates Entwined: boxed set - 2024

www.ingramcontent.com/pod-product-compliance
Lightning Source LLC
Chambersburg PA
CBHW031151050726
47495CB00019B/1429